THE GUARDIAN

WHEN THE LAST DRAGON DIED
BOOK I

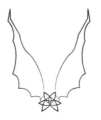

ERIN LEE

Copyright © 2021 by Erin Lee
Cover art by Toni Infante
Cover design by Allison Davis Salcido
Epigraph by Tab Fischer
Pact symbols by Deb Lee Toth

The text of this book is set in 11.35-point Palatino.
Book design by Allison Davis Salcido

ISBN 978-1-7358483-0-3 (paperback) – ISBN 978-1-7358483-1-0 (hardcover) – ISBN 978-1-7358483-2-7 (eBook)

Trade Paperback Edition: April 2021

www.erinleewrites.com
www.twitter.com/HappiLeeErin

For my daughter, who hugged me and said,
"Mommy, I can't wait to read your book."

Here you go, baby girl.

Awake the glowing ashes

For we were once at peace

Protected by fire and magic

With the growing of the trees

We sought out to teach them

And our claws became a ladder

To reach us on their journey

When all their hope was shattered

Instead they took our calling

And reformed it with their swords

For fire once protected us

But now our pleas were ignored

Yet one last soul remains

With a child no one sees

And with her star, she entrapped them

With the power from the Queen

PART ONE

THE DRAKON

CHAPTER 1

ALVIS WITT WAS TROUBLE.

He was almost always at the center of it, and when he wasn't, trouble was always close behind him. He was a dangerous boy. He grinned at the sight of blood, tossed out bruises for fun, and spent his days searching for people to fight.

At least that's what you'd think Alvis was like if you went off his dad's version of things.

No, Alvis did not "grin" when he saw blood. In fact, it kinda made him gag and it was annoying to get out of clothes.

Yes, Alvis "tossed out bruises" but he'd had his fair share thrown right back, so that one cancelled out.

Oh, and that whole "searching for fights" thing?

Well . . . maybe that one wasn't too different from his dad's account of things.

Still, it wasn't like Alvis was some thug needing a thrill—he was *helping* people. So what if once or twice a month he took a few extra back alleys on his way home from work and stumbled upon a robbery? Was he *not* supposed to apprehend the thief? And maybe he sometimes (okay, always) kept a bandana in his pocket to cover his face if kids his own age harassed a family of Guardians and needed to be knocked down a notch or two. What was so bad about that?

"You need to stop drawing attention to yourself," his dad always said when Alvis came home with another bruise and bloodied knuckles. "No one in Bellow should use magic. One of these days you're going to accidentally use your attribute in front of the wrong person."

"Guardians use their magic all the time."

"You aren't a Guardian. You're one of Ellowyn Clark's descendants."

AKA a "Chosen One." Around the age of nine, Alvis realized that meant being a sheltered hermit. "What's the point of having magic if I can't help people with it? If I join Linless, then—"

The genius mechanic, Michael Witt, would level Alvis with *that* look—the one caught somewhere between daring Alvis to finish his sentence, and the exasperation that only comes from raising a teenager. A repetitive excuse often followed the look, like the one about Alvis's mother keeping herself hidden as a Chosen One, too. Or how joining the resistance group, Linless, was too dangerous. Or that Alvis's impulsive attitude was guaranteed to ruin Linless missions.

Impulsive. Can't really argue with that, Alvis thought, as he dropped from the fire escape onto a skinny blonde with greasy hair and a knife in his hand. The boy groaned as he slammed into the icy concrete. Alvis dug his heel into the guy's back, earning him a pained gasp. He looked at the shocked faces of the five other punks who thought ganging up on an older Guardian woman was a good use of their time.

Without bothering to take turns, the kids were on him, weapons and fists swinging. A lucky punch connected with his stomach, followed by a knife slashing across his bicep, but he barely noticed, too lost in familiar movements—dodging, kicking, and punching. With grunts and groans, bodies knocked away from him. If his fist was making contact, he didn't care about the details.

"Why are you defending her?" one kid growled, wiping at his bloody lip. "She's a filthy Guardian!"

The locket flared warm beneath his shirt and against his chest. Alvis tightened his fist—the slight surge of extra power made his fingers tingle. But somewhere between leaping at the guy, and watching him fall to the ground, unconscious, regret hit him.

Shit, that was overkill.

The gang members didn't seem to notice Alvis's extreme use of force—they were too busy gathering themselves up and scattering, dragging their unmoving comrade along with them. They shouted threats of payback over their shoulders as they ran away, and Alvis would have thrown up his middle finger if he weren't heaving and panting.

Adrenaline still flowed through him, setting his nerves on fire and making his fingers itch for more. The wound on his arm stung, but his coat and sweater had taken the brunt of it, keeping it shallow.

Alvis approached the older woman he'd defended, and crouching, offered her his arm, gently helping her from the cold, filthy ground. He never trusted his hands with older folks—their bones were too fragile against his strength. "Are you okay, ma'am?"

The older lady was barely able to balance on shaking legs, but still she nodded, and softly thanked him. Her deep blue, reptilian eyes focused on him for too long. "Are you a Guardian as well, child?"

Panicked, Alvis gave her a tilted smile behind his bandana, and pulled his hood back over his head. "No, I'm just good at fighting." It wasn't a lie, not exactly. Whether the woman believed him, Alvis didn't wait to figure out; he sprinted down the alleyway, tossing her a quick wave over his shoulder.

The bitter cold stung his lungs as Alvis darted through the crowded streets and dingy back alleys of Bellow. He was already rehearsing his cool, collected, I-did-absolutely-nothing-against-your-rules face for when his dad inevitably noticed the cut in Alvis's coat, and they had that same old conversation all over again.

CHAPTER 2

WITH A JERK, RAE WOKE UP with tears on his cheeks, and his sister's face stained in perfect detail behind his eyelids.

He shot up off the thin, tattered mattress, choking on a gasp. Nausea like a tidal wave made his stomach lurch into his throat. He swallowed it back with practiced effort and folded forward to bury his face into his knees. The tears dampened his prison uniform. The memory of blood beneath his nails made his fingers twitch.

Breathe, Rae reminded himself. *Breathe like you're blowing out a candle.*

He grabbed at his white hair, tugging harshly at the tangles to ground himself. Deep breaths made the raw wound on his chest scream, every uncomfortable stretch of skin causing sweat to drip down his temple. Each slight twist of his body made him want to sob. Blood was once again leaking through the fresh bandages, staining his already filthy clothes.

The pain wasn't something he had missed these past ten years.

The Hanah from his nightmare still hadn't faded. He uncurled himself and tilted his head back, throwing his eyes open to try to banish it. The harsh lights of his cell were blinding, but he resisted squinting against them, letting the white spots in his vision cleanse the darkness he was close to losing himself in.

Rae's cell was three bare white walls, the last wall a line of metal bars. It was empty besides himself and his bed. And it was freezing like always. The rapidly cooling sweat on his uniform clung to his back, sending a wash of goosebumps over his grimy skin.

Fighting a shiver, Rae grabbed the thin blanket from the ground where he must have kicked it off in his restless sleep and wrapped it around his shoulders. The gentle weight of it made him feel small and weak, but he was used to feeling weak by now.

As Rae shifted the blanket, the shackle around his right wrist slid down his forearm. He sucked in a pained breath as it scratched against the fresh gash there. Rae slid the chain back up and gently ran his thumb over the bandage. He hadn't been awake when they cut open his arm to insert the tracking device. Once the injury healed, it would join the other longer scar beneath. It had been the last scar he ever received before being given his gemstone ten years ago.

The old and the new. Both tethered him to the past

more than any chain ever could.

"Hey, Bloodied Champion."

An ugly fury burned in Rae's chest at the title. He forced his expression to remain neutral.

Metal scraped against the tile floor, sending a grinding screech into the cell. The guard pulled her sword back off the ground, clearly annoyed that Rae ignored her taunt.

Rae didn't recognize her—not surprising, as he received a new guard daily. But he didn't need to look to know she was smirking in the pompous way *Drakon* did when one of their own became a "mere *Kon*."

"Answer when you're spoken to."

With a short, exasperated exhale, Rae finally turned towards her. He kept his face blank, but he tilted his head in a way he knew was calculated as it was condescending. "You didn't ask a question."

For a prison, Trailor was bizarrely bright; the guard had no chance of hiding the angry flush on her cheeks. She hit her sword against the bars, scowling when Rae continued to remain unphased. "You really are as stuck up as they say."

Rae remained silent and unblinking as he watched her bravado. When she finally found the courage to step against the cell bars, her scowl slid into a snarl with barred fangs. Yellow and red eyes flared. One hand gripped a bar, and gray smoke began to swell from between her fingers, sending the heavy stench of iron into the air. "You think you're so important because you were the highest Ranker. But how many of us did you kill, just so you could throw it all away?"

Rae's heart picked up at the accusation. The truth of it struck deep into his guilt, like long claws sinking between his ribs. He forced his breathing to even out, and his quiet voice was hoarse and rusty. "Any *Drakon* who becomes a Ranker knows the risks."

"*Peera drakon ah!*"

That grotesque phrase—Rae wanted to scrawl it across every mansion in Nerwen City, simply so he could smash it to pieces.

"You were a symbol of power," the guard growled, green scales rapidly covering her skin, glistening when they caught the light.

"It was never my intention to be."

Under her hand, the metal glowed an angry orange. "You betrayed us, Bloodied Champion. You betrayed Zen!"

Finally, Rae eyes flashed dark—the blanket fell to the mattress as he stood and walked to the bars with blind intent. The guard was taller than him, and still gripped her sword in one hand, but Rae could see fear creeping into her face. "If anyone has betrayed you, it's Zen itself," he spat, bitter and unafraid of how blasphemous the words were. He couldn't care less—he was already going to be executed, hope of escape growing dimmer by the day.

There was no risk in declaring that his loyalty no longer belonged to the country that had lied to him, used him, and taken his sister from him, despite every promise she would be safe. "I will not be a hero to anyone who doesn't realize that Zen has reduced our race to mere puppets."

The guard's eyes watered, burning bright with anger at the truth of Rae's words. Her body began to stretch, bright green wings slowly pushing their way from her back, and her hand gripping the bar transformed into a claw. Rae and the guard's hybrid dragon race was far smaller than their ancestors, but they were still taller than most humans and continued to be far stronger. Rae braced his feet against the tile, prepared to spring forward once the guard's clawed hand ripped the cell bars free from the ceiling.

"My, my!" A voice chided, playful and smooth, silk curling around every word. "What a fascinating turn-around of beliefs."

The hallway was suddenly so cold Rae swore he saw his own breath.

The guard's dragon form retreated in a snap—taking Rae's chance of escape with it. She stumbled back, acting like she hadn't stupidly put herself within Rae's reach, or nearly ripped open his cell. She bowed to the approaching figure. "Captain Cian."

Cian ignored her.

He looked the same as always; skin eerily white and tinted blue, veins lurking too close to the surface. Diamond blue eyes flashed beneath white eyelashes, and his long ice-blonde hair was perfectly tied in a low braid. A dark blue, finely pressed suit and silver tie covered his strong, slim build and long poised limbs.

Cian walked with his back slightly curved, his shoulders pulled back too far to be considered natural. It was a posture he felt struck the right balance of casual and menacing, no matter how many times Rae told him it wasn't. Cian came to a stop in front of Rae's cell, hands informally tucked in his pockets.

"To think, Rae, little more than a week ago, you were so desperately fighting for your country."

A little more than a week ago, Rae had considered Cian one of the people closest to him.

Cian knew who Rae had spent every match fighting for, and it most certainly had never been Zen.

The guard sneered. Cian's mocking of Rae was fuel meant to ignite the *Drakons'* rage against their disgraced hero. Their contempt of him was why Rae would never again find peace is Nerwen City, even if he could escape.

Rae remained silent.

Cian hummed, eyeing Rae's chest. A smirk quirked his pale lips when he saw the blood soaking through Rae's shirt. "Nine days without your gemstone! How hellish is it without your magic? Without that impenetrable shield? How does pain feel now that you are powerless to prevent it?"

Unimaginable. Like losing part of your very soul.

"Why so bitter, Cian?" Rae responded. "Are you heartbroken you'll never get the chance to beat me without underhanded tricks?"

The guard made a choking noise, shocked at Rae's insolence.

In a blink, the door to Rae's cell flew open and Cian's freezing hand wrapped around his throat. His back slammed into the wall—head snapping backwards with a painful crack. Rae blinked away the spots blurring his vision, but he was powerless against the thin, sharp ice twisting into needles and pricking his neck. Rae tried to call his magic to harden his skin—to throw up that protective barrier he always depended on—but nothing happened. *Of course, nothing happened.*

Pride twisted Cian's frown into something sinister— he had never successfully used his attribute against Rae before. His mouth split into a victorious grin, all freezing sharp edges. Rae forced his face to remain stoic; he would never again give his former family the satisfaction of seeing his pain.

Cian's face faltered. Then he chuckled—it was shaky and mirthless. With one hand still clamped around Rae's throat, he set his other hand against the bandages on Rae's chest. His touch was like a caress, gentle and careful. Then suddenly, the ice surrounding Rae's neck retreated into Cian's freezing palm and slid out of the hand on Rae's chest. Hot pain sliced into the raw hole above Rae's heart like a hundred papercuts. Rae cried out, finally unable to stay quiet.

"Don't act so irreverent, Bloodied Champion. You should feel fortunate you've been sentenced to death, instead of spending the rest of your days without an attribute."

Rae tried to push away, but Cian pressed more slivers of ice into his chest, forcing another gasp from him.

"You are nothing without your gemstone. You're a disgraceful *Kon* now, a fallen *Drakon*. A dragon without his magic. *A Guardian.*"

With a sharp yank, Cian pulled his hand away from

Rae's chest, the ice ripping away from the bandage at a cruel angle. Then the hand around Rae's throat released, and he slid to the ground, gasping for air. Rae felt bruises purpling his neck, already tender when he trailed his fingers over them. They hurt far too much—why did something so simple as a bruise *hurt so much?*

"You're right about one thing, Rae. You won't die a hero. You will die showing all Guardians what happens to those who betray Zen."

Cian knelt in front of him—he rubbed his thumb across Rae's damp cheek, his eyebrow perking when Rae didn't resist the touch. Cian's sharp grin flashed again, his blue eyes drinking in a Rae he hadn't seen in years. Committing it to memory. Reveling in it.

"Peera Drakon ah, Rae."

CHAPTER 3

THROUGHOUT THE WORLD'S HISTORY, there have been many misconceptions and untruths held as fact. Perhaps the greatest of these was this: dragons had always longed for the destruction of humanity.

Dragons had been the first creatures of the Earth. They had sought to do nothing but sow the love they were brought to life by, and nature had looked kindly on them because of it; air gave their wings flight, fire protected them, water nourished them, the green of the world gave them near immortality. In loving harmony, they had danced with the magical abilities the spirits of the Earth had granted them.

When humans appeared, dragons had roared in celebration, knowing they were to live side by side with another of Earth's magnificent beings.

Humans were made to be curious. They were brought

to life to search for wisdom and use their gifts for the good of future generations. But as their knowledge grew, so did their lust for war. Countries began to fight amongst themselves. And as humans' destruction grew, it took with it the world that had given the dragons strength; sprawling forests of green turned to dust, lakes and oceans became deserts of desolate winds, clouds turned from white to a fraught gray as they were overcome with smoke instead of storms.

The dragons' powers had begun to fade.

The leader of the dragons had been known as the Dragon Queen. She'd been a kind and dedicated leader, who had ruled their land since the beginning of time. She'd witnessed her brethren—her children—falling one by one into an eternal sleep, as their life force waned. With each child she had lost, the Dragon Queen wept.

And her anger had grown.

For the first time, humans had learned what it meant to fear a dragon.

The destruction to the world was irreversible, and the dragons' desperate attempt at survival had been their final fight.

Near the end, a young woman, armed with nothing but determination for peace and her grandmother's spell book, had appeared before the ailing Dragon Queen. "I met one of your children. She spoke of what we humans have done," she had said, shock pulling her voice into barely more than a whisper. "Is it true?"

"You humans appeared in numbers, and as your numbers swelled, so did your wars and destruction," the

Dragon Queen had snarled, her voice worn and rough as gravel, but sturdy as steel. "Fire cannot burn a dragon, but it can destroy us just the same. I was alive to see the first of my kind born, and now I shall be the last of us to die. It is a pain you can never begin to imagine."

Upon hearing this, the young scientist had begun to cry. "Let me help you live on," she had said, desperate and well-intentioned. The knowledge of what her kind had done to bring the dragons to extinction filled her with a deep dread and anguish. "The country I come from is Quint. We have scientists!" She had held up the worn spell book. "And mages! We haven't been successful with magic yet, but if we work together, maybe we can find a way for dragons to survive. If it is humanity's fault, then it is also our responsibility to fix it. Please, help me make this right."

The Dragon Queen had silently watched the small creature before her. She had sensed no fear in her, instead an honesty she did not know humans were capable of. It had given her hope she never thought she would feel again, for at its core, her heart was still kind.

She had struggled forward, her long limbs slow as she drew closer to her final breath. The young woman had been awed at the magnificent beast looking down upon her.

"Tell me, human child. What is your name?"

"Ellowyn Clark."

"Ellowyn, do you carry something precious to you?"

Ellowyn had crinkled her brow, then her eyes lit up. She had reached beneath her shirt and pulled out a locket.

For a moment, she'd watched the way it dangled from its chain. The new, crookedly engraved "A" had caught the little bit of light available. Tears had begun to fall, but she bit her lip to fight them back and held the necklace up. "This was given to me by someone very important, as a reminder of who we used to be, and who we can become."

"My trust in humans is damaged," the Dragon Queen had whispered, the air of her words still a forceful wind. She had bent her neck, close enough for Ellowyn to see the beauty of her scales. It had taken all of Ellowyn's willpower to stop herself from reaching out a hand to feel them.

"I have dwelt many years in anger. However, justified or not, it is exhausting. And I am not so proud as to take it to my grave."

The bright blue of the Dragon Queen's eyes had turned into a magnificent array of colors, then her entire body had begun to glow. The light had compressed and burst forth, racing into the locket between Ellowyn's fingertips.

"This is the last of my magical power. May it pass down through generations as worthy of it as you," the Dragon Queen had said, and bowed her head before Ellowyn. "The age of dragon is ending, but perhaps a new age can begin. An age where man and dragon can truly co-exist. If you are capable of such a feat, human child, then you have my blessing." The Dragon Queen had rested her body against the ground, her muscles settling as though a great weight had been lifted from them.

Hand shaking with regret, Ellowyn had traced her

fingers across the Dragon Queen's scales; they had been chilly to the touch, but there'd been a warmth beneath them, a comfort she had never known before. Closing her eyes, Ellowyn had rested her forehead upon the Dragon Queen's cheek, as high as her height allowed.

"I promise my life, mighty Dragon Queen. I will find a way for dragons to exist again. And I will find a way for humans and dragons to live in peace."

The Dragon Queen had breathed her last.

CHAPTER 4

BELLOW WAS A SHADOW; a large collection of slums stretching along the outside of Nerwen City's Untouchable Wall, a barrier created with *Drakon* magic to keep out those deemed unworthy. Some were born in Bellow, like Alvis, while some settled there from other cities in Zen, leaving their war-torn homes for the promise of one day being invited into the so-called paradise that was Nerwen City, the shining capital of Zen.

The technology of Bellow was rustic at best; gas lamps and flames were more common than the electric ones used in the capital. The ones that were electric in Bellow just meant burnt out bulbs that were never quickly replaced.

Crime was high and common, almost numbingly so. Brothels and bars numbered higher than classrooms, their frequent customers mostly business suits and officers from Nerwen City who condemned the sinners of

Bellow by day, then took advantage of the crime by night.

At the shore were docks where fishermen worked to capture fish, the best of which they would never eat themselves. Bellow was filled with the factories that Nerwen City refused to have within its walls. The bigwigs claimed this was because they wanted the citizens of Bellow to have employment opportunities, but they simply wanted the profits without getting their hands dirty.

None of this bothered Alvis though—Bellow was his home; all he knew and everything he would ever know.

Calling where he and his dad lived a house was far too generous. A thin, single story building, it rested tightly in the nook of an alleyway behind the abandoned butcher shop his dad had converted into a workshop and store. On the other side of their home was a sloping apartment building, whose tenants came and went as quickly as the months slid into each other.

The white paint on the outside of their house was chipped and faded. The inside was simple and compact, with barely any furniture; a couch with numerous holes and a cushion missing, a dining table and chairs in the kitchen, two mattresses in two tiny rooms. Their fridge was dingy, but in good working order, thanks to his dad's incredible mechanical skills.

Across the hall from Alvis's bedroom was a bathroom, so tiny that Alvis needed to duck to avoid hitting his head. And there was a stool by the bath he sat on to bathe because he couldn't fit in the tub properly. They had running water, which meant they were luckier than most of the town, but it was often frigid, and they could only use it a few times a week to avoid the bill being too high.

The shop out front was twice the size of their home, but no less worn down. Aside from the door, the glass windows lining the shopfront had been painted black prior to their arrival, making one wonder what exactly the former "butcher" really dealt in. Beyond the addition of colorful graffiti from who knows which gang, the windows had remained that way since. A wooden sign with the words "Mechanic Michael" in intricately painted letters, hung above the front entrance.

When Alvis reached the shop in the late afternoon, he didn't even think about unlocking it; when he pushed at the door, it opened easily like it always did. Alvis used to sigh and shake his head because not locking the front door was an open invitation for thieves to waltz in and take what they pleased. Then he got older and realized an unlocked door told strangers that Michael Witt had nothing to hide. If the front door was open, no one would assume how tightly secured and hidden all the other entrances were.

Aside from the standard dust being blown around by his entrance, the shop was empty as usual. He made his way through the store, past the aisles with the few cases of items for sale, to the door separating the sales floor from Michael's workshop. Alvis grabbed the chain around his neck, pulling it out from under his shirt. The metal key clanked gently against the locket next to it when he slid it into the lock and twisted.

"I'm home," Alvis said into the darkness, closing the door behind him. He slid the latch of the lock back in place, then twisted the knob to lock it, too.

The wooden stairs below him were steep, and at the bottom lay an unmoving form, one hand outstretched towards the top of the staircase.

Unbothered, and with a complete lack of sympathy, Alvis descended the stairs, and nudged his boot against his dad's ribs. "Why're you sleeping here, old man—"

Suddenly, Alvis's world spun as a hand gripped his ankle and pulled. He landed hard against the cement on his stomach, one of his arms bent painfully around his back.

"You really should stop calling your dad 'old.' At least not while I can still get you into a chokehold," Michael playfully chided. He tugged at Alvis's bent arm for emphasis.

Alvis groaned, smacking his free hand on the ground in defeat, until his dad released him. He pushed himself up, and shook out his shoulder, glaring up at his father. "That was completely unnecessary."

Michael flashed him a cheeky grin. "That's your punishment. What kind of son insults before checking if their father is okay?"

"The one who knows how dramatic you are."

In most people's opinion, Michael was strange, but oddly approachable. He wasn't exactly who people expected when they thought of his position in the rebel group, Linless. He grinned so often it felt weird when he didn't. His tan face was constantly peppered with uneven scruff, and his shoulder-length black hair had streaks of gray. It was always pulled back into a loose and messy ponytail, tangled and sticking up everywhere from when he pulled and scratched at it in frustration over his latest project. His clothes were dirty and untucked, his olive skin was always covered in streaks of grease, and he would lose his thick-framed glasses if they weren't fastened to his head with a red elastic band.

What Michael lacked in appearance, he more than made up for with his unrivaled engineering and mechanical work. He was, by far, the best mechanic in all of Bellow.

Even though work was sporadic, and sometimes came from less-than-stellar people, he had many loyal customers. But he never asked for credit; when a customer was satisfied with his work, and promised to spread the word about him, he would politely ask them not to.

"I'm a simple mechanic," he would say, with a humble chuckle and sheepish smile. "People talking like I'm someone renowned is too much pressure for a guy like me."

I'm part of the rebellion and would prefer not having the wrong person showing up on my doorstep, is what he was really saying. Especially if you had the right ears and knew how many members of Linless walked through his shop door.

Michael was the best type of person. Sometimes he worked with sketchy people, but more often he worked with those who couldn't afford it. Alvis and his father, with the little they had, looked exceedingly privileged next to many of those around them. When the heater of the family down the street broke, Michael spent fourteen straight hours without sleep, fixing it. He even went so far as to improve its efficiency and decrease the risk of it starting a fire.

And when most businesses in Bellow shunned and refused service to Guardians, Michael welcomed them so openly that every other project he was working on took a backseat to whatever need they had. Occasionally, disgusting gossipers would whisper about Michael's "abnormal" urge to help "*those* people." Maybe he helped Guardians because of the whole his-son-was-secretly-a-human-with-dragon-magic thing. Or maybe it was his way of atoning for what he'd done while working in the prison and science facility, Trailor. Whatever the reason, Michael treated Guardians and *Kon* the way other humans in Bellow refused to: special and gentle, like they were of far higher importance than himself. Not trash, merely because they were dragons without their magic.

Michael suddenly grabbed Alvis's arm, yanking Alvis out of his thoughts, and inspected the slice across his son's bicep, despite Alvis's pained yelp. "How did you get into a fight? All I asked you to do today was search for a new job."

"You can't really call it a fight if the other guys didn't have a chance."

Michael scoffed, "You don't need stitches this time, luckily." He dropped Alvis's arm—like he couldn't be bothered to worry about it ever again—and set back to work, perching on a stool to inspect a gear through a microscope. "Should I even bother telling you not to do it again?"

"Only if you think saving old ladies is a bad thing?"

Michael leveled him with a look over the rim of his glasses, but still shook his head with a soft smile, like he was proud of Alvis, but couldn't say it out loud without encouraging his behavior. "Did you use your magic?"

Alvis pulled out that "what, no, of course not, I would never" face he'd practiced all the way home. But his dad's unimpressed stare was a blatant give away that Alvis hadn't gotten any better at lying since the last time he tried. "Only for a punch, okay? No one even noticed."

" 'No one'?"

"Nope," Alvis answered, because the old lady hadn't been an opponent, which meant she didn't count.

The legs of the spare stool scrapped obnoxiously against the concrete as Alvis pulled it up to the table. "What are you working on?"

Caught between pressing the argument over Alvis's fighting and knowing it would play out the same way it always did, Michael dropped the subject. "The same project as yesterday."

"The generators?"

Michael hummed in the affirmative. "Charlie stopped by and dropped off some more parts this afternoon. Apparently, his client ordered an extra dozen."

"Wants them in the same amount of time, I bet."

"But of course."

That explained why his dad hadn't taken time to sleep or eat. It was a common occurrence when Michael took a job from his broker-slash-Linless operative, Charlie; he would come in with a job that seemed innocent and simple enough, only to exponentially increase the workload after Michael had already started on it. Since an incomplete job neither paid, nor made the clients Charlie promised the goods to very happy—and those clients weren't exactly the kind of people you *wanted* to piss off—Michael was constantly at the mercy of ridiculous deadlines.

Setting his elbow against the cool metal of the desk, Alvis leaned forward, and rested the palm of his chin in his hand, leisurely observing the way his dad worked on the generator.

For as goofy and flippant as his dad presented himself, Michael's hands were always focused and careful when it came to his work. Calloused fingers delicately maneuvered a metal cylinder against the surface of the desk, while his other hand worked on attaching a thin copper wire to the center. His dad's hands were rough, nails dirty and broken, but he was patient with a care that made it seem like he was working with a fragile newborn, rather than a lifeless piece of scrap metal.

A familiar pang of envy filled Alvis.

Ever since he was a boy, Alvis would watch his father and dream of doing what he did. He had memories of sitting in his dad's lap on the dusty workshop floor with a homemade, wooden screwdriver in his hand, while a heavier, metal version twisted between Michael's fingers. And of standing on tiptoe at the desk, in awe, as he watched his dad work, fingers moving fast and graceful from one part to the next. He would replicate the movements. But then his mom died when he was seven and his magical attribute was awakened. Replicating became watching and mesmerizing, as another piece of wood cracked, or metal crinkled in his palm, or glass shattered between his hands. Alvis used to cry about it when he was younger, frustrated to the point of tears when yet another drill shattered, simply because he tried to use it.

His locket had fallen out of Alvis's collar during their tussle by the stairs. He ran his thumb over the unevenly carved "A," a soothing motion he'd done since his mother died, and he'd inherited it from her.

While everything else cracked in his hands, the locket never did. Sometimes he wondered if it was fate—there were only ten Ellowyn Clark Talismans in the world, each controlled by a Wielder, and he had ended up with one that was indestructible.

Attributes were endless and creative, and Alvis had gotten the short end of the stick when it came to originality. His magic wasn't creating pictures out of breath—like his mother had been able to do—or shooting lightning bolts from his feet, or healing broken legs with some fancy molecule manipulation, or something.

It was just . . . *strength*.

Somewhat controlled, but mostly simmering beneath the surface, waiting for him to get the slightest bit emotional, so it could peek out at the most inconvenient times.

At least his strength helped him fight, since that was really the only thing he was good at. Sure, he could paint okay, and he was the most efficient worker when he wasn't, y'know, getting fired. But throwing punches, reading opponents' movements, and knocking people onto their asses? *That* came as naturally to him as breathing, and Alvis could appreciate that his attribute might have a slight hand in that.

Other people didn't seem to appreciate it, though.

Like his dad, who was holding a small generator and motioning for Alvis to take it.

"This needs the cover put on it. Screws are in the box to your left, and the extra screwdriver is—oh shoot, where did I put that stupid thing?"

With one last squeeze, Alvis let the locket slide from his fingers and delicately took the collected ball of wires and copper from his dad. All he wanted to do was to shove it back into Michael's hands, and go find a roof he could practice dodging an enemy's fist. "I'm gonna mess this up. You'll just have to fix it."

"Then we'll come to that when it happens—aha!" Michael straightened, and triumphantly held up the spare screwdriver. He lightly tapped the handle of it against Alvis's forehead.

"Stop worrying about unnecessary things. If I need to fix something, I'll fix it. Simple as that." He grinned. "That's what I'm here for, after all."

CHAPTER 5

ZEN HADN'T BEGUN as a country of blood sport.

Zen had, however, always been a country of greed. And of war; it utilized its ferocious military power against others when their money wasn't enough. This led to distrust from other nations, and fear of being Zen's next invasion.

When word of the Guardians—the incredible dragon and human hybrids— had reached the King and Queen of Zen, the temptation to monopolize them became far too strong to resist. They decided to do what they did best: conquer.

As powerful as Zen's military was, they had found they could not stand against the mighty force of Quint's Guardians, as the hybrids flew into battle with their Charges, the power of their Pacts releasing the Guardians' devastating magic.

For the first time in its history, Zen had tasted defeat. Treaties of peace had been written and agreed upon. And as Zen had bowed its head, the King and Queen asked for one thing: a Talisman to create their own Guardians.

For years, their request had been denied, even as Guardians from other parts of the world made their new home in Zen. But as Ellowyn Clark grew older, her belief in the good of the future had remained strong. She had felt that Zen's years-long promise to treat their new Guardian citizens as equals would be followed through. So, despite facing disagreement from the monarchy and state council, Ellowyn had finally granted her last Talisman, the Bowl of Reparation, to Zen.

Her belief in Zen had borne true, for a time.

Years had passed, and Guardians were welcomed into Zen's society, both within the capital of Nerwen City and across the rest of the country.

Every human citizen and Guardian had been given the opportunity to create a Pact, if they desired to, even in the poorest parts of the nation. A Pact was a powerful, magically binding connection; the strength of a human's soul—a Charge—paired with a Guardian's dragon power.

It didn't take long for greedy eyes to focus on the power of a Pact.

Beneath the ruling class's façade of equal opportunity, they had grown bored during peacetime. Simply counting their riches had no longer been enough, and soon they'd looked elsewhere for entertainment.

And thus, the sport of Rankers had been born.

The wealthy twisted Pacts into something new, something rich neighbors used to measure their wealth and power. Guardians and their Charges were pitted against each other as Rankers in fighting tournaments, some legal, some not. Some Guardians fought of their own accord, some against their will.

However, it had not taken long before impoverished and poor Pacts had begun to rise in the rankings, defeating those of the rich and powerful, until even the King's Rankers had been defeated. It had been then that the elite proved that the wrath of the prideful knows no limits.

The formation of a Pact could not be influenced by money, education, or birthright. So together, the King, politicians, banks, and wealthy, had released a new decree: Pacts beneath a certain societal status were now illegal, and punishable by death.

This decree had soon led to the most atrocious act ever committed by Zen, forever staining the country red.

It was a night that became known as the Massacre of Charges.

CHAPTER 6

LATER THAT NIGHT, as the two Witt's sat around the dinner table eating stale bread and cold eggs, there was a loud, heavy knock on the front.

Alvis and Michael tensed briefly, a reflex from living in Bellow, and Michael doing what he did. But when Michael glanced through the peephole, he breathed out an annoyed sigh, moved to unlock the two deadbolts, and opened the door.

On the other side stood Charlie. His coat collar was tugged up to his ears and his hat pulled low. The light from his cigarette was the only reason his face was visible. His hands were in the pockets of his trench coat, obviously trying to look poised despite the freezing cold.

He grinned at Michael from around his cigarette. "Evening."

Charlie was a picture boy for suave confidence. He

wore crisp suits and ties and walked with a smooth conviction that was as enticing as it was suspicious. He looked even younger than his twenty-nine years, with rugged features, and a strong jawline consistently covered in a five o'clock shadow. The beard always stood out against his snow-white skin. His voice was like an aged whiskey, strong but sweet, and he spoke in a convincing Eastern accent to lend himself a certain enticement that put you at ease with a simple word. Whether Charlie was actually from the East or it was simply another part of his well painted character, Alvis didn't know because Charlie never let anyone close enough to know. He acted like a familiar book, with the cover worn and pages bent to mark favorite passages, but in reality, he was sealed shut and locked, the key long lost.

Alvis didn't dislike Charlie, but the best part of Charlie was who tagged along with him.

"Alvy!" Miller sang and jumped out from behind Charlie, his short stature making it seem like he'd appeared from nowhere. Miller's tight curls were free from hair ties today, and his familiar dark features caused a little flutter in Alvis's stomach.

Crooked smile as big as always, Miller settled into the seat next to Alvis and the two exchanged a fist bump with practiced ease.

Miller had been in Alvis's life since they were ten. He had ended up at the orphanage down the street. One day, Alvis saw him surrounded by three older kids, holding his own despite being outnumbered. He'd jumped in to defend him, only to have Miller punch him, too, right after the last kid had fallen because he had figured Alvis was backup for the other kids. Miller had offered to buy him fruit as an apology, but didn't have any money, so Alvis had paid for it instead. He hadn't minded because Miller's parents had been former gang members before they were killed by the Royal Police. Miller had offered to show Alvis what fighting techniques he'd learned from them, which was the best payment Alvis could've asked for.

A year ago, Charlie needed some new brawn to help him deal with less-than-pleasant clients. No one was particularly surprised when he hired Miller, despite him being barely seventeen. Miller was levelheaded, sly, and focused. He was short and lanky, with the face of a cherub, despite the long scar across his left cheek.

Cocky men were never prepared to fight someone who looked as innocent as Miller, and that made Miller dangerous.

Miller's hand dropped to Alvis's leg under the table, brown eyes twinkling playfully. Alvis flushed, and threw a warning glance at him, because they weren't exactly alone, but he didn't pull way, either.

Like Alvis said. *Dangerous.*

"What brings you by tonight, Charlie?" Michael asked after they sat down in their chairs. "We agreed on extra time for the generators."

Charlie waved a hand absentmindedly, dismissing Michael's concern. Charlie leaned his chair back on two legs, threw one arm over the back, and crossed his legs, his ankle resting atop his knee. He took a long draw from his cigarette, tilted his head back, and blew it out slowly.

"Got me some news from the capitol. Seems the Bloodied Champion is set to be executed."

Despite the heater beneath the table, a chill filled the room instantly.

"Can't imagine Linless will be too happy about it, considering the plans they have for him."

Alvis straightened at the mention of Linless. "What plans?"

"Don't know the details, but I hear they've got plans to get him a Charge—"

Michael's glass made a loud clink as he set it on the table. "That's enough, Charlie."

Charlie's chair slammed back to the ground. The broker looked annoyed, almost offended by Michael's interruption. "Oi, this won't be an easy one, Mikey. We need all the help we can get." He jammed a thumb in Alvis's direction. "Don't you think it's time to stop your unnecessary coddling, and let him use his powers?"

Mouth dropping open, Alvis looked from Charlie to his dad. "Dad, what the hell—"

There was a scraping of wood, as Michael harshly slid his chair back and stood. He smiled at Alvis, too playful for the tense atmosphere in the room.

"Charlie and I need to have a conversation in the workshop. You two stay here and enjoy the rest of dinner."

Alvis shot up from his chair, so fast it tumbled backwards to the floor, nearly sending Miller with it. His knee banged against the table, making the dishes clatter.

"You can't just expect me to leave it like that! What

happened to all that 'keep it hidden no matter what' shit? Why does *Charlie* get to know about me—" Alvis gestured to Miller, almost smacking him in the face. "When I'm not even allowed to tell Miller?"

"This isn't the time for us to have this argument again," said Michael.

"But Charlie's right! If I can use my powers to fight, then I should! I don't get why you won't let me—"

"*Alvis.*"

Alvis's breath stilled. A chill ran up his spine.

As Alvis grew up, he felt many things for his father; respect for the work he did, admiration for how kind he was, annoyance for how he babied Alvis.

Never, not once, did Alvis feel fear.

His dad's expression right then—so cold, intense, and threatening; jaw tightened, and lips pulled into a thin line, eyes unblinking—*terrified* him.

Charlie's cigarette slipped from his mouth to the floor. He hastily pressed his heel into the butt, as though he intentionally let it fall. He sent a pitying look Alvis's way, before he trailed out the door after Michael, walking like a lamb to the slaughter.

Alvis's heart pounded, throwing out alarms to his brain to—for once—run, instead of fight.

CHAPTER 7

"I GOT THE invitation," Miller said.

He settled back onto the thin mattress Alvis called his bed and stretched his arms over his head. The sleeves of Alvis's oversized sweater slid down toned forearms, and the collar fell off one shoulder, revealing smooth black skin glowing from light of a small lamp on the nightstand.

Miller always stole Alvis's clothes after they found themselves here in Alvis's bed, satisfied and laughing over stupid jokes. But he left them smelling like smoke and cinnamon, so Alvis didn't mind.

When Alvis did nothing more than blankly stare, Miller pinched his side, annoyed. "Did I break you earlier? I'm talking about *the* invitation. Into Nerwen City."

"Oh."

Miller's frown deepened. "Can you act like you'll actually miss me?"

Like a fuse lighting off, Alvis pounced. He wrapped his arms loosely around Miller's waist and nuzzled his face into his stomach.

"Of course, I'll miss you, dumbass. Sorry. I'm just distracted."

Miller relaxed instantly into his arms with a soft, relieved chuckle. Fingers scrapped through Alvis's hair and mused the ebony locks. "You thinking about what happened earlier?"

Alvis loosened his hold and rolled onto his back, sticking close enough for Miller to continue stroking his hair.

He stared up at the cracked ceiling of his bedroom and sighed.

"I don't get it. I could defeat every bad guy in the world and Dad would still find some excuse to keep me out of Linless. It's not like they don't have other kids my age. The *leader* isn't much older than me. What's the difference between me and her?"

"Don't say details like that out in the open, dumbass. And the difference is: she doesn't have Michael Witt as her father. He knows the risks of being in Linless more than anyone else. Obviously, he's gonna stop his only son from getting involved in all that."

"Dude, he's fucking Linless's top guy in Bellow. I've been involved since I was born *because* of him." And that whole magic-of-the-Dragon-Queen thing.

It didn't matter that his dad had been so hypocritical—telling Charlie without even discussing it with Alvis first. The secret had just been so ingrained into Alvis that saying it out loud still felt wrong. If he couldn't say it to

Miller, Alvis wasn't sure he would ever be able to say it to anyone.

And Miller was the same Miller he always was. He understood Alvis had kept it for a reason and he knew Alvis wasn't good at lying, so he let the subject alone.

"I don't need him to protect me," said Alvis.

"Doesn't matter. He's your dad." Miller's next breath was shaky, no doubt knowing what fatherly sacrifices could cost. His fingers paused before resuming their previous pace. "He's gonna protect you whether you think you need it or not."

"Why should he get to decide what I do with my life, just because he thinks it's dangerous?"

"So rebellious."

"If I *wanted* to be rebellious, I could be rebellious."

Alvis held up his hands, spreading his fingers and reaching for the ceiling. "What's the point of being strong if I can't do something important with it?"

Miller snorted.

Alvis's arms went limp, flopping next to him on the bed. He tilted his head back and pouted up at Miller. "I'm serious."

"I know. How many times do I have to tell you how corny that line is?"

Slowly, Miller slid his hand from Alvis's hair down his neck. His thumb traced Alvis's jawline, then his collarbone and the scar just beneath it. Under his touch, Alvis's skin grew hotter, his breathing shallower. Miller's hand continued down his bicep, then his forearm and wrist, until he finally intertwined Alvis's fingers with his own.

"An act of grandeur isn't the only way to be a hero, you know. Sometimes saving one person can be as important as saving everyone."

Talk about cheesy lines. But unlike Alvis, Miller rarely said cheesy things. They sounded more important when he did.

Alvis held up his hand again, eyes trailing over the lines and scars on his palms, each one crossing, connecting, and blending into the next. On his knuckles, Alvis felt every punch he'd ever thrown; every broken nose that stained his clothes with another's blood, every bandage his dad wrapped around them when a fight went wrong . . .

There were endless attributes, many way more creative than increased strength. There had to be a reason why he, out of everyone, was born with *his* magic. There had to be more to all those impulsive fights and small-time victories. Was he strong just because he was a good fighter? Or was he strong because he was destined to save people?

There had *to be more.*

Miller flicked Alvis right in the middle of his furrowed brow. "Stop thinking so hard."

"I'm not." But Miller's rude attack had its intended effect, stalling Alvis's train of thought. "What about you with your 'grandeur?' Where'd you pick up a fancy word like that?"

Miller flicked him again. "I've been practicing. I hear people who speak better get higher paying jobs in Nerwen City." Miller's other hand was still intertwined with his, and Alvis resisted tightening his fingers.

"You're really leaving, aren't you?"

"Yeah."

"Does Charlie know?"

Miller shook his head.

"When do you leave?"

Uncharacteristically hesitant, Miller chewed on his bottom lip until Alvis gently dragged it free. His answer was a breath against Alvis's thumb.

"Tomorrow morning."

No one from Bellow who accepted an invitation into Nerwen City ever came back. They didn't make contact, they didn't visit. They left all of Bellow behind them, a dark mark on their past.

A plea sat on the tip of Alvis's tongue, but he knew how pointless it would be to say it. Ever since Miller's dad and stepmother were killed by the Royal Police for their association with the mafia, Miller had been determined to get into Nerwen City to find the ones who did it and take them down from the inside.

Alvis couldn't win against revenge like that.

This was it then.

No more skin touching skin, and smiles meeting smiles. The two of them would never be together like this again.

Nauseous and weighed down, Alvis said, "I love you."

Miller's hand in Alvis's suddenly felt ten degrees warmer. "I don't get how you can say that so easily, every time."

"I'm serious."

"I know."

Miller's eyes searched his; they reflected the ache in Alvis's own.

"I love you, too."

Alvis slid his hand across Miller's jaw and caressed the curly black hair. Alvis tugged Miller down to him and their lips met, gentle at first.

Alvis wanted to cling tighter, but desperation always dampened the control over his strength, so he knew he couldn't.

It worked out, though; with a grip that knocked the air from Alvis's lungs, Miller held on tight enough for them both.

SOMETIME PAST MIDNIGHT, Miller breathed softly against Alvis's neck.

Alvis could describe in detail every line of Miller's face, but his eyes still traced the rounded cheeks, the wide nose, and every other feature that made it perfect; memorizing them once more because this would be the last time he could.

Alvis's throat tightened. He needed to get away before he started crying.

He carefully unwrapped himself from Miller's arms, slid from the bed, and paused until Miller relaxed and buried himself into his pillow.

Alvis pulled on his necklace and the same pants and green sweater he had worn the day before. He made his way out of the bedroom, closing the door gently behind him.

The hallway's floorboards creaked beneath Alvis's feet. The rest of the house was still dark, and his dad's bedroom was empty.

The workshop was empty, too, when Alvis peeked into it.

He fiddled with his key and debated if eavesdropping was worth the price of his father's wrath. It wasn't the first time he'd had this argument with himself. Michael hosted countless Linless meetings; his workshop was the main spot in Bellow for them, and would continue to be, until they were compromised. Alvis lost track years ago of how often he stood outside the locked door, desperate to know what was happening inside. Each time he walked away, something deep in his bones told him it wouldn't be worth it. Not yet.

But something was different tonight. Those same bones were screaming, *this is it. Linless is the path you're destined for.*

The sound of twisting the deadbolt back into place echoed in his ears.

The shop was pitch black, giving the illusion of emptiness, but light was peeking out from beneath the door of his dad's workshop.

Alvis's breathing felt too loud. He tiptoed across the floorboards, gently stepping over the ones he knew creaked extra loudly. He pressed his ear to the door, but the metal was too thick to hear anything but a few whispers of things like, "Bloodied Champion," and "Trailor."

Quiet, quiet, quiet, Alvis told himself, as he slid the workshop key into the lock. All he needed to do was open the door enough to hear what they were talking about. It wouldn't need to be much—barely a sliver, really . . .

He swallowed, and tugged the door, praying the hinges hadn't suddenly started squeaking since that afternoon. Alvis sighed, relieved, when the door opened without a sound.

Lights from the workshop below cast a warm glow across his face. Not daring to risk a glimpse down, Alvis turned his back to the door, and settled onto his knees to listen. Soft voices carried up the stairs.

"The Bloodied Champion's execution is set for tomorrow afternoon."

That one was his dad. A flash of panic sent Alvis into flight-mode at his voice, but he tapped his locket, and kept himself from backing away.

Michael continued. "Commander Volos called for a public execution and—understandably—King Mel followed her suggestion. Our greatest chance of success, with minimal chance of exposure, would be to infiltrate Trailor before he's taken to the coliseum. However, knowing what we do about both the Bloodied Champion, and Zen, they have no plans to truly execute him."

"Then why are they making such a spectacle of it?" asked a boy Alvis didn't recognize. "Is this guy *that* important?"

"He's never lost a fight as a Ranker since he was fourteen. Rae is one of the strongest *Drakon* Rankers in Zen. He has the potential to be one of the most powerful

Guardians in the world," said a woman with a raspy, soothing voice. "And he's a twin; Zen's scientists aren't foolish enough to give up a research subject like that."

"Guardian experimentation? Shit," the boy muttered, echoing Alvis's own thoughts. "Figured killing humans for gemstones would be enough for them."

"As for why they're putting on such a show, it's to maintain order," Michael said. "Not only is his supposed death a major loss to us, him staying alive threatens the order of Zen's society. If their strongest *Drakon* can successfully rebel, then why can't other *Drakon*?"

The boy spoke up again. "Even if we are successful, can we truly trust he will be on our side, or trust him with a human Charge?"

"Not every *Drakon* is a blind sheep, Tahtsu," another voice said. The high pitch of it did nothing to dampen its bite. "Plenty of them know the truth, even if it takes time to understand it."

There was a disagreeing huff, but Tahtsu said nothing else.

"The matter of his powers remains," the woman from before said, steering the conversation back to a safer topic. "Rae won't have one of Zen's artificial gemstones or a Charge, but his underlying magic is strong. If, at any point, he becomes unconscious, his defenses will activate, and none of us will be strong enough to carry him to the checkpoint in time."

Someone responded, but Alvis couldn't hear it over the loud pounding of his heart in his ears.

Linless needed someone *strong*.

Alvis was strong.

Which meant: *Linless needed him.*

He didn't know when he opened the door wider, or when he started to grin, or when he took that first step down—all he could think about was, *this was really it.* This was his opening. His invitation towards his dream— His second step never happened.

The rotting wood beneath his feet suddenly transformed, curling around his legs and arms. He was yanked harshly backwards, back slamming into the wall at the top of the stairs. Alvis gasped, the breath knocked out of him. He tried to shake the spots from his vision, so he could figure out who the hell was attacking him on his own turf.

In the dim light, there was a woman with gray hair pooling around her feet, and wrinkles around her lips that were barely visible in the limited lighting. She knelt on her knees, hand pressed against the floor—with each move of her fingers, the wood of the stair followed, like it was at her command.

Alvis realized very quickly what this woman was: a *Drakon.*

"*Drakon*" was the term Zen's government created, to set Guardians with gemstones above every other Guardian. Zen—especially Nerwen City—didn't believe in Pacts. They believed in power. And few things were more powerful than a Guardian with a gemstone.

A *Drakon* in Bellow usually meant the Royal Police were nearby—*Drakon* only ever meant bad things, especially for something like a freaking *resistance.* Alvis realized he'd just opened the door to the one place that Nerwen City could *never* know about, if they all hoped to live.

"Who are you, intruder?" the *Drakon* growled, her gravelly voice bearing down on him, like the wood digging into his body.

"What the hell? *I'm* not the intruder here. Why is a *Drakon*—" Alvis replied without watching his tone. He bit his tongue because taunting a *Drakon* was stupid, and contrary to popular belief, he didn't have a death wish.

The woman twisted her hand against the floor, and the wood's hold tightened, splinters pricking at Alvis's skin.

"Do not dare call me by such a name, boy."

Alvis crinkled his brow—*Drakon* were rarely humble. They prided themselves, and their title, and how it showed their status. Alvis had never met one who got offended by the name.

Maybe Alvis was wrong. Maybe this woman wasn't a *Drakon*. But if she was using magic *without* a gemstone, then she could only go by one other name—

The twisting wood made its way up towards Alvis's throat.

Oh shit, he thought, the chill running down his spine a reminder he was facing a truly powerful enemy for once. Panic hit him like a glass of cold water, then his locket flared warm, pushing the fear back.

He flexed his arm, and yanked, breaking out of the wood easily.

The woman's eyes widened. She twisted her hand again, and the wood would have grabbed Alvis's leg, if he hadn't—in a breathtaking display of clumsiness—slipped on the top step.

He rolled down the stairs, and into a room full of shocked faces he didn't know.

The one he did know didn't look happy to see him.

"Dad!" Alvis pulled himself to his feet, despite the ache from falling. "A Guardian! Upstairs—"

His words were cut off when his attacker reached the bottom of the stairs. She slammed her hand against the bottom step, and it turned into a large spike, pointed directly at Alvis.

"Ellian, retreat." Michael said.

Ellian obeyed without hesitation, the spike withdrawing into the stairs like it had never existed.

Alvis's body nearly went limp when the threat vanished. But a whole new threat appeared as his father grabbed him by the arm and harshly pulled him up. Without a word he began dragging Alvis back towards the stairs—unnatural desperation made his grip stronger than Alvis was used to.

A new voice with a playful but sharp edge said, "Michael, is this your son?"

Michael froze, making Alvis stop as well. His eyes shut tight, his jaw working, and he exhaled slowly, like he always did when trying to maintain his composure. The fake smile he usually plastered on when he was keeping secrets pulled at his lips, but it quickly slipped away, like he knew there was no point to it.

Across the room, lounging with her hip against the corner of the table, was a young woman.

She gave off an otherworldly air: She was tall, easily Alvis's height, with smooth brown skin, and full lips painted dark red. Her black bangs parted in the middle of her forehead. The rest of her hair fell in loose curls around her shoulders. She wore a bright yellow pant suit, and pure white, closed-toe shoes with undone, golden laces. Her smile was tilted and sly, and there was only one person who could look so powerful in a meeting of Linless's strongest.

"You're Meera?" Alvis said, awed. "*The* Meera? The *Leader of Linless*, Meera?"

Michael roughly grabbed Alvis's head and pushed it down. "*Princess* Meera. Greet her properly."

Alvis gave the quickest bow in the history of bows, determined to ask Princess Meera every question about Linless he ever had before his dad could force him out of the room. But what stumbled out first was: "Are you really breaking someone out of Trailor?"

Michael grabbed Alvis's head and forced his son to look at him.

"I know what you're thinking, and the answer is—*No*."

Alvis pushed his dad's hand away. "You said that Rae guy will be experimented on for the rest of his life. If I can help him, then you can't expect me to sit here, and do nothing."

"A kid like you won't be of any help to us," said Michael.

Teeth grinding together, Alvis wanted to scream. His dad wasn't even giving him a chance; he was still concerned with keeping Alvis hidden away, refusing to believe he could be trusted with his magic.

Alvis didn't want to be hidden. He wanted to *fight*.

Alvis dragged his eyes across the faces of the Linless agents, settling on Meera. He could do it. He could spill the secret he had kept hidden his entire life. Right here, and now, in front of Princess Meera, and Linless, and his father wouldn't be able to explain it away. Then Linless would want him to fight for them. He could join the rebellion and go from Alvis—the wannabe vigilante—to Alvis, an actual rebel hero.

His father wasn't glowering at him anymore; the warning was now a deep crease between his eyebrows, his frown sending a desperate plea. Alvis's confidence almost fell apart at the seams, but he refused to let it completely unravel.

"You know I'm not just any kid. I'm—"

"Fascinating."

Suddenly, Meera was in front of him—uncomfortably close.

"You broke out of Ellian's attribute, didn't you?" she asked.

Mutely, Alvis nodded, his determination suddenly un-focused. He hadn't been wrong before about her height: Meera's eyes were at the same level as his. Alvis was caught in their mixture of brown, green, and gray.

Her eyes fell to the sliver of chain visible on Alvis's neck . . .

Holy shit, Alvis thought with a sharp inhale. *She knows.*

He shot a glance at the rest of the Linless members, but they were all merely stuck between confusion and curiosity. None of them seemed to know as much as their leader did.

"Princess . . ."

To anyone besides Alvis, Michael sounded calm and distant, like this was another piece of the heist for them to discuss. "Alvis has never been on a mission before. We can't take someone as inexperienced as him on such an important one."

"We need someone strong, in case Rae becomes unconscious," Meera replied.

It was almost like a cat and mouse game; their sentences a string of innocent words, casting an illusion, and hiding the truth from everyone but the three of them.

Meera continued, "We need someone who can break himself out of a Guardian's attribute, should they encounter trouble while carrying Rae."

"I can't let my only son go somewhere so dangerous, like Trailor," Michael said cautiously. "The Royal Police still have a bounty on my head. They won't be kind to Alvis if they find out who he is."

"Some secrets can't be kept forever, Michael," Meera purred, her ruby lips curved in excitement and intrigue. She walked back to her spot at the table, every movement elegant and smooth.

It was happening, Alvis thought. *It was finally happening—!*

"Alvis," Meera said. "How would you like to be the Bloodied Champion's escort?"

CHAPTER 8

MILLER WAS GONE when Alvis went back to his room.

Looking at his bed properly made up dampened Alvis's excitement. Here Alvis was, finally getting what he wanted most, and he would never get to see Miller's face light up for him.

But still. *Alvis was getting what he always wanted.*

Alvis was finally going on his first mission with Linless.

The excitement built up again, twisting together with the longing to see Miller, until Alvis couldn't tell which was making his stomach hurt more.

Alvis made his way over the wooden chest to dig out some new clothes. As he reached for a clean shirt, he heard his name being called from the doorway.

Honestly, the most surprising thing about it being his dad, was it had taken him—what? Twenty minutes to come and scold him? But his dad's uncharacteristic delay didn't really matter now that they were alone and out of Meera's sight. Michael could rip into him now like he wanted to, express his disdain, and order Alvis to stay home.

"Alvis, you can't use your attribute on this mission. I know you've used touches of it here and there . . ."

Alvis's eyes widened—he thought he'd kept that secret *really* well from his father.

"But inside Trailor *cannot* be where you fully utilize your attribute for the first time. It's far too dangerous. Any of Zen's top *Drakon* will be able to recognize who you are if you use your magic."

And there it was: not quite the "you can't go" speech, but close enough.

Alvis had about thirty snappy comebacks ready to fire off, until his dad held up his hand to stop him. His other hand rubbed at the ridge of his nose, as he took a deep breath. Then he sighed—this sigh was usually reserved for when his dad knew he was fighting a losing battle.

"When you get back from the mission," Michael declared, "we'll figure out together how you can use your attribute."

The lid of the chest slipped, almost slamming onto Alvis's fingers. He spun around, jaw open and speechless. "*What?*"

Michael wasn't completely thrilled by the turn of events, but he smiled softly. He always looked so much younger when the lines of his face were smoothed out like that.

"We'll most likely be relocating to Princess Meera's

homeland after this mission. I'm sure we can find someone in Quint to help you learn to use your attribute. So, promise me, Alvis: beyond rescuing the Bloodied Champion, promise me you won't use your magic."

Secret, secret. Alvis wanted to be done hiding behind that bandana. But one more time . . . he could keep his secret hidden one more time.

"Promise."

Michael stared at Alvis for a moment, before nodding, satisfied. He moved forward into the room and picked up the locket from where Alvis had set it on his bed. He ran his thumb gently over the engraving, like he wanted to transfer it to his own skin, and Alvis knew who he was thinking about.

Alvis's mother, Belle, wasn't an off-limits topic for them; her picture was the only one framed and hung in the living room with countless of Alvis's paintings taped around it.

Alvis was seven when she died, but he was old enough to remember clearly what she looked like: short, with long black hair, and one ear weirdly pointed at the tip. And what it sounded like when she laughed: boisterous, with snorts in between each giggle when Michael and Alvis really got her going. Alvis had her green eyes, and the same spirited way of facing situations head on (she called an officer an unfavorable name on more than one occasion). These were barely more than minor details, but Alvis kept them close to his heart.

"Have I told you how much your mother disliked her attribute?"

Alvis glanced up at his father. That information was new; confusing new. She had used it in front of Alvis all the time. And she would smile each time Alvis grinned, watching a wispy horse move around his head, and nuzzle his cheek in a warm brush of air, like his mother was passing along a kiss.

"The power to turn breath into art—Belle always thought it was worthless, until you were born. We couldn't figure out why you were screaming nonstop, then she made one hundred stars, and swirled them in a circle above you. You stopped crying. She'd mesmerized you with her magic."

Eyes misty, Michael smiled fondly, first at the locket, then up at Alvis. "I think for the first time she found its purpose."

Alvis had never heard this story before. It didn't seem fair of Michael to share it now, when Alvis was riding high about Linless, and low about Miller—he was tilting over the line into crying territory.

"If I'm being honest, I always hoped you would grow out of wanting to join Linless. It's like I'm hand delivering you to the enemy. I can't—" Michael bit off with a sigh. He gestured for Alvis's hand, then set the locket into it, and folded Alvis's fingers around it. "I'm terrified of losing you, but you deserve to find the purpose for your magic."

And there was that tilting feeling again, pushing him into the tears-and-warmth-in-your-chest kind of happy.

Permission. His dad was finally giving him permission to figure out his attribute—to let it out, wear it out, until it was exhausted, and he knew by muscle memory his magic's limitations.

The locket burned in his hand, hotter than Alvis knew it could get. But his dad was always great at letting Alvis ride out his emotions, giving him space to cry without pressuring him to stop.

After a moment, Michael ruffled his son's hair, pressing down hard enough to bow Alvis's neck. And then Alvis returned the tightest hug his dad had ever given him.

"I'm proud of you, Alvis. Please come back home safe."

MOST OF THE PLANS for Rae's rescue mission flew over Alvis's head.

He couldn't keep up with everyone's name, could barely connect which Charge belonged with which Guardian, and couldn't visualize how they were planning to pull off the whole thing in the first place.

Meera told Alvis he didn't need to know every detail. He was grateful for that because, yeah . . . He might have been waiting to get into Linless *forever*, but no one had time for coddling, and Alvis knew he'd feel like a child if they did.

Alvis did clue in on one very important thing, and that was this Bloodied Champion must be really, *really* important to warrant such a freaking large rescue—he was *six* teams, and *thirty-five* Linless agents kind of important, to be exact.

One team would stay behind at Michael's workshop; another was in charge of flying everyone in, and out, with invisibility attributes; the third team would stay hidden in Crimson Forest, and maintain communication, keep Charges safe, and prepare for retreat. Six Guardians and their Charges would man the front lines, to distract who knew how many Trailor guards. And there were two *Drakon*/Linless spies on the inside: one to get them entry through Nerwen City's wall, and the other to guarantee Rae's whereabouts within Trailor.

Finally, there was the rescue team—*Alvis's* team— responsible for getting Rae safely to where Zaile, a Guardian, could teleport him to the checkpoint within the Crimson Forest.

"Your magic is teleportation?" Alvis asked her, eyes damn near sparkling in awe.

Zaile grinned and pushed her oversized orange glasses back up her nose, her light gray eyes with flecks of dark red sparkling in excitement. She was built like a gymnast, and sported fiery red hair and freckles scattered across her skin like a starry sky. "Hell yeah, it is! As long as it's within distance and if I can see the destination, I can send anything and everything!"

"As long as you have the time to focus on it," scoffed her Charge, Lamont. But to Alvis he sounded proud, like acknowledging Zaile's limitations made her attribute that much more impressive.

From what Alvis had picked up on, Lamont was one of the top officials there. He would ask permission before offering Princess Meera his opinion and wouldn't hold back after he was given space to speak his mind. When outlining the plans, he was the one who stated which attribute would be needed where, and what attributes could counter them.

"Why aren't you coming with us?" asked Alvis when he learned Lamont would wait behind at the checkpoint in the Crimson Forest.

Zaile chirped up, "Guardians need their charges to Release their dragon forms. I'm responsible for teleporting Rae out, and shouldn't need mine, when Ellian and the others will be there with us. It would put Lamont in unnecessary danger. Besides, he needs to be my eyes in the Crimson Forest. If we're in range, I can teleport people to his location."

The stars in Alvis's eyes returned. "That's so freaking cool."

Before her departure back to her home country of Quint, Princess Meera took the hand of each of her subordinates, one by one, placing a delicate kiss on their knuckles, head bowed like in prayer.

When she got to Alvis, she did the same act of gratitude, without hesitation.

"With the love of the Dragon Queen, you are Linless," Princess Meera said, against Alvis's skin. "Let the rumors of its rebels soar."

CHAPTER 9

HANAH HAD SPENT most of her time in Trailor's medical ward. Her sharp mind limited to a frail body that was unable to handle a gemstone. Rae had spent his time with her any chance he could get away between training, matches, and classy dinners, where he—and other prized Rankers—were paraded around by their owners like show horses.

"If you want to survive, you must entertain — give them the confidence to place their bets on you."

Hanah's room had never felt like a cell. To Rae, the room had always felt warm, simply because Hanah was in it. Hanah had always been his home, even before their owner—Mr. Bremmet—had found them, cold, and dirty, in an orphanage in Bellow. Hanah had thought the same of Rae, as well.

Rae couldn't pinpoint when that stopped being true.

Even as she had endlessly encouraged Rae and taken care of him, Hanah's bitterness towards being the twin without an attribute had simmered beneath the surface. When they were young, Rae had sensed it was there but never touched on it. It terrified him to think that the truth would have been revealed—that one of the only people he loved, had hated him deep down for something he couldn't control. It terrified him, until he shook, and couldn't breathe. He wanted to run as far away from that truth as he could.

So, on the day Rae had been given a gemstone—when he turned from a mere Guardian into a true *Drakon*—he had made Hanah a promise: if she didn't have an attribute herself, Rae would use his own for her.

Yet, the longer Hanah had been confined to her cell, and the longer Rae fought and killed other Rankers for her sake, the less talkative she became with him. Her questions about Rae's days became fewer and farther in between. When Rae offered up the information on his own, she rarely responded with more than a hum, or a short sentence laced with sarcasm. She smiled at him less.

Commander Volos, though—*she* had earned a smile and laughter, every time Rae showed up and saw them together.

Breathe, Rae told himself. One breath. Two breaths. Three breaths.

Each reminder of Hanah he encountered, as he walked down the hallway towards his execution, grew higher pitched in his head. Rae's hands were bound, but he was still able to lift them—he craved hitting his palm against his head to knock the screeching away, but he couldn't lose face in front of the six guards escorting him. Or Cian, who was enjoying the sweat beading on Rae's brow.

Nine days ago, Rae had thrown his claws so hard against the privacy glass of Hanah's cell that it shattered, sending shards flying through the room. The glass had been cleaned up and he had had plenty of time to second-guess his timing, intrusive thoughts coming and going. But some thoughts he failed to shake . . .

Why didn't I break the glass before it was too late?

Rae might have thought Cian and his escorts were lost, leading him the wrong way on accident. They should not have been there, standing outside the glass that let doctors and scientists steal away Hanah's privacy as they slowly stole her life. The medical ward was nowhere near the back exit they should be heading towards, where a black car, with black tinted windows, waited to take him to the arena—where his death sentence would be carried out, in the same space he had spent the last seven years fighting for Hanah's life.

Cian had brought him to Hanah's old cell on purpose.

"I know you never had the chance to say goodbye," Cian said.

He said it like he was disconnected, uninvolved—as if Cian and Rae hadn't grown up together the last seven years. Like Cian hadn't been the one to break the final string holding Rae's sanity together, the day he found out Hanah was dead.

Of all the people I thought would hate me, Cian, Rae thought. *I never thought one of them would be you.*

Rae bit back tears and kept the bitterness from his voice. "Won't this detour delay my execution?"

A human guard scoffed—Jazz, if Rae recalled correctly. Not that it mattered—he wasn't particularly invested in learning people's names anymore. "You that impatient to die, Bloodied Champion?"

Rae spared him a glance, and when Jazz caught his attention, he crinkled his brow. Jazz gave Rae a nod, eyes darting between him and the windows.

"Is there something you're nervous about, Jazz?" Cian asked, mildly. His tone was less playful than before, showing that the sting of Rae's words must have had an effect.

Jazz's jump was subtle—but not subtle enough. He shook his head, metal head piece tilting awkwardly to one side. *Too obvious.* "No, sir."

Cian stepped closer, neck twisted and hand on his sword. The hilt slowly turned to ice. "Is that so? You've been checking your watch quite often. It seems to me you're awfully concerned with the time—"

The windows exploded.

A black dragon roared, shrill and intimidating, announcing their presence. Snout adorned with robust horns; their short neck immediately retreated back through the cavern in the wall they had just created.

Before the glass settled from the first impact, more windows burst, and a second dragon dove through. Surrounded by thin sparks, the small beige dragon wrapped their jaws around one of the human guards. A young girl leaned off the dragon's back and slammed a silver staff through the guard's chest. Electricity buzzed through the metal and into the guard. The dragon reopened their jaw, letting the body fall—still twitching—to the ground.

The girl slid from the beige dragon's head and grasped the staff, pulling it free—while the dragon curled protectively around her, a warning to their enemies. On the girl's bare arm was a tattoo—black lines that were sharp-edged, like static.

Charges, Rae realized. *Here, in Zen—in Trailor.*

With trained instincts, Rae's *Drakon* guards transformed in colored flashes of light. Their bodies stretched and grew into their dragon forms—magical attributes immediately activating—and fought back the intruders.

The remaining human guards rushed to Rae's side, harshly grabbing his shoulders, and throwing him behind them. Their swords went up, prepared to attack—when the first dragon who'd broken through, smashed another hole into the windows. From that same dragon's back emerged a tall boy, with striking black hair, broad shoulders, and a chain around his neck.

The boy leapt into the air, and Rae found it hard to focus on anything else.

Trailor had never been breached like this before, but even its human guards were well-trained. They hardly paused to process the boy landing elegantly on the ground before they were on him. He dodged fists, and twisted from swords, returning the attacks with his own punches. He threw people to the ground—one after another—with practiced ease, and too little fear.

Barbaric, is what Rae would usually call the display—

beautiful, is what he thought instead, captivated by the blood splattering against the boy's tan skin, and his wild, green eyes. When those eyes turned to him—moved towards him—and knelt before him—they were bizarrely alight with excitement.

"I'm Alvis Witt," the boy said, breaking the chains on Rae's wrists with his bare hands. "And I'm here to rescue you!"

CHAPTER 10

SOMEWHERE IN THE BACK of his head, Alvis thought, *Oh, fuck—did I just say my name out loud?*

But this Rae guy was staring at him with wide-eyed wonder, the same face Alvis's rescues earned him in Bellow—but ten times more fulfilling and addicting.

Alvis thought he knew what an adrenaline rush felt like—he'd been wrong.

Throwing some jerks over his shoulder was *nothing* compared to *this*: Riding through frigid air on a dragon's back, clinging tight to Crew's dark horn; Crew's Charge—Idrin—holding fast to the other, as Crew dipped and twisted around balls of flame. Alvis's mouth hanging open in awe when the Guardian next to them forged a crystal spear from moisture in the air and threw it, gutting the enemy flame-*Drakon* through the stomach. Watching Ellian slam into the windows of Trailor like they were paper, shattering them. His gaze connecting with violet eyes—then leaping from Crew's back towards victory, like every jump from a rooftop had prepared Alvis for this moment—

Something slammed hard onto the ground next to them.

Startled, Alvis and Rae both turned. But when they saw the limp, unmoving, dragon body, Alvis was the one who choked on a gasp.

Ellian's eyes were open and staring—glossed over in a way Alvis had never seen before. Blood trailed down the older Guardian's snout and into her mouth, her teeth turning crimson. Buried into the scales of her long neck were icicles—long and clear—slowly melting from the warm blood painting them red. The woman, who had only yesterday jumped Alvis on the stairs, now lay bleeding at his feet. And like a kick in the head he didn't see coming, Alvis realized this was death.

Ellian was dead.

Across the hall, a tall blonde *Drakon* cackled. "Oh dear, it seems Rae's caught the eye of someone important—I suppose we should have expected it. You Linless pests do enjoy surprises, after all."

Alvis's mouth wasn't functioning—Ellian still wasn't moving, even after Alvis touched her claw and gently shook her. Out of the corner of his eye, he vaguely caught movement—something heading towards him quickly. He wouldn't be able to react in time—

Zaile's wind wrapped around Alvis's limbs. He either blinked or blacked out—or maybe both—because suddenly he was at the other end of the hall and the icicles that had been baring down on him were gone.

Nausea—like a punch to the gut—made him stumble to his knees, but he had no time to puke, before Zaile shouted his name. She raised her hand towards Rae and he vanished. When he reappeared, he was slamming into Alvis's arms—nearly knocking them both over.

Zaile teleported the ice-*Drakon*'s next icicles into one of his own guards. "Go!"

Alvis bit at his cheek—prepared to refuse leaving Zaile behind—but the look in her smoldering gray eyes behind her glasses scolded him before he could open his mouth. *I'll be right behind you*, her eyes said. Even though Alvis didn't know Zaile, he could tell she understood the importance of her role—she wouldn't leave until she saw it through to the end.

Alvis needed to focus on his role, too.

He pulled Rae's smaller body closer. "Can you run?" Rae's answer was a harsh shove against Alvis's chest, pushing himself out of Alvis's arms, and back onto his own feet. Only the slightest bit off-kilter, Rae sprinted forward—forcing Alvis to catch up with him.

The last thing Alvis heard as they ran, was the ice-*Drakon*'s taunting laugh.

"NORTH HALL," ALVIS SAID, when Rae impatiently asked where they were supposed to be going. "As close to the Crimson Forest as possible."

Rae didn't acknowledge Alvis's answer, but he took a sharp left immediately after.

How much time had Rae spent in Trailor? For sure, longer than the week he'd been imprisoned—no one knew which corner to round or where guards would be unless they had the opportunity to memorize them. Just like how Alvis knew what fire escapes where sturdy enough to hold his weight, and which roofs let him do a rolling landing.

Through the windows to their right, the edges of the Crimson Forest grew closer, its ever-glowing red leaves like a torch lighting their way. Above the forest was a sky full of *Drakon* and Guardians dancing a deadly waltz.

"Holy shit," Alvis mumbled, breathless—he and Rae came to a stop, and stared at the battle raging outside.

From story books and photos, he knew what dragons looked like. But back in Bellow, would anything like this ever happen? Guardians didn't battle there because Guardians with dragon forms were *illegal*. Hell—he'd never even *seen* a dragon up close, until an hour ago— but seeing a dragon up close was *nothing*, compared to watching at a distance, while dragons fought claw to claw, attribute to attribute. It was brutal, bloody, and fascinating.

They watched as a blue dragon froze midair—the dragon had been hit with magic. One second, they had been gripping an enemy dragon's throat, and the next, they froze and fell—heavy and limp—towards the ground.

Shit, Alvis thought. *Did that mean the group of Charges and Guardians in the forest below had been ambushed?* Another dragon fell. Then another. *Was that a Linless agent, too? Shit, shit! Was Linless winning or losing?*

Next to Alvis, Rae murmured, "Is this all for me?" There was a disconnect between Rae's unaffected stare and the softness of his words, as though he was stuck somewhere between relief and disbelief.

"Yeah," Alvis replied, just as softly.

Rae stepped back from the window—like the glass and sky between him and the battle still wasn't enough distance. Without another word, he turned on his heel and took off running again.

Watching Rae's small back retreat, Alvis had an answer to his question—Linless was *winning*. Rae was the reason for all this fighting; he was the end goal—and Alvis had him. He was going to get Rae to the checkpoint and protect him until Zaile came. He wouldn't even need to use his attribute.

Suddenly, Alvis's neck felt too light—he reached up to touch it.

His necklace was gone.

Frantically, Alvis ran his hands over his neck—his pockets—every piece of himself—refusing to believe he made such a huge mistake at such a critical time.

Fuck, it really wasn't there.

Alvis's legs were double the length of Rae's and his adrenaline was in overdrive, so closing the distance between them was easy. He grabbed Rae's uninjured arm and yanked him to a stop—probably giving the smaller boy some sort of whiplash.

Rae spun on him—sweat and dirt smeared against

his temple. His confused but elegant curse demanded an answer. "Shit—What the *hell?*"

"My locket isn't here!" Alvis explained—the rush of his words turning the sentence into practically one word. "We need to go back!"

Rae stared at Alvis like he had sprouted fifteen heads. "You can't be serious."

Alvis ignored him and tugged on his arm. Rae immediately dug his heels into the floor.

"Dude, stop it—we're going back!"

"If it's so important, then you shouldn't have lost it in the first place." Rae tore his arm free. "And why do I need to go with *you?*"

"Because I'm responsible for getting you to the checkpoint."

"Thus far, a clearly *brilliant* decision. You've already told me where I need to go—'North Hall, as close to the Crimson Forest as possible.' I will get there myself."

Like hell, Alvis was gonna let Rae out of his sight. He'd already made one major mistake and he couldn't afford another. "But *I* don't know where to go. And if you pass out, I'm the only one who can carry you."

Rae was momentarily petrified, mouth dropping open, then his eyes narrowed. "How the *hell* do you know that about my attribute?"

"Not the time." Alvis grabbed Rae's arm again, earning him a startled gasp and a flinch because Alvis was too panicked to keep his power entirely controlled. "We need to stick together."

"I'm not risking my freedom over some silly necklace."

"It's not just *any* necklace, asshole!"

Still trying to shake Alvis's grip, Rae's frown was caught between confusion and suspicion. "Then tell me why it's so special," he demanded through grinding teeth.

Alvis grabbed at his hair with his free hand, roughly running his fingers through it and tugging. He growled—loud and long—making Rae jump the tiniest bit.

It felt like Alvis had too many options and too few at the same time. Going back to get his necklace meant taking longer to get to the checkpoint and putting Rae in more danger. Would they be able to escape from that ice bastard a second time?

But losing his necklace was dangerous, too. How long had he spent hiding the truth about his identity? Could he really just drop that big secret right there—in the middle of enemy territory—to some stranger narrowing his eyes and planting his feet, just because he was prepared to run off and leave Alvis and his failure behind in the dust? But if Alvis didn't reveal the secret now and left the locket behind, he *would* be a failure.

Alvis couldn't risk failing, not when he was so close to his goal that he could taste it. He dangled on a ledge—once he said the words, he would fall over, and there would be no going back. But he couldn't risk playing it safe anymore.

Some secrets couldn't be kept forever.

Heart in his throat, and stomach plummeting, Alvis somehow kept his voice from shaking. "You ever heard of Ellowyn Clark?"

Apparently, one way for Rae's stoic expression to slip was to make him feel patronized. *"Obviously."*

"It's *her* locket."

Rae stopped struggling against Alvis's hold, and the realization smoothed the furrow between his brows. "A Talisman?"

"And I'm a *direct* descendant."

"But that means you're a—"

Sirens rang throughout the building—people shouted; Guardians roared.

Yet nothing was louder than when Rae's lips moved, and he called Alvis by that title he'd kept hidden for so long. It was like a weight had been lifted, and Alvis suddenly remembered how to breathe again. He never thought the person he would share his biggest secret with would be a complete stranger, but regret was nowhere to be found. Alvis never believed in fate, but when Rae said it again—a breathless whisper of *"Chosen One"* into the chaos around them—Alvis's destiny had never felt more real.

"So, yeah, there you go," Alvis said to ground himself again. "Seems like you've got amazing deduction skills. And if you're so smart, you know what it means if that locket gets into the wrong hands. So, would you just come with me alread—Whoa! *What the hell are you doing?"*

"I'm going with you," Rae said, holding onto Alvis's wrist and pulling him along with surprising strength. "I'm your responsibility, right?"

"WHERE DID YOU lose it?"

"If I knew where it was, do you think I would be this freaked out?"

"Can you feel for it?"

"How should I know?"

"How could you *not* know?"

"I've never lost it before." And what a terrible time to do so for the first time. He'd been so lost in the exhilaration of an actual battle he'd become too distracted. Dammit, he wanted to cry. "What do I do?" he groaned.

Rae's expression didn't soften, but his voice was the slightest bit less annoyed. "I don't know the difference between a human with a magical attribute and a *Drakon*, but losing your magic is like losing a piece of yourself. Do you feel that way?"

"Enough to notice the locket is gone." He flexed his hand. Power, warm and familiar, still flowed into the tips of his fingers. "I still have my power, though."

"Then the locket must still be here. Focus and find it." If Alvis had the capacity to think about anything besides finding his locket, he might have noticed the sharp edge of Rae's tone.

Sensing his locket sounded complicated and simple at the same time. He had never done it before—granted, he had never been more than a couple footsteps away from the locket since he'd inherited the Talisman. He'd never *needed* to focus on it. Was there some chant he should say?

"Lockeeet?" Alvis ventured, first to himself, then raising his voice and saying it again.

Rae's expression twisted into something indiscernible.

"Why are you speaking out loud?"

"I'm focusing."

"Focusing generally does not involve talking."

"Stop distracting me. This was your—"

A subtle warmth suddenly filled his chest—the same kind he always felt when the locket was responding to him. It was dull, but after he took a tentative step forward, it grew the slightest bit stronger.

Alvis sprinted forward. Without confirmation, Rae was quickly on his heels. Alvis didn't know where he was going, but he didn't need to. His feet were carrying him quickly back to the hallway they so narrowly escaped from. But it was there—Alvis *knew* it was there, and a quick slide around another corner later and Alvis saw it.

Warm, soothing, and familiar, the locket was glowing. And it was glowing in a palm with tinted blue skin, and long, slim fingers like icicles.

"My, my! Aren't you two in a rush."

In the center of the hall, the ice-*Drakon* from earlier stood alone. Around him the other guards—both dragon and human—lay dead and defeated, no doubt by the Guardians they had underestimated. But Linless wasn't without casualties: Ellian's body had been tossed aside, twisted like an abandoned doll, and Zaile was slumped against a wall. In one hand, the ice-*Drakon* held Alvis's locket above his head, taking in its details, while his other arm rested leisurely on the hilt of his sword, impaled into

Idrin's back.

The tattoo on Idrin's arm was gone. She was reaching desperately towards Crew in front of her. Though no wound was visible on Crew, she was lifeless just the same. Crew stretched her fingers—trying to touch her Charge one last time—but they had to settle for taking their final breaths together instead.

Rae sucked in a worried breath. "*Cian*," he hissed at the ice-*Drakon*.

"That locket's not yours," Alvis growled at Cian. He stepped forward, but Rae grabbed his arm, stopping him from blindly marching into the reach of Cian's sword. "Give it back, asshole!"

"So rude," Cian replied. He licked his lips like he could taste Alvis's growing fury. "A necklace that doesn't crack even in a dragon's claw. Legend has it there's only one Talisman capable of that. And it must be special to you as well if you stupidly brought Rae back here instead of escaping."

Cian rolled the locket between his fingers like a coin and pulled his sword free from Idrin's back. More blood rolled down Idrin's shoulders to join the puddle under her, the red bright against the white tile.

With a casual sweep, Cian pointed his sword to each fallen Linless agent around them. "Rescuing Rae was the point of all these lives, was it not?"

Alvis's chest suddenly burned hot. The bitter taste of vehemence was a calming encouragement Alvis felt in his fingertips, as his nails dug into his palm. It was new, and familiar, and overwhelming. Somewhere in the back of his head, his father pleaded desperately for him to stop, but Alvis couldn't stop.

Rage. Hot, white rage. The purest rage Alvis had ever felt.

Power electrified his skin, like he was caught in the moment of flying across rooftops, high on conquering his limits, but one slip and the world would crash into him. He recognized this magic—how many times had it brushed his knuckles when he punched? Or glossed over his fingers to break paint brushes between them? Every day it was with him, simmering below the surface, waiting to break free. And now it called his name louder than ever before—and Alvis was finally ready to answer.

The locket grew hotter, too. The heat of it met Cian's icy skin, sending steam into the air. Cian hissed and dropped it.

Fists clenched, Alvis took his first step towards Cian, then another.

"I *said*, that locket doesn't belong to you."

It was clear Cian didn't fear Alvis. Why should he? Cian was a *Drakon*—and Wielder or not—Alvis was a human, so when Alvis continued to stalk forward, Cian didn't bother stepping away.

"You really are a Wielder, aren't you?" Cian hissed wickedly, awed. "Maybe even a Chosen One?"

Alvis didn't like Cian saying those words; they could never compare to the light and truth he felt when they were spoken from Rae's lips. On Cian's tongue they were a vile and grotesque venom.

Alvis's feet moved faster. Cian still didn't falter.

lace burst into a blinding flash of light. Cian
..ing his eyes against the glare.
_ nim.

Alvis leapt, and connected his fist with Cian's right
eye—it squished beneath Alvis's knuckles, then burst,
sending fluid and blood into the air. Cian went from
growling to crying out in pain, as he backed into a wall.
He slumped to the ground, unconscious, one eye rolled
back and the other empty and bleeding.

With a jerk, the intense strength left Alvis's body. He
fell to the ground, dry heaving. Gagging, he used his shirt
to wipe away the blood and mucus—and whatever the
hell else eyes were made up of. He would burn the shirt
later because a destroyed piece of clothing was much,
much better than the stickiness now clinging to his skin.

There was a cough, followed by a groan. Then a familiar voice moaned Alvis's name—he raced to Zaile's side,
legs heavy and dragging.

"Zaile, are you—"

A wheeze interrupted him. Zaile's right arm was
hanging useless, her red hair was askew, and her orange
glasses were gone. Alvis steadied her when she attempted
to stand.

"I'm fine—give me a second. Lamont's group was
ambushed, I need to—" Zaile squeezed her eyes shut, a
focused crease in her brow. It suddenly evened out, and
she fell further into Alvis's hold, relieved. "Lamont says
he's okay, but we need to hurry. I don't know how long
he can hold out with the pain, and I don't have much
strength left."

DESPITE HER INJURIES, Zaile managed to transport the remaining Linless operatives to the checkpoint. Rae disappeared in Zaile's wind first, followed by Alvis. He was struck again by the flash of darkness and an intense jerk in his stomach. Zaile must have been exhausted, or maybe it was harder to aim from a longer distance, because Alvis reappeared half his body height above the ground. He gave a startled yelp, and crashed next to Rae in the snow, elbow narrowly missing the smaller boy's face.

Zaile appeared last, and collapsed into Lamont's arms, immediately burying her face into his chest with a wail.

Tahtsu, sweat on his brow from escaping the guards who had attacked them, stepped out from behind the trees. "Where's Ellian?" he demanded. His eyes were swollen. Despite the freezing temperature, the left sleeve of his shirt was ripped off. His arm was filled with red fading lines that had once been Ellian's mark. "Zaile, where the fuck is my grandmother?"

Tahtsu already knew the answer, but when Zaile shook her head, Tahtsu asked again. Then again, and again—until Lamont pulled Zaile closer, and softly hissed, "*Tahtsu.*"

Tahtsu grabbed onto his own arm, hand running down the skin where his Charge tattoo should have been. His other hand went to his mouth to cover his scream.

Next to Alvis, Rae was starting to shake. Whether it was from the cold or the desperate cries he knew came from his rescue, Alvis wasn't sure.

Linless had completed their mission.

But at what cost?

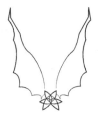

CHAPTER 11

THE NEXT FEW HOURS RUSHED by in such a blur, Rae could hardly process them. He remembered the chill of snow soaking through his prison uniform, and the sting when a Linless operative tore away the bandages on his arm before gripping it. Electricity crackled beneath her fingers, short circuiting Rae's tracking device there.

Then he was ushered forward, escaping with strangers through the Crimson Forest and out the underground tunnels, past the wall, into Bellow—a place he hadn't been to since he was ten, and wore rags instead of pressed suits.

Rae was led through alleyways and side streets. Alvis quietly shuffled Rae along with him, until they reached a storefront with windows painted black and a sign that read, "Mechanic Michael."

When Rae stepped over the threshold, his breathing

doubled, the anxiety from their escape leaping onto his chest and pressing down—dizziness overtook him and he stumbled forward. But strong arms wrapped around him before he could hit the ground.

RAE OPENED HIS EYES, the movement slow and heavy. In the dim lighting, he could make out shelves full of tools, boxes, and crates, some protected by metal bars. The room was in a sort of organized disarray.

He ghosted his fingers across the floor; they bumped into what felt like scraps of metal. The ground beneath him was hard, and a single thick quilt separated Rae from the freezing concrete. A wool blanket was thrown over him, and he was no longer wearing his Trailor uniform— he'd been changed into a pair of sweatpants, and a shirt so large the sleeves fell to his elbows.

Despite the lack of bedding, Rae was still warm. A heavy, oversized coat was wrapped around him, snug and grounding, and Rae couldn't help nuzzling into it for the slightest bit of comfort he hadn't felt since Hanah died.

"Twenty-one operatives died . . ."

Above him were faint voices he didn't know. Rae's instincts immediately went on high alert.

"Bloodied Champion . . ."

" . . . leave for Quint immediately after sunset, before Volos can find us . . ."

The conversation trailed off. A door opened, and heavy

footsteps made their way down the stairs.

Rae stumbled to his feet. He grabbed a near-by hammer, and crouched low to the ground, prepared to fight even as his vision threatened to go black.

A disheveled man with a reassuring smile appeared from the doorway.

"Oh, you're awake! Great!" the man said, voice deep yet cheerful. His untucked, loose fitting shirt made it difficult for Rae to gauge his strength. "I apologize for the lacking accommodations. I would have put you in my room, but this is the only one with a hidden space. The Royal Police are on high alert right now—"

"Who are you?"

The man held up his hands casually, unnerved by Rae's interruption.

"Hey, hey—it's okay. I'm sorry if I startled you. I'm Michael Witt. I'm a member of Linless. You're safe here."

" 'Witt'?" Rae relaxed the slightest bit. "Are you related to Alvis?"

"I am. I'm his father!" said Michael proudly.

"Are you also a Chosen One, then?" Rae quickly realized he wasn't meant to know that information when Michael steeled his expression into a stoicism Rae was used to wearing himself; calculatingly blank, testing the waters.

"Would you mind being more specific? I'm not sure I know what you're referring to," Michael replied.

Rae responded with caution of his own. "Alvis told me he is a Wielder as well as one of Ellowyn Clark's direct descendants."

Another combination of expressions dashed across Michael's face—shock, to anger, to fear, then back around again to shock—until he made the same loud, obnoxious groan Alvis had howled in the hallway before admitting who he was. Michael seemed prepared to storm up the stairs and scream Alvis's full name, but he settled for running a hand over his face.

"That *dumbass*."

"Are you, then?" Rae pressed, refusing to let the topic fall away easily. "Are you a Chosen One?"

A look of endearment at Rae's curiosity passed across Michael's face, then he sighed, resigned. "No, I'm not a Chosen One *or* a Wielder. A Talisman can only belong to one Wielder at a time. When one dies, then the magic moves on to the next in line." The harsh lines of Michael's frown softened into a fond smile. "Alvis's necklace belonged to his mother."

Rae's curiosity didn't end with Michael's words, but he knew his questions needed to. It wasn't his place to pry into someone's death when he barely knew these people's names.

These people. Linless. People he had never met, many of who he would never get the chance to thank.

Rae shivered, pulling the heavy jacket tighter to him. The hammer dangled from his fingers.

"Did twenty-one people really die to free me from Trailor?"

Rae expected immediate blame, or the taunting, hostile glare most wore when they reminded him of every life he'd taken. But Michael Witt gently pulled the hammer free of Rae's grasp, and gave him a kind smile. Michael walked to a wooden table and pulled out one of the chairs, gesturing for Rae to sit. "Now that you're awake, do you mind if I take a look at your arm? The tracking device should be deactivated, but we still need to remove it. We can talk while I work."

Michael reached for Rae's right arm, but Rae yanked it away. He cradled it to his chest, barely suppressing the animalistic flare of his nostrils. Too many people had touched his arm in the past week with ill intentions. But the offered hand was steady and patient.

"I'll go as quick as possible," Michael said. "I promise."

There was a soft, honest kindness in his voice. Rae didn't know whether he should feel comforted by it, or on edge. But Alvis's father was right, and Rae wasn't a fool. They couldn't risk keeping the tracking device intact in case the scientists of Trailor had a way to reactivate it. But removing it meant Michael cutting along the gash used to insert the tracking device, the one above his scar . . .

No, Rae reminded himself. *Keep your emotions in check like you've been taught. Don't be sentimental about an old scar.*

With one last, protective press of his arm to his chest, Rae sat down in the chair and let Michael gently take his arm. He set it on the table that was covered in trinkets, tools, and a metal tray full of broken needles.

Michael chuckled, genuinely amused. "Your magic is truly something else. No gemstone or Pact, but you can still use your attribute."

Rae leveled him with a look. "It only works when I'm unconscious."

It was cruel, honestly. If his powers were going to linger just out of reach, he would rather not have them at all.

Michael hummed, and wiped the dried blood away from Rae's wound. He softly scrubbed at it with a cloth soaked in a numbing agent, no doubt crafted with a medicinal attribute. Rae wondered if it was procured legally. Within seconds, his entire forearm was numb, and suddenly Rae didn't care anymore whether it was legal or not. The pain was muted, not gone entirely, but enough for Rae to sigh in relief.

He watched Michael carefully cut into the perfect line of glue holding Rae's skin together.

Rae and Hanah were born to Guardian parents in Bellow. He knew how humans acted towards Guardians, especially the fallen ones. He would argue the abuse towards Guardians rivaled how the *Drakon* treated them. The only place Guardians found fair treatment was with each other. They were familiar with what it meant to be tossed aside like yesterday's newspaper or born without the hope of ever spreading their wings and flying. Kindness from humans, like the type Rae felt in Michael's touch and the way he sat at Rae's side, as though they were equals, *that* was rare.

Unable to stop himself, Rae asked, "Are you a Guardian?"

"Is a Guardian the only person who can help another Guardian in need?" Michael replied, not angry, simply curious about Rae's answer.

Rae's next words were slow but still suspicious. "No, I suppose not."

Michael pried Rae's skin apart, eyes concentrating behind his glasses, and dipped his gloved finger in. The numbing medicine hadn't soaked all the way through. Rae hissed when Michael scraped out a small, slim piece of metal. Michael's face softened, apologetic. He held up the tracking device.

"Would you like to do the honors?" Michael asked.

Rae held out his palm without a word, then set the device on the table. He grabbed the hammer he'd picked up before. The sound of the tracking device shattering was exhilarating.

Michael threaded string through the head of a needle. He tapped it against Rae's skin, and nodded when he didn't react, then set about sewing up the wound. "Growing up in Nerwen City would convince you every non-Guardian hates all Guardians."

Rae furrowed his brow. "How could a simple mechanic from Bellow understand what happens in a place like Nerwen City?"

Michael chuckled. "I'm glad calling myself a 'simple mechanic' is catching on." He pulled down the collar of his shirt, revealing the recognizable brand of a Trailor employee beneath his collarbone. "Nerwen City needs mechanics, too. Sometimes their mechanics work in Trailor and are important enough to get high security clearance." Michael readjusted his collar but, like the rest of his shirt, it was too wrinkled to flatten completely. "And important enough to do things I can never be forgiven for."

Rae barely held back his shock. Someone like Michael had escaped Trailor, and lived under the radar for this long? And to become a leader of Linless . . . Who exactly was this man? Definitely not a simple mechanic like Rae had thought a moment ago.

Rae wanted to ask if Alvis knew about Michael's past, but he could read between Michael's words. They were laced with guilt of unspeakable sins he committed at Trailor, and the fear of Alvis ever learning of those sins, of who his father was. What was it like, Rae wondered, to have someone protect you from truths you're better off not knowing?

"Is that what led you to the rebellion?" Rae asked.

"Part of it. I'd say having a child was a bigger motivator." Michael finished stitching, the snow-white skin now pulled back in place. Now that it was unwrapped, Rae noticed his entire forearm was a grotesque array of colorful bruises.

"Rae, do you know why Linless broke you out?"

"To make use of me." Rae wasn't so naïve to think they would rescue him for anything else. "Though I'm not sure what for."

"Linless has a single goal: to liberate Zen, and give Guardians back their own autonomy." Michael glanced up from wrapping gauze around Rae's arm, the scar becoming hidden once more. "I know what you've been taught about Pacts, Rae. Ever since the Massacre of the Charges, Guardians and humans in this country have feared them. They believe they're taboo and dangerous. But if we can show them that isn't true, then Nerwen City will lose control over every Guardian in Zen."

"That all sounds like a pretty picture." And, to Rae, it

sounded impossible, no matter how much he would love to see it come to fruition. "But you aren't explaining why Linless rescued *me* instead of any other *Drakon*."

"Because you're the only one who can fill the final missing piece," said Michael. The dressing over the wound was pulled tight and Michael patted it once to signal he was finished. He gathered up the dirty tools and walked to a sink against the back wall. With barely a sound, he dropped the supplies into it, then grabbed a spare wet rag, and wiped Rae's blood from his fingers. He leaned back against the lip of the sink, arms crossed over his chest, and ankles thrown casually over each other. Any semblance of comfort was gone; when he met Rae's eyes, Rae felt every defense he'd let down rise again with such force his body trembled.

"The world's strongest *Drakon* loses his gemstone, then becomes the strongest Pact in the world, a face of hope for the rebellion. Has a nice ring to it, doesn't it?"

Like being pulled to a stop, Rae's stomach jerked. *Him*? In a Pact? Pacts were primitive. Tying one's life and magic to a human who could easily be killed was such a ridiculous risk, when a Charge's death meant the Guardian's death, as well. There was a reason they'd been so easily extinguished a hundred years ago once gemstones were created. The word always tasted vile the few times he allowed himself to say it out loud.

Alvis's face flashed through his mind. He remembered that fire in Alvis's eyes as he broke Rae's chains.

Michael watched him, taking in every miniscule shift in Rae's expression. Rae realized this was more than

Michael laying out Rae's intended role in Linless—this was a test.

"I have no loyalty to Zen," Rae confirmed.

"Then can you forget everything you've been trained to be as the Bloodied Champion, and become a Guardian?" Michael asked.

Michael had to know any answer Rae gave would be shaky at best. How could Rae possibly understand what being in a Pact meant? But did it honestly matter if he did? The result would be the same: Hanah was gone. His powers were unreachable. All he had left was making Zen pay for their sins, so he could be forgiven for his.

It became clear that he was being given one hope of making that happen.

That hope was a Pact.

Rae straightened his shoulders. He convinced himself that this was something he could handle, needed to handle, *would* handle. And he could convince Michael as well. But a silent scream roared to life in his mind when he was about to answer, so shrill he flinched. It formed a pressure against his temples and behind his eyes; a harsh shiver ran through his body when he pushed back against his own voice screaming at him.

You'll get your powers back, but at what cost? You're already weak, Rae! You can't protect anyone ever again!

"If it means Zen will fall," Rae said, needing to speak before he fell victim to his own thoughts, "I will become whatever I need to."

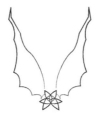

CHAPTER 12

ALVIS GOT AN EARFUL. Actually, Alvis got *two* earfuls. No, scratch that, Alvis's ears would be stuffed full of his dad's yelling for at least a month.

It was almost impressive, really. Two hours ago, Alvis heard more swear words come out of his dad's mouth than he had his entire young adult life.

"Trailor has cameras!" Michael shouted, not at all caring about the volume, or that other Linless agents could probably hear every word. "They know your fucking face, Alvis! Did you make sure the *Drakon* you hit wouldn't remember who you are, or which Talisman you Wield? They know you're part of Linless! How could you *do* this, son? After you specifically promised me you wouldn't display your magic. The only thing that could make this worse is if they knew your name."

Maybe Alvis should have come clean at that part, but

he was already frustrated that his dad was angry, instead of proud.

A lot of things had gone wrong on the mission. Why was Alvis using his power the one his dad chose to be pissed off about? And why did breaking the little promise he made to his dad bring them back to Alvis "not being mature enough" to handle his attribute?

Alvis's mind jumped to the image of Ellian's lifeless, dull eyes staring out into nothing. How was he not mature enough to handle his attribute, when he had faced death?

Alvis growled and picked up another abandoned, concrete slab. He tossed it into the air—higher than he needed to—and prepared his punch. Once the slab was at the perfect height, Alvis threw his fist forward and it connected dead center. With a loud slam, the concrete slab cracked and exploded. The broken pieces fell to join the growing pile he'd started an hour ago.

The skin of his right hand was scratched open, and blood spread across his knuckles. He ignored it. He'd just practice with his left hand.

He reached for another concrete chunk but came up empty.

Of course, this would be the day his two hundred blocks would finally run out. Alvis had gotten them from a previous construction job—he had pleaded with his manager, promising to work extra hours for them. Eventually, he'd worn her down enough that she had tossed in an extra ten if he promised to never ask her again.

Alvis frowned, staring down at his unintentionally

finished pile. With a groan, he slid his gloves back on. He made his way to the edge of the building and slouched forward over the railing.

This roof was a few blocks away from Michael's workshop. It had been abandoned long ago. The building next to him was a bike shop, loud and screeching with engines of cheap, scraped together motorcycles. Thanks to the shop's noise, no one could hear Alvis letting off steam with a little extra strength. Now, though, without the satisfying crack of the exploding blocks, the revving of bike engines was giving him a headache.

Time to head home, Alvis thought. He ran to the side of the roof and jumped.

The sky was a gorgeous orange and gray as he leapt through it, the sun starting to set across the horizon. The chilly air cut his lungs and chapped his lips, but each perfect jump was worth it.

The building across the street from the workshop was three stories tall. It was what Alvis considered *his* roof; it was where Alvis watched pretend customers—AKA Linless operatives—come in and out of his father's store, always there for meetings Alvis wasn't allowed to attend. Sometimes he had brought Miller up there. Other times he sat alone, remembering his mother's voice as she told him a bedtime story.

As Alvis made the last perfect jump, a shine of silvery white on the rooftop caught his eye. The distraction was enough to have him *completely* screw up his landing. He landed in the wrong spot of his foot, stumbling until he tripped, palms scratching against the rough rooftop, his wool gloves saving them from being scraped to death.

Rae stood, staring at him with large, unblinking eyes, not at all startled or worried by Alvis's remarkable entrance. Showered and out of the dirty, blood stained prison uniform, Rae was practically swimming in clothes he was wearing; a pair of jeans Alvis hadn't worn in years, a wool sweater with a deep V-neck, and Alvis's extra jacket.

It took ten breaths for Alvis to steady his jolted nerves and shake away the stinging in his hands. He walked up to join Rae at the concrete wall bordering the roof.

"You're awake." he said, too loudly.

"Obviously," Rae replied.

"How are you feeling?"

Briefly, Rae frowned, startled by the question like no one had ever asked him how he was doing before, then the lines on his face evened out, and he dragged his eyes away.

Rae subtly shifted from one foot to the other, then covered it up with a few determined steps that put more distance between them. He stared at the ugly buildings on the street, and countless people crowding by, the snow a dirty black beneath their feet.

Where Alvis had to slouch onto the wall, Rae was the perfect height to fold his hands on top of it and stand straight, shoulders pulled taught and proper.

"I'm fine," Rae said, in a snappy reply. His tone left no room for the conversation to continue. But Alvis was pretty good at diving ahead when he wanted to.

"I'm gonna guess Bellow isn't as pretty as Nerwen City, huh?"

Everyone knew Nerwen City was pretty. They didn't need to visit to know that—it was beaten into Bellow's people from the second they were born. And it was what made those special invitations to the capitol of Zen so irresistible. Who wouldn't want to stay in a captivating metropolis of fancy houses and skyscrapers. It had a city square with golden fountains and the ground painted silver, ready to impress the countless royalty, leaders, and the posh visitors attending one of Zen's countless Ranker tournaments. The castle sat above the city, the expansive forest and Tailor behind it. But for being the home to the King and his family and head officers, the castle was a far second to the most important building in the city—no—the *country*.

Like most stadiums in the world, the Calamity Stadium was a new addition in the past one hundred years, when Guardians—battling as Rankers—first took off. It was the largest stadium in the world; neighborhoods were bulldozed to make room for it. It was renowned as the biggest and best stadium; made of white marble, it was adorned with gold paint and expensive screens, giving the audience—and those within a ten-mile radius—a closer look, as Rankers battled to prove they were the best.

Private, closed-off booths were built into the top of the stadium to give the richest spectators a bird's eye view of the action from behind a shatterproof, near-invisible wall. The wall was always pristine—every scratch and smudge cleaned off after each match.

Calamity Stadium's inner ground was a grassy field

that sprawled for a mile. This extra space meant the amount of supplies available for Rankers to enhance their attributes—and excite the crowds—was far greater than other countries. And Zen needed it to be; the country thrived on tourism. Ever since Zen had gained Guardians, the bored rich and powerful had invented the bloody Ranker tournaments and twisted them into a profitable, horrifying hobby. Banning Pacts only put more power into the wealthy's hands as they invented gemstones that could turn Guardians into their dragon form without a human Charge.

The closest Alvis had ever gotten to Calamity Stadium was through his dad's stories, and watching Rankers howl and fly, as far above the stadium as the rules allowed. That was, until Alvis and his fellow Linless agents had snuck through the tall wall separating Nerwen City from Bellow under the cover of night.

Alvis stared out at the distant wall. The polluted and foggy sky mixed with the approaching dusk and blocked out what lay beyond. He'd memorized the wall, and distantly what was behind it, years ago, but it felt like he was seeing it all again for the first time. Like the picture had gone from flat to dimensional, the detail of each side completed. Alvis now knew what the Crimson Forest looked like from above; how beautiful those bleeding, red leaves were, and the towering trees as they climbed up the hill, hiding Trailor away. And he'd seen the forest disturbed when bodies of dragons and humans fell, breaking branches, and crashing to the ground.

"I lived here until I was ten," Rae finally replied. "I

know what Bellow is like."

It took Alvis a few blinks to remember what question Rae was replying to, then Alvis raised his eyebrows, surprised and sheepish at the same time. "Oh, sorry. Didn't mean to jump to conclusions. I thought all the *Drakon* in Nerwen City were born there."

"Most are, but there are always exceptions." Rae focused on the tall, sprawling wall in the distance, too. "Though I can't say I'm comfortable here after living in Nerwen City for so long."

Alvis felt a twinge of overprotection for his city, but he bit it back. "How long were you in Nerwen City?"

"Seven years."

"Holy shit—you're *seventeen*?"

Rae didn't reply. There wasn't even anything on his face Alvis could consider emotion.

Seventeen . . . That meant the two of them were the same age. And Rae had been out winning championships with his attribute, while at the same time, Alvis wasn't even allowed to use or speak about his. "And *you're* the strongest Ranker, *ever*?"

Finally, Rae looked at him, but he focused onto Alvis's shock, instead of his awe. "Are you always this curious about people you've just met?" He ground out in annoyance.

"Yeah, when they're interesting."

"Most people don't appreciate hundreds of pointless questions from someone they don't know."

"We're traveling to Quint together," Alvis said, beginning to get annoyed by Rae's unnecessary snappiness.

"It's not like we're gonna be strangers for long."

Rae looked at Alvis from head to toe. Alvis couldn't figure out what Rae was searching for, but he felt a weird, sudden spike in his heartbeat. He was all ready to shove Rae away, but then, like every word was highly considered before spoken, Rae said, "I suppose that's true."

Alvis snorted a laugh. "You talk like a sixty-year-old rich dude."

"There's nothing wrong with talking properly."

"I suppose that's true."

Rae's tiny glare felt like a small victory.

Alvis held his eyes for as long as Rae would let him, taking in the bright violet and slight crimson of them, the kaleidoscope of colors evidence of dragon's blood.

"So . . . Strongest Ranker Ever. What got you locked up in Trailor with a fancy title like that?"

There was a pause, as Rae tapped his fingers against the concrete wall, deciding what details Alvis should know. "I interrupted the annual tournament to attack my owner."

Well, damn. That would do it, Alvis thought, awed.

Alvis landed a heavy pat of respect between Rae's shoulder blades, causing the smaller boy to gasp and nearly tumble over the roof's wall. A regal face like Rae's shouldn't be capable of glowering, but the glare he sent Alvis was too impressive not to respect.

"What's your attribute, anyway?" Alvis asked. "Is it earth based?"

Rae's eyes turned cold, sliding into bitterness caused by whatever wound Alvis was poking at.

"What does it matter?" said Rae. "I'm a *Kon* now, I can't use it anymore."

"Uh, but you *do* still have it. It still goes off when you're unconscious," Alvis pointed out. "Just because you can't use your magic on purpose doesn't mean it's *gone*, dumbass."

"It might as well be the same thing. An attribute is the most important part of a *Drakon*. Without a gemstone to unlock their magic, they are just a Guardian, a pale shadow in comparison. I may as well have no magic at all."

"They really do brainwash you over there, don't they?" Alvis gestured below them to the sidewalks filled with people—some, no doubt, Guardians—with heads down and shoulders slouched, marching forward towards their destinations. "You're telling me that a Guardian is powerless and worthless without a gemstone? A Guardian always has their powers; it's not like a gemstone and being a *Drakon*, or forming a Pact with a human Charge, is what makes their magic real. Becoming a *"Kon"* isn't such a horrible fate."

They fell into another silence. Alvis didn't feel like filling it this time, annoyance simmering. Former *Drakon* and battled-hardened Ranker or not, Rae didn't get a pass to imply Guardians—Alvis's co-workers, his neighbors, his friends—were any less important because of their ability to use their magic or not.

Rae exhaled, heavy, like he was barely biting back a bitter, unconvinced laugh. "You sound a lot like your father."

When Alvis remained silent, Rae's focus fluttered back

to him in time to see Alvis's anger disappear, and his eyes go comically wide. "What?"

"You're the only person in the world who's ever thought that." Alvis said.

"I don't mean literally. I was just expressing my surprise that you can sound so philosophical, despite speaking the way you do."

If Rae was bothered by Alvis's squawk of protest, he didn't show it.

"My attribute is metal based," Rae continued, hesitantly. "It's impenetrable, but if I don't concentrate it can increase my weight exponentially."

Alvis raised his eyebrows, impressed. "Is that why you're so heavy when unconscious?"

Rae nodded.

"And without a gemstone, or Pact, too. That's crazy."

Rae sighed softly, probably used to hearing that line anytime he talked about his magic. He opened his mouth to reply—but then froze, petrified, looking into the distance.

"Rae?" Alvis asked. "Are you okay?"

Panicked, Rae dropped to the ground, pressing as far up against the roof's wall as possible. Alvis knew enough about what that fear in Rae's eyes meant to immediately follow.

For two minutes, nothing happened. Alvis furrowed his brow at Rae. His chest was starting to rise and fall, trying to control his breathing. Rae had yanked the jacket's hood over his head, and shushed Alvis when he asked what he'd seen.

A roar sliced through the air. Then another.

Alvis tried to count and track how many *Drakon* were approaching their location, but the eager wails were overlapping too much, the harsh flapping of wings echoed between buildings as they flew over Alvis and Rae.

Two *Drakon* banked back and landed heavily onto the shorter buildings next to them. Concrete cracked beneath their claws, the noise drowned out by more howls, intimidating and declaring their presence. A single turn of the head and either of them would see Alvis and Rae flattening themselves against the roof wall.

The *Drakon* to the left roared again, so shrilly, Alvis could feel it in his bones. The buildings shook, windows threatening to crack. Alvis wasn't sure when he'd thrown himself down onto his stomach, but he opened his eyes when hands pushed hard against his chest.

Their faces were so close, Alvis could feel Rae's breath. Pressed into the concrete, Alvis was half covering him with his much larger frame. Rae's curls were soft under his palm, hand gently pressing Rae down, his other arm thrown over him.

"I don't need your protection," Rae snapped, shoving Alvis away, not caring that he might draw attention.

"It was a fucking reflex! Calm down," Alvis hissed back, then refocused on the threat around them.

How had Nerwen City found them so quickly?

Bellow was huge, and Alvis and his dad lived on the most southeastern edge. Nothing Michael ever did gave any indication of his rebellion involvement.

So how had they been discovered?

He chanced a glance at the *Drakon*; they still hadn't noticed him and Rae. And that's when Alvis realized the *Drakon* weren't searching for them—their gazes were focused across the street on his dad's shop.

Sudden panic made Alvis want to puke.

In bursts of colored lights, the *Drakon* on either side of them took on their human forms. They leapt from the roofs and out of sight. Alvis and Rae covertly looked over the roof wall, and Alvis had never released his breath so fast—only to choke on his next one.

Covered in a light blue hue, another *Drakon* landed heavy on the ground next to the other *Drakon* from the roof. The claws of their hind legs dug into the pavement, breaking it into shards. The blue *Drakon* stood with their back drawn straight, a large, glistening blue sword covered in ice resting between their shoulder blades. Their wings flared around them, a sharp whistle cutting through the air.

The blue *Drakon* slammed into the surrounding buildings.

Screams erupted, but the *Drakon* didn't give them a second thought. One eye was clenched shut, the other a glistening diamond blue. Together, Rae and Alvis caught each other's eyes.

Cian.

Cian roared; a monstrous, terrifying declaration, as he reshaped into his human form.

Alvis and Rae needed to get off the roof before they were spotted, and before the *Drakon* attacked Michael's shop. Before Alvis was out of chances to stop them. He nudged Rae with his elbow and nodded towards the fire escape to their left. Like he did when Alvis had raced towards his lost locket, Rae moved with immediate understanding.

The city around them was in an uproar, but Alvis's heart pounded in his ears, making it hard to hear anything else. He glimpsed his dad greeting Cian enthusiastically, cheerful and welcoming as he always was to everyone.

Alvis climbed halfway down the ladder, then slid down the rest, the sting on his palms from falling earlier flaring up. Rae clambered down after him, but before Alvis could sprint around the corner and out of the alleyway, Rae gripped his arm to stop him. "You can't rush out there without a plan."

Alvis stared at the blue eyepatch stretched across Cian's face now that he was human. "My plan is to knock Cian's other eye out before he can hurt anyone else."

"That isn't a plan."

"There isn't time for a different one! I've already beaten Cian once."

"You had surprise on your side then. Cian knows to be careful with you now. He's one of the highest officers in the Royal Police for a reason." Rae nodded towards the line of enemy *Drakon*. "Why do you think he brought so many *Drakon* with him? You can't possibly believe you can handle them alone."

"I've got my Talisman."

"Do you actually know how to control it?"

Alvis pressed his lips into a thin line. Rae didn't look smug, but he was obviously relieved Alvis took what he was saying into consideration. When Rae went to say something else, a loud clattering interrupted—the sound of something metal being thrown onto the ruined pavement. Rae and Alvis cautiously looked around the building's corner.

In the snow was the headpiece Jazz had worn when Linless broke through Trailor's wall.

"Clever!" Cian hollered, ensuring every person in their neighborhood heard. "Gaining *Drakon* from inside Trailor—hiding right under our noses! I must say, Commander Volos seemed almost impressed, despite how furious she was." He clicked his tongue, looking at Jazz's headpiece with a mocking frown. "It is unfortunate poor Jazz wasn't more immune to torture. Were you truly planning to put Rae into one of your dirty Pacts? I've never heard of something so cruel and vile."

Michael played innocent with natural ease, as he looked at the dented and bloody helmet at his feet. "I'm not sure what this has to do with me. I'm a simple mechanic, sir."

Cian was tall, and his sword was long; together it was more than enough reach to tap at Michael's sign.

"Am I correct that *you* are the owner here, Michael *Witt*?" Cian's tone was deceptively playful and smooth, as he emphasized their last name. With sudden horror, Alvis figured it out—he knew how Cian had found them.

Fuck.

I'm Alvis Witt, and I'm here to rescue you!

Fuck.

The mirth in Cian's voice turned resentful. "If you're

going to send your child on a mission, you should warn him what he should keep secret, and what he should shout from the hilltops."

"I'm afraid you're mistaken, sir," Michael said, "I don't have a son."

"Sure, you do!" Cian replied. "Tall, an excellent fighter."

Cian lifted his sword and rested the dull side against his shoulders. He took three hops forward, like a child playing a game, then flicked his wrist. A burst of ice flew towards Michael, a breath away from slicing his cheek. Michael stood still, unperturbed.

Lowering his sword back to his side, Cian pulled himself to his full height once more. Slowly, he licked his lips and continued, "Dark hair, green eyes, olive skin just like you. *Chosen One.*"

From behind the building, Rae pulled at Alvis's shirt sleeve. "Your dad is buying us time to escape," he harshly whispered. "We need to go."

Alvis shook him off. "I'm not going to sit here while my dad takes the fall for something I fucked up. You're their goal, so get the hell out of here while I—"

"You heard how Cian talked about you. You're as important of a capture as I am. Your father understands this. If you ignore what he's trying to do, and try to play hero, then you will only make things worse."

Alvis rounded on him. If it was anyone else, they would have stumbled to their knees, and backed away from his searing glare. "What the hell do you not *understand*? I'm *not* leaving without my dad!"

"Alvis, you *have* to—" Rae broke off in a gasp. But he wasn't fast enough to grab Alvis again, as Alvis dashed around the corner.

Alvis froze.

Beneath the sign with "Mechanic Michael" painted so intricately by Alvis's hand, his father was on his knees, a sword sharpened by ice sliding further into his chest. It carved out his back, spilling blood onto the snow. His father's blood.

No.

No.

No, no, no.

Rae's hand covered Alvis's mouth before he could scream.

Suddenly, in a wisp of air, Zaile appeared in front of them. She wrapped her freckled arms around them both, flinching at the twist of her broken arm. "I'm sorry, Alvis. I'm so sorry," she whispered against his shoulder.

Before Zaile could teleport them away, Alvis's eyes met his dad's. The light in them was fading and it was wrong how glossed over they were. *Fuck*, it wasn't true, *this wasn't happening*— Alvis's frantic hands reached out for his dad, but the freezing air was the only thing his fingers could grasp.

Red painted Michael's lips as he smiled at Alvis like he always did, his mouth forming his final words.

"Go. Find your purpose."

PART TWO

THE BLOODIED CHAMPION

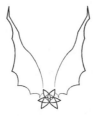

CHAPTER 13

A GROUP OF LINLESS AGENTS, including Alvis and Rae, fled Zen in a frenzied rush; their goal focused on escape and reaching Quint before they took anymore casualties.

Flying on the back of a Guardian that Rae didn't know, he observed as the land gradually turned from snow and ice, into desert, then wide stretches of green forest.

Rae had visited many countries for Ranker tournaments, but he'd usually flown himself and never made the time to appreciate the scenery passing below.

They arrived in Torne sometime at night. Or perhaps it was early morning. Rae wasn't sure. Exhaustion had pulled him in and out of sleep as they fled with minimal stops.

Ahead of them a palace rose into the twilight, starstrewn sky. The warm glow from several windows made it twinkle like a jewel above the city below. The Guardians glided to a tired landing on a flat roof, obviously designed to accommodate the palace's flying guests. Rae slid off the back of the Guardian he'd been riding, but still felt like the stones under his feet were moving. Strangers appeared from the palace door, words were exchanged, and he found himself and Alvis being ushered down opulent hallways to a medical bay. He was too tired to protest the instructions he was given, or the new clothes he changed into. Glancing at Alvis, Rae decided he looked even more haggard than he felt. *And Alvis had just lost his father* ... Rae's heart squeezed when it brushed up against the familiar hole in his chest where Hanah had been. He looked away.

They were escorted next to a bedroom. The two soft, clean beds made Rae want to cry, he was so tired. He didn't even recall his head hitting the pillows.

THE SUN WAS FLIRTING WITH THE HORIZON again when Rae woke up. It felt like a sunset, but he was still a bit disoriented, head hazy and heavy. He didn't feel rested. Every muscle was sore, even moving his fingers was difficult. The blankets were kicked off him, but he still felt warm. Too warm. Rae hadn't felt this warm in weeks—he'd spent so many days enjoying Zen's cold season freezing in a Trailor cell—and the balmy air reminded him he was now in a strange land, in a strange bed.

Rae rubbed his face. But he was *here*. They had made it to Torne, the capital of Quint. And he had arrived a fugitive—Zen would never be his home again. He couldn't decide if that made him want to cry, or shout for joy, or break into panic. Despite Zen chewing him up and spitting him back out, it had still been his home. There was a twisted safety in staying with the devil you knew, even when you hated them.

But it was time to let go, time to grab onto something new and push back the fear of how terrifying that could be.

Rae traced his fingers over the soft cotton sheet on the bed. He'd forgotten beds could feel this nice. Sunlight danced through the window to his left, past the gauzy curtains, and illuminated the comfortably dim room with its high ceilings, regal reclining chairs, and two beds.

Two beds.

Rae's eyes snapped to Alvis laying on the second bed. His back was to Rae, shoulders rising and falling in an easy rhythm. It was surprising how quietly he slept; Rae had figured Alvis would be as loud in his sleep as he was awake. Watching the other boy rest made Rae feel calm and overly aware at the same time. After a moment, a small noise escaped Alvis's lips. Rae looked back at his clean sheets. He understood all too well the shape of Alvis's dreams, and couldn't fault him for those whimpers of loss.

Rae pulled his knees to his chest and curled his face into them. All the lives he had taken, not being able to protect Hanah, and every person who just died for him to escape—would becoming a Guardian really be enough to atone for being the Bloodied Champion of Zen?

A low, gruff voice pulled him from his thoughts. "Oh—hey."

Rae glanced over to the other bed. Green eyes still glossed over with sleep stared at him. Sucking in a quiet breath, Rae straightened his shoulders, pretending his momentary display of weakness didn't happen. "Good evening," he replied.

Alvis groaned and swiped a hand across his face. Rae saw the tear stains on his cheeks. There had been little time for talking after Michael Witt's death. And the lost look on Alvis's face had been too familiar. Rae hated seeing it on Alvis as much as he hated wearing it himself, but he wasn't sure if it was his place to sympathize. Rae debated if he should say something—offer condolences? Apologize? What could he possibly offer that didn't sound contrived?

"Shit, you're right," Alvis said, glancing towards the window, and Rae's chance to broach Alvis's loss was gone. "The sun is going down—how long were we asleep?"

"All day, I assume."

Alvis snorted and rolled his eyes. Rae didn't have the energy to question how Alvis could find amusement after all that had just happened. Rubbing the tightness out of his shoulder, Alvis's head twirled on a swivel. With every turn, a new layer of shock made his eyes grow wider. "This room is *huge.*"

Alvis began a rambling account of the room; how every detail of the painted ceiling was so incredible. How the chairs and two desks were so simple but elegant. How their beds were far too big for one person each. When Alvis began pointing out the large bedroom door and questioning if people could peek through the tall windows, Rae finally interrupted, "I can see the room just fine."

Alvis quieted. Rae expected a glare or one of Alvis's favorite four letter words, but Alvis simply shrugged, and continued looking around the room and stretching his neck. Rae's eyes snagged on Alvis's large hands, which were wrapped in bandages. Then on the dark, purple circles painted beneath Alvis's eyes. With a yawn, Alvis fell backwards against his pillow, no doubt feeling the same bone-deep exhaustion of the past forty-eight hours.

With a dancer's quiet grace, Rae slid from his bed. The marble was chilly beneath his feet as he treaded to the large windows. The glass was spotless; he could see his own face staring back clearly. Rae thought Alvis looked exhausted, but he wasn't faring much better.

The light gray pajamas were far too large on him—a growing trend apparently. They reminded him too much of what he'd worn in Trailor, and he had a sudden, urgent need to rip them off. Rae dragged his thumb over his bandaged scar to stop himself. His breathing picked up, and in his reflection, the purple of his eyes deepened, red flashing and white flaring—

"Hey, what're you looking at?"

Rae jumped, his breath catching and evening out. He saw Alvis's reflection instead of his own, violet eyes meeting a curious green through the glass. "I'm looking outside."

Alvis seemed torn between shoving Rae and rolling his eyes again. He reached for the latch of the glass door by the window.

"What do you think you're doing?" demanded Rae, like Alvis was about to release a cage of demons.

"There's no point in staring at the outside when you can, y'know. *Go outside.*"

Rae opened his mouth to protest, but Alvis had already undone the latch. The door opened easily, and suddenly the room smelled like clean, salty air. The warm light of the setting sun painted the sky in a beauty that stole Rae's breath.

"Why're you still standing there?" Alvis was already outside, leaning against the balcony's marble railing. "This view is crazy."

A gentle, balmy breeze brushed Rae's bangs across his face. He could taste the saltwater on his lips but couldn't recall crossing the threshold into the open sky around them.

Below, sprawling green gardens flourished around the royal Palace. A tall, impenetrable looking stone wall surrounded it. Clear and calm, a glistening ocean disappeared beyond the horizon to meet the setting sun; red and orange mixing with the cobalt blue waves. In comparison, the waters bordering Nerwen City were dreary and gray, decorated with jagged rocks and ailing piers. Torne's snowy, white sands supported well-cared for docks, where ships of every shape and size were moored and bobbing with the incoming tide.

From this height, Rae could also see down into the

city of Torne. It was even more compact than Nerwen City, buildings pressed together with hardly any space between. But where Nerwen City had drab buildings that blended easily into the next, making it difficult to tell your way around, and an endless supply of people smashed together— bumping shoulders and exchanging glares— Torne's narrow, cobblestone streets weaved through city like veins in a leaf. And Rae watched as Quint's citizens leisurely strolled past colorful houses and shops, heading to their evening destinations. It was like looking at a box of assorted candy Rae had been gifted after a particularly well-received performance, the calm flow of foot traffic like so many ants weaving around the jeweled treats.

Beyond the city proper was more endless green, dotted by excessively large houses, and to the north—an arena.

It was large enough to rival Nerwen City's, marbled sides glowing orange and red in rays the sinking sun. Rae felt his awe shrink, and the reality of his situation peg him to the spot. The arena glared at him like a bloody eye, reminding him of who he had been, and what he would need to become to make Zen pay for its crimes.

Next to him, Alvis sniffed and pawed at his eyes. "There are worse places we could call home, I guess," he said, the genuine optimism in his voice a stark contrast to his face breaking down.

Once again, Rae's tongue felt wooden, as any reply he could offer Alvis would come off resentful or dismissive. He wasn't sure Quint would ever be home, but they both desperately needed it to be a new beginning.

CHAPTER 14

A SERVANT KNOCKED on their door, luring Alvis and Rae off the balcony with a dinner that smelled of spices and oils. Alvis had to wipe drool from his chin when he saw the still sizzling steak—he'd had steak, what? Once, maybe twice in his entire *life*, but it had *never* looked like the masterpiece sitting on his plate.

Rae's attempt at being unaffected was laughable—the smaller boy licked his lips and grabbed his fork at the speed of light. Yet he still had the gall to act disgusted when Alvis shoved half his steak into his mouth in two bites.

Rae was about as talkative as a wall. The silence was suffocating, so Alvis sat out on the balcony to eat, the sounds of the city filtering up into the growing night. For a smaller city, it was impressively noisy; high-pitched laughter, music from performers in the town's square—

and closer to the Palace—Guardian sentries flapped their wings, the sound snapping the air anytime their patrol brought them close.

Tears blurred Alvis's vision—why the hell was he crying? Was it because of a dragon flying by? Or was it because vaguely somewhere in the distance, that lullaby his dad sang to him was being played?

The metal spoon in Alvis's hand folded in his grip, then broke in two. *"Shit,"* he hissed, dropping the pieces onto his tray. He pushed it and the small table away with too much force, sending the dishes clattering against each other and spiling his water.

One time, his mom and dad had teased him about the crush he'd had on a neighbor boy. Alvis was so flustered, he threw his hands out and knocked over a full pitcher of water, soaking their entire meal.

Goddammit, Alvis thought as he moved from the table to the ground, bracing his back against the marble railing. Did he really need to go through this whole thing again?

He was never given a chance to find his footing beneath the grief before a random association and memory would knock him back: The flapping of wings—flying on a dragon's back twelve hours before his dad would die. The smell of garlic—his dad always combined it with burning eggs. Bandages wrapped around his hands—how many rolls of white tape had his dad gone through over the years to cover similar wounds? His mind swirled with memories of snowball fights, and the handmade, metal kitten his dad gave him for his twelfth birthday, and how much his dad had hated spiders. Eventually—maybe days, maybe months from now—these memories would represent the stolen chance to create new ones with his father. Alvis didn't know which he hated thinking about more—the memories, or the fact there would never be any more to make.

He flexed his fingers, trying to shake away the imprint from the broken spoon. He was strong enough to break metal, but not strong enough to hold onto what had mattered most—it had slipped between his fingers and fallen to where he couldn't get it back.

Warmth pressed against his chest. He ignored it at first, but it grew hotter with each tear dampening his cheeks, and he wanted to scream at his magic to leave him alone—just for once. He wanted to snarl at it and his locket to stop pretending to be a comfort when it was the reason his dad was dead. If Alvis hadn't dropped the Talisman, or if he hadn't tapped into his power in front of Cian, or he hadn't shouted his name like a fucking *moron*—or, or, or.

Alvis pulled the locket free from his shirt and over his head. He tightened it in his palm. *Destroy it*, he thought. *This is why he's dead. It's the reason dad is dead!* But the locket didn't crack. The locket never cracked. And the next brush of heat from it felt like a scolding, like his dad was sitting next to him and saying, *"How many times do I have to tell you?"*

Alvis let his head fall back against the marble railing with a gentle bump. What was he thinking? Alvis's lineage wasn't what led to his father's death. If Alvis weren't a Chosen One, would it have changed anything?

Cian still would've tortured Jazz; still would've showed up at Michael's shop; still would've killed his dad for stalling until Rae could escape.

But his head understanding this didn't mean his heart did. And he wasn't sure when his heart would ever catch up.

Sobs shook him, and his chest burned with heavy breaths, but holding back felt worse. The subtle buzz of power from his Talisman now felt comforting, like an old friend that had been with him through thick and thin. More memories washed over him—his fingers spreading paint along canvases; his dad's hand patting his hair after a nightmare; his mom's breath creating smoke rings of jumping foxes.

Find purpose in your own power—his dad's last wish. But how was he supposed to do that in the face of all these memories and this guilt?

The grotesque popping of Cian's eye suddenly brushed against his knuckles, a memory he wouldn't be able to shake out. Right now, he didn't mind it; it made him happy to have taken something important from Cian, to have left a physical reminder that also served as a promise of more pain to come.

Across the balcony, in the room, Rae was back in bed, facing away. Alvis remembered their rooftop conversation before the world fell on its ear. And the way Cian had sneered at the concept of Pacts, like the word was trash in his mouth.

No more. No more spilled blood. No more humans and Guardians dying by Cian's icy magic or falling under his sword. Alvis would not let it happen any longer. He still had his magic. And he had allies and Linless. But most importantly, he had a purpose.

And it looked like Cian, dead at his feet.

IT'S SO FREAKING HOT, Alvis thought, wiping the sweat from his brow.

The early morning sun was still low, but it didn't stop Alvis from feeling like he was about to pass out as he and Rae were led to a courtyard. Every time he peeled his shirt from his stomach, he grew more grateful for the thin clothes he'd been given that morning by Boam, a servant assigned to them. The idea of having a *servant* was so weird, it still made Alvis pull a face when he thought about it.

There *was* one thing Alvis enjoyed about the heat, though.

"I know you're trying not to laugh, so stop acting like you aren't," Rae said for the third time since they had woken up. Nothing about his posture or tone of voice said he was aggravated, but his frown was deeper than normal as he smoothed back his hair.

It was no longer soft waves that gently framed his face; it had soaked up so much humidity that it was now alight on his head like a white puff pastry. Of course, it wasn't Rae's fault—Torne was so stupidly humid that even Alvis's own barely wavy hair was beginning to take on a life of its own. He did pretty good at keeping himself composed, until the first thing Princess Meera said after Alvis and Rae greeted her was, "Rae, would you like help tying back your hair?"

Alvis had continued snickering at Rae's slightly mortified expression, but his next laugh came out choked because Princess Meera expertly weaved Rae's bangs into a braid away from his forehead—it made Rae's eyes more pronounced, his cheekbones sharper, and showed off the flush dusting his cheeks from the heat.

Rae cast a sharp glance towards Alvis as they followed Meera to the courtyard, daring him to say something else. Alvis quickly looked away. His ears *burned*, and it wouldn't be fair to blame it on the temperature.

The courtyard was flooded with color; green trees, full bushes, and countless flowers. Unoccupied tables lay scattered around it, granting space for Alvis and Rae to talk privately with Princess Meera.

They chose a stone table with benches under a large, leafy tree that provided merciful shade. Alvis almost fell to his knees in joy, even the stone seat under him was thankfully cool.

Rae eyed Princess Meera's Charge—Luca—who took up a position some distance away from them, leaning against a tree, arms crossed, gaze sweeping across the courtyard. Her black hair was pulled back into a tight bun, and cotton uniform was buttoned up the front, a sword with a golden hilt rested at her side. Sporting thick arms and broad shoulders, she was short in stature but commanding all the same. Her right arm was covered in burn scars, while her left featured a gentle curl of black flames that wrapped from her shoulder to her fingertips.

Focusing on Luca's tattoo, Rae asked, "Your Charge is the leader of Linless's combat team, correct? Isn't that dangerous?"

"Most certainly," Meera said, with a fond smile. "Which my mother never fails to remind me of." She rested her elbows on the table, hands folded in front of her. "But Luca was not meant to sit on the sidelines. She is a leader and has been for as long as I have known her. She is my Charge, yes, but she is also her own person. I would be a failure as her Guardian if I were to stop her from doing what makes her feel fulfilled."

Rae frowned down at the pale stone of the table. "Is that how every Guardian should act?"

"Every Pact is different, because every Guardian and human is different. What they want, who they are now, who they will be in the future. The bond between Guardian and Charge may be unique and strong, but it is the same as any other relationship." Meera's hair shifted across her shoulders as she tilted her head. "Are you interested in forming a Pact, Rae?"

Before Rae could answer, a new voice said, "I hope you aren't speaking of hypotheticals again, Princess."

Meera's slow smile dropped, eyes cooling. She stood, elegant and poised, and gestured for Alvis and Rae to follow suit. She managed a curtsey that felt disobedient. "Queen Deyn."

The Queen of Quint carried herself less like a royal and more like the warrior she'd been trained to be. Despite the limited knowledge Zen allowed in about other countries,

Alvis still knew enough about Quint's queen to know she was a legend. She was the country's most dedicated champion and became King Mitt's bodyguard early in her twenties. Even after their marriage, Deyn was the head of King Mitt's security detail. But she couldn't protect him from illness, and he died shortly after newborn Meera was adopted and became the heir of the royal family. On the queen's chest, she bore the natural Gemstone Mitt had given her as he took his last breath.

Queen Deyn's hair was black, dusted with silver and pulled back into numerous box braids. Charming laughter lines lingered around her lips and eyes. Her skin was darker than Meera's, a deep, rich brown, and her lace and silk clothes spoke of elegance. They were a sharp contrast to Meera's casual white pants, loose black top, and bright yellow shoes.

Once they were all seated again, Queen Deyn extended her hand to Alvis, fingers long and adorned with jewels. "It's wonderful to meet you, Alvis Witt. We are honored to have a Wielder visiting Quint, and a Chosen One at that."

There it was again: *Chosen One*. The name now felt defiled since it had dropped out of Cian's disgusting mouth. Alvis bit his cheek to keep himself from pulling a rude face. "Nice to meet you, too, Queen Deyn."

Queen Deyn's hazel eyes softened. She brought her other hand up and patted Alvis's bandaged hand gently between them, her touch reminding Alvis of his own mother's. "I am sorry to hear about your father. He was a great man."

Alvis relaxed into the touch. "Thank you."

Deyn gave Alvis another small smile, then she turned to Rae, but made no move to take his hand. If she had looked at Alvis with a calming warmth, then the way she looked at Rae was colder than ice. "Bloodied Champion."

Rae quickly bowed his head. Before Rae could greet her back, Queen Deyn continued. "I find it necessary to inform you I did not authorize your rescue. If it were my decision, you would have been left to the consequences of your crimes. However, what is done is done. My daughter has argued for you to hold an important position within Linless, and I agree only because it is a roll we need filled, having suffered the loss of twenty-one agents in your rescue." She paused, eyes narrowing. "I suggest you fulfill your duty to ensure their deaths were not in vain."

Holy shit—talk about a hefty responsibility. Alvis wasn't sure which threw him off more: the unexpected harshness of her words, or the way Rae didn't defend himself. Alvis was close enough to see Rae's subtle reaction: a flinch and twitch of his fingers, his stable stare faltering, and his chest heaving the slightest bit harder. Alvis wondered if Rae was fighting back the urge to touch his forearm, like Alvis had caught him doing several times now. Was Rae's jaw working like that because he wanted to argue with her, or was he fighting back tears?

Alvis didn't get an answer, because all Rae did was bow further and say, "I promise, Queen Deyn."

Deyn waved a hand at him, dismissive. Out of the corner of his eye, Alvis caught Meera's jaw working, biting back some choice words, no doubt—probably the same ones Alvis was thinking to himself. Weren't they in Quint now, the country most welcoming of all Guardians, no matter their past? The queen's attitude towards Rae left a sour taste in Alvis's mouth, and he wasn't sure the look had left before she focused on him again. "If you have any questions, Alvis, the princess and I are more than happy to answer them."

Alvis did have questions. *Am I officially part of Linless now? When do we kick Zen's ass? When can I learn how to use my power?* But instead of asking those, he returned the queen's smile and pointed to Rae. "Rae's got more than me, so he should go first."

Rae finally lifted his head, eyes shooting towards Alvis. An awkward silence settled around them, until Deyn tilted her head, a signal for Rae to speak before he lost his chance.

Alvis reached over and patted Rae on the back—too hard if Rae's startled gasp was anything to go off. "Go ahead, dude."

Hands folded too neatly in his lap, Rae cleared his throat. "I am curious about a number of things."

"Of course," said Princess Meera, with a wide smile before her mother could speak. "You were thrown into this whole thing quite suddenly. And I'm sure Zen doesn't teach you much about what happens beyond the walls of Nerwen City."

The tension in Rae's shoulders loosened slightly. "That's correct. I know Linless is a resistance group at the forefront of the rebellion, but I'm unclear what your goal is."

"Linless's goal is complete liberation of Guardians,"

Meera said easily, in a matter that suggested repetition. "Not solely in Zen, but throughout the entire world."

The center of the table glowed orange, until a flame simmered to life. Heat bathed Alvis's face. The flame curled around itself into small creatures—young dragons playing together; they moved like they were alive, twisting, rolling, and full of expression. When Alvis reached out a finger, the two dragons paused to nuzzle against him without so much of a sting, and Alvis realized they didn't just move like they were alive—they *were* alive. They were creations exactly like his mother used to make. Those always seemed alive, too. Maybe they had been, he realized.

Princess Meera twirled her finger, and the baby dragons roared small, cheerful squeaks, before hopping back to the center flame, melding effortlessly into it. The flame separated again, this time into a dragon towering over a human woman. "Thousands of years ago, dragons were on the edge of extinction. Understanding humanity's role in their deaths, Ellowyn Clark promised to right their wrongs, and find a way for dragons to continue existing, and live in peace with humans. The Dragon Queen trusted Ellowyn Clark with the remainder of her magic—enough to create an entire new race."

Princess Meera turned her hand palm up and crooked her fingers, encouraging the flames to twist into ten distinct pieces. They rotated slowly in a circle above the table. "Ellowyn divided the magic into Ten Talismans and traveled throughout the world. She gave one Talisman to a Wielder in each part of it, giving birth to a new Guardian race. Zen was one of those chosen countries."

Princess Meera paused, staring into the flames. "Your homeland has always been hungry to dominate: their history is comprised of more war than peace. However, Ellowyn believed in the good of people. She trusted Zen would treat its new citizens with respect and bring peace to the land. But she was wrong. And one hundred years ago, Zen committed a most atrocious act."

The fiery replica of Alvis's locket floated past him. "The Massacre of Charges," he said. His dad had taught Alvis about it, once he was old enough to understand why the senseless murder of over a million Charges and their Guardians was still only talked about in hushed whispers and within small circles.

Meera's voice was heavier now, anger simmering. "Once details of the massacre reached my great-grand-mother's ears, she could not continue standing by. However, due to treaties agreed upon by Zen and Quint, making any straight-forward move against Zen would be a declaration of war. Zen had also grown economically, and their favor with other countries of political strength meant Quint could not afford to begin a war it would most certainly lose. Instead, with her most trusted and loyal councilmen and soldiers, she created Linless to be the force of change she and Quint couldn't be. To do things she couldn't openly do: forge alliances with other countries, creating a network of spies to infiltrate Zen's top agencies—doing the dirty work leaders of countries cannot sign off on—all while keeping a low profile until the moment is right."

Rae frowned. "Wouldn't breaking me free count as a high-profile move? Why wouldn't such a thing cause Zen to retaliate against Quint?"

"You think too highly of yourself, Bloodied Champion." Queen Deyn's reply cut sharp as a knife. "As the princess stated, Linless is more than Quint; it has sects and operatives within multiple countries. And Linless's origins have been intentionally blurred for generations, ensuring it cannot be traced back to Quint. Zen is powerful, but it also has enemies, so Zen would not move so boldly over something like a jail break."

"But it is still possible they will make a move," Meera interjected. She didn't drop her eyes when Deyn's dark orange and green eyes snapped towards her in warning. "With Commander Volos at the helm, Zen is getting bolder about its stance on Pacts. And if our sources are correct, they have plans to spread the magic in their mass-produced gemstones throughout the world. If they succeed, another massacre will be inevitable, this one on a global scale."

Deyn waved a calculated hand towards Rae's chest. "Unlike yours, a true Gemstone is not created by stealing a life for its soul. It is a sacred gift from a human to a Guardian with consent from each party." Gently, she touched her Gemstone, fingers tracing it. " 'No purpose is greater than giving someone else a reason to continue living.' Those were my husband's last words as he gave his life for mine." Like a tiger narrowed on its prey, her eyes were back on Rae. "Your role within Linless is to become a Guardian people can look up to. You must quickly learn how different an artificial Gemstone and a Pact are."

"How?" Rae paused. He looked like he was trying to decide whose eyes he should hold: The queen's and risk appearing defiant? Or the princess's and risk belittling the queen's words? He glanced at Alvis, but Alvis raised an eyebrow. Rae turned away and smoothed his pant legs. "How should I go about finding a Charge, if it's so dangerous for one to be with me?"

"Well," said Princess Meera, like she had been anticipating the question and was overwhelmed at finally getting to answer it. "All you need is to find a strong Charge." She made quick movements with her fingers and flames returned to the table, taking the form of yet another dragon. Unlike any of the other dragons, Rae seemed to recognize this one, violet eyes going doe-eyed with shock and longing. The new little flame dragon had jagged horns like a scythe, and spikes running from head to spine. Around its small face was a mane, like a lion's.

Princess Meera's pointer finger moved again, and the dragon flew, circling Alvis until he held up his palm and it settled in, sitting proper and powerful. "Luckily, Rae, you are already friends with one of Ellowyn Clark's descendants—a Chosen One."

Um, what? Alvis thought.

"Um, *what?*" Alvis said.

" '*Friends*'?" Rae choked out.

Princess Meera's grin grew. "Sometimes the best way to take down an enemy is to beat them at their own game. A phenomenal new Pact would send hope to Guardians throughout the world—"

"Meera." Queen Deyn's voice cut like a blade. A silent conversation happened quickly between mother and daughter. Alvis recognized the look in both of their eyes and knew it wasn't the first time they were having this unspoken back and forth.

The little flame dragon turned in Alvis's hands to stare at the queen, its wings stretching and tail twitching. Queen Deyn was unbothered by the small dragon's menace, her sharp eyes returning her own threat. The dragon's wings pulled flush against its back.

"Alvis," Deyn began. She was using the same tone of voice from earlier, motherly and welcoming. But Alvis found the little flame dragon and warmth from his locket far more reassuring. "It would not be beneficial for you to enter into such a dangerous Pact."

"Rae's role in this rebellion is to fight in matches," Meera quickly countered. "Being Rae's Charge means you'll fight in them as well, Alvis."

The offer was everything Alvis had ever wanted. It dangled from Princess Meera's perfectly painted nails. Flawless bait. From the little fire dragon to the perfect recreation of his Talisman floating before him, Meera knew what she was doing. And she knew how Alvis would answer.

But Queen Deyn interrupted again, exasperation pinching her brow. "Chosen Ones and Wielders have their own parts to play. Perhaps you could find a role better suited for you. Our engineering corps would be more than happy to find you a position. Your father was a spectacular mechanic. Surly he passed some wisdom of his trade onto you—"

"Are you shitting me?"

The words were out of Alvis's mouth before he had finished thinking them. But his brain finally caught up, and his eyes widened. No matter how pissed off the suggestion made him, saying *that* to a queen wasn't going to end well for him.

"Oh, *shit*. Uh, I didn't mean to—that isn't what I meant to say. Or how I meant to—I just meant—"

Queen Deyn's earlier softness for Alvis was now hidden behind a small frown. "Do tell. What *did* you intend to say, young man?"

"It's impossible for me to become a mechanic," Alvis quickly explained. He wasn't normally this uncomfortable with authority, but he knew when he was walking a tightrope, and this wasn't the time to snap that rope. "Believe me, I've tried since I was little. But my magic is uncontrolled. Well, mostly uncontrolled."

Gently, Alvis shook his hand, and the fire dragon flew back to Meera's shoulder, nuzzling into her neck. Alvis clenched his hand into a fist, the comfort of the little dragon's flame lingering. "I can't make things with my magic, but I can fight with it. And I'm *good* at fighting."

"Your father spent years hiding your ancestry, even from us—Linless, his greatest allies. Do you believe putting yourself in danger as a Linless operative, and a Charge, is a choice he would approve of?"

Alvis met the Queen of Quint's keen gaze. "No, he wouldn't like it." He smiled and blinked back tears, steeling his confidence. "But with everything that's happened over the last few days, he would've got it. Because he knew me better than anyone, and knew what I want to do, even if he wouldn't have approved."

Alvis bowed his head, hoping it was deep enough. "Sorry, your Majesty. I don't want to be a mechanic. I want to join Linless as a fighter."

Silence.

Alvis *hated* silence.

Queen Deyn's expression didn't shift when she finally said, "I see. If that is your choice, I will not stop Meera from allowing you to join Linless. *However,* I forbid you from revealing that you are a Wielder and Chosen One to *anyone* who does not already know. Friend or foe."

With a relieved exhale, Alvis nodded slowly. Not revealing who he was meant continuing to keep his magic secret , instead of learning how to use it. That would be a bridge he crossed when he got there—right now, he needed to get into Linless, no matter what.

But Deyn wasn't done laying out her terms, apparently. "One month from today, the city-state of Tarley will hold their annual tournament."

"Mother," Meera said—sounding for the first time like she wasn't the one in control of the direction of the conversation. "You can't possibly expect—"

Queen Deyn held up a hand, silencing her. "If Alvis and Rae decide to follow through with this ill-advised Pact, then show me, at the tournament, that it's possible for it to succeed."

One month, Alvis thought. That sounded easy enough.

"The Pact is more than a mere incantation," Queen

Deyn said, as she stood. "It is the ultimate connection of trust. I suggest you consider whether or not such a trust can exist between the two of you." When Deyn drug her gaze from Rae to Alvis, it was scrutinizing and doubtful. "Before one of you loses your life."

CHAPTER 15

"OH . . . WHAT THE HELL?"

With his back turned, Rae allowed himself to roll his eyes. He figured being in entirely different areas of their room would force Alvis to stop talking to him, but it hadn't lessened his unnecessary commentary on every bullet point of their respective Pact contract since they started reviewing it.

"Are you to the part about telepathic powers?" Alvis said, unhindered by Rae's lack of replies. He was out on the balcony in the muggy night, lounging against the stone railing. Rae wasn't sure when Alvis had removed his shirt—probably after the sixth time he'd whined about the heat. A thin layer of sweat had appeared across his upper body, making his light tan skin glisten in the light spilling from their room. His locket on his wide chest glinted. Rae tore his eyes away from it.

" '*The telepathic link makes it easier for a Pact to communicate.*' That sounds like it would feel weird. Do you think we're able to turn it off, or is it always—Oh wait, here we go: '*One another's thoughts cannot be read at will; the Guardian or Charge must open the line of communication.*' "

"You don't need to read out loud. I've already gone through the papers twice."

Shocked, Alvis's eyes shot up. Rae made a point of restacking his copy against the desk—*his* desk. If he joined Linless.

"Show off," said Alvis with an annoyed sigh, and dropped his attention back to his own contract resting in his lap. "Just stay the hell out of my thoughts."

"I doubt you have many to begin with." Rae hadn't missed the way Alvis's words implied a Pact between them was inevitable. It made his stomach clench and the air in his chest constrict. "Aren't you worried that you're getting ahead of yourself? We haven't even committed to a Pact, yet."

Alvis wasn't looking at him, but Rae caught the amused quirk of his brows. Ignoring it, Rae set his papers—perfectly stacked—back onto the wooden desk, but kept his hands on them. It felt like the contract would disappear if he let go.

With the contract read and scanned a second time, Rae wasn't quite sure what to do with himself. He had always appreciated the quiet; constant interaction with people he wasn't close to was exhausting. And talking too much made his throat uncomfortably parched. He had always preferred spending time with Hanah or Cian, where he didn't need to watch his tongue. Then, near the end of being a *Drakon*, Rae's hours spent with Cian and Hanah dwindled, until he spent days alone with only his thoughts to keep him company.

But Rae wasn't alone anymore.

He stole another glance at Alvis. Even with his short-lived silence, Rae couldn't dismiss the taller boy's presence. He was entirely too aware of him. Energetic and comfortable in his skin, Rae doubted he was the only one whose attention Alvis easily stole. Rae was used to drawing eyes himself—thanks to expensive clothes and being a top Ranker—but the wandering eyes towards Alvis were different. They weren't leaching or distrustful; Alvis drew smiles and easy conversation. He had a bizarre innocence that put people at ease. That would certainly be a benefit for Rae—if his Charge was well-liked, then maybe people would see Rae in that same positive light.

Still, Alvis was impulsive, and Rae didn't do well with spontaneity. He operated with details, plans, and thorough calculations. Not idiots who ask a queen to her face if she was "shitting" him. Or being forced to speak when it was more than obvious his voice wasn't welcome. And what was Alvis thinking, declaring he would be Rae's Charge without a second thought?

A headache was building behind Rae's eyes. Unsurprising, with how exhausting the past two weeks had been. He rubbed his temples and mumbled, "Dammit."

Now that he was done reading the Pact contract, there was no need for him to remain awake. He could crawl into the bed he wasn't chained to and sleep peacefully.

Yet, here he was instead, replaying Alvis's every word from that afternoon, despite finally getting some silence out of him.

"You say something?"

Another curse slid out around his sigh. "No," replied Rae. He turned in his chair, shoving his headache behind a neutral expression. Alvis was sitting on the balcony railing, facing the expanse of Torne below and the ocean beyond. Despite the late hour, the city was alive; lights still burned, laughter and music filled the streets, and he could hear the sound of distant waves breaking against the shore.

When Alvis spoke again, Rae nearly jumped at how close his voice was—he wasn't sure when his own feet had carried him out of the room and to Alvis's side.

"Torne is hot as hell, but it's so pretty. I wanna paint it."

"You paint?"

Alvis wiggled his fingers. "Finger painting. I can't really use brushes because if I don't concentrate hard enough, they break. And there's no point in painting if I can't even get paint on the canvas, y'know?"

Rae wasn't sure he did. He had never been good at fine art. Music he could do, as Mr. Bremmet had forced him to master the piano and countless sonatas, preparing him to perform at the drop of a hat, no matter who he was trying to impress. He'd been forced to learn singing and dancing as well, though the former made him so nervous he rarely did it. Despite becoming accomplished in these talents, he didn't have a natural interest in them, like Alvis seemed to have for painting. Rae wondered what it must feel like to be so inspired by something, or someone, that it drove you to create beautiful art.

"Do you wanna go explore?" asked Alvis, grinning at him like a goofy kid. His sense of adventure was another trait Rae didn't particularly like keeping up with. How could someone just decide to go out with no plan? "Princess Meera gave us the go-ahead to leave the Palace as long as we don't tell people who we are."

"No."

Alvis seemed ready to complain, so Rae pointed to Alvis's contract. It sat abandoned near the windows, breeze threatening to blow it away. "Do you have time to play, when you haven't finished reading your paperwork?"

"For your information, Mr. Highbrow, I *did* finish it."

Rae folded his arms. "What is a Pact?"

"Seriously. You're freakin' quizzing me?" Alvis swiveled around on the balcony to face him, apparently fearless of the long drop into open, night air beside him. He folded his long legs in front of him. "Fine. A Pact is when a human lends their soul to a Guardian, so they can unlock their dragon form and use their magic."

They were eye to eye now. Rae took a step back. "What happens to the Guardian if their Charge is injured?"

"Guardian gets hurt, too. If I die, you die."

"And if a Guardian is the one injured?"

"Charge feels it, but not as bad."

"What are the possible points of Release for a Guardian's seal?"

Alvis wasn't as quick to answer that one, but still sounded sure of himself when he said, "The heart, and the hand."

"Heart, and *forehead*," Rae corrected, allowing himself to be the slightest bit smug when Alvis glared at him and rolled his eyes.

"Okay, so I didn't memorize *every* single detail. Still doesn't mean I didn't read it." He leaned forward, annoyingly closing the distance between Rae and himself again. "My turn. Where does the term 'Pact Partner' come from?"

Rae searched his tired brain for the answer but came up short. He couldn't remember the term from his reading, and his headache was protesting again. It wasn't until he turned to rush back to his contract and search through its pages that Alvis barked a loud laugh directly into his ear, and Rae realized he hadn't missed a thing.

"That isn't funny." Rae couldn't remember the last time his cheeks had flushed from embarrassment. He had half a mind to push Alvis over the ledge. "I'm trying to be professional about this, you idiot."

"Professional, my ass. All you're doing is overthinking." Alvis stretched, cracking his back, annoyingly casual and calm. "I want to join Linless. You want your powers back so you can fight against Zen, right? We become a Pact; you get what you want, I get what I want, and Linless gets us. Everyone's happy."

It sounded so . . . *possible*. And tempting. Far too tempting. But there were still too many unknowns; plans like this were rarely as simple as they seemed.

"You heard Queen Deyn earlier," Alvis continued, despite Rae's lack of response, but he was probably used to Rae's silences by now. " 'Can't put a Chosen One in danger.' Yadda, yadda. Bullshit, bullshit. I'm *going* to fight, whether the queen wants me to or not. It's not her decision."

Rae knew what Alvis's tone meant, the unconcealed, stubborn defiance. "That seems like a passive aggressive way of saying you plan to use your powers. Are you admitting you lied to the queen?"

"Shhh—dude, shut up! What if someone hears you?" Alvis glanced around nervously. When he deemed himself safe from Deyn's retribution, he sighed. "I'm not *planning* to use my magic. So technically, I'm not lying."

"I'm not sure queens enjoy technicalities in the face of direct orders."

Alvis's green eyes darkened, looking almost black in the low light. "Cian stole the most important person to me, and I'm gonna make sure he doesn't do it again to anyone else. No matter what I need to do, or say, I'm joining Linless."

Alvis slid from the railing to the balcony with cat-like grace, his heavy gaze locked on Rae's eyes. Rae felt pinned to the spot, heart pounding in his ears. Alvis roughly pushed a finger into his chest. "Right now, I can only do that if I'm with you."

Alvis was standing so close again, continuing to state possibilities like they were facts. The sensible side of Rae listed everything to dispute them: A gemstone and a Pact were vastly different. Becoming someone's Guardian was more than physical pain—emotions could pass through as well. And Alvis was all feeling, and no logic. Would Rae be able to handle that? What if Rae couldn't keep control over the screaming inside his own ears? Not to mention there was too much they didn't know about each other, and Pacts created out of desperation were the most short-lived and dangerous.

"See?" Alvis said. "That, right there, is what we call overthinking." But he stepped back and looked off into the mild, star-jeweled sky. Music from the city below still lilted on the briny air, and Rae realized that, even though Alvis desperately wanted the hope their Pact would create, he was giving Rae the space to decide for himself. He wouldn't pressure Rae into a Pact. And if Rae said no, would probably find some other means to use his magic to clobber Cian again and get in trouble. For such a bull-headed guy, it was irritatingly considerate of Alvis.

Rae watched as a bead of sweat slid down the ridges of Alvis's neck. He took in Alvis's broad shoulders, and the scars scattered along his chest and torso, testaments to the enemies he had bested. Ellowyn Clark's Talisman gleamed, its edges limned by the room's yellow light.

If Alvis was offering to be his Charge with no questions asked, would it be so wrong to accept? Even if Rae's mind was full of sharp edges and phantom screams? But he saw an emerald fire behind Alvis's eyes when he spoke of his goal, and of their Pact. Those searing eyes turned to him now, and Rae felt flames igniting and simmering inside himself. They shared this, Alvis and him. This burning rage for Zen. And the need to repay the country that had scarred them and ripped their loved ones away. Zen needed to pay. Zen would pay. They would make sure of that.

CHAPTER 16

TO ALVIS'S AMUSEMENT, Rae couldn't hold someone's gaze when he was nervous. He would stumble over words and try to hide it with two-word sentences and an extra dose of sarcasm. It was probably why Rae had chosen to memorize his incantations for the Pact Ceremony, and why he hadn't spoken a word since they left their room.

Still, Alvis couldn't exactly blame Rae for being nervous. Even his own heart was starting to pick up speed, knowing that his soul was about to become more than just his own.

Torne used their gardens for everything, apparently. He and Rae sat under another blessed patch of tree-shade, while Dr. Sienya—the head of the Palace's medical team—finished looking over their signed Pact contracts.

They were in the center of the garden this time, sitting across from each other on a large blanket made of the softest material Alvis had ever run his fingers over. The morning air was sticky as ever, but plump clouds grazed across the sky, casting slow-moving pockets of cool shade. It managed to cool the air the slightest bit, and Alvis would greedily take whatever break the weather threw at them.

Dr. Sienya sat at a stone table a little distance away. It felt like it took her a century to turn each page of the contract in her hand.

"What's the ugliest insect?" Alvis asked Rae. They had been sitting here in silence for over ten minutes, at least. And Rae must have gone over the incantation at least four times by now. Alvis was getting antsy. He scratched his nose.

"I'm not answering such a stupid question," Rae replied, without looking up from the paper in his lap.

"Fine, we'll go with a cockroach."

Rae scrunched his nose.

"Picture a cockroach in the shape of a very big human," Alvis said. "Now think of the human-sized cockroach, naked and dancing, his cockroach junk just swinging around . . ."

Despite his pretense of ignoring Alvis, Rae still jerked like Alvis had pinched him. Rae bit off a curse, much to Alvis's disappointment. "Do *not* make me picture things like that."

"It's better than drowning in nerves, though, right?"

Rae clamped his mouth down on whatever argument he was about to start. "I'm not nervous," he finally pushed out, his mouth in a near pout.

Alvis smiled, reassuring. "It's fine if you are. But we're doing this Pact thing together, y'know."

The words had the opposite effect he intended. If anything, Rae now looked even more uncomfortable than before. Great.

"If you make me think of another naked insect, I'm leaving." Rae interjected, when Alvis opened his mouth to tell him another stupid joke.

Apparently, nerves also made Rae scary.

Dr. Sienya stood over them. "I'm curious what that means, but we've got a Pact Ceremony to perform." Leave it to the respected doc to appear right as a mortifying sentence comes out of poor Rae's mouth. At least it was distracting Rae better than Alvis had been.

They were lucky to have Dr. Sienya here with them, overseeing their ceremony. She was the most renowned and trusted healer in all of Torne. Her crisp, white coat flared around her shoulders, and her tight, brown curls were like a soft cloud around her face. The collar of her blue shirt dipped low between her breasts, revealing a soft, white Gemstone that glittered in the light. Though she came across as all business, she had an excellent bedside manner.

Alvis had met Dr. Sienya briefly after he first arrived in the Palace of Torne. He remembered how her bright eyes—one brown and the other pink—moved swiftly while she used her attribute to ease the sting of cuts on his injured hands. She'd even apologized for being unable to heal them entirely, the space of time being too long since the injury occurred.

Dr. Sienya trailed those same dual-colored eyes from Rae to Alvis, then back to Rae. "Have you reviewed the incantations, Rae?" she asked. "Do you have any questions?"

"I don't believe so," said Rae, smoothing out invisible wrinkles on his paper. "I think I understand what to say."

"And you both know what you need to do during the ceremony?"

Rae nodded. "I place my hand on the center of Alvis's chest where my Guardian mark will appear."

"And I'll keep Rae's head pressed to mine," Alvis added. " 'Cause both trigger points need to be activated and it's dangerous to break that contact, even though I'm about to be stabbed with freaking dragon claws."

Rae leveled him with a look that clearly said, *Then why did you agree to do this?*

I already told you, dumbass, Alvis glared back.

Dr. Sienya knelt on the blanket next to them, then patted Alvis's shoulder, soft and reassuring. "That's what I'm here for," she said. "I can't heal the wounds from a Pact Ceremony, but I've got plenty of magic to help with the pain, afterwards."

Unsurprisingly, that made Alvis feel only *slightly* less worried.

Dr. Sienya nodded, signaling it was time to begin.

Without another word, Alvis pulled his left arm out of its sleeve, revealing the upper part of his chest, and shuffled forward on his knees, knowing he would need to be the one to close the distance. This close up, he could see Rae had small freckles on his nose. When Rae glanced down at his paper one last time, Alvis noticed that his eyelashes were long and white as they feathered against his flushed cheeks.

Rae rested the palm of his right hand against Alvis's chest, directly over his heart. Alvis gently grasped the nape of Rae's neck with his right hand, their arms forming a kind of embrace. Together they moved in and their foreheads met.

Breath shaking, Rae began to speak. "In accordance with the laws of the Guardians, I, Rae Bremmet, hereby accept your life force as my own."

Warmth radiated from where Rae's hand met his chest. Alvis was vaguely aware of a silver glow emanating from where their bodies touched, but he was too entranced by Rae's eyes to question its purpose. Rae's pupils shrank to dots, such small specks that Alvis would have thought they had vanished completely, if he weren't so focused on every little detail of Rae. His purple irises flashed white, then silver, then back to purple, the cycle repeating over, until the colors swirled and burst into a dazzling, spinning, amethyst flame.

The hand pressed against his chest grew hotter and sharper—Alvis tore his gaze away and glanced down. Rae's hand was no longer that of a human. Now it had scales, shining white and tinted with red. The nails of the claw dug into his flesh, blood rupturing around them. Intense, stabbing pain sliced through him, and he couldn't stop the cry of pain that ripped from his throat. But Rae's next words were soft and warm against Alvis's cheek. "With this contract, I bind us with the promise to protect your body and soul, as if they are my own. I swear my loyalty to you, and you alone. Your death is my death; your pain is my pain."

Alvis felt like Rae's claw was burying into his chest, grabbing his heart and squeezing. Agonizing heat shot through him, bursting from the claws in his chest, and down his left arm. It swirled and burned, like a hot metal was branding his skin. He heard his voice screaming, sweat and tears streamed down his face, and he felt bile clawing up his throat. His grip on Rae's neck was tight—he strained to control his strength against the onslaught of pain, his nails biting crescents into Rae's cold, smooth skin.

"Alvis Witt," Rae breathed.

The command peal through Alvis like a bell.

Rae's eyes were still a burning kaleidoscope of color; his focused gaze made Alvis feel naked and bare, as if Rae could see every piece of him. Suddenly, the searing pain began to transform into a comforting, soothing warmth.

Rae's lips parted. "I will be your Guardian."

A light flashed around them, engulfing Alvis, drowning him. The pain was back, and he fell into it, then everything went black.

ALVIS GRINNED. He was in the stands of a stadium, watching the empty field. He had never seen a Guardian battle before, and he didn't know who would be fighting, but *god*, he was so excited for it. He felt like he belonged, and he hadn't even had a match of his own, yet. It felt so right looking down to the field and knowing he would get to stand there soon.

The chattering around him suddenly went silent.

A thousand heads all turned towards him. Necks twisted at grotesque angles, like flowers on withering stems.

Alvis blinked.

He was standing in the center of the field now.

He swiveled his head. The crowd was still watching him, thousands of black eyes tracking his every movement. He stepped to the left and they followed. He turned and ran in the other direction, but eyes were there, too. His skin crawled. He wanted to peel it off, maybe run for cover—*anything* to feel less exposed and displayed.

The chattering was back. It turned to shouts. To screams. To a cacophony hurtling towards him:

"Kill her!"

"Rip her throat out!

"Champion! Champion! Champion!"

"Peera Drakon Ah!"

What the hell was going on? His hands felt sticky and warm. He glanced down to find them painted maroon, blood leaking from the lines of his palm, oozing from beneath the bed of his nails.

It didn't hurt. Because it wasn't his blood.

Alvis whimpered, and tried to wipe the mess off on his shirt, but the blood kept coming. And now there was some splattering onto his face, like it did sometimes when he was beating someone's nose in—

A girl with a dusting of freckles across her nose, and dark, violet eyes stared up at him. He tilted his head—something made her red hair look unnatural, like it was meant to be a lighter shade. She was pale and crying, clawing desperately at his face and trying to push him off her, but he couldn't move. *Wouldn't* move. His hand was clamped around her throat—it felt familiar and right. One of her eyes was bloody, and on closer look, it wasn't even there anymore.

Suddenly, she wasn't a human but a dragon, and she no longer looked scared. She didn't look like anything anymore. It wasn't until Alvis saw his claws buried into her neck, and the blood coloring the glistening white of his scales, that he realized she was dead.

He reeled back. The sickening sound of his claws ripping her skin as he pulled away made him scream, but it came out as a roar that didn't belong to him.

"Champion! Champion! Champion!"

He needed to get away—get away—*get away.*

He flew. Alvis knew he wasn't supposed to have wings, but he didn't question how to use them. He expanded them as far as they would go, then further, until the tendons stretched and threatened to snap. He whipped them forward, climbing higher and higher into the beautiful sunset.

He was yanked to a stop. His tail flailed, fighting against whatever force pulled him back every time he gained air. His bloodied hands scrambled desperately for something to grasp, but there was nothing. Absolutely nothing. Not even air.

He gasped, his lungs constricting.

He couldn't breathe. Where had the air gone—he couldn't breathe!

"Champion! Champion! Champion!"

Something slicked up along his spine. He gagged. The cold, damp touch made him want to puke. He wanted to feel anything else, anything else but that slimy touch. It didn't stop, the phantom force slid over every ridge and nub of his long spine. It left goosebumps in its wake. Alvis had never felt something as gross as this.

The smell of oil filled his senses. It smelled like his dad's workshop. He wanted to cry. What he cherished was tainted. All because of what he had done.

Wait, what *he* had done? What did he . . . ?

A cruel, chiding voice breathed into his ear, *"You shouldn't have come back here."*

He was falling now. Down, down, until he was swallowed by pitch blackness. He landed atop soft grass. It was too soft. Too soft and warm. It smelled like metal and curdled milk.

The sun was back, like a lit match.

He screamed. He began rubbing at his skin, desperate to wipe the soft tissue away, until his arms were blistering and raw. He frantically pushed to his feet, but slid against a rotting liver, or was it a lung? The human organs piled around him were bloody and torn. He was sinking into them. Desperately he struggled, tearing at the soft tissue, but the carnage pulled him down faster.

A soft chanting in the distance filtered through. He stopped struggling, half-submerged in the mountain of gore. He was going numb. But it was a welcome relief. He closed his eyes.

Something wrapped around his neck, and he forced his eyes back open.

The body parts were gone, and the girl from before was in front of him. She looked happy now. *She looks good when she's smiling*, he thought. Red stuck to her pale skin and the white of her dress where it pressed to Alvis as she hugged him.

"Welcome home," she sighed contently.

Home. He had made it back.

"Welcome home, Bloody Champion."

ALVIS JOLTED AWAKE with a cry.

The sheets were wrapped around his legs, trapping him, holding him down. He kicked and twisted free, slamming into the bedframe. The wood dug into the divot of his spine, and the movement pulled at the raw Pact tattoo.

Pact tattoo.

He paused, reigning in his breathing. The repetitive tug of pain from his new tattoo grounded him. There were no bodies. No crimson claws.

Alvis's hands shook as he dropped his face into them. Wetness in the corners of his eyes grew and spilled into his fingers.

The nightmare hadn't felt like his, but at the same time

it did. He couldn't shake the images away. He still smelled the rotting flesh and heard the bloodthirsty chants of the arena crowd and felt the sweat sticking his shirt to his skin like honey.

There was a gasp. Alvis looked over—Rae was across in his bed, almost mimicking Alvis perfectly. He was breathing heavily, wiping at his cheeks to hide the evidence of his tears. Sensing Alvis's stare, he turned, and they caught each other's eyes. Engulfed in purple, the pupils of Rae's eyes were gone, and the violet of them reminded Alvis of the girl in his dream. Rae's hair was the same color as hers, too.

Suddenly, the puzzle pieces fell into place.

"You had the same nightmare, too?" Shit, Alvis's throat was so dry, the words were coming out hoarse. "Was that your sister—"

A shrill screech in Alvis's mind made him gasp and squeeze his eyes shut. He shook his head, sending the jarring noise away. When he opened his eyes again, Rae was half-way across the room, walking casually, despite the sweat matting his hair to his forehead.

The bathroom door closed softly, but Alvis saw it for the barrier it was. Rae was shutting him out, refusing to acknowledge what he and Alvis had seen.

Another spectral scream rattled in Alvis's mind. Rae's twin sister. Her pale face, so like her brother's, flashed behind Alvis's eyes. The person Rae had probably cared for most, who was also lost to Zen's corruption. The realization of her identity brushed uncomfortably close to the fresh hole in his heart where his father had been torn away. He didn't want to open that bag of pain and guilt right now.

On the heels of that thought, Alvis realized that maybe Rae wasn't shutting him out.

Maybe he was protecting him from what he thought was much, much worse.

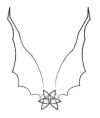

CHAPTER 17

THE DAY AFTER THE PACT CEREMONY, Rae felt an inkling of Alvis's emotions. It was easy to tell they weren't his own. Like the brush of a stranger's shoulder as they rushed past you on the street, the foreign feelings were fleeting. It made them easier to ignore. But Rae quickly came to understand that he couldn't push Alvis's emotions away when they hit him unexpectantly. And the stronger they were, the longer they made themselves at home in his mind.

Rae felt raw, tingling pain like pinpricks as Alvis stared out through teary eyes at Torne. He was remembering Bellow, his father, and someone named Miller.

Occasional panic would hit Rae when Alvis woke up from a nightmare—either Rae's or his own—grasping desperately for his locket and gasping for air. Rae had also felt Alvis's annoyance when Rae refused to engage with any of his icebreaker questions.

But no matter what he felt from Alvis, it was never malicious. Anger, hurt, sadness . . . They were all painful, but always pure. Rae's own mind had a way of twisting these into something horrible, a reminder of what would happen if he let the emotions be more than ghosts in his head.

THREE DAYS. For three days now, power had raced within Rae's veins. His mind, for once, was satisfied into silence, knowing his wings were back and he could soon fly again. He would once more experience that familiar glow and bone deep warmth as he hardened his skin with his shield—a protection against the outside world, pain once again not allowed in.

There was a sudden, sharp sting in Rae's cheek. He hissed, rubbing at the pinch like it was physically his own. He glared at Alvis from across the room. "Please stop doing that." He was barely keeping the displeasure out of his tone.

"You first," Alvis replied, releasing the skin of his cheek. He steadied himself against the mirror in front of him. "I still feel like I'm gonna pass out every time you use your magic."

Jaw working, Rae let his attribute go, and the warm glow on his chest retreated.

Alvis returned to his reflection, twisting his arm this way and that to catch every inch and detail of the new tattoo on it. A pile of ripped, dirtied gauze sat at his feet. Rae could already hear Dr. Sienya scolding Alvis for taking the bandages off so soon.

"Why are you looking at the Pact tattoo again?" Rae asked. His left arm was stinging with every stretch of Alvis's skin.

"Because it's pretty," Alvis replied, easy and quick.

A bizarre swell of pride made Rae catch his breath. Was it cocky to find his own Pact tattoo gorgeous? He wasn't sure he deserved credit—their design was as big of a mystery to him as it was to everyone else.

Black with a tint of red, the tattoo began over Alvis's heart and stretched across his collarbone and shoulder, then down the entire length of his left arm, into his palm. The lines were stationary now, but Rae remembered how they looked during the ceremony, slithering and burning across Alvis's skin. They were now branded on Alvis, like they had always been a part of him.

Alvis touched at his chest where the tattoo began. It was raw and sore, more so than the rest of him. The tattoo's design there was formed in the shape of a flower, forged from metal: Six petals flared with sharp edges, linking together like chains in a loop, until they became too small to see. Two lines below formed a delicate stem that flared into a hook.

The tattoo was the mark that tied Rae to Alvis as his Guardian, and Alvis to Rae as his Charge. Though it caused them both considerable pain to obtain, Rae couldn't help but find the overall design *breathtaking*.

But bitterness still burned the back of his throat.

That mark was also a reminder that dragon blood was awake and stirring within Rae's veins, an addicting sweetness. Its warmth had always been his greatest and most consistent comfort. Yet, whenever Rae tried to use even the slightest bit of his magic, Alvis became too winded to function.

The first day had been the worst. Rae had caught Alvis's weight at least five times, before Dr. Sienya ordered Alvis to get back into bed.

"Give it another day or so," Dr. Sienya had told Rae, while Alvis snored. "The stronger the Guardian, the more power they need from their Charge. It takes a while for a Charge's body to get used to the demand. If you rush it, Alvis could get hurt. You two have plenty of time to figure out the right balance." Rae wasn't so sure about that. Three days had already passed, and they had less than a month to get their act together before the Tarley tournament.

Rae's magic had come rushing back to him easily, but could he really call it his? He looked at the tattoo running along Alvis's skin again. What was so pretty about something so cruel?

He turned away before his head could roar.

ZAILE VISITED LATER THAT SAME DAY with a basket of pastries. She smiled, gray and red eyes warming behind her new pair of orange classes when she saw that

Alvis was still asleep. Her red hair was tied back in a high bun with a mint green bow, loose strands framing her freckled face. She quickly dropped into the chair across from Rae at his table, ignoring his obvious discomfort at having to entertain company.

"It took Lamont two weeks after our Pact ceremony to be able to unlock my dragon form without fainting." Zaile began. Her arm was still in a cast; there had been too much time after the initial injury for Dr. Sienya to do more than basic pain management. "Don't tell Lamont I told you, though. I'm his best friend, and he would *still* never let me transform again if he found out I said that. He needs people to think he's flawless, being a top teacher at the university and all."

Zaile offered Rae a muffin. He took it but didn't plan on eating it. He wasn't sure if the revelation about Lamont's training as a Charge was comforting or worried him more. They couldn't afford for Alvis to take weeks to unlock Rae's dragon form.

Around a mouthful of her pastry, she added, "Our attribute training was almost as bad."

"Attribute training?" Rae asked mildly. He was already more than familiar with his magical ability. And he was rather confident no one else could teach him something he didn't already know.

Zaile nodded. "Oh, I think it's called '*transference*' in the contract. In the tournaments you're used to fighting in, you've only faced *Drakon*, who don't need a Charge because they have an artificial gemstone to unlock their powers. *Drakon* only have to focus on defending themselves. But when a Guardian and their Charge fight together, it's up to the Guardian to protect both of them. Attribute training is focused on learning to use your magic on Alvis to defend him as your Charge, until it's as natural as using it to defend yourself."

"But most attributes can't be used on multiple people at once," Rae countered. "Wouldn't a Guardian using their magic on a Charge during a fight make the Guardian too vulnerable?" Rae wasn't sure why the question made Zaile's lips turn down into a frown. Her next words made him quickly realize where he'd gone wrong.

"If you want to survive as a Pact, Rae, it's your job to be vulnerable for your Charge." Zaile's eyes fell to Rae's chest, and Rae knew she was considering what lay hidden under his shirt: the deep, circular scar of pink where his *Drakon* gemstone had so recently been embedded in his chest. "Unless the Bloodied Champion is all you're ever planning to be."

CHAPTER 18

ON THE SIXTH DAY since the Pact Ceremony—and only three weeks until the tournament—Rae pushed open the large, wooden doors to exit the Palace library. Before they could open all the way, Alvis appeared out of them, grabbed his arm, and dragged him away down a hallway.

Rae immediately jerked himself free. "You're supposed to be resting."

"If I rest any longer, I'm going to find new ways to annoy you through the Pact link. You want that?"

No, Rae really didn't.

"Where are you taking me?" Rae said, instead of answering Alvis's question.

"Not sure. Just exploring. And stop looking at me like I've betrayed you. Locking yourself up in the room with a bunch of old books you keep stealing from the royal library isn't good for your health, dude."

"I'm not *stealing* them. And I fail to see how that is any of your business." Rae didn't have time for this. There was a stack ten books deep on his desk he needed to read through. Books about Pact history, stories of exceptional and famous Pacts, the types of relationships between Guardians and their Charges. If he learned every detail about being a Charge's Guardian, he could prove he deserved to be one. And he could better protect himself and Alvis. Something about that last thought made him feel terribly vulnerable.

Rae walked straight into a wall, only to realize it was Alvis's back as he froze. Alvis grabbed Rae's shoulder to steady him without taking his eyes off the door in front of them. Before Rae could complain about Alvis's inconsiderate, sudden halt, Alvis said, "I think this is the door to the Palace's engineering warehouse."

Rae cast an uninterested glance towards the door Alvis was pointing at. "Didn't you tell Queen Deyn you have no interest in mechanical work?" he asked.

"I don't," Alvis replied evenly.

Sadness. The emotion suddenly clutched at Rae's heart. Like being blindsided, Rae understood why Alvis was staring at the door with such longing. "Let's go back, then," Rae said softly. "There are plenty of other places to look at. We don't need to go in there."

"Yeah, I kinda do," said Alvis.

Why? Rae wanted to ask. Why would Alvis purposely walk into what would bring unwanted memories and pure pain? But Alvis was already walking towards the entrance. The clench in Rae's chest tightened even further. He took a breath, having no choice but to follow his Charge.

The warehouse's lights were bright fluorescent, and the scent of metal lingered in the air. A row of large shelves crowded together, forming a small aisle in the center to walk through. Behind their locked bars were countless instruments, creations, and weapons. Some of the weapons were unique, and others were replicas of one another, or simple swords for a foot soldier's hand. Rae traced his fingers over the small inscriptions running along the bottom of each bar, musing over the small symbols he didn't always recognize. Alvis paused to take in a few of the shelves, but he was quick to head for the end of the narrow aisle.

Their feet barely cleared the final cases when a hail of arrows greeted them.

Alvis tensed in place. Rae rolled away, but as he stood up, an arrow floated in front of him, daring him to move again.

"Please step away and raise your arms."

In the center of the room was a white boy with jet black hair, cut short and parted to the right. His face was long, with a light flush dusting across his cheeks and a slightly crooked nose. His large, blue eyes were narrowed in a focused, but not hostile warning. His torso and legs were long, and even in the mechanical wheelchair he sat in, Rae knew he was tall. His entire body was thin and narrow, with protruding collar bones and lanky arms, the left one covered in a telltale Charge tattoo. In his hands was a bow, at least half his height, and pulled taut, an arrow aimed steadily at them. Rae could feel his claws begging to break free.

"Wait a minute—" Alvis began.

The arrow flew at Alvis's face. Then it halted just shy of his nose. Stunned and crossed-eyed, Alvis watched the arrow float.

Now standing beside the boy was a girl with her left hand raised, two fingers bent. She had beige skin and golden eyes, hooded by long lashes. Her soft brown hair was cut short at her chin, brushing against her cheekbones. She was petite and thin, but the sleeveless, flowing dress she wore displayed toned muscles. Besides the laser focus of her eyes on Alvis, her expression was blank, almost solemn. The girl tilted her head slightly and her pointer finger twitched. The arrow crept closer, the tip brushing against Alvis's nose, a declaration of who was in control of it.

Another man stepped up beside them. "Do what you've been asked. Aella is as good at ramming arrows into people's eyes as she is at stopping them."

Alvis made a startled noise, but took a step forward. "Aren't you—"

The soft whoosh of another arrow, then another and another, shooting through the air, until Rae and Alvis were surrounded by them. Two positioned themselves at Alvis's eyes—one pointed at each—while another two scratched at the pulses of each of their necks, not hard enough to pierce skin, but enough to set their hearts racing.

"You're Tahtsu, aren't you?" Alvis tried again, foolishly unphased by the gravity of the situation. "You were in Nerwn City on the mission to rescue Rae."

The boy with the bow didn't falter his hold, but he glanced at Tahtsu, confused. "Really? Tahtsu, why didn't you say something sooner?"

Tahtsu's arms were crossed over his chest, not a single look of apology to be seen. His gaze hadn't dropped from Rae, pure disdain in his black eyes, then he took note of Alvis's tattooed arm. The scowl turned into a sneer, and he scoffed. "You really went through with it." He stalked forward.

Tahtsu and Rae were about the same height. He leaned into Rae's space, their eyes meeting easily. "Hey, Bloodied Champion, what's it like trying to be something you've been taught to hate?" He tapped Rae's temple. "I bet there's a lot of shit going on up there."

Claws pounded at a door in Rae's mind. It took every ounce of restraint for him to not growl and break Tahtsu's finger.

"Did you know an unstable Guardian can kill their Charge?"

Breathe. Breathe. Breathe.

"But you probably wouldn't care much. You've already killed plenty of other people." Tahtsu tapped the fletching of the bow at Rae's neck, and pressed it harder into his pulse. He frowned when Rae's skin hardened in response. "Someone attacks you, and you don't even check to see if your Charge is okay. Do you really think you can protect anyone—"

172

The arrows floating around Alvis and Rae suddenly flipped and shot away, narrowly missing Tahtsu's temple. Tahtsu flinched, startled, and whirled around to glare at the Guardian across the room.

"What the hell, Aella?"

"You talk too much, Tahtsu," replied Aella, fingers now flipped downwards. Her voice was deeper than Rae expected, with a long drawl on the vowels that he almost recognized but wasn't sure how.

The arrows returned and piled neatly into the pale archer's open palm. "It's not your place to question what happens between a Guardian and their Charge."

Tahtsu's hands flexed tightly at his side. "That's not what this is about, Tal. This guy is the reason my grandmother—*my* Guardian—is dead. You don't get a say in how I feel about him."

There was a flare of anger Rae didn't recognize as his own; it forced itself on to him. He struggled to push it back.

Calm down, he snapped at Alvis through their Pact link. But Alvis was already stepping forward in between him and Tahtsu.

Tahtsu narrowed his eyes at Alvis. "You got a problem with it, too? Surprising. Your dad died also because of *him*."

"Dad died *protecting* Rae and me," replied Alvis. "There's only one person responsible for my dad's death, and he sure as hell isn't Rae. Everyone deals with this shit differently, but grief doesn't give you a pass to be a total asshole."

The two stared at each other, anger sparking between them. Then Tahtsu turned away with a snort. He stomped over to a nearby metal table and slammed himself down on the stool. He pulled his legs up and curled over them, somehow perfectly balanced.

"Why did you say that?" Rae shot at Alvis. But Rae might as well have asked Alvis to solve a complicated math equation: Alvis's face scrunched up, perplexation making his green eyes narrow. Slowly, Rae clarified, "Why did you defend me?"

"You didn't deserve what he was saying."

The unspoken *"obviously"* was heard clearly. Rae didn't know what to do with it.

"I apologize for threatening you," said the archer boy—Tal—distinctly not apologizing for Tahtsu's actions.

Aella gently took the bow and arrow from Tal's hands and set them on a side table, delicate and careful. He grinned at her, grateful. Once his hands were free, the boy pressed a button on one of the armrests and the chair moved forward, until he stopped in front of Rae. He held out his hand, face bright and eyes sparkling.

"I'm Tal. It's nice to meet you!"

"Hello," replied Rae, slipping his hand into Tal's frail, calloused one. "I'm Rae."

"Alvis Witt," Alvis said, when Tal offered his hand to him next. "Nice to meet you, too."

"Oh, you're the new recruits!" He pointed to himself, then Aella. "We're Linless agents, too. Our main thing is partaking in tournaments to find new Pacts that Linless can recruit." Tal moved to a table and picked up a metal frame. "As for my job here in the Palace, I do the hardware for things, while Tahtsu does the software, technological part and . . . um, are you alright, Alvis?"

Confused, Alvis wiped at his own cheeks, surprised when they came back wet.

"Oh, uh, my dad was a mechanic." There was an unmistakable quiver in his throat. "He is . . . *was*, the best mechanic back home."

Was. Rae knew what the correction felt like. Tal seemed to as well, offering Alvis a kind, understanding smile. "You'll have to tell us more about him. Do you want to stay here while we work? Unless that's too difficult. Then we could go get food instead."

Alvis's face brightened in a way Rae hadn't seen before: in excitement, relief, lighter simply because someone offered him a place to talk. It was a distinct reminder that Rae hadn't checked in on Alvis at all. But if Rae felt every one of Alvis's emotions, did he really need to ask about them? Something about that question left a bitter taste of guilt in his mouth.

CHAPTER 19

EIGHT DAYS AFTER ALVIS AND RAE became a pact, Alvis's bandages were no more. Bedrest was a thing of the past. And so long to falling asleep in the bath and almost drowning . . . hopefully.

"Do it, do it," Alvis excitedly chanted to Rae the instant Dr. Sienya said they could test Rae's attribute. "Use your magic. I can handle it."

Rae's neck began to give off a soft glow as the skin tightened, becoming impenetrable.

They both sighed, relieved, when Alvis didn't pass out on his feet.

LAMONT WAS WAITING for Alvis and Rae as they made their way to the center of the Palace of Torne's training field. Arms crossed over his chest, he was ever-frowning, and just as handsome as the last time Alvis saw him. His skin a radiant brown, black hair just long enough to curl at the edge around his pierced ear, one side slightly shaved. His harsh jawline was dusted in the shadow of a beard. And his arms were bared by the sleeveless uniform he wore, showing off not only his Pact tattoo, but the needle-inked ones on his right arm.

Lamont nodded at them—AKA the most unenthusiastic greeting ever—and started towards a large supply of weapons, some of which Alvis didn't even know the names of, but it gave him a nice view of—

"If you're going to gawk at him," Rae interrupted, causing Alvis to very nearly jumped out of his skin. "The very least you could do is keep those thoughts to yourself."

Alvis exploded in a fierce red blush from his hairline to his collarbone. It was one thing to accidentally say his thoughts internally, but for Rae to call him out where Lamont could freaking *hear* him was entirely unnecessary. "You *dick*—"

A metallic ring cut through the air, and a silver flash swung past Alvis. He dodged, narrowly avoiding a cut on his cheek. He sputtered and planted his feet in preparation for another swing of the thick, short sword Lamont was angling at him, but Lamont didn't move. He stood still in his stance with the sword poised forward. "That was even more pathetic than I expected," he said.

That sort of statement would normally have Alvis already punching the guy in the jaw, but instead, all he thought was, *Oh no, his voice is still hot.* And he was also struck with the realization that it wasn't him Lamont was talking to.

Rae was a few steps back, knees bent, and posture that of a man on complete defense. He looked equally taken aback by Lamont's words, the tension in his shoulders loosening slightly.

"A Guardian who doesn't protect his Charge?" accused Lamont, taking a step in Rae's direction. He moved like a man who had rehearsed every shift of his limbs, a casual show of confidence and precision. He moved his wrist, spinning the hilt of the sword around with practiced ease, warming up his wrist, until the sword was upright in his grip. He pointed it in Alvis's direction. "Have you no sense of self-preservation?"

Lips pursed into a thin line, Rae said nothing. His gaze dropped to the sword, then followed the line of it to Alvis. He stared at Alvis with a mixture of surprise and resentment, like remembering Alvis was there left a bad taste in his mouth.

And it didn't leave a particularly good one in Alvis's either.

"The hell's with that look?" Alvis moved into Rae's space. "Why do you look like you're blaming me for your screwup?"

"That isn't what I'm doing." Rae collected himself, but his lack of patience spoke volumes about how right on the mark Alvis's accusation was. "I'm simply trying to decide how I'll assess the situation next time—"

In a blink, Alvis was tumbling backwards, the sky spinning above him. A strong, warm pressure wrapped around his middle, slamming the breath out of him. The ground was unforgiving as he landed on his back with a groan, a stupidly heavy weight settled on top of him, squeezing the last piece of air he had from his lungs.

As Alvis shook away the stars, he realized the weight was Rae who was sprawled across his chest, violet eyes with specks of white staring down at him. For a brief second, he seemed as caught off guard as Alvis, like he had no idea how they ended up in the mess of limbs in the dirt, despite being the reason they were there.

A shadow loomed over them. They both glanced up to see Lamont, sword poised and catching the sunlight. "Better," he said.

Rae hadn't been trying to escalate; he was pushing Alvis out of danger. Alvis started to apologize, but Rae pushed his hands against Alvis's stomach—ignoring Alvis's pained "oof"—and hurried to his feet, cheeks slightly redder than before.

"Princess Meera's plan is for the two of you to become the strongest Pact in the world," Lamont began. "She wants you to stand as a direct threat to Zen's laws against Pacts. I've been instructed to lead your training and ensure you become that Pact. I suggest you not waste my time."

The next words seemed to tumble out of Rae's mouth unintentionally. "Am I able to use my dragon form now?"

Lamont's watchful eyes narrowed. "A little impatient aren't we, Bloodied Champion."

"Let's do it," Alvis said, before the light of anticipation in Rae's eyes completely deflated. "I want to see your dragon form." And Alvis really did. More than he'd wanted to see many things in his entire life. Ever since he'd learned Rae's name, and learned who he was, Alvis craved to see his dragon form. He'd seen the reflection of it in the nightmares he and Rae shared, but never the full picture. He understood that Meera's fiery replica in the garden showed Rae's general form, but Alvis craved to see the color and shape that only the real thing could reveal. And the sooner he figured out how to release Rae's dragon form, the sooner they would be ready for the approaching Tarley tournament where they could prove he and Rae were ready to show Zen they'd pissed off the wrong Pact.

Blushing, Rae said out loud, "That's cheesy. Don't ask so eagerly for my dragon form like that."

Alvis kicked him in the shin, yelping when his toes met rock solid skin, sending an instant burst of pain through his entire foot. Rae's eyes widened, jaw clenching, the only sign he was experiencing the same pain.

Lamont rubbed at his temple, their childish antics clearly not impressing him. "What did I just mention about not wasting my time? Turn towards one another. Alvis, put your left hand on Rae's head."

"Like this?"

Rae made a sputtering noise, like a disgruntled cat, as Alvis smacked his hand into his face. He mumbled something that sounded like, "don't break my nose," but it was too muffled beneath Alvis's palm to really know for sure.

Lamont paused, mouth opening and closing for a moment.

"No, that's incorrect," he finally said. He reached out

and wrapped his hand around Alvis's wrist and slid it up, correctly positioning it so his palm rested only against Rae's forehead. "Loosen your grip. You aren't trying to crack his skull."

Alvis did like he was told, to find Rae glaring up at him. "Uh, sorry."

Rae's nostrils flared and he looked away.

Lamont continued, "The Release Point in the head and heart require the same incantation. However, because of how much power is released through the heart, it's too dangerous for most Charges to maintain. It should only be used as a last resort. Once your hand is in place, say, "*Release*," and his dragon form will be unlocked." Lamont backed away once more.

Alvis was oddly nervous: Like he was standing on a cliff and ready to jump. Like how he felt when he stared at a blank canvas for the first time, and the fear of the paintbrush cracking in his grip trembled through him, but the possibility of it not breaking making his stomach jitter excitedly. He was suddenly very aware of Rae beneath his hand—he was colder than expected, as if pulling the heat from Alvis without any intention of returning it. The curls of his pale hair were soft and mussed against Alvis's fingers. And when Rae raised his eyebrows, questioning why Alvis was hesitating, Alvis felt that under his hand, too. It was weird but exhilarating—feeling Rae like this. He wondered for a moment if Rae could hear his heart pounding, even though they were only an arm's reach from each other.

Alvis felt a prod of anticipation in his mind. Then a

strain of dread caught him off guard. Alvis looked at Rae to find his gaze downcast. His face betrayed nothing, but Rae reached for his own arm, then dropped it away. His fingers twitched, annoyed he hadn't followed through.

You okay? Alvis asked silently through their Pact link.

Rae tensed and searched Alvis's face for a moment, looking confused and anxious. But he quickly shoved his emotions behind that neutral mask Alvis distained so much.

"Any day now," Rae challenged, before Alvis could press him further.

Alvis opened his mouth to tell Rae off because Alvis didn't appreciate his concern being pushed away so easily.

"If the next words out of your mouth are not the incantation to Release Rae's dragon form," Lamont interrupted. "Then this training is over."

Alvis's mouth slammed shut. He took a deep breath, felt Rae do the same, and flexed his hand one last time. "*Release,*" he breathed, closing his eyes.

Alvis wasn't sure what he expected to happen. He'd only seen a Guardian in their dragon form the day Linless rescued Rae, and when Alvis had ridden through the skies on a Guardian all the way to Torne. But the pain of losing his dad had numbed him to the experience, though he recalled the warmth of the dragon's scales under him.

Behind his eyelids Alvis saw a flash of purple light and felt a pull on his magic, like someone measuring out ribbon from a spool. It didn't tire him like before. He felt the wind stir around him, picking up to match the pace of the magic. Anticipation clenched his stomach, and the air was pushed out of his chest. Suddenly, the pressure lifted, and the wind settled.

Alvis slowly opened his eyes.

A large cat eye, deep violet and familiar, stared back at him.

His hand was no longer pressed to the Release Point on Rae's forehead. Instead there was the leather nose of a beast, long and arched.

The dragon Rae shifted slightly, pressing against Alvis's hand. Alvis would have called it a nuzzle, but it was too affectionate of a word, so he read it for what it really was—a sign for Alvis to drop his hand. He complied, despite his entire body demanding otherwise.

There was a bizarre feeling of exhilaration that came along with being this close to such a magnificent dragon—a dragon *he* had helped summon. Alvis felt lost the instant his hand fell away from Rae. There was warmth radiating in his chest now, so strong he thought he might cry; he felt whole and complete, and it took him a moment to realize the feeling wasn't his.

Rae didn't roar. He simply raised his elegant, horned head, slow and deliberate. Stretched his long, scaled neck, to reveal a soft mane of purple fur. As he tilted his head back, the sun sparked off the scythe-sharped horns crowning his head. His pearly scales were like the wet snow Alvis had spent his life playing in, pure white and throwing rainbows against the light. Alvis was just tall enough to fit perfectly beneath his chin.

Rae slowly blinked, and then his wings stretched out

as far as they could go, the sun filtering purple through the transparent layers. He breathed deep like a man touching the warmth of the sun for the first time after days in the dark.

A disbelieving laugh startled out of Alvis. He'd never seen something so *beautiful*.

Then the awe was quickly being replaced by a numbing chill spreading from the Pact tattoo on his chest. Alvis's body seized, a sudden fear gripping him. It rooted him to the spot and drowned him. He fumbled to regain control, like his heart was trying to beat out of his chest and escape. His skin was freezing and on fire at the same time.

Alvis clutched at his chest—what the hell was happening? And was that *him whimpering like a child*? It was hard to tell as a shrill ringing engulfed his ears. Alvis squeezed his eyes shut, fighting to gain control over the consuming fear, but it was like balancing on a patch of ice and he couldn't find purchase. He registered a thud as his knees hit the ground. A shock of light pierced through his eyelids, and then his face met the grass.

Alvis opened his eyes as wide as he could manage, and Rae in his human form stumbled to his knees next to him, barely catching himself from face-planting into the ground. Rae gagged, and a stab of nausea made Alvis want to do the same. Rae fell onto his side, close enough for Alvis to clearly see the sheen of sweat matting his bangs to his forehead. Rae must have it bad, if he wasn't actively putting more than an arm's length between them. Alvis still felt like throwing up. If he didn't focus on breathing through it, he was going to end up puking in Rae's face.

Two perfectly polished boots stepped towards their heads, and a shadow fell over them. "Well, you aren't dead," Lamont commented. "Which is a positive."

"Yeah, well, I feel like I wanna be dead," Alvis groaned. Rae snorted in agreement next to him, then immediately regretted it, and curled further in on himself, arms wrapping around his stomach.

"I would say you had an adequate warning." Lamont crossed his arms and stared down his nose at them. "Tomorrow at dawn, you two will begin training together, until you learn how to fight as a team." Lamont turned on his booted heel, heading towards the entrance to the training field. He paused just long enough to say over his shoulder, "I wish you luck. No other Pact will need it as much as you."

"Okay, he's hot, but he's kind of an asshole," Alvis grumbled into the dirt.

Then he rolled over and puked into the grass. Rae groaned and did the same.

CHAPTER 20

SOMETHING ALVIS DECIDED ON very quickly after living in Torne, was that he *really* liked living in Torne. Sure, the Palace could still be uncomfortable—he'd declined having the staff wait on him hand and foot because that was seriously *too* much. And sometimes the ceilings were too high, and his bed was too soft, but he was slowly adjusting.

And not searching for a job that he would immediately get fired from was nice, because Linless gave their operatives allowances, which was surreal. The amount of money was far more than Alvis had ever seen, and most of it sat unused because spending too much stressed him out.

Also, the goddam *heat*. It was hard to get use to sweating immediately after he stepped outside. It was gross. But Bellow's bitter cold—stinging his cheeks and ears until they were red—hadn't exactly been fun, either.

Alvis found he could get easily lost in Torne's winding streets, and not mind it at all. Well, as long as he remembered to bring along his Palace identification card. Which he'd forgotten at least five times by now. Rae hadn't appreciated Alvis using their mind-meld thing at midnight to come bring it to him at the gate.

Alvis discovered that every nook and cranny of Torne was a splatter of color; flowers, and street art, and even the houses themselves burst like paint on a canvas. Everything was bright, inviting, and so *alive* compared to the bleak gray he'd grown up surrounded by. At night, the cobblestone streets lit up with laughter, and bombastic music flowed from the bars and taverns. His favorite part of the city was the South Market; street vendors always lined the roads with crisp spices, drool-worthy meat, and sweets like warm caramel and vanilla. Alvis had only tasted them three times in his life, and the scents pulled him back to the happy memory of eating candy with his father.

Oh, and the most important reason Alvis liked Torne and its Palace?

It was a place for *fighting*.

Maybe that term was more primitive than what Lamont or Queen Deyn would describe their city, but it was true. The Palace alone had weight rooms, training rooms, and rooms strictly for attribute training. Outside were long fields with space for Guardians to fly and fight against each other. There were different sorts of terrain for Charges to practice on, which could be changed and fixed by Guardians with specialized attributes: Sometimes the ground was smooth stone. Other times it was rocky and uneven. And sometimes it was simply grass.

On the third day of being able to Release Rae's dragon form, Alvis's limbs were heavy with exhaustion, but not as much as they had been the week before. He was slowly figuring out how to control the amount of energy he gave to Rae, and when to breathe deeper. He found controlling the spike of intense fear the Release caused was surprisingly hard, but wanting to see Rae soar had Alvis determined to master it in the next day or two.

Despite how tired Alvis felt after training, he still hadn't been able to stay in his room to rest afterwards. Today was no exception. He'd tried to relax on his bed, but thoughts of the last time he saw Miller, along with his father, kept interrupting any attempt at calm. It wasn't the first time he couldn't shake the restlessness, so he quickly searched for an outlet and found it by sneaking off to one of the Palace's practice fields. It was the smallest one and the furthest away from the Palace, the distance made it safe to use his powers openly. But only a tiny, *little* bit, though. Or at least, that's what he would swear by, if Queen Deyn caught him.

When he arrived at the small field, smooth, gray concrete was spread across it. A relieved grin stretched Alvis's lips, so wide his cheeks began to hurt. Concrete was what he always trained with back home, specifically when Miller was on a job, or when his dad couldn't get away from a new project. It had been barely three weeks since he'd last punched through concrete, but it felt like that day was an eternity ago—the day Alvis and Rae hid on a rooftop, while Cian's roars tore through Bellow's chilly air, and his father took his last breath.

Slowly, movements almost mechanical, Alvis knelt onto the concrete. He slammed his fists into the stone in front of him.

"So rebellious," the memory of Miller said.

Would Miller be proud of him now? What would he say if he knew Alvis was finally in Linless, but at the cost of so much? Would Miller shake his head with that same, endeared smile?

One punch. Two punches. Three.

"When you get back," his dad had declared. *"We'll figure out together how you can use your power."*

But what could his dad and him figure out about Alvis's power now? There was no time left. That, *we will do this,* could never become, *we did that.*

The stone cracked and fractured beneath Alvis's hands, until slabs became bricks, then bricks became dust. He stood and dragged his feet to a broken slab, grabbing it. He raised it above his head. When he slammed it back down, the harsh collision masked Alvis's choked scream.

"Do you believe putting yourself in danger is something your father would approve of?" Queen Deyn's voice asked in his mind.

Was Alvis's father hiding him away supposed to be a good thing, simply because he did it to protect him? Because it wasn't. It fucking *wasn't.* Nothing about losing the most important person to him was *good* for him. Nothing about how he would feel fine one minute, and utter emptiness the next, was *good*.

Alvis stomped. Lifted his foot and slammed it down onto a fresh patch of concrete. He stomped again, and again, like a child who didn't understand why they couldn't get what they so desperately wanted. The shattered pieces slowly took the shape of a face with an eye missing, a cold smile, and frosty blue veins beneath pale skin. Then the face twisted into two bodies: one with a sword sliding into the skin of his stomach, the other holding the sword and ending his father's life.

Power—more than Alvis had ever felt—surged through him. The locket against his chest flared, searing hot like it had when Alvis destroyed Cian's eye. Alvis's fist slashed through the air again, his mind white from seething rage. In the back of his mind, there were loud screeches he knew belonged to Rae, but he could barely hear them. Every bit of strength settled into his knuckles, desperate to break free, to release without consequence. But before his knuckle could graze the stone, Alvis forced himself to freeze.

There would always be consequences to using his strength.

The rage vanished like a wisp of smoke.

Hands raw and bloody, Alvis let himself drop to his knees. He pressed his palms tightly against his eyes, hoping the black pressure would somehow ground him, but the tears refused to be held back.

Are you okay? Rae asked through their Pact link, hesitantly, sounding winded. The screaming had quieted.

The cuts on Alvis's hands stung. They reminded him

that Rae had felt every single one of them, too. Guilt twisted in Alvis's gut from knowing he'd unintentionally hurt Rae.

Yeah, Alvis managed to say. *Sorry.*

Rae didn't reply, but Alvis was too focused on slowing his breathing to notice.

"Wow, you're sure training hard today."

Alvis's entire body jerked. He stood, stance immediately en garde, and spun around, glare already in place.

Princess Meera stood just outside the pile of rubble Alvis had created. Dressed in a white, sleeveless shirt and high waisted beige shorts, her dark hair fell in soft waves around her shoulders. Her red shoes were a stark contrast on the white concrete—concrete that was very broken, and very, *very* obviously broken by someone who shouldn't have been using his magic to do so.

Alvis began to say either an excuse or an apology— he wasn't sure himself which would come out of his mouth—but Meera shooed his concern away with a gentle wave of her hand. "There's no one else here," she said. "If security *did* notice, I'd order them to keep it a secret. I do advice you see Dr. Sienya after this, though, and have her heal your hands."

Alvis smiled, relieved, and gave a little bow of appreciation.

Meera bent her legs, delicately balancing on the back of her heels. She rested her left arm across her knees, while her right hand slid over the cracks left by Alvis's loss of control. "Grief is an unusual thing, isn't it? That's what my grandmother used to often say."

Embarrassed, Alvis rubbed at the back of his head. "Uh, sorry about that. I was having a moment."

Meera smiled softly at him, understanding. "Are you doing alright, Alvis?"

Alvis wiped at his face with his shirt, doing his best to avoid adding blood to the dirt and tears mixed on it already. "Yeah," he replied, surprising himself with how true it was, now that he'd let off steam. "I just . . . needed to use my powers a little. They're all I have left from my past, y'know? They're comforting."

"That's very mature of you," Meera said.

Well, Alvis wasn't sure about *that*.

"And unlike my mother," Meera continued. "I believe Wielders should be free to practice their attributes, instead of hiding them away. There's something otherworldly about their magic. I always enjoy seeing it in action."

Alvis's eyes lit up. "You've met other Wielders? Really? *Really*, really?"

"Really." Meera laughed. She stood, clapping her hands to rid them of dust. "Chosen Ones, as well. Though you are one of few I've ever heard of entering into a Pact."

"Why?" Alvis asked, surprised.

"Unlike solely being a Wielder, Chosen Ones have incredible magic inherited directly from Ellowyn Clark, in addition to a Talisman that contains enough magic to be a soul itself. What benefit could come from subjugating all that power to a Guardian as a Charge?" Meera's smile faded. "Not to mention, even now, Chosen Ones and Wielders live in danger: when their soul becomes a Gemstone, its more powerful than any other. Add in

192

how their power still transfers into the next Wielder, and Gemstones created from Wielders are the most powerful in the world. Some never use their magic in fear of being hunted by those who want to create Gemstones from them."

Furrowing his brow, Alvis tried to think back on all his conversations with his father. But despite the hundreds of times they had repeated the disagreement about Alvis's powers, his dad had never mentioned anything about Chosen Ones and Wielders becoming Gemstones.

"Y'know," Alvis said, "Chosen One or not, no one makes being a Charge sound particularly nice."

"There are downsides to both the Guardian and Charge. Compromise and self-sacrifice must happen on both sides for a Pact to truly succeed." Meera paused, carefully studying Alvis's reaction. "Does hearing that all make you want to change your mind?"

"Change my mind about what?"

"About being a Charge." Meera gestured towards the Palace. "About joining Linless. Wouldn't you rather return to hiding your power to avoid unnecessary danger?"

"Hell no."

Meera didn't seem caught off guard by the speed of Alvis's reply. "Do you mind telling me why?"

Slowly, Alvis grabbed at his necklace and lifted it over his head. Holding it delicately in his palm, he ran his thumb over the unevenly carved "A." "My mom hated being a Chosen One, so she never tried learning more about her power. But I'm different. I want to know *everything*. How to use it, how I can help people by using it, and why I'm the one who was given this sort of attribute. I don't think I've ever used more than fifty percent, and though I'm a little scared of using it, I'm even more terrified of never finding out the depth of my magic. I want to know what I'm capable of."

When Meera didn't reply, Alvis glanced up. She was staring at him, something unreadable in her expression. Then, slowly, her lips broke into a smile. It reminded Alvis of the one his dad had worn whenever Alvis did something that made him proud. "You truly are interesting, Alvis Witt."

Before Alvis could respond, two fire dragons appeared at Meera's sides, each reaching her waist. Meera gathered her hair into a high ponytail, then bent down, and with both hands, picked up a medium-sized slab of concrete Alvis had broken earlier. With no hesitation, she tossed it into the air directly above her head. One of the fire dragons immediately spread its wings and leapt to grab the concrete in its teeth. Squeaking happily, the dragon flew over to Alvis, floating a few feet above him and ready to let the rock drop.

Meera's smile was playfully calculating. "Now, would you care for a little moving target practice?"

CHAPTER 21

THE NEXT MORNING, Alvis and Rae walked together towards the training field. Aside from Alvis's yawns, and the sound of their shoes on the marble, the two were silent.

Out of nowhere, Rae made a weird, half-chirp noise, like a kitten's broken meow. When Alvis glanced at him, Rae's lips were pursed, as he pointedly stared at the ground. His fitted, black shirt wrinkled as he clenched and unclenched his fingers into the hem. Rae tried to speak again, but that same noise came out, and he cut himself off again.

Alvis didn't know if the sound was intended to be cute, or if it was because stoic and proper Rae was the one making it. Then Alvis noticed the pink tinting Rae's ears, and decided maybe it didn't matter, and it was just *cute*. "Are you trying to say something, or is that just a noise you make sometimes?" He asked to stop himself from meowing back, probably saving his own life.

Clearly annoyed, Rae asked, "Are your hands okay?"

"Oh?" Alvis said, starting to smirk. "Is that actual concern I hear in your voice?"

The crease between Rae's brows deepened, his frown turning into more of a pout.

"I'm kidding." Alvis wiggled his fingers to show there was nothing wrong with them. "Dr. Sienya healed them right up. Sorry again for hurting you."

For a split second, Rae's eyes widened. Alvis couldn't tell if the look was from shock or what, but that neutral expression was back on Rae's face before Alvis could figure it out. Rae nodded and, once again, silence settled between them.

"TODAY, WE'LL BE DOING transference training," Zaile said enthusiastically from Lamont's side, once Alvis and Rae made their way onto the field.

Transference. Alvis remembered the term from that long-ass contract. It was the act of a Guardian using their attribute on someone or something else. Unlike using it on oneself, transference wasn't a skill that came naturally, but it was incredibly important for battling when a Charge was actively in danger. Alvis frowned. "Aren't we going to let Rae's dragon loose first?"

"No, and this will give you time to rest. The Charge is more of a passive actor at the start of transference training," Lamont explained. "Now, Alvis, what weapon do you fight best with?"

Alvis raised his bare hands, waving them slightly. "These."

Lamont stared at Alvis like he was standing on his head. "I'm . . . assuming you mean close combat."

"Why are you saying it like it's a bad thing?" Alvis huffed, offended.

"It's not bad, but inconvenient; most opponents you fight will be armed. But if you don't need to worry about being injured, you could fight much more efficiently without being hurt." Lamont turned to Rae. "Using your attribute to guard Alvis against oncoming weapons ensures your safety as well. A defensive attribute used on an offensive fighter—honestly, you two have skills that complete each other."

Alvis brightened. Rae glanced away.

Lamont unsheathed his sword and pointed at the grass beneath Alvis's feet. "Sit down."

Alvis eyed the sword. "Uh, I don't know if I want to."

"Transference is easier to start learning on a stationary target. Now, *sit*."

Still wary, Alvis followed the directions. He leaned back on his palms, jaw clenching to stop himself from arguing further.

Zaile turned to Rae, red hair shining like a torch in the sunlight. She raised her hand towards Lamont, swirls of white air dancing on her fingertips. "You can't send transference in his general direction and hope it lands. You're using your magic on him the same way you would do to yourself. You need to be precise."

Zaile's freckled fingers twitched, then curled into

a sudden, tight fist. The air she was playing with shot forward. It spiraled around Lamont's body, growing and spinning, until it encompassed him and he was gone. She turned her fist over, three fingers unfolding then bending again in a single fluid motion. Lamont reappeared across the courtyard, mere inches above the large water fountain. Lamont started to curse Zaile's name, but then he vanished again, and landed in the same spot he had been before, the rest of Zaile's name returning with him.

"Zaile," Lamont started again in a growl. "What have I told you—"

"Bye!"

A burst of wind tousled Alvis's hair as Zaile disappeared. She reappeared next to Rae, giving him a harsh pat on the shoulder. "Don't mess it up, Rae! And Alvis— Lamont is going to stab you now. Have fun!"

"What—"

Zaile was gone, probably teleporting as far away as her attribute allowed.

Slowly, Alvis turned his head back towards Lamont. As expected, his frown was deeper than normal on his rugged face, and with that look in his black eyes, he didn't need the sword in his hand to straight up *murder* someone.

Eyeing said sword Alvis said, "Uh, I'm gonna take a pass on the stabbing thing."

Lamont took a calming breath, running his hand through his black hair and pushing it behind his pierced ear. "Replicating a situation where Rae needs to use his power is the fastest way to motivate him."

"Okay," Alvis groaned. "Very little of this has been fun so far."

Rae, who was experimenting with different finger movements, looked half tempted to flick them against Alvis's forehead. "Could you please stop being annoyed about this whole thing? You're making it hard to concentrate."

Lamont's eyebrow rose. "Rae, are you feeling Alvis's emotions?"

"He's what?" Alvis twisted his neck back towards Rae. "You're *what*?"

Looking like he'd been caught with his hand in the cookie jar, Rae avoided Alvis's eyes, and gave a hesitant nod.

"That may make things slightly more difficult for you," Lamont said, giving Alvis's protests no mind. "But it's good you're aware of it. You must learn to focus, despite any outside factors, including the mental state your Charge is in. You will need to ensure his emotions don't impact you."

For a split second, Rae's shoulders seemed to slump. He quickly recovered with another nod. "I understand."

Alvis did vaguely remember reading about how a Charge's emotions could be as painful as anything physical. Setting aside that it had been his bad for sharing his emotions, that wasn't what pissed Alvis off about this little revelation.

It was that Rae hadn't said a damn thing to him about it.

Alvis swirled his annoyance into a ball and released it.

His heckles rose when Rae swallowed again, the emotional stab obviously affecting him.

Calm down, said Rae. Alvis wondered how someone could be so dismissive when they were trying to be reassuring. *Lamont most likely won't hurt you until we've practiced a little more.*

Oh, so you can *tell what I'm feeling. Thanks for letting me know, you —*

"Son of a bitch!" Alvis yelped in pain, as he jerked backwards, grabbing at his arm where Lamont had pricked him with the tip of his sword. "Rae!"

Rae frowned, showing only mild surprise. "You distracted me."

"Distracted my ass—ow!" Alvis growled at Lamont, as he casually readjusted his grip on his sword, like he hadn't just sliced a new cut into Alvis's other bicep. "Stop it!"

"Focus," said Lamont. "I will aim for Alvis's right clavicle next. Focus your attribute there, Rae, and protect Alvis from the cut with transference."

With a hesitant nod, Rae raised his hand, exhaling a shaky breath out through his nose. His fingers wobbled with the barest hint of nerves.

Torn between watching Rae's hand and Lamont's sword, Alvis closed his eyes. The darkness was soothing. Reading moves before they happened came naturally now, and sometimes taking away a sense made them easier to focus on; it lent him a heightened sense of an opponent. Alvis's ears twitched at the air splitting as Lamont raised his sword. His fingers gripped his knees to stop himself from tackling Lamont before he could make his move.

There was another scratch to the sensitive skin right above Alvis's collarbone—he hissed. It didn't hurt as bad as the previous one, but it was still a startling sting. Then another scratch came. Then another, and another. He knew where each one was going to land—they were easily avoidable—but he let the strikes land anyway.

"Rae, c'mon," Alvis grumbled in exasperation ten minutes later, after he finally had to duck away from Lamont's sword, or risk stupidly grabbing the blade. He'd lost track of how many times the goddam thing had pricked him. "How many times are you going to let him hurt me?"

In a bizarre mix of frustration and apology, the corners of Rae's mouth pulled back into as big of a sneer someone like him could make. "I'm not doing this on purpose. You don't know how difficult casting my attribute onto you is."

Alvis heard a screech far back in his mind; raw and wild, a rabid animal slamming against bars, determined to break free. The slamming grew, and Alvis finally recognized it from those nightmares he often had since him and Rae formed their Pact. The screech was a reminder that Rae was feeling every scratch, too.

Finally, an hour in, it happened—Alvis felt a new sensation unlike anything he had before. It began as a pressure beneath the skin of his neck where Lamont had decided his next target would be. Then the pressure felt like a heavy brand burning against his skin, until it finally turned soothing cold. In the same instant, Lamont's sword struck him, but the only evidence of it was a gentle tap against Alvis's neck and the soft sound of metal-on-metal.

Alvis immediately snapped his eyes to Rae's. He expected to see excitement or maybe relief that his attribute had *finally* manifested onto Alvis, that he had successfully used transference. Instead, Alvis found Rae staring at his own hand like it had betrayed him.

The cool sensation on Alvis's neck slipped away, replaced by the sharp, familiar touch of metal against Alvis's skin.

The small, proud smile on Lamont's lips slipped away. He pulled his sword back from the thin line of blood it had drawn. "Again."

THE SUN WAS CASTING PINK HUES into the sky when Alvis cornered Rae in a hall on his way to dinner. "Hey."

Rae stepped around him without a word, but Alvis shuffled his feet until he was sidestepping in front of Rae again.

"*Hey*," Alvis repeated, harsher this time. "You wanna take a guess at what I'm feeling right now?"

"I prefer not to," Rae said.

"More like you don't need to. Since you already know. Apparently." He aimed all of his annoyance, frustration, and numerous other feelings at Rae.

Rae sighed, a heavy exhale. He was finished with the conversation before it even started. "It's not like I'm feeling them on purpose, or that I want them at all. Figure out how to control them if you prefer they stay secret." If Rae didn't know any better, he would think the look on Alvis's face was pity.

"I don't care that you know them. What I care about is, if I'm making whatever you're trying to deal with, worse."

So, it wasn't pity. It was consideration. Rae was in no mood to handle either. "I'm not 'trying' to deal with it—I *am* dealing with it."

All the softness in Alvis's expression immediately vanished as his frown deepened. His jaw clenched, and his fists shook with the effort to keep them at his sides. Part of Rae wouldn't mind if Alvis grabbed him by the collar and pushed him against the wall. Then Rae could push back and tell him, in Alvis's own language, to back down before he poked at the part of Rae he could barely control.

But Alvis pushed him in a way Rae didn't want him to. "Don't lie to me, Rae," Alvis accused. "How the hell can I fix something if you don't *tell* me I need to fix it?"

"Now you know," Rae replied. "Go ahead and work on it."

"That's not—" Alvis groaned, rubbing a hand over his face. "That's not what I want! I want us to *talk*, Rae. About your nightmares. About why you glared at me when you used transference earlier. If you talk to me about it, then we can get our shit together."

"No," said Rae, backing away. He didn't do talking,

especially not about things like this. "There's nothing 'we' can do. I'm handling it. I don't need you to be part of it. We can simply go about doing our own thing. You focus on the Charges, and I'll focus on the Guardians."

The anger on Alvis's face turned into hurt. His mouth dropped open like the rejection had physically slapped him. After a struggled silence, he managed to rearrange his expression into stone, and replied, "Fine."

A chill ran down Rae's spine. The word coming from Alvis sounded so *wrong*.

"Sorry for asking," Alvis muttered, then pushed Rae aside. His footsteps were heavy as he walked away. They echoed in the empty hallway, reminding Rae he was alone once more.

CHAPTER 22

ELLOWYN CLARK KEPT HER PROMISE of continuing the dragon race as best she could.

Quint was a country known for their science. Once Ellowyn returned from her expedition to the dragon's land, Quint finally had magic, as well.

But what led to the dragon's extinction also hindered the Guardian's creation. With so much of the world in ruins, the life energy that dragons had depended on to exist was limited. The idea of combining dragon DNA with that of a human's as a solution was an offhand comment a younger scientist might say. Not something anyone thought would be a serious answer to how to sustain a dragon.

Eventually, Quint's scientists found the combination could be pulled off: The human-half of the DNA would give the dragon-half enough energy to survive. As a result, the dragon-half was able to manifest the physical glory their ancestors had bathed in.

At first, Ellowyn found the results an insult to the dragons; to create a new dragon race with the essence of humans—the beings who had forced the dragons to extinction—left a vile taste upon her tongue and weighed on her conscience. But as she held the locket in the palm of her hand, brimming with the Dragon Queen's magic, she reached a conclusion: if creating a race of dragon-human hybrids meant keeping her promise, perhaps it was a choice the Dragon Queen could forgive her for.

Ellowyn had still felt unworthy of the Dragon Queen's magic. The locket had always been warm, inviting, and tempting, but Ellowyn had resisted it. Yet, she believed in the promise she had made to the Dragon Queen: she believed humans could prosper and grow in harmony with a new race of dragons.

For the first time, Ellowyn opened the locket. She allowed the magic to flow through her. With every fiber of her being she believed in the knowledge of scientists, in the power of the Dragon Queen's magic, and in the good of people's hearts.

And thus, the first Guardians were born.

However, the team of scientists quickly learned that Guardians were unable to actively pull life energy into their souls from the nature around them to manifest their magical attributes, as their mighty dragon ancestors had done. Their human DNA was simply keeping them alive and could do no more than that. Eventually, Quint scientists found a solution by joining a human's soul to a Guardian's. The combined power of the human's and Guardian's souls was able to awaken a Guardian's full potential: they could use their magic at will and transform into their dragon form. This incredible bond became known as a Pact, and the bonded human became known as a Charge.

But a Pact was far from a perfect solution: A Charge whose soul was too weak to provide enough energy risked exhaustion, to the point of death. And every injury the Charge received, the Guardian did as well. Luckily, the Guardian's pain wasn't inflicted on the Charge quite as heavily. A Guardian could also only change into their dragon form as long as the Charge was available to unlock it.

Never could Ellowyn have imagined that later, humans would seek another solution that stood in contrast to Pacts: artificial gemstones created from human souls, imbedded into the chest of Guardians to unlock their powers, without the perceived drawbacks of defending a human Charge. The *Drakon* were the country of Zen's greatest creation and tool of propaganda.

ONCE ELLOWYN FELT ASSURED she was fulfilling her promise to the Dragon Queen, she traveled throughout the world, spreading the knowledge of Guardians, Charges, and Pacts. Along with her, she brought Ten Talismans, each bearing a name and portion of the Dragon Queen's power: the Unbreakable Locket, the Golden Arrowhead, the Broken Flute, the Book of Spells, the Rainbow Hair Piece, the Dragon Scale Key, the Silver

Quill, the Heart of Glass, the Topaz Earrings, and the Bowl of Reparation.

Wielding the Book of Spells for Quint, Elloywn gifted a Talisman to other Wielders in nine different countries so that they too could create Guardians. She provided this gift with a single command: Guardians were to co-exist with humans and be treated as equal beings in every way.

RAE RESISTED THE URGE TO GROAN and drop his face into the open book in front of him. Even with no one around to see him in this quiet area of the Royal Library, the combination of actions was too childish. His frustration was serious, though.

How many times had Rae read about the creation of the Guardians, Pacts, the Ten Talismans and their Wielders? He understood the drawbacks to a Pact for Guardians and Charges: Alvis could die if Rae overpowered him, and they would feel every scratch the other received. But all these texts he was reading were too *literal*. Normally, Rae liked straightforward explanations, but none of this was telling him *the how's*: how to stop forcing his dreams onto Alvis; how to overcome the dripping terror in his stomach anytime he tried to use transference; how to fight the temptation calling him to escape before he stepped foot in another arena and did something he would regret.

Drawing his fingers across the scar on his chest, he was struck by a longing to have the missing *Drakon* gemstone back. With a gemstone he could turn into a dragon at will. And he could use his attribute to its full ability, without considering how someone else's death meant his demise as well. Not being able to transform at all had been difficult enough—somehow knowing he now needed Alvis to do it was even more difficult, especially when he was simply expected to learn how to share what had always been his alone.

Rae focused his attribute onto the scar: the skin of it hardened, but the physical hole in his chest remained empty.

"Hey—Rae!"

Rae barely stopped himself from jumping. He glanced up to see the brightest smile in the world, and he froze. For a blink, his vision turned white. Then his mind was full of flashing memories. All of them were Hanah with her lips pulled back in a grin—the smile she always gave him when he needed it most. Pushing its way to the forefront was the memory of Hanah patting his head after the first time he killed another Ranker. *"Breathe like you're blowing out a candle stick,"* she had told him at the time. *"Breathing is natural, so it's scary when you forget how to do it. But if you take it breath by breath, then the hard moments won't seem as bad."*

But smiling at Rae from a few tables down wasn't the Hanah he remembered. It wasn't Hanah at all.

Tal furrowed his brows, his long face looking concerned. "Are you okay?" he asked. "You look like you saw a ghost."

Rae tightened his posture, quickly composing himself.

"Yes, I'm fine. Nice to see you again, Tal."

Tal and Rae hadn't talked since they'd first met a few days ago, but Tal pressed a button on the armrest of his wheelchair. A soft buzzing sound emitted from the tires. The mechanical chair quickly and smoothly slid forward. Tal's big blue eyes sparkled, like he couldn't contain his excitement to see Rae again. "Good to see you, too!" Tal replied energetically. His black hair was still parted to the right, and the locks shifted as he slid himself to the edge of his wheelchair and let his feet settle onto the ground. He braced himself against the handles of the wheelchair, then, with a soft grunting noise, pushed himself up to stand. He was shaky at first, but patiently waited for his legs to steady themselves. Once they did, he pumped his fist, like a silent congratulations to himself.

Taken aback, Rae couldn't stop his mouth from dropping open. When Tal met his eyes, Rae quickly looked away until he heard a gentle laugh. "Wow, you and Alvis are way different!" Tal said. "Alvis asked me straight up why I was in a wheelchair if I could still walk. You're pretending you aren't wondering why. And that's okay! I know it's kind of jarring for someone to go from *fup* to *hup*, then back to *fup*."

At Rae's crinkled brow, Tal dropped heavy back into his chair. "*Fup*," he said, then slowly stood up again. "*Hup!*"

"I . . . see," Rae replied, watching Tal walk to the bookshelf, steps slow, shaky, and determined.

"I'm sick," said Tal, as he scanned the titles. "Basically, my entire body is slowly shutting down. My legs just happen to be the first part to be really affected. I won't be able to use them much longer, so I'm doing as much as I can with them for now." He let out an excited cheer when he found the book he was searching for. "I'm grateful I can still hold my bow at least!"

Rae recognized Tal's positivity and optimism. The first few years after Mr. Bremmet adopted him and Hanah, Hanah would welcome Rae with the same kind of glowing enthusiasm. While her slight resentment was always there beneath the surface, she would still reassure him that she was simply happy to be alive, and happy that Rae was trying so hard for her. Rae would have assumed this memory would send him spiraling, but instead he felt secure. Safe. Like he was being taken back to his favorite moments with his sister, before the light in her eyes had dulled.

"Wow," Tal said, after glancing at the stacks of books on Rae's table. "You really are reading a lot!"

Suddenly self-conscious, Rae ventured, "Did Alvis tell you that?"

"Yeah," Tal replied. "He talks about you a lot when he's at the shop."

"I'm sure he has only nice things to say."

Tal's face fell for the first time. "Uh . . ."

"I'm not upset," Rae said quickly. "I'm sorry. I didn't intend to make you feel awkward. You don't need to explain. I know how Alvis feels about me. Nothing you tell me would be a surprise." Rae turned to the next page in his book, more to distract himself than to truly read. "I can guess it's not much different from what other people here are saying about me."

Silence settled heavily between them. Then the table jostled slightly as Tal used it to steady himself into the chair opposite Rae. Rae could see the way Tal's breathing grew heavier with the effort, but Tal seemed unbothered. "You're doing great," Tal exhaled. "You wouldn't be doing all this research if you weren't trying!"

"I think you're the only one here who would say that," Rae replied, once he shook himself out of his stupor from Tal's words.

Very matter-of-factly, Tal set his book onto the table and flipped it open to the table of contents, humming while he did so. "I'm not sure about that. Alvis complains, but he never insults you—not seriously, at least. And, y'know, it's okay if you're struggling. The Guardian in a Pact can sometimes get lost in the scheme of things. And you're a former *Drakon*, too. Letting go of everything you grew up learning isn't easy. There's nothing wrong if you don't figure it all out right away—not in my opinion, at least."

"I'm not struggling," Rae said, because it was the only part of Tal's words he felt safe replying to. Relief threatened to push him to tears if he focused on the rest of the sentiment.

Tal searched Rae's face. Rae knew his expression was neutral, but he still felt like Tal could see through him. He expected Tal to push, like Alvis did. Or treat his apparent apathy with sarcasm, like Cian had. Or look at Rae with pity, like Hanah always had.

Tal's lips stretched into a wide, genuine grin. "Okay," he simply said. He dropped his gaze back to his book, leaving Rae momentarily speechless. No more than five seconds passed before Tal looked back up, practically jumping in his seat with excited curiosity. "So, what was being a Ranker like? Is it true you're basically a celebrity? Oh, and you don't have to answer if you don't want to. It's just, I was born in Amberstate—you know where that is, right? It's right along Zen's southern border, and we're a *Drakon* sport country, too. But we're a lot smaller, and don't really have many gemstones—the one's from Zen or the real ones. So, growing up I heard a lot about Zen's Rankers and how cool they are."

Rae had barely adjusted to Alvis's straight forwardness—now here was Tal, blunt in a different way. Rae wasn't used to receiving so much information at once. Yet, for some reason, every fact Tal offered up about himself felt important and easy to retain. Rae felt obligated to the conversation, but not like he was trapped. "I visited Amberstate a few times," he offered. "Their arena was nice."

A brief look of surprise shifted Tal's features. He quickly pushed it away with an excited nod of his head. "Right? I mean, that's kind of because they put all the tax money into it. But still, it was always fun to watch battles in it!"

Rae offered him a small nod of assent. "To answer your other question, Rankers do tend to be treated like celebrities, depending on where they are in the rankings, and how long they stay there. I've never liked calling myself a celebrity, though."

"You were number one, right?"

"Yes."

"How many matches did you have to win to get there?"

"Five hundred, consecutive."

"Whoa! Was your face on, like, billboards and stuff?"

"Unfortunately."

"Did you get to eat a ton of amazing food?"

"Yes."

"What was your favorite?"

"I enjoy spicy dishes."

Tal crinkled his nose at that. "Then you'll have to go visit Papa Bob's restaurant with us sometime," he said. "His booth is always popular during the annual festival. Aella—the Guardian I'm a Charge to—loves spicy food as well, and he's her favorite."

There was a brief pause as Tal pursed his lips. The silence was jarring compared to the chipper conversation. Hesitantly, he continued, "Did Alvis tell you where Aella is from?"

Crinkling his brow, Rae shook his head. "No, he didn't."

Another second of quiet. "Aella is from Nerwen City, as well."

Rae stilled as he took in this revelation.

Aella was a Guardian from Nerwen City. Like himself. She was also in a Pact with Tal, like Rae was now struggling in a Pact with Alvis.

Swallowing against the sudden dryness in his throat, Rae whispered, "If Aella is a Guardian from Nerwen City, was she also a . . ." But saying the next word out loud felt dangerous, like speaking it would make it untrue, and would smother the small hope in his chest that there was finally someone in the Palace who could understand him, even a little, and what he had gone through and done for Nerwen City.

Tal reached out to pat Rae's hand, but pulled back, unsure if comforting Rae would make him feel better or worse. He still offered him a warm smile. "When I say I understand how hard it can be to forget what being a *Drakon* means, it's because I've seen firsthand what that's like. If you ever have any questions, Aella and I would be happy to help you, Rae."

Questions were suddenly drowning Rae. Just as much as he was drowning in the piles of books around him. Perhaps it was time to search for answers outside of these pages. "Tal," he said, stomach twisting in anticipation. "If you don't mind, could you tell me where I can find Aella?"

INSIDE ONE OF THE PALACE'S GARDENS, Aella sat alone in the crisp green grass, surrounded by bushes of white roses. Her beige skin glowed in the warm sunlight where it dappled from the fronds of the tall palm trees ringing the rose garden. Her short, brunette hair brushed forward along her cheeks as she made graceful movements with her fingers. Slowly, the soft wind of her magic plucked the white roses one-by-one from the bushes. They floated through the air with a gentle grace, until they landed in front of her. Her golden eyes were soft as she carefully watched each rose come to her.

Rae lingered at the entrance of the rose garden, simply watching. How could she do transference so flawlessly and controlled? She made it look so simple it was breathtaking.

One of the newly plucked roses suddenly flipped and pierced through the air. In a breath it was at Rae's throat. He threw up his shield, hardening his skin, and the stem bent and cracked against his neck on impact. As the pieces of the pale rose fell to the ground, Rae caught Aella's eyes. She watched him carefully for a moment but didn't try to attack him again.

With a soft exhale, Rae approached her, stopping a cautious distance away. "Tal said you might be able to help me," he ventured. His and Aella's arrow-strewn introduction in the engineering room had been unconventional, but Rae knew he needn't bother with another one.

At the mention of her Charge's name, Aella's defenses fell, like Tal's blessing of the conversation was all that mattered. She resumed pulling more roses free from the bush with her magic. "What can I help you with?"

Now that he was in front of Aella, Rae hesitated. The questions were piled in his head and he had trouble deciding which to lead with. Which ones may be too painful for Aella? Rae needed answers, but he also didn't want to pry; he knew firsthand how painful the topic of being a *Drakon* could be.

Finally, Rae settled on, "Tal told me you used to live in Nerwen City." That question felt relatively safe and general.

Aella was now weaving two long rose stems together between her nimble fingers. She let go and the bundle floated, suspended in the air in front of her. She began to twist another flower into it. "Yes. I was born there," she replied, too casually. She then tugged down the front collar of her loose, pink cotton shirt—far enough for Rae to see the beginning of a large scar. Exactly like the one on Rae's own chest where his *Drakon* gemstone had been.

Desperately, Rae wanted to reach out and touch Aella's scar to confirm their shared trauma. "You really were a *Drakon*?" Rae said, his words cracking.

"Briefly." Aella allowed her shirt to settle back into place. "I was exiled when I was ten."

Rae's eyebrows shot up, taken aback. "*Drakon* don't receive a gemstone until that age," He swallowed against the dryness of his throat. "I've never heard of . . . But then, why were you exiled so quickly afterwards?"

Aella continued building on the floating half-circle, flower creation in front of her. She clicked her tongue when she snagged her thumb on a thorn but selected another rose without pause. "No one wanted me."

Rae couldn't understand how there was no pain in Aella's golden eyes as she spoke. Losing your gemstone was agonizing, like losing a part of yourself. Yet, Aella mentioned the loss of hers with ease.

Rae tightened his hands into fists, nails digging into the skin of his palms. "Does it get easier to be in a Pact, instead of having a gemstone? To no longer have full control over when your power can be used?"

"Our circumstances are too different for me to give

you an adequate answer," Aella replied gently. "I wasn't a *Drakon* long enough to know the difference between a gemstone and a Pact." Aella was watching him over the flowers suspended between them. "However, if you ask me how hard it is to overcome hating myself for needing a Pact, I would give you a different answer: Pacts feel like dying, at first. *Drakon* were trained to never rely on humans. We were taught that those with gemstones are the true children of the Dragon Queen. *Peera Drakon Ah.*"

Blood of the Dragon Queen. Rae could never forget.

Aella absentmindedly brushed a white petal with her thumb. "Perhaps I have never truly experienced a gemstone, but the hatred instilled in me is the same that was instilled in you. Entering into a Pact took years for me to accept. If it were not for Tal, I most likely never would have joined into a Pact at all. I do not envy the weight you must be carrying, but I understand it."

Her graceful hands added more white roses to the flower crown taking shape beneath them. "Tal once told me that knowing someone believes in you can make changing easier, even if you don't trust in their belief."

How? Rae wanted to ask. He recalled Alvis's frustration every time Rae hesitated to stop Lamont's attacks; Zaile's cold stare each time Alvis asked Rae to go out with them and Rae declined; Lamont's barbed reminders that Alvis and Rae were running out of time before the Tarley tournament, and Rae was running out of chances to prove Linless needed him, and was no longer the Bloodied Champion.

How could Rae trust someone's belief in him, when no

one here in Quint honestly believed in him?

A gentle breeze brushed past Rae's cheeks. He glanced up at Aella, the finished crown of roses floating above her cupped palms. Slowly, it lifted and gently rested on Rae's snowy curls.

Aella offered the barest hint of a smile. "Keep fighting, Rae."

CHAPTER 23

EXHAUSTION MADE ALVIS'S MOVEMENTS slower than normal.

Maybe he should have been resting in bed, but instead, Alvis was out in the crowds of Torne and into the South Market before he thought twice about it. Alvis had started coming down here with Zaile, but he hadn't thought about asking her to come along this time before he stormed out of his and Rae's room.

All Alvis wanted was a drink or two, and to not think about his latest argument with Rae, that emotionally constipated *ass*.

Alvis picked the first tavern he recognized. It was a single story, slightly less pristine place, filled to the max with patrons of all kinds. There was music dancing between the packed tables—something with a stomping melody that didn't exist in Bellow and set his heart tapping along.

Patrons were toasting or hunched close to hear over the din. In the very back corner, far away from the stage and crowds, Alvis spotted the only free table and chairs. It wasn't the most sociable spot, but it would have to do until he loosened up a bit more.

After flagging down a waitress to place his drink order, he settled into the chair closest to the wall with a sigh. On the table were carvings in the wood. There was no unity to them, but they made a map he could trace. His finger slid from one line to the next, the motion relaxing, until he thought of Rae and got riled up again.

Nineteen days into this Pact training, and Alvis and Rae were falling further and further behind, while the tournament drew closer. Alvis could Release Rae's dragon form perfectly now, without getting winded. And when they sparred against some of the Palace's soldiers for transference practice, they both held their own.

Held their own *individually*.

When Alvis and Rae tried to work together, though?

It was a freaking *shitshow*.

Today had been their first practice match against students from the Palace of Torne's training school, and Alvis and Rae had lost *embarrassingly* quick. The loss shouldn't have been that big of a deal; normally Alvis would bite the bullet and accept it. But the loss was the cherry on top of the collection of dismissed attempts, denied bonds, and everything Alvis couldn't deal with from Rae right now.

The knife-wielding Charge they sparred against had left Alvis with scratches across his forearms. After the match, the medical lab had been empty, so Alvis had set about trying to wrap up his left arm with only one hand and pure, pissed off determination.

"I can do it," Rae had offered the third time Alvis failed.

"Fuck off."

"I was trying to win," Rae replied without missing a beat. "Why couldn't you listen to me? We lost because you seem to think lack of strategy is the same as being on the offensive. I didn't become the best Ranker in Nerwen City by jumping in without thinking—"

"And I didn't become the best fighter in Bellow by running away," Alvis had snapped back. "Don't give me some bullshit line about being strategic. You were too scared to even *move* out there."

"You were trying to catch knives with your bare hands. How was I supposed to focus—"

"Then *tell* me that's what's happening, instead of shouting orders!"

Bandages successfully wrapped, Alvis had dropped the roll back onto the table and whirled to face Rae. "Maybe if you dealt with your shit, instead of pretending it doesn't exist, then feeling something wouldn't be such a huge deal."

Rae's eyes had lit up, the flecks of white flashing and the purple nearly glowing against his pale skin. Alvis remembered thinking, *Yes—give me something to work with!* But then Rae pulled back like he always did and stormed off without looking back.

Like Alvis said. *Shitshow.*

He groaned and dropped his head onto the table. *God, he needed that drink.*

As if summoned, a cold, blue, and foaming drink mercifully slid to a stop in front of him. When he glanced up, it wasn't the waitress or some deity delivering it.

Standing over him was a guy in a loose, dirtied white shirt, which stood in stark contrast to his deep russet eyes. A sleeveless, leather coat hugged his frame, not much different than Alvis's own, and his brown hair was parted to one side, bangs behind his ears. The sly twist of his lips showed off yellowed teeth, sharp canines giving him a playful, wild look, despite the five o'clock shadow on his jagged cheekbones.

"Uh," Alvis said, all coherent thought momentarily stalled, simply because a good-looking guy was smiling down at him. But he recovered quickly and gave the man a grin of his own. He picked up the drink, grateful for the coolness of the glass. "Thanks."

It wasn't intended as an invitation, but Alvis didn't mind the guy taking it as one, as he slid smoothly into the seat in front of him.

"The name's Rival," the man said, his voice like whiskey with an Eastern drawl.

Alvis took his offered hand, giving it a firm shake. "Alvis."

"Fellow Charge, I see," said Rival, eyeing the Pact tattoo visible under Alvis's left sleeve. "Where's your Guardian?"

"Around," Alvis replied vaguely. *A Charge should never give the impression they're alone.* It was one of Lamont's very emphasized teaching points. Alvis crinkled his brow at Rival's bare arm. "If you're a Charge, why don't you have a tattoo?"

"In between Guardians right now."

" 'In between?' How many Guardians have you had?"

"Ah," said Rival, voice taking an upward tilt. "You're new to this. The last one made five."

Alvis squeaked, shocked. "Five? You've done the bonding thing *five* times?" Alvis ran a hand over the Pact tattoo through his shirt; it still burned from time to time, the memory one he wished he could shake off forever, but it clung to him. "It *hurts*."

Rival snorted in agreement. "You'd think they would figure out how to make it better." He shrugged, brushing away Alvis's shock with a casual wave of his hand. "I'm doing what I need to get by. You get used to those sorts of things after a while."

"Why would you *want* to go through that so many times, though?"

"People change." Rival took a long sip from his ale, sizing Alvis up from behind it. "Their desires, their intentions, their goals. No point in staying attached if you're no longer compatible." He set his cup back onto the table and leaned forward, keeping Alvis's attention as he smirked, a slow, attractive draw of the lips. "But I'm sure that won't be the case for you and *your* Guardian."

Alvis opened his mouth to argue against Rival's sarcastic tone, but promptly shut it. He didn't *have* an argument. Rival was right: Alvis and Rae had never agreed to be more than mutual steppingstones for each other to reach their goals. But Alvis figured it was implied they needed to become more than that. Pacts were intimate bonds, built on trust. Even Rae had to know that, with all those books about Pacts and Guardians that he consumed, instead of engaging Alvis in any sort of comradery.

Parting ways after being so connected to another person . . . Alvis couldn't picture it. It didn't make sense. But maybe to Rae, it did. Maybe that's why opening up to Alvis was so hard for him, because not connecting would make breaking off their Pact later that much easier. After Cian was defeated, and Zen was torn down, would Rae give a second thought to ending it? The thought caused his stomach to clench.

"That's a pretty jaded way of looking at it," Alvis finally said, trying to sound less deflated than he felt.

"Jaded isn't the same thing as untraditional," Rival corrected. "Proper people like to believe Pacts can only happen between those with *deep* connections or some shit like that. And it's not true. The trust thing is, though."

Rival tipped his glass towards Alvis's. "Glarin' at your drink isn't nearly as fun as drinkin' it, by the way."

Rival's challenge rested somewhere between flirtatious and simple fellowship, and if it helped Alvis stop thinking about Rae, it was as good of a distraction as any. Alvis threw back his drink, finishing the cool liquid in two gulps. When he slammed the empty, glass mug back onto the table, Rival was smirking, impressed.

Alvis wiped at his mouth with the back of his hand and sent Rival a grin of his own. "What d'you say we go for round two?"

RIVAL, IT TURNED OUT, was the perfect company Alvis could hope for. He was easy to talk to and an attentive listener. They shared a lot in common: both were Charges, both enjoyed a good fight, and both were driven from their homelands. Rival's clan had been destroyed after his father had made too many deals with the wrong people, leaving only Rival alive.

"Guardians are selfish *dicks*," said Alvis, four drinks in and unable to let the topic go. " 'None of your business.' 'I want nothing to do with you unless I wanna go dragon.' 'Why do you keep telling me to get a hobby?' Fuck, you'd think I was asking Rae to unleash every dirty little secret he has."

"If you're that frustrated with him, why not get a different Guardian?" suggested Rival again, the words sluggish.

"Because . . ." Alvis trailed off, unsure about the real answer. Something about it made his stomach churn and ache, or maybe that was the drinks. His locket flared hot like it was telling him he already knew the answer, though, but he readjusted the chain to tell it to calm down. "Whatever. It doesn't matter. I don't wanna talk about other guys with you."

Rival offered him a sheepish smile, the canine's making it seem less genuine. " 'Bout that . . . Not gonna lie, I sat here 'cause there weren't any other tables. You're actually not my type."

If Alvis weren't so sloshed, the sting of disappointment might have hurt a bit more, but tipsy Alvis paid it no mind. Why Rival sat wasn't important; Alvis would never say no to more friends.

Still, he raised an eyebrow, incredulous. "What was with all the flirting earlier, then?"

Rival raised an eyebrow right back.

Fair enough, Alvis thought with a shrug.

Rival gestured with his drink towards a guy not much older than them, short and skinny with black eyes. It took Alvis a second of squinting against the impending dizziness to realize it wasn't Tahtsu.

"What about you?" asked Rival. "What's your type?"

"Most guys, but it depends on what he's like as a person." Alvis wasn't against flings, but he knew he didn't prefer it. Miller's face and cheeky grin appeared in his mind. Alvis couldn't help but smile sadly. "I had a boyfriend back home but . . . lots of things happened, and I'll probably never see him again."

"What about your Guardian? What was his name—Rae?" Rival mused, easily steering the conversation back into something less melancholy.

"Yeah. What about him?"

"Most guys are your type. Does that mean *he's* your type?"

"Uh." Alvis squinted. Everything about Rae came to mind. Suddenly Alvis couldn't tell if his face was red from the alcohol or his racing heart. "He's my Guardian."

The answer was too slow. Rival's eyes brightened and he smirked. "Oh damn, he *is*. How far have you gone?"

"Nowhere," Alvis said adamantly. Some part of him didn't want to be drunk the first time he thought about this. "Rae is . . ."

"I'm what, exactly?"

Alvis had lost his reflexes about two drinks ago, but he still managed to snap his head towards Rae's voice. "Fun sucker? Emotionally constipated?"

If Rae would stop moving around so much, Alvis might be able to make out his expression, but he sounded unimpressed and unbothered. "You're drunk."

Alvis nodded and poked Rae in the forehead. "And *you're* insightful."

Rae batted Alvis's hand away. "Even an idiot would be able to tell."

"So, you're Rae, huh?" Rival said it like a laugh, open and loud. "Alvy was just talkin' about you."

"Alvis talks about a lot of things," Rae countered, even and emotionless.

Alvis kicked him in the ankle, or tried too, he wasn't sure if he made contact.

"So, how would you describe your relationship?" Rival continued, bemused.

With an exasperated grunt, Rae replied, "He's my Charge."

"Ah." Alvis had only known him for a few hours, but he could already tell what Rival sounded like when he was smirking.

Rival pushed his chair back, the shake of the table a sign that he stumbled slightly. "Well, if that's all he is, then you should make sure to play your part better. He said you've been together for almost a month now, but you still can't use transference on him. I've had Pacts for a fourth of the time you have, and they can always use it in days."

There was a long pause before Rae answered, "I'm not those people."

"Obviously not."

"Hey," Alvis said, the word drawn out like an impaired, musical note. "What we talked about is a *secret*, Rival."

Rival looked Alvis over, understanding his barely coherent mumbling over the revelry of the tavern. "All's I'm sayin' is compatibility is important. Huh, Rae?"

If Rae replied, Alvis couldn't hear it over the tavern noise. But he heard Rival's low laugh in response.

Rival patted Alvis on the head with another toothy grin. "See ya around, Alvy."

CHAPTER 24

"HE WAS REALLY NICE."

"He got you drunk."

"I'm the one who got me 'runk, thank you much, Raenold. And 'runk or not, it's nice to make new friends."

"Friends." The two had seemed a little closer than that already, with the way Rival leaned into Alvis space when they laughed. But it wasn't Rae's business who Alvis decided to socialize with. But what had he been blabbing about all night? If Rival was scolding Rae for his lackluster display at being a Guardian, Alvis had obviously spilt some frustrations.

Rae bit back a sigh. He had no right to be annoyed that Alvis was seeking other people to vent to about him. Rae was the one throwing up the wall to keep Alvis out.

A small part of him was curious about the end of Alvis's sentence, before he had walked up and interrupted him in the tavern. What did Alvis think of him? He found his fear of the answer outweighed his curiosity.

Rae readjusted Alvis's weight on his shoulders, as they weaved their way to the Palace through the revelers still enjoying the mild, Torne night. The softly lit stones under their feet were uneven, and Alvis was finding a way to stumble over one every few steps, causing them both to jerk and falter to a stop, before continuing their trudge. Finally, Rae gave up, and coerced Alvis onto his back so he could carry him, and they could return to their room before noon the next day.

No one had warned Rae that becoming a babysitter was part of a Pact, but here he was. Once the clock had struck eleven that night, and Alvis still hadn't returned, Rae finally crawled out of bed and wandered into the South Market for the first time. The boisterous nightlife was nearly overwhelming at first; it was nothing like the high-class, extravagant clubs he was used to. Rae was grateful at least that Alvis's alcohol-ridden mind had replied to him through their Pact link, slurring his location, even though Alvis didn't seem to remember doing so.

Giving someone a piggyback ride when they were considerably bigger wasn't easy, especially when you weren't used to this much contact with another person. But it was better than the embarrassing, stumbling mess they had been. Alvis hadn't even made it to the tavern door before he tripped into a couple lost in each other, causing them to spill their drinks all over one another's clothing. Rae had apologized profusely and pulled Alvis through the door. Only for Alvis to stumble again into some sleeping chickens perched on boxes, sending them in an uproar of feathers and squawks. Yes, despite his pride, it was more efficient to just carry his drunken mess of a Charge. And Alvis had been far more excited about letting Rae carry him than any normal person would be.

Drunk Alvis was a clingier Alvis. His arms hugged almost too tightly around Rae's neck. He rested his head on Rae's shoulder, not caring that his messy hair kept tickling Rae's cheek, or that his breath smelled like a dead animal. The heat Alvis radiated against his back was more intense than high noon in Torne.

Alvis lifted his head, only to plop it back down, bony chin digging into Rae's skull. "I'm sleepy," he slurred.

Rae didn't bother repressing his sigh. He ignored Alvis's long whine—far too loud and directly into his ear—then huffed when Alvis tightened his arms. "Don't grab on so hard, idiot."

"I'm not grabbing. I'm hugging."

Rae didn't have the energy for this.

"Hey!" If Rae hadn't spent his life learning how to repress things like surprise, his head would have slammed right up into Alvis's chin at his Charge's shout. Not that Alvis would have noticed; he squirmed and flailed an arm out in a sweeping motion that encompassed the colorful buildings packed tightly around them. "This is my street right here!"

Rae halted in the middle of the intersection. He looked over his shoulder at Alvis, baffled to find him beaming at the street to their right. Rae hadn't spent enough time in Bellow to memorize what the Witt's neighborhood had looked like, but he was hard-pressed to find any similarities.

"Alvis, we aren't in Bellow. We're in Torne."

"No way! I don't live in Torne—see, look!" Rae followed Alvis's finger to the sign hanging from the roof of a store. From this distance, it was too dark to make out any details on it. "That's Dad's sign! I was the one who painted it, so I would recognize it anywhere."

Rae sighed again, and adjusted his hold on Alvis's knees, hiking him further up his back from where his squirming made him slip. He needed to get Alvis back to the Palace and deposit him into bed, before he made them do something crazy like break into an unsuspecting bakery. But, when he started in the opposite direction, Alvis used his hold on Rae's neck to yank him backwards.

"What are you doing?" Rae choked, barely stopping them from both flopping backwards on to the hard cobblestones.

"What are *you* doing? Why are you going the wrong way?" Alvis tugged at Rae's neck again. Rae was one more press to his larynx away from dropping Alvis on principle alone. "I want to see my dad!"

Gritting his teeth, Rae attempted to start forward again, but Alvis refused, putting enough strength into his hold this time that Rae glared at him over his shoulder. "That isn't your street, dumbass. Michael isn't going to be there—"

Alvis interrupted him with a giggle, like Rae was the silly one out of the two of them. "What are you talking about? Dad is *always* home!"

"Alvis . . . he's dead."

Rae wasn't sure what threw him off balance more: how suddenly the wiggling stopped, or how heavy his unthoughtful words hung in the air. He could feel Alvis holding his breath by how his chest constricted, and by how Rae could no longer smell Alvis's alcoholic breath against his face.

The arms around Rae's neck finally loosened, but the relief he should have felt was hollow and wrong, as Alvis went limp against him. "Dammit, I forgot," Alvis muttered, voice cracking. Rae felt tears against his neck, soaking into the collar of his shirt. "I hate when I forget. Does that ever happen to you? Do you ever forget your sister isn't alive anymore?"

"I don't think that's any of your business," snapped Rae, more caught off guard than defensive.

Silence.

Then Alvis sighed and mumbled, "Fuck, you're such a *dick*."

Alvis pulled himself back, forcing Rae to release him. When his feet met the street, he stumbled but stood upright. "Gettin' pissed for no reason. What's so bad about talking? Why is it so hard for you to just give me something here?"

Clingy and drunk Alvis hadn't given any sign he was still angry about their earlier conversation; it had taken Rae a moment to decipher the meaning of the slurred words. "I don't understand what you're expecting I give to you."

I've given you control of the most important part of myself.

"Something! Anything!" Alvis leaned forward and jabbed a finger into Rae's chest. "Show me you want to be in this fuckin' Pact."

"If I didn't want to be in this Pact, then I wouldn't be."

"You sure?" Alvis accused. " 'Cause you're doing a real shit job of showing it. I'm over here trying to make it happen, and you're, what? Reading all about technicalities without using them when it fuckin' matters most."

Rae knew what Alvis was doing; trying to rile Rae up, and push a reaction out of him. His intent wasn't malicious, but Alvis was still always pushing Rae. And the more he pushed, the closer to the edge of his control Rae became. It was the edge Rae was tiptoeing every second of every day since he had turned from a *Drakon* to a Guardian.

With a clenched jaw and no response, Rae pivoted on his heel. Behind him, Alvis let out a half-groan, half-growl of frustration before stomping after him, his long strides easily overtaking Rae.

The rest of the walk to the Palace was tense, as they both silently stewed in their feelings. Luckily, the guards gave them no trouble, despite Alvis forgetting his identification card. Again.

When Rae unlocked the door to their room, Alvis pushed past him with a huff, boots heavy on the marble. He threw himself down on his bed without changing his clothes, back pointedly facing Rae in the darkness.

Childish, thought Rae, sitting on the side of his bed and slipping out of his shoes. But not unwarranted. The list for becoming a successful Guardian was growing longer and harder to keep track of. Like a balancing act he wasn't stable enough to carry. The pressure to live up to everyone's expectations of him made the tension in his head scream.

I'm failing again, Rae thought. *I can't protect anyone. Not Alvis. Not Hanah—*

The shoe Rae had been holding dropped, the mass of leather and string slipping unintentionally from his fingers and landing hard onto the marble. The voice in his head was getting stronger. If Alvis noticed what was going on, who else did? He couldn't let this happen. He *needed* to be a Guardian. He needed his powers. He needed to get revenge on Zen.

Breathe. Breathe. Please, breathe.

Rae startled as a light touch feathered against his leg. He opened his eyes and glanced down.

Despite being drunk and a bigger buffoon than normal, Alvis had quietly crawled out of bed and was kneeling on the floor in front of Rae. He lifted his fingers and began gently running them through Rae's hair. Rae could feel the heat radiating from Alvis's fingers as they weaved between the strands. Time seemed to slow, and something in Rae's chest unfurled.

"Alvis?" He murmured.

"Hmm?"

"What are you doing?"

"Comforting you."

" . . . Why?"

" 'Cause you're scared."

Rae crinkled his brow, trying to focus. "I'm not scared."

"Yeah, you are. You always remind yourself to breathe when you're scared."

Rae stiffened. Alvis knowing Hanah's precious word of comfort would make Alvis see him as weak. "I thought you were mad at me." Rae snapped, defensive.

Alvis gave a long blink, like he couldn't understand what Rae was asking, then smiled. "Yeah, I am mad. But if you're scared, then I can be mad later."

Rae reached out to tap at Alvis's emotions, and was unnerved to find Alvis wasn't lying. "I said, I'm not scared," he repeated.

The pressure on Rae's head increased as Alvis ruffled his hair harder, like he was trying to create static with it. "Shut up. It's okay to be scared. Or sad. Or angry. Sometimes feeling that stuff is the only way to feel better."

Alvis's breath was still heavy with alcohol, and his clothes smelled of smoke and the tavern, but Rae couldn't remember how to push him away. Alvis's hand still stroked his hair, exploring the soft, white locks.

Rae found his hand reaching up to trace the lines of Alvis's mouth, noticing for the first time the small scar on his top lip. Rae's cheeks suddenly felt ten degrees warmer than they normally did. If he allowed himself to focus, he might have thought Alvis's fingers scraping against his scalp felt *nice.*

Rae dropped his fingers from Alvis's face and pulled back, frowning when the next swipe of Alvis's hand ran along his jawline instead. "You can stop now."

Alvis gave another slow blink. Then he made his way back to his bed, flopping gracelessly onto his mattress, eyes already closed. He mumbled something else, but it was too incoherent for Rae to understand. Within moments, his breathing evened out, and the only noise in the room was his soft snores.

The touch from Alvis's fingers lingered, but when Rae ran his own through his hair, it felt hollow. He didn't understand what was making his stomach twist in a way that was more pleasant than not. He forced himself to sleep before he could put a name to it.

CHAPTER 25

LIKE ALVIS HAD SEEN HIM DO nearly every day the last few weeks, Lamont unfastened his jacket and slid it off his slim shoulders, folding and setting it aside.

"No more student Pacts today?" Alvis asked, pointedly ignoring Rae's jaw clenching in annoyance.

Lamont said nothing. He simply adjusted his gloves, unsheathed his sword with his right hand, then held up his left. "Zaile."

Zaile appeared in front of Lamont, her forehead meeting his palm at the perfect height and angle. There was a burst of red light. When it faded, Zaile hovered in her dragon form above Lamont, agile, orange body upright and poised, before landing gently on the ground. She was smaller than the other Guardians Alvis had seen so far—about the size of Rae's dragon form—but she was playful and quick, which was reflected in her dragon's nimble form.

After Alvis Released Rae's dragon form, he couldn't stop staring at him. No matter how many times he'd puked because of it, Rae was still breathtaking.

The air around Alvis swirled, Rae's wings kicking up dust without regard to the human next to him, making Alvis cough. A roar above him pulled his attention upwards, but in the breath it took to look up, a flash of black came out of his blind spot. Alvis gasped and twisted his feet to narrowly dodge Lamont's elbow aiming for his chin. "Your opponent isn't above you," said Lamont.

The dirt beneath Lamont's heel crunched as he spun then jumped, sword swinging down. Alvis had no time to step aside, but the sword disappeared before it could connect. Lamont was now behind him, digging a boot into Alvis's unprotected side. Alvis groaned, but he had experienced worse; he barely stumbled at the contact.

Lamont raised an eyebrow, the slightest bit impressed. It quickly lapsed, then he slammed the hilt of his sword into Alvis's shoulder, wrenching a pained gasp from him. Alvis stumbled forward to the ground with a curse.

Would you stop letting him hurt you? snapped Rae. *I thought fighting was your specialty.*

Shut up, Alvis fired back. Fighting always helped Alvis let off steam, but there wasn't anything fun about getting knocked around because his Guardian wasn't doing his job. Alvis wasn't in the mood to put up with unnecessary scolding. *Just go back to not giving a shit.*

I can't concentrate if you keep getting injured—move!

The desperate command had Alvis rolling onto his back right as Lamont's sword swung down. Alvis managed to get a leg up. It would have connected with Lamont's ribs if he hadn't *vanished* right before. What the absolute *bullshit—*

Lamont reappeared behind him. He grabbed Alvis's right arm, twisting it painfully behind his back and forcing him to his knees. Alvis's socket threatened to pop. Growling, a burst of Alvis's magic ignited within him, more than enough to break himself free of Lamont's hold. Alvis clambered to his feet, and when Lamont materialized a short distance away from him once more, it was an infuriating reminder Alvis still hadn't landed a single blow on him.

Alvis tightened his stance, shaking his fists and smirking with the confidence breaking free had given him. It was cocky, and Lamont called him on it with a disbelieving shake of his head. Lamont dropped into his own defensive stance, waiting to see what ridiculous, pathetic move Alvis could possibly attempt next.

Alvis had to admit, the current fight was getting him nowhere. He'd fought against knives plenty of times, could recall like second nature what to do: maintain distance until they come to you, stay perpendicular, focus on the weapon and not the opponent. But swords could reach further, and even though Alvis liked Zaile, teleporting Lamont away the moment Alvis could get close to him was *annoying.*

I need you to make sure Zaile stops teleporting Lamont, he said mentally to Rae.

You say that as though I haven't been, Rae replied tartly.

Obviously, you haven't, if Lamont can disappear this

much. I need it to be constant. Like, teleport, teleport, teleport, teleport —

The ground beneath Alvis shook. Rae slid past, claws digging into dirt to drag himself to a stop after being knocked from the sky. Rae righted himself instantly, but instead of jumping back into battle, he looked at Alvis. Dragons were expressive, but Rae's glare was on a whole different level. He growled and leapt back into the air, the force of his wings sending Alvis backwards onto his ass.

"I have a *plan*, dumbass!" Alvis yelled after Rae's retreating form.

If you can force Zaile to drop her attribute before she's ready, I can catch Lamont by surprise. Then you can use transference on my hand, while I smash his sword.

Jumping at an enemy with a sword is foolish. Just stay away.

Like hell I'll do that!

The next time Lamont teleported, Alvis caught the briefest shimmer of him reappearing and leapt aside. He clamped Lamont's forearm in a grip so tight, the pressure made Alvis's hands burn. Alvis grinned when Lamont's eyes widened, and he used the surprise against him, yanking him off balance and twisting his arm into a hold that would force him to drop his weapon—

But then the only thing between his fingers was air, and when Lamont reappeared, it was with a perfect punch to the side of Alvis's mouth. Alvis groaned as he found himself on the ground. *Again.*

There was a hissed sigh through their Pact link. Alvis felt the brush of Rae's attribute across his cheek right as Lamont aimed another punch. But Zaile's orange body flew towards Rae, and the transference shield dropped like Rae hadn't bothered with it at all, forcing Alvis to take Lamont's fist full force.

Dammit, how much more of this was Alvis supposed to take?

Another half-assed shield on his arm. Another shallow cut on his bicep when the shield faltered immediately. Rae's quick removal of his attribute was a constant distraction. It left Alvis with bruises and cuts he could have avoided. If Rae was going to be so inconsistent, Alvis might as well fight like he believed Rae would never use his magic at all.

Forget about transference, Alvis finally snapped. *Keep your magic to yourself. I don't want it.*

There was no response.

Alvis concentrated on his locket, willing it to boost his magic. He wiped at his bleeding lips with the back of his hand. He was done with this. No one could say he didn't try his best. His hands felt raw and bloodied from tearing at the wall Rae had built around himself. But enough was enough. Alvis had sustained enough damage to know it was a lost cause a while ago. If Rae wanted his damn wall so much, then so be it. Alvis steeled his grip and aimed himself toward Lamont.

He was clearly better off anyway.

AFTER NIGHTMARE NUMBER fifteen, Alvis found out the name of the girl whose white hair always turned red.

"Hanah," Rae said, sitting opposite her in a cell made of glass. Blood was splattered across his white skin and expensive, crisp gray shirt. He held Hanah's hands in his own. Blood coated his fingers; it was still fresh, thick and dripping.

"I won today, Hanah."

Hanah pulled her hands away. Disgusted by the blood. Disgusted by Rae's touch. Next to her was a bowl of water. It pooled over the sides when she shoved her hands into it, rubbing the blood away and turning the water pink.

"What did you bring me?" replied Hanah.

"I told you." Rae gave her a small, proud smile.

Alvis didn't recognize this Rae. This Rae was openly meek and desperate, not hiding behind stoicism and calculated words. "I won again. Mr. Bremmet said he will bring you a new gemstone to try this week."

Hanah sneered. The purple veins beneath her skin were beginning to turn black, pushing their way to the surface, until they slid through her pores and dripped dark ichor down her face. Rae grabbed Hanah's hands again. Her upper lip twisted up and she yanked them away once more, immediately returning to the bowl of water and rinsing them like she wanted to peel the skin raw.

"Hanah, please . . ."

The water slid from pink, to crimson, to black, as the black liquid dripped from her chin. "You say you've won, but you didn't save me," Hanah scathed. "You will *never* be able to save me, Rae. You are weak. You cower beneath that Ranker name you've earned, the name you deserve. *Bloodied Champion.*"

Rae shook his head, grabbing at his hair, pulling and screaming, then screaming louder and louder. From the white of nothingness, a dragon took form. It wound itself around Rae, a protective barrier until it wound too tight, and Rae's screaming slid into gasps for air.

And Alvis only watched.

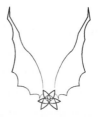

CHAPTER 26

AFTER THAT FIRST NIGHT in the tavern two weeks ago, Alvis ran into Rival a second time. And like it had the first time they drank together, the conversation carried on like old friends, not new acquaintances.

Once Alvis found out Rival was an extremely capable fighter, their friendship was solidified with a toast and spar that same night. By the time Alvis crawled into his own bed, his sides hurt from laughing and taking Rival's powerful kicks.

Alvis began to often find himself at Rival's place when he needed to let off more steam than the disaster that was he and Rae's Pact practices could offer.

Rival lived in a little one-bedroom house a few blocks outside of South Market. He wasn't much of a decorator. The walls and shelves remained empty despite Rival living there for over a year. He was also surprisingly tidy; the house barely looked lived in. It was almost like Rival planned to skip town the second he wanted to and leave no trace he'd been in Torne at all.

"It's boring to be tied down," Rival had told Alvis and Zaile one night after a few drinks. "Traveling and meeting different people is better. More opportunities for a challenge."

A challenge Rival looked for in tournaments all over the continent, since his entire village was killed five years ago. Apparently, he was a pretty sought-after Charge who had made a name for himself in towns like Tarley. Alvis had nearly jumped off the ground in excitement when he found out Rival would be at the Tarley tournament the same time as him. It was in those places Rival thrived, connecting with Guardians and fighting alongside them, until they parted ways for whatever reason.

Rival wasn't humble, but he wasn't annoyingly arrogant either. He reminded Alvis of Miller in a lot of ways, never boasting confidence without the evidence to back it up. Particularly in lack of restraint. He kicked Alvis to the grass with a heel to the ribs, slamming Alvis out of his daydreaming.

"What's with you today?" Rival asked, watching Alvis groan and rub at his side. "Why are you spacing out so much? You could've dodged that kick." Rival slid his twin knives back into their sheaths and wiped at the sweat on his forehead with the back of his hand. "And why are you acting like I maimed you? That was barely a love tap."

"Cut me some slack," Alvis grumped. "I got hit there like, fifty times during training today."

Rival snorted. "Rae still hasn't figured out transference?"

"*No*," Alvis answered, and flopped back into the grass with a moan.

Aella, Tal, and Zaile had already had the pleasure of his oncoming rant, but the words still fell out in a jumbled fit. "All he does are half-assed shields and acts like *that's* trying. And when I try to strategize with him, what's that asshole do? Ignores me. Runs away!"

Rival took a drink from a glass water bottle. He passed it to Alvis and sat down in the grass next to him. "Why don't you just end the Pact?"

Lips on the rim of the glass, Alvis blew, making the bottle whistle, his anger quickly deflating. Rival casually tossed out that question whenever Alvis had a real good rant session. Alvis didn't think Rival's way of thinking was wrong. Honestly, it was perfectly logical. But not being in the Pact with Rae . . . Simply thinking about it left a vile taste on Alvis's tongue.

"I need Rae if I want to get revenge for my dad," Alvis finally said. It was the same answer he always gave. After another sip of water, he added, "And I don't know what he's gone through, but I feel like if I went through whatever happened to him, I would want someone to not give up on me, either. Even though I really wanted to."

"So, you're just gonna wait until, what? He spills his heart out to you? What if he never does?"

"He will," Alvis said, though the words seemed more and more like a lie the longer the tension between him and Rae dragged on.

Rival shook his head, disbelieving but not surprised. "You're patient when it comes to the stupidest things."

"Yeah, yeah," Alvis mumbled back.

Alvis stretched his arm out in front of him. No matter how often he drew his Pact tattoo, pictured it in his mind, or watched the way it stretched when he twisted his arm, it always seemed new. But whenever Rae did manage to use his attribute shield on Alvis, the marks felt like they had always been part of him.

Drawing his eyes across the design that reminded him of a chain link, Alvis pondered, "Haven't you ever, I don't know, just felt like you're supposed to be where someone else is?"

"Only sexually."

Caught off guard, Alvis flushed, the water bottle nearly shattering in his hand. He jabbed it into Rival's ribs, but not nearly as hard as he could have. "*Not* what I meant!" he snapped.

Rival cackled and grabbed the bottle free from Alvis's grip. "Seriously, I've got no idea what you're talking about. I've had all different kinds of Guardians, but I'd never stay in a Pact because I felt bad for mine."

Alvis leveled Rival with a *don't bullshit me* look. "Didn't you call your third Guardian a 'pitiful aristocrat'?"

"Yeah, but I didn't stay with Jal because she was pitiful. I stayed with her because she could throw lightning bolts." Rival's mischievous smile grew smaller. The harsh lines of his face soften into a sadness Alvis had never seen Rival wear before. "Jal reminded me of my sister, Ida," Rival said. "At first I thought that would be a good thing."

Rival rolled the bottle between his hands, then softly set it down. He stared at it like it was turning into someone familiar. "Jal did become something like an older sister, but once I realized she would never be Ida, I couldn't stay with her."

The humid air settling over them was almost suffocating, but Alvis didn't mind. He wanted to know more, as much as Rival was comfortable telling him.

Gently, but without hesitation, Alvis asked, "Hey, Rival, how did your clan die?"

"A Chosen One."

"A . . . *What*?!" Alvis shot up, eyes wide, making Rival jump, confused. "Are you sure—I mean, how do you know they were a Chosen One?"

Rival must have mistaken Alvis's panic for awe. His expression darkened. "Don't tell me you're one of those people who think Chosen Ones and Wielders are special just because they're born with powers."

"Uh," Alvis blinked, slowly, hoping Rival wasn't clued in enough to know it meant he was desperately searching for a coverup. "No. I wouldn't say that?"

"Good, 'cause they aren't." Rival unsheathed one of his knives again. He unfolded an oiled cloth from his pocket and began polishing it, movements rougher than normal. "The Chosen One who killed everyone in my village wasn't special but bragged like they were," Rival continued evenly. "They were some fucker who took money in exchange for killing children. One day I'll find them and break that hairpiece in front of them. Make them regret ever letting me live."

Under Alvis's shirt, the locket suddenly flared at the threat. Alvis resisted the urge to touch and comfort it.

Slowly, he asked, "Do you hate *all* Chosen Ones now?"

Rival glanced up from his blade, eyebrow raised. "Why does it matter?"

"It's just . . ."

I forbid you from revealing who you are to anyone who does not already know, friend or foe. Alvis's mouth slammed shut as Queen Deyn's words echoed in his mind.

In the Palace, surrounded by a handful of people who knew his secret, Alvis had forgotten the whole your-powers-need-to-be-a-secret thing. There were some people he couldn't reveal the truth to. Just like he had to hide his powers from Miller, he had to hide them from Rival, too. And now that Alvis knew about Rival's family, the lie was impossibly heavier this time.

"Never mind," Alvis said, sighing.

Concern pinched Rival's brow. He returned the dagger to its sheath and tucked the oil cloth away. "Seriously, Alvy. Are you okay?"

Quickly, Alvis stood and dusted off his pants, more to seem casual than actually caring about the dirt. He stretched his arms out over his head and cracked his back, working out the muscles that had tightened after his and Rival's spar session. Alvis eyed the tattoos on his hand again, then dropped his arms back to his side.

"Like I said, it's nothing. I think training is getting to me. Wanna go get food?" Alvis was already walking backwards towards the gate.

Rival studied him, then shrugged and grinned. "Only if your rich ass is paying, Palace Boy."

CHAPTER 27

PRINCESS MEERA WAS WHINING before Luca finished opening the door. "Lucaaaaa," she said, voice muffled by the table she was draped over. "Help, I'm dying."

"You shouldn't say things like that," Luca chided, unconcerned. She adjusted the folder of that day's reports in her thick arms, the door to Meera's room closing with a heavy slam behind her. Her ebony hair was in a severe bun, as always. The golden hilt of her sword caught the light as she entered the room. "If I were Pelia, I would be running to your mother right now, crying about how I think you're sick. *Again.*"

Without lifting her head, Meera pushed off her Charge's words with a lazy wave of her hand. "Pelia is a pure, innocent handmaid. *You* are the only one who opens my door like some bear. So, of course, I know when it's you."

Luca quirked an eyebrow, amused. And, considering she now knew what mood Meera was in, she was half-tempted to open the door again, just to see what other insults Meera would come up with. Meera peeled her forehead off the table before Luca could try. "Mother made me attend the Counsel meeting today," she explained, huffing to blow her bangs out of her eyes. "And all those old assholes could complain about was how improper it is for me to sleep with people during the day. We're on the brink of Zen declaring war on us but, yes, my personal life is so much more important."

"That sounds about how most of your meetings with the counsel go," Luca replied. She gestured towards the mess of papers and books scattered over Meera's desk. "What did you do to earn all this?"

Pouting, Meera swirled her finger in the air. From it a little, red flame dragon took shape, hopping playfully on the table, excitedly squeaking. Meera held up the book she had been reading, and the dragon jumped and grabbed it from her. With quick flaps of its flaming wings, the dragon made its way across the room and dropped the book into Luca's waiting hands.

Luca glanced down at the book in her hand. *The Rules of Decorum*, the title read. It was the first book all members of Quint's royal family were read, and the first they learned to read by themselves. The rules inside were pressed into the royal reader's memory from infancy.

"It's been a few months since Queen Deyn last ordered you to review this," Luca commented.

Meera called the little dragon back, and it extinguished

in a flicker on her fingertips. "She only does it because she knows I hate it," she complained.

"She does it when you've acted childish."

"You're supposed to be on my team."

Luca chuckled softly. "What did you do this time?"

A proud grin, dimples deep, told Luca all she needed to know before Meera even began to speak. "I told them it was fine if they wanted to focus on who I'm in bed with. Then they wouldn't be as preoccupied with what else I have my hand in."

"*Meera!*"

"Oh, not you, too," Meera groaned. She relaxed back into her chair, long legs stretching out in front of her and arms crossing over her chest. "Honestly, I thought it was clever. But enough of the counsel complained to Mother. They're so obvious in their dislike for me, it's boring. You would think after eighteen years they would accept that an adopted daughter will be receiving the crown."

If they knew who Meera was, they might be more accepting, Luca thought.

It was a thought Luca could never say out loud.

But Meera knew immediately what that slight quirk of Luca's left brow meant. Reading people, their emotions, and their intentions was a dangerous strength Meera had trained over the years. Luca stood no chance against it.

Meera's pout smoothed into a straight line. Eyes locked with Luca's, Meera slid her fingers across her lips. She twisted them, then tossed the imaginary key Luca's way. Luca made no move to catch it.

"Luca," Meera whined. "You're supposed to catch it!"

Luca sighed. Without a word, she walked over to Meera's bed and sat down at the foot of it. She set the packet of papers she was holding next to her, then gestured for Meera to come to her. Meera popped off the chair with a grin and was across the room with impressive speed and settled happily into the space between Luca's legs. Like this, their height difference was more even, with Meera's head at the perfect level for Luca to calmingly stroke her hair, without having to tilt the princess's head too far back or down.

"Is this your report on Rae and Alvis?" Meera asked, excited anticipation making her practically bounce. She twisted, ignoring Luca's grunt of protest when the twist slid Meera's hair from her fingers. Meera reached around her Charge and grabbed the papers off the bed, then cuddled back into her spot like it was home. "How were they today?"

"Alvis is doing well."

"And Rae?"

Luca went silent. Her hands in Meera's hair slowed. Meera groaned and let her head fall onto Luca's knee.

"*How?*" Meera said, more to herself than Luca. "It's been almost a month. Any Guardian of Rae's caliber should be more than capable of using transference by now. All the other former *Drakon* didn't have it easy, but even they figured out within the first two weeks."

Meera's breathing shook for a moment until Luca gently tucked a shorter piece of hair behind her ear, pulling it away from Meera's face.

"The tournament in Tarley is one week away," Meera

said slowly, like she would be admitting defeat if she wasn't careful with her words. "If those two don't figure out transference before then, Mother isn't going to let them keep their Pact. Ellian, Crew, Jazz, Michael . . . All their deaths will have been for nothing."

A heavy silence settled over them. Meera pictured the face and name of every member Linless lost on their mission in Nerwen City. For a moment, she curled in on herself, unable to find her footing beneath the weight of the deaths her leadership had led to. Then Luca delicately combed her fingers through a larger batch of Meera's curls, twisting it into a fishtail braid, and Meera straightened her shoulders once more.

"Luca," Meera said. Her voice was soft but not delicate. "Between Alvis and Rae, who do you think is more important for my plan to succeed?"

"That's a cruel question," Luca replied.

"Which is why I'm asking you. You won't judge me for thinking it."

Becoming each other's safe space was something Luca and Meera had done since childhood. They had begun not long after Luca was selected to be Meera's Charge when they were only five years old. Between them was no judgement, and no holding back honesty.

"Alvis is a Chosen One," Luca stated. "With or without Rae, he still has that power, even if it is untamed. Rae is important as a symbol to all Guardians that a Pact is as strong as an artificial gemstone from Zen. But while Rae is the best *Drakon* to play that role, he isn't the only one who could."

"But what has Rae gone through?" Meera whispered. "What happened to make him so terrified of protecting someone?"

"Is that something we have time left to consider?"

"Ugh," Meera mumbled. She nuzzled her cheek against Luca's leg, wiping away the tear she couldn't quite keep back. "Being a cold-hearted leader is hard."

Luca laughed softly. "Your grandmother didn't pick you because you're cold hearted. She picked you because you're calculated, determined, and have always understood why Linless needs to do the things we do."

Luca tied the braid and let it fall softly against Meera's neck. Then she wrapped her arms around Meera's shoulders and pulled her to her chest. "She picked you because *you* are the leader Linless needs."

Meera's next breath was a shaky sigh. She let her fingers slide over the tattoo on Luca's left arm, then the scars on her right. Scars that Luca had had since before Meera knew her. Scars from the night Lamont and Luca were the only two to escape the fire that killed the rest of Counsel Bolhm's family. Scars that reminded Meera of how terrifying Luca found flames. Scars that sang to Meera of how much Luca trusted her with her life.

"And, for what it's worth," Luca continued. "I do think your joke to the counsel was clever."

Meera was already smiling when she tilted her head back, black bangs falling across her forehead and eyes glistening with tears and gratitude. "Grandmother picked you for a good reason, too," Meera said.

Luca never did well with being told she was important,

so she simply smiled in response.

Cuddling further into Luca's arms and the sturdiness of her chest, Meera whispered, "Hopefully Alvis and Rae's next test won't be the final one."

CHAPTER 28

"WOULD YOU STOP WORRYING," ALVIS TOLD RAE the next morning. "Just because it's our first time against another Linless Pact doesn't mean you gotta look like you're ready to puke."

Rae watched Alvis stretch out his legs, then his arms, warming them up. Alvis had been brimming with excited anticipation since Lamont told them they would finally partake in a spar against someone from Linless, in front of a crowd of students from the Palace's training school, no less.

When Alvis caught Rae staring at him, not speaking, he sighed. He did that often nowadays whenever the two of them trained. "It's a *practice* match, Rae. Like I've already told you, just do what you always did in matches back home."

If Rae "did what he always did," too much blood

would be spilled. The second to last time he'd fought, Rae had slammed his head into a Ranker's stomach, then enclosed his mouth around his neck. The flesh was easily torn away, and he could taste the salt of tears mingle with the heat of blood—

The screeching in Rae's head was growing louder than normal. Next to him, Alvis let out a soft gasp and flinched. But Rae missed it, unable to stop himself from digging a palm into his eye, forcing the next screech back. Then Rae's scar on his chest screamed, too, demanding to be scratched in relief, telling him to run away before someone could see him do it. But Rae couldn't leave. He couldn't back down. This was his opportunity to move forward. To put distance between who he wanted to be and the person everyone still believed he was.

They would be sparring on the training grounds and not in the arena, but that was no comfort to Rae's panic. An entire class of students their age, but much more experienced with Pacts, was observing them. Rae was under the scrutiny of all those eyes, surrounded by mindless chatter that would soon evolve into cheers.

Soon became suddenly. Shocked gasps turned into excited hollers and applause. The reason for it became immediately evident.

There, walking from the sideline towards Alvis and Rae, were their opponents—Princess Meera and her Charge, Commander Luca.

"Holy *shit*," Alvis squeaked with terror.

Rae swallowed against the sudden lump in his throat. "Should I start worrying now?" he asked to distract himself or risk passing out.

When Meera and Luca finally made it to the center of the field, Meera grinned at them. "Hello!" She curtsied, yellow dress flowing playfully around her. "Please take care of us!"

"Wait, wait, hold on—wait," Alvis sputtered, a hand frantically gesturing between themselves and Meera and Luca. "You're joking, right? We aren't actually going up against you, are we?"

"Why?" Meera replied wryly. "Are you scared?"

"Obviously!"

"Well, *you* aren't going against me." Meera laughed. When she looked at Rae, her prismatic eyes of gray, brown, and green rested somewhere between playful and imploring. "Rae is."

Fight-or-flight sent Rae's mind into overdrive. He had not felt a stare like Meera's since his last match as a *Drakon* Ranker in the arena. It was the stare of a true dragon. Someone so far above him that he had no hope of competing against them and winning. At least, not without falling back on how he used to win.

There was a scratching deep in Rae's mind; dizziness threatened to tilt the ground under him, and a black ring was trying to creep around his vision. He pinched his leg, forcing himself to stay focused and not fall into the luring spiral of anxiety.

If Rae was incapable of fighting like a Guardian during this simple practice match, and instead fought like the Bloodied Champion . . . What would that mean for his place here in Linless? For his place as Alvis's Guardian?

Alvis raised an eyebrow at Luca when he noticed she was empty handed. "You aren't using your sword?" he asked.

"I needed to give you some sort of a chance," Luca said, touching the empty space on her left hip where her sword usually rested.

The challenge made Alvis's eyes light up like a torch. The excitement grew when Luca placed her left hand on Meera's forehead, and in a flash of gray light, Meera was transformed.

Princess Meera's dragon form was tall. Her regal neck was long, and two sharpened, black nails rested on the curve of her thin, expansive wings. Spread wide, the wings nearly engulfed her when she retreated them against her back. Her thin tail flowed behind her, nearly twice her body length. Meera's dragon skin was a glistening cascade of scales, orange, gray, and beautiful.

Too distracted by Meera's dragon form, Alvis was hardly paying attention when he held up his hand, waiting for Rae to step into it. Rae stared at Alvis's palm for a few heartbeats, his dizziness growing and his panic condensing into a stabbing pressure in his chest. He placed his forehead into Alvis's palm, but the simple word of *"Release"* Rae might normally be relieved to hear felt hollow and distant.

Lamont called for the match to begin.

ALVIS HAD NEVER SEEN Commander Luca in combat, but he wasn't surprised she was talented at hand to hand fighting. She was fast and had a mean left hook. But she was playing at being predictable and didn't have as long of a reach as Alvis did. It was easy for Alvis to sidestep her third punch and land one of his own, sending Luca stumbling back.

The ground in front of him bursting into flames. The fire quickly took shape: First, a pair of wings stretching. Then, a long back and tail. Next, a snout and burning teeth. The flames condensed into the new reptilian being now protectively crouching in front of Luca. Its black hide was matte, as if it were made of thick, choking smoke. And its red, slitted eyes glowed like two hot coals.

Princess Meera's attribute—dragons made of flames.

Some distance away, dragon Meera sat, posture perfect, her claw settling back onto the ground after calling on her attribute. The way her tail casually glided across the packed dirt was too prim to be called a wag. With a steady gaze, her eyes never wavered from Rae. Alvis cursed under his breath. How could Meera's control of the flames be so tight without a mere glance at the destination?

For his part, Rae was still crouching behind him, attention never leaving Meera, but making no actual move to do anything. Alvis clenched his teeth but kept himself from saying the first words that came to mind.

Luca also annoyingly stood still, showing no intention of going on the offensive. She wiped away the blood on her lip Alvis had drawn with the back of her hand. Alvis took a step forward, but the black flame dragon reared, blocking his path. He tried to step to the side. Again, the dragon mirrored the movement and cut him off. It let out a warning growl, like a raging bonfire. Alvis growled right back. He wouldn't be able do a single thing if he couldn't get within arm's reach of Luca.

Well, sometimes the best way around, is through.

Rae, Alvis said. *I assume it does, but does your shield guard against fire?*

Silence. Followed very quickly by Rae snapping, *I know what you're thinking, but Meera and Luca could be planning something. It would be better to figure it out before jumping in.*

No shit, they're probably planning something, Alvis replied, gaze shifting everywhere to look for an entrance to Luca. *That's why we need to move before they do.*

No reply.

Fine, Alvis growled.

He tapped at his locket beneath his shirt, letting its magic warm his chest and stir his own attribute, before concentrating the enhanced magic into his fists. He knew he was about to break the rule Queen Deyn had given him, but what the hell else was he supposed to do, if Rae wasn't going to bother with him?

Resentfully, Alvis told Rae, *Guess we'll do our own things like we always do.*

But when Alvis refocused his attention on the flame dragon, it wasn't standing in front of Luca anymore. It was now circling the ground around Alvis, slowly at first. Then it picked up speed, faster and faster, until it was no longer a dragon but a circle of fire. The spinning stopped and suddenly the flames burst up, taller than Alvis could reach.

The magic in Alvis's hands dispersed, quickly shifting into a defensive stance. Eyes watering, Alvis squinted against the heat. From the other side, he caught the flames reflecting in Luca's black eyes just as she leapt into the circle. Alvis dodged, but jerked to stop, back so close to his fiery prison he could feel it lick the fabric of his shirt. He swiveled and danced away, then the hard heel of a boot met Alvis's lower back, making him grunt. Luca wrapped her arms around Alvis's waist and pushed him to the ground. She managed to land two punches before Alvis growled and flipped them both, readying his own fist.

Move!

Fire rained from the sky. Alvis rolled away and watched it scorch the dirt right where he and Luca had been. He glanced up. Above him was another of Meera's dark flame dragons, circling him. Then the dragon screeched and from its mouth another burst of flames shot down, but instead of aiming for Alvis, it landed on Luca, engulfing her in the fire.

Luca rose to her feet, unbothered. The collar of her buttoned shirt was now open. Beneath it, the Pact tattoo over her heart glowed the brightest blue.

MAKE. MEERA. STOP! Alvis yelled at Rae through their Pact link.

Stopping Meera would be easy—Rae could fight against the flame dragon with his own shield, landing on it and smothering the dragon until it was extinguished. He could pull Meera's attention to him so she couldn't use her attribute on Luca, and instead be forced to use it against Rae. He could use his claws to hold Meera against the ground, while Alvis took Luca on in hand-to-hand combat and possibly sealed their victory.

Stopping Meera *should* be easy, but Rae couldn't move his legs.

Fine, said Alvis harshly. *If you're not going to do anything, I'm jumping through the flame wall. I'm not going to sit here like a freaking damsel in distress while you have a strategy crisis.*

Don't— Rae gasped at a sudden, harsh pain on his arm. Alvis must have gotten burned. *Alvis, you can't jump through fire!*

Watch me!

"Use transference, Rae," Meera prompted, snatching Rae's attention back to her. "Protect Alvis. You cannot call yourself a Guardian if you cannot protect the person giving you your power. Use it. *Protect your Charge.*"

Rae tried. He tried to use transference. Tried to move his limbs from the dirt. Tried to stop the piercing scream in his mind—he had to fight the urge to slam his head against the ground to knock it away. His lungs were constricting into a tight ball, it felt like a spear was sliding between his ribs, impaling him to the spot.

Below him, Alvis's hands covered his ears.

Rae could feel that the smoke from the dragon's flames was making Alvis dizzy. He was doing his best against Luca's attacks, but the ash was blurring his vision and forcing him to cough.

Then it wasn't Alvis surrounded by red fire, but Hanah.

Hanah covered in red. Rae's claws covered in the red of Hanah's blood.

Red. *Red. Red, RED—*

The next thing Rae knew, he was back in his human form. Alvis was next to him on his knees, coughing and smelling of ash.

"Rae," Meera pronounced, now in front of them, her large dragon form retreating. "You've been given weeks to improve, yet you refuse to use your magic consistently on Alvis. You stop yourself before you can commit, leaving Alvis vulnerable. This was never a match I expected you to win. This was a test I hoped you would pass. Unfortunately, that isn't the case."

The words were bold and commanding, but Rae could hear something behind them. Something like heartbreak.

"Despite our plans, I cannot, in good conscience, leave a Charge in your hands, Rae. You still think of yourself as a *Drakon*, not a Guardian. And because of that, I pass my judgement."

A chant began to spill into his consciousness before Meera finished. Rae's one-word mantra of *"Breathe,"* but it rushed from a dark, shrieking, yawning opening inside his heart. The word repeated, spiraling out of him, spinning endlessly like Meera's dragon flame surrounding Alvis. He barely noticed the shock slapped on Alvis's face and his growing alarm.

Princess Meera looked at them both solemnly.

"Tomorrow, the Pact between you and Alvis ends."

CHAPTER 29

Breathe.
Breathe.
Breathe.
Breathe.
Breathe.
Breathe.
Breathe.
Breathe.
Breathe.
Breathe.
Breathe.
Breathe.
Breathe.
Breathe.
Breathe.
Breathe.

CHAPTER 30

WHEN THE SUN SET IN TORNE, it brought with it a relieving coolness at the ocean's shoreline. Torne didn't sleep. As usual, streetlights were still lit and blazing all down the main roads. The bustle from the taverns and general pedestrian merriment of the city square could be heard, but it was mere background noise to the breaking waves. The salty breeze settled on Alvis's tongue when he licked his lips, and it tasted almost sweet against the sour taste left behind from Meera's decision.

Unsurprisingly, Rae had vanished immediately afterwards. Just Rae doing what Rae did best. Disappearing right when they could work things through. And now he wasn't replying to Alvis, no matter how annoying Alvis was through their Pact link.

Alvis kicked at the soft sand, sending a burst of it into the air to quickly be swept away by the night wind. The beach was empty aside from the docks, some of which had boats and some that didn't. When he couldn't get to a training field, he came down here when he needed fresh air. Something about sitting on the sandy beach, or sitting at the end of the long dock, feet dipping into the water, helped clear his head. And damn, if he didn't need head-clearing right now.

What Meera said had been right, of course. Rae had had weeks to get past whatever was holding him back, and he hadn't been able to. Alvis had no reason to believe they ever had a chance to become that "Face of the Rebellion" Pact that Princess Meera's plans called for.

Then why did ending his Pact with Rae cause Alvis's stomach to drop?

Alvis's locket grew warm.

The full moon was partially hidden behind clouds, but there was enough light for Alvis to catch the distant but familiar head of hair sitting at the very end of the closest dock. *Shit, speak of the devil*, thought Alvis, starting to feel every ounce of built-up anger trying to free itself from inside him.

Feet dangling over the dock, Rae had his arms wrapped around himself. His white hair was glowing, and he looked somehow smaller, watching the water kiss his toes.

Alvis didn't bother talking himself down and stomped his way out of the sand and onto the dock. The boards protested beneath his loud footfalls.

Rae turned around; eyes wide. He shot up as Alvis moved like a lion zeroing in on his prey. Rae didn't look scared—he met Alvis' glare head on. He started his own hurried stride towards him, but when they met near the middle, Rae pushed past Alvis, shoulder knocking against his. With a growl, Alvis swirled on his feet, catching up easily with his long strides because Rae was a dumbass if he thought he could outrun him.

"Let me pass. I have nothing to say to you," said Rae, when Alvis moved in front of his path.

"Like hell you don't. You're just too chickenshit to say it. Meera told us that our Pact is over. And instead of—I don't know—*talking* to me, you take off running?"

"You heard Princess Meera: tomorrow this ends," Rae stated, glaring off to the side. "She's already made the decision. What's the point in talking about something that is inevitable?"

"You told me before we did this whole thing that you wanted your powers back. That you wanted to make Zen pay and become more than the Bloodied Champion. Was that just a bunch of bullshit?"

Rae's anger seemed to be simmering below the surface. Alvis wanted to make it boil over. To finally break through the bullshit, to get to the heart of the matter, without having Rae blow him off *again*.

"You know very well it isn't bullshit," seethed Rae.

"Really? Then why can't you use transference?" countered Alvis. The heat of his Talisman turned ugly; a warning he was pushing too hard, but he ignored it. "Why can't you communicate with me in matches? Why can't you let me in? You can't because you aren't trying to, at all."

"I *am* trying!" Rae's voice was beginning to tremble.

"You can't possibly understand what I've gone through. I'm not a Chosen One, like you. You inevitably have a home here—" Rae threw an arm towards the Palace of Torne on the hill above the city. "While I need to overcome everything about myself to earn my place. You do not get to act like we both have the same hurdles to jump, when yours are so much shorter than mine."

There was a shrill shriek. Both of them flinched, then Alvis's eyes flashed. He closed the distance between them and forced Rae to tilt his head back. Rae's breath was hot and quick as it fanned across Alvis' neck. And if it were any other time, Alvis might have traced the lines of Rae's face to see if his cheekbones really were that defined, or if the shadows made them look that way.

But this was dirty fists and seeing who could break the other first, so he matched the fire in Rae's eyes with his own and said, "You want to know what *I* think? I think you don't want to be a Guardian because you *like* being the Bloodied Champion."

Rae's eyes widened, then he was pushing at Alvis, and it gave Alvis the permission to push back. They pushed and pushed until they were tripping over each other's feet and ripping at each other's clothes to see who would be the first to fall.

Alvis didn't know what meaningless taunt tumbled out of his mouth next, or why he decided to wrap his fingers around the scar on Rae's right forearm, but Rae's violet eyes burned violently in response and he snarled, all unrestrained anger and broken masks.

In the moonlight, slivers of light reflected off Rae's

white skin in a blinding burst, as his attribute grew too strong, his Guardian defense ability activating. It turned his skin to stone, and wrapped around every part of him, from where Alvis gripped Rae's now smooth, cold arm, to the solid tips of his ears. Rae may have still been in his human form, but it seemed like his dragon form was the one solidifying to marble. The wood planks under their feet creaked and snapped beneath the sudden, colossal weight. Together, Alvis and Rae fell through them.

The sea water was a cold punch, knocking the breath from Alvis's lungs. He was being dragged down against every instinct in his body. He was heavy—*too* heavy. And then he felt the cold arm still locked in his grip and Rae's solid body tugging them steadily lower. Lungs already burning, Alvis wrapped his arms around Rae and tugged, struggling against the weight pulling them both down, down, down.

His lungs were screaming now, and pressure was building against his ears, but the thought of letting Rae go into the black water was far more terrifying. Adrenaline like a live wire shocking his system, Alvis demanded himself to do just freaking *do something!*

His locket began to glow, suspended beneath his floating shirt and Alvis instinctually pulled its warmth and magic to him. The surge of strength was a level of his attribute he'd never dared to try before. He kicked his feet. Each powerful kick was like a turbine cutting the water, closing the distance to the moonlit surface above. With a gasp, Alvis's head broke into the air, his lungs gulping hungrily.

Salt burned his eyes. Alvis needed to get Rae and himself to the shore. Getting his bearings, he began to slice through the water with his free arm and his legs. Finally, his feet found purchase in the shallows, and he dragged and pulled himself and Rae to the sticky, wet sand. With a final heave, Alvis collapsed on top of him, his chest heaving and his magic retreating in a sudden rush.

After a moment, Rae sputtered and coughed sea water from his lungs. He slowly opened his eyes. The thin pupils grew and shrank as they adjusted to the lack of distance between his face and Alvis's. They stared at each other, their quick breaths mingling and chests meeting with each rise and fall. The sand was cold under Alvis's palms, braced beside Rae's head, but he barely noticed, too lost in the way Rae's eyes were glowing like they did during their Pact ceremony: violet and red and crystal white all at once. Unlike any color combination Alvis had ever seen.

Whoa, Alvis thought, too lost to keep it to himself.

For a split second, he was positive Rae echoed it.

But with a harsh shove, the moment was broken. Rae pushed Alvis off him and stumbled to his feet, shedding sea water. He walked jerkily away before Alvis could even regain his footing.

"See?" Alvis shouted after him. "You're running away again!"

Rae froze, spine perfectly straight in an eerie, mechanical way. Alvis barely heard Rae speak over the waves breaking under him.

"Five hundred," Rae repeated, a little louder.

275

"Five hundred? Five hundred what?"

Rae spun, the stoicism gone. Suddenly he was in front of Alvis again. Alvis must have ripped Rae's shirt at some point because the wind pushed the tatters apart, allowing Alvis to see the deep, circular scar on Rae's chest for the first time. It stood red and stark in the moonlight against the rest of Rae's unmarked, white skin.

Alvis gasped when Rae slammed his hand against the Pact tattoo on Alvis's chest. "I won five hundred matches as a Ranker. Consecutive. I was number one. I was the highest earner. I was the most sought after. I was who every other Ranker trained to defeat. I was the one they looked up to. Now, I don't even pose a threat because you control my power. Do you know how painful it is to have the single most important part of yourself stolen away, and when you get it back, it isn't *yours* anymore? Yet, everyone expects you to use it in the same way you always have, and when you fail, they look at you like you're the only one responsible for it!"

Rae fell to his knees, hands covering his ears and tugging at his own hair. Alvis watched as he tried to dig his fingers into the scar on his forearm, clinging to it like a lifeline. "Protect, protect, protect. Never mind the last time I tried to protect someone important, I sacrificed everything about myself, and I still lost her. Fight like the Bloodied Champion but don't *be* the Bloodied Champion. The Bloodied Champion isn't a Guardian, but if I'm not the Bloodied Champion and I'm not a Guardian, then who the hell am I supposed to be?"

The words tumbled out of Rae in a rush like the shrill

roar of a wounded animal. Like its desperate cry cutting across the sky, searching for someone who would care enough to listen for it.

Finally, Alvis heard it.

The Bloodied Champion. What about that name did Alvis even know? What did he *need* to know? Here Rae was, trying to move forward from it, and Alvis had grabbed him by the arm and jerked him backwards without understanding anything. *Do what you always do in matches.* That hadn't been fair, demanding he be more than a Ranker, while telling him to fall back into the role everyone hated him for.

Alvis crouched and watched drops of water slide from Rae's hair and down his neck, leaving goosebumps in their wake. Gently, he pried Rae's hands away from his ears. "Breathe, Rae."

Rae's wrists were far smaller than his. Alvis could feel his pulse, too quick and refusing to slow down. "*Breathe*," murmured Alvis again, soft but insistent. "Rae, it's okay. I need you to breathe."

Alvis wasn't sure how many minutes passed, or how many times he said the word, but it didn't matter. He waited and repeated it until Rae's shoulders relaxed, and his inhales deepened, and his sobs slowed.

Alvis's heart ached for him. "I'm sorry," he whispered. "I'm sorry for calling you by that name. I won't ever do it again. I Promise."

Rae's breathing began to even out.

"There you go, you've got it," Alvis encouraged, rubbing his thumb over Rae's palms, soothing. "I'm sorry for pushing you too far. Whatever you're dealing with from being a Ranker—from losing your sister—I'm not going to force you to face it if you're not ready. But it doesn't need to be only your pain anymore."

Rae finally lifted his head. Tears still ran down his cheeks to his chin, but he looked at Alvis like he was an anchor.

"You need to trust me when I say I want to help you," Alvis continued. "But I can't if you don't let me. If you don't trust me back."

Frantically, Rae shook his head. He choked out, "You can't possibly have forgotten how it's not the Charge's job to take care of the Guard—"

"Stop," Alvis interrupted gently. "Guardian, Charge—fuck all that. I don't care what the rules are. If you're going to protect me, it's only fair I protect you, too. That's all there is to it."

A blush turned Rae's blotchy face redder. "You're being stupid—"

But Alvis refused to let him run away.

Not this time.

He grabbed the collar of Rae's shirt, holding him in place. " 'Alvis Witt, I will be your Guardian.' That's what you said to me when we made this Pact, right? As your stupid Charge, I'm telling you this—" Alvis's hand slid around to the back of Rae's neck, until damp hair chilled his knuckles, and he heard Rae's sharp inhale when he pressed their foreheads together. "From now on, you aren't fighting as the Bloodied Champion. You're fighting as my Guardian. And if you start to forget that, I'll make sure you remember."

Moments passed silently. Alvis wasn't sure how long he and Rae knelt, leaning against each other, simply being in each other's space. Finally, Rae relaxed under Alvis's touch and pressed his forehead the slightest bit harder into Alvis's. "How do you plan to make me remember?" Rae whispered. Skeptical. Hopeful.

"I don't know," Alvis replied, wiping away a stray tear from Rae's cheek with his thumb. "I'll stab myself, or something."

A comfortable silence stretched between them again. It was punctuated by the bustles of the city at their backs and the tide breaking against the shore. By Alvis's own heart pounding in his ears like a drum finding its rhythm for the first time.

Rae softly pushed him away—and laughed.

Alvis had never heard Rae laugh before. He had glimpsed it, watched it disappear behind Rae's hand as he stifled it like it was something he needed to be ashamed of.

There was nothing shameful about Rae's laugh. It tumbled out untamed and unbidden, so happy to finally be let free, it couldn't contain itself. It wound around all the noises of the night and whispered, "I'm what ears deserve to hear most." It was the chime of bells in the Spring air, and what the glittering of stars must sound like under a warm desert sky, but still none of it came close to conveying what Rae's laugh did to his heart.

The moon illuminated Rae's smile. When he smiled that wide, there was a dimple at one corner of his mouth. He looked younger, the lines on his face smoothed out.

The specks of white in his eyes danced. Alvis had forgotten about the freckles on Rae's nose, but he couldn't stop looking at them now.

"You're ridiculous," Rae finally said with a disbelieving shake of his head. He wiped at the tears. Alvis still hadn't stopped staring at Rae's freckles, so when Rae lifted his head and turned his smile directly to him, their eyes met easily. "You never change, do you?"

"Apparently not," breathed Alvis.

A gust of wind tousled Rae's hair and he laughed again. With sudden conviction, he held out his hand. "Please give me your arm."

The request yanked Alvis out of his trance. He let Rae take him by the wrist, hoping Rae wouldn't notice the quick, uneven staccato of his pulse. "What are you doing?"

"I'm giving you something." Rae's touch was barely a whisper. He drew his finger across the plain of Alvis's hand from his knuckles up the wrist and forearm. The skin in the wake of his touch shone brightly, just like Rae's scales did when his attribute was activated.

"I know it's not much," Rae said, "but I want to show you I'm trying." Rae was tracing the lines of the Pact tattoo, but Alvis couldn't look down. He remained transfixed on Rae's face. It was impossible Rae didn't pick up on the open admiration, the childlike wonder Alvis stared at him with, because Alvis was too overwhelmed to hide it away.

Rae looked up at Alvis from beneath his lashes. "This is as much of a promise as I can give right now."

"I think it works just fine," Alvis managed to reply, voice almost cracking.

Hesitant but genuine, Rae flashed a small smile. It was easy for Alvis to return it with one of his own.

PART THREE

THE TOURNAMENT

CHAPTER 31

CIAN

CIAN WAS WHAT A *DRAKON* SHOULD BE.

Born in Nerwen City, his parents were renowned, high-earning Rankers before they were retired from arena tournaments. Cian had excelled in all combat training, was a dedicated student and at the top of every class he attended, and his Attribute Reveal Test showed extraordinary potential for his ice magic. By the day of his gemstone ceremony, Cian's loyalty to his home country of Zen was steadfast. It had been carved into his bones and written into his blood. He had understood the responsibility of representing Nerwen City as a *Drakon* Ranker, and he'd known the worst offense he could commit was to bring shame to his owner.

Every owner in the city had kept their eye on Cian throughout his first thirteen years of life, but it had been his parent's owner, Mr. Bremmet, who'd won out against every other, very generous bid. "I've got great plans for you, Cian," Mr. Bremmet had said proudly, after Cian's first victory in a Ranker battle. "You may become the greatest Ranker I've ever seen."

And Cian almost was. Until, one year later, when Rae had appeared.

Rae.

With his torn clothes, anxious twitching, and worried, violet eyes. *Rae,* who had grown up in the slums with no distinguished training. *Rae,* and his so-called "unrivaled" magical potential.

Rae had manifested like a ghost you didn't know was haunting you. One who hid in your own shadow, until he overtook you, throwing you into his shadow instead.

But Rae had been far from terrifying the first time Cian met him. Whimpering, Rae had hidden behind Mr. Bremmet, his dirty fingers shaking as they clutched onto the Ranker owner's pristine pant leg, wrinkling it. Cian's stomach had dropped when he realized Mr. Bremmet wasn't kicking the boy away like he normally would have.

"Cian, this is Rae. He will be living here from now on." Mr. Bremmet had beamed. He'd taken Rae's small hand and gently pulled him forward, and Cian had his first good look at him: tiny and frail, gray hair a sullied mess of soot and grime, dirt smeared across his cheeks, right forearm bandaged.

"His gemstone ceremony is tomorrow," Mr. Bremmet had continued. "Cian, I want you to look out for him."

Shocked, Cian had barely kept his mouth from dropping open. He'd covered it with a frown. "Look out for him, sir?"

"Right now, you are my most talented Ranker, Cian. I trust you to give him guidance in addition to what he will be learning elsewhere." Mr. Bremmet squeezed Rae's shoulder reassuringly, ignoring the way the young boy had flinched. "I have a feeling Rae here will become the best Ranker this world will ever see."

Anger had simmered hot through Cian's body, intense enough to melt the ice beneath his skin and push tears into the corners of his eyes. *Right now?* he'd thought. *Best the world will ever see?* Hadn't it been only a year since Mr. Bremmet said those words to him? Why was Mr. Bremmet looking down at Rae the same way he had normally looked at Cian? Who was this *Rae*—

"Do you understand, Cian?" Mr. Bremmet's eyes had become hard. The left sleeve of his dress shirt had been rolled up his pronounced forearm, revealing the golden bracelet underneath. The blue jewel within it had caught the light, twinkling like an evil eye. When Mr. Bremmet had touched it, the tap was feather light, but the threat was loud and clear.

Cian had quickly reminded himself of every lesson in obedience he had gone through. "Of course, sir."

"Then compose yourself," Mr. Bremmet had instructed coldly. "What have I told you about allowing your emotions to control you?"

"I apologize, sir," Cian had replied, quickly bowing and using the motion to conceal his face to blink back a few tears. "I promise to take good care of him."

"Good," Mr. Bremmet had said, dropping his hand from his wrist. "The Headmistress will be expecting Rae.

See him to her office."

"Yes, sir."

Cian didn't speak again until he and Rae had been two hallways over from Mr. Bremmet's office. Rae had trailed behind him, focus never leaving the ground, until Cian had knelt in front of him, making him jump and stop. His lips had trembled as he stared at Cian, who was now at his eyelevel.

Up close, Rae's skin had been even filthier than it first appeared; black oil stuck to Rae's cheek, his nails were broken, and his lips were dry and cracked. The scent of ammonia and rotten fish had started to hang in the air. Even if they were only three years apart, Cian could tell the younger boy had been short for his age. "What is so wonderful about you?" he'd asked, balancing his elbow on his knee, resting his chin in his palm. "What makes Mr. Bremmet so excited about you?"

"Um . . . I'm a twin," Rae had said quietly, suppressing a shake at the snide anger in Cian's tone. "Mr. Bremmet said that's something good?"

Twin Guardians. They were almost as rare as Ellowyn Clark's direct bloodline descendants. Those *Chosen Ones*. They were always born with one twin inheriting the magical power, leaving barely—if any— magic for the other twin, and never enough for an attribute to call their own.

"My twin sister, Hanah, is here, too. But she's in . . ." Rae's eyes had shifted, and he'd wrung his hands together, trying to recall his words. "Trailor? We were born in Bellow, and Mr. Bremmet found us in the orphanage—"

"I didn't ask for your life's story," Cian had snapped coldly.

"O-oh," Rae had replied meekly, dropping his eyes and looking like he was ready to cry.

An unexpected guilt had struck Cian's heart. But he'd resisted the urge to apologize—Rae would have to find a backbone sooner or later. "What attribute do you have?" Cian had asked instead, anger slightly receding into annoyed curiosity.

"Huh?"

"What magic did the Attribute Reveal Test say you would have after receiving a gemstone?"

"I—I didn't take a test..." Rae's eyes had lit up slightly. "Oh, but I get *really* heavy when someone tries to move me, and I don't want to be moved."

Cian's stomach had twisted for the second time that night. "Magic? *Without* a gemstone?"

"I guess, yeah."

" 'Yes'."

Rae had crinkled his brow.

"We answer with 'yes' in Nerwen City. Unless you want to embarrass Mr. Bremmet, you should learn to speak properly." The words had come out snappier than he'd intended but hearing about Rae's power . . . Cian had quickly shaken his head, ridding himself of what it meant and what it would mean for him. He'd glanced down at Rae's right forearm, covered in a fresh bandage. Casually he'd reached for it, and Rae had shivered at the touch, the chill of Cian's attribute no doubt penetrating through the bandage. "What happened here?" Cian had asked.

"Um, when the people found me and Hanah, one of them got mad and tried to cut her. So, I . . . moved and they got me instead." Rae's voice had dipped lower as he continued. "I didn't want them to hurt her."

The words had settled like a warning to anyone daring enough to try again. A sudden, dark determination had hardened Rae's eyes for the first time. Cian had known Rae's stare wasn't intended for him, but a shiver still ran down his spine. It had taken all of Cian's focus to keep his next breath from shaking in response. Instead, he'd pulled his lips back in a mirthless smile. "Oh, my. What a little hero you are," he'd remarked.

With his thumbnail, Cian had pressed lightly into the bandage until a patch of red stained through and Rae whimpered. "Well, you're lucky your gemstone ceremony is tomorrow. Becoming a *Drakon* will heal this right up. Now . . ." Cian had reached forward and grabbed Rae's other hand, delicately folding it into his. "If you plan to stay here, it is critically important to follow every order, understood?"

Rae's expression had turned more dutiful and hopeful at his words. Rae's hand had tightened in his, searching for comfort in Cian's icy fingers. "Okay. I—I mean, yes."

Cian had smiled back, like an indulgent older brother. He would play the part Mr. Bremmet had assigned to him. He would perfect it, memorize his lines, learn his marks. Cian was Mr. Bremmet's favorite Ranker, after all. Some filthy boy from the slums could not replace him so easily.

Cian would not lose.

ONCE CIAN HAD DROPPED OFF RAE with Headmistress Applesten, he'd assumed he would have the rest of the evening to himself. He had read information on the next day's matches, showered to wash away the sweat left behind from his afternoon training, then painted his nails to fix any chips. The sun had fallen by the time he relaxed into his pillow.

Then had come a knock on his door. A soft, hesitant tap Cian was immediately annoyed by.

He'd considered ignoring it, figuring Rae would leave eventually. With Cian's luck though, Rae would curl up outside his door like a lost puppy. Then Cian's servant would find Rae there in the morning and scurry off to report it.

Another slow knock, just as soft as the first had been.

Cian had groaned, then sighed. "Come in, Rae."

The door had opened slowly. Rae was acting like he didn't belong despite asking to be let in. He'd closed the door with a soft click.

Dressed in silk purple pajamas, Rae had looked much better now that all that grime on his skin and in his hair had been scrubbed away. Headmistress Applesten had tenderly taken care of all of Mr. Bremmet's Rankers. To turn Rae's hair from dark gray to near white—Cian hadn't doubted it took her hours. In that short time, Rae had gone from street rat to looking like he belonged in the same room as Cian.

Cian had pushed himself up to sit and ran a hand through his long blonde hair, pushing it out of his face. "Well? What is it you want?"

"Um," Rae had paused. Apparently, it was the only word he had no trouble saying. "I—I'm not used to sleeping alone."

"And? What does that have to do with me?"

"Um. I—I was wondering . . . If I could sleep with you tonight?"

Cian had barked out a laugh, making Rae's shoulders droop. "Are you serious? Why in the world would I let you sleep in here with me?"

"Because . . . Mr. Bremmet said you would help me?"

Cian had frowned, earlier amusement nowhere to be found. "Why is everything you say a question?"

"Um . . ."

"Mr. Bremmet made no mention of sleepovers in his orders."

Rae had shifted from foot to foot, wringing his hands, first together, then into the hem of his pajamas. Despite the distance between them, Cian had been able to tell Rae's bottom lip was shaking as he chewed on it. Cian's odd guilt from earlier had returned.

With a sigh, Cian had moved to one side of the king-sized bed and held up the covers. "*Fine.* Come here. Stay on that side and don't dare to touch me."

With impressive speed, Rae had been across the room before Cian had finished his terms. Rae had cuddled under the blankets, nuzzling his face into the fluffy spare pillow, his clean, snowy curls billowing around him, until all Cian had been able to see was half a smile and one large, purple eye.

The room had become silent. Cian had figured Rae had fallen asleep, but then Rae quietly asked, "Can I ask you a question about Mr. Bremmet's bracelet?"

"What of it?"

"Why were you scared of it?"

Rae was surprisingly perceptive, Cian had thought. Yet, hopelessly clueless. With a huff, he'd replied, "You don't even know what an owner's bracelet is for?"

Rae had given a small shake of his head.

"Every *Drakon* family is connected to a specific bracelet. It ensures we *Drakon* never lose control."

Rae had paused for a moment. "Doesn't that sound more like *Drakon* are being controlled—?"

Quickly, Cian had pressed his hand over Rae's mouth before he could finish the sentence. "In private or not, I wouldn't say things like that if I were you," Cian had hissed in his ear. "Especially if you want to become a Bremmet. Understood?"

Rae had given three quick, terrified nods.

"Good," Cian had grunted. He'd pulled his hand back, wiping it on Rae's shirt to rid himself of any saliva from Rae's mouth. "Now go to sleep. You're annoying me."

"Can I ask one more question, Cian?"

"*What?*"

"Do we . . . do Rankers really have to kill people?"

"Obviously. It is the easiest way to win both in the present and the future: if you kill opponents now, it will be unnecessary to worry about competing against them later."

But the question had peaked Cian's curiosity. He'd rolled onto his side, facing Rae again. "Honestly, why are you becoming a Ranker if you can barely tolerate the thought of killing, when it's the thing you need to do to win?"

Rae had chewed on his bottom lip. "He—Mr. Bremmet—he said he'd make Hanah all better."

"Is she sick?"

"Uh-huh—I mean, yes. They don't know what she has so they have to study her for a bit. Mr. Bremmet said if I win him a lot of money, he'll use it to find a way to make Hanah better and maybe find her a gemstone."

Cian's eyes had narrowed. Some of the best doctors and scientists in the world worked at Trailor. What kind of rare illness could this girl possibly have that they needed to study it before she could be healed? In addition, Mr. Bremmet had never been known for compassion or being moved by sob stories. Why would he have brought a dying girl along in the first place?

Cian had remembered the amethyst fire in Rae's eyes from earlier when he'd spoken of defending Hanah. It had been the only time conviction overcame fear in them. Rae hadn't seemed like a boy motivated by money—his dear, sickly sister was the key to his cooperation. No doubt, it was what Mr. Bremmet was using to his full advantage.

Rae had laid unblinking, studying every part of Cian's face, making Cian uneasy. "Stop staring at me," Cian had said, curtly. "You're coming across as weird."

"Oh—sorry. It's just . . . You don't look like someone who kills people."

"What happens in the arena is survival. I do what I

need to. What I was *raised* to do."

Rae had blinked. "But don't you feel guilty?"

"No."

"How?"

Cian had sighed, "Listen, Rae. If you want to succeed here, you cannot hold onto things like guilt. It's understandable you wouldn't understand this since you haven't gone through *Drakon* training. But those feelings you have about guilt? You need to either rid yourself of them or push them as far back into your mind as you would your darkest secrets."

Cian had wrapped his fingers around Rae's bandaged wrist again. He'd slid thin blades of ice into the wound, inciting another whimper from Rae's lips. *What a lamb.* "You will do horrible things. You will rip throats apart. You will break wings. You will do whatever it takes to succeed, or risk sacrificing what you fight for."

Cian had dropped Rae's wrist. It had fallen heavy onto the mattress between them. *"Peera Drakon Ah,"* Cian had whispered into the space between them. "Understood?"

Rae had swallowed, no doubt suppressing a sob. *"Peera Drakon Ah,"* Rae had whispered back.

CHAPTER 32

ALVIS AND RAE SAT TOGETHER inside the Linless conference room for the first time. Before them was a long table that featured a built-in screen, capable of three-dimensional video that Linless used for mission briefings and plans. Rae knew it must have cost a small fortune and spoke to how well funded the Linless rebels were.

Sitting opposite of them at the table were Lamont and Zaile. Charge and Guardian sat with perfect posture, stares unrelenting as they took in the lack of distance between Alvis and Rae. Rae resisted the urge to pull away and allowed Alvis's gentle hold on his wrist to keep him steady.

From the head of the table, Princess Meera stood, watching Rae and Alvis, her expression inscrutable. "Are you certain?" she asked.

Alvis nodded. "Yes."

"You're willing to go against my direct orders and continue your Pact with Rae?"

Meera wasn't pleased with Rae; he had fought like a *Drakon* Ranker, insulting the very nature of what being a Guardian meant. Her faith had been betrayed. Every vouch she made for him had been pointless and an embarrassment.

But Alvis was . . . Well, he was *Alvis*. He stood confident in the face of Meera's displeasure, while Rae shifted uneasily.

"Yes. And Rae has something to say, too." Alvis elbowed Rae in the side, signaling him like they had practiced.

No more hesitation, Rae told himself, as he stood and gave Princess Meera a short bow. He looked into her impassive eyes and began. "I am sincerely sorry for my actions. I understand my behavior has not been that of a Guardian. I know I have betrayed your trust, Princess Meera. But I'm determined to make it right. If possible, I would like another chance to prove I can be the Guardian that Linless needs."

Hesitantly, Rae broke his gaze with Meera and looked down at Alvis. Even sitting, Alvis came up to his shoulder. "I want to become the Guardian I believe I can be."

A strained silence stretched after Rae finished his formal apology, long enough for Rae to fear his words wouldn't be enough. Meera had taken his apology without a single shift in her expression; her lips remained pursed and eyes betrayed nothing of her thoughts or feelings.

When Rae's eyes shifted to Lamont and Zaile, he breathed a small sigh of relief to see Zaile was smiling at him, pleased.

"The Tarley tournament is next week," Meera finally said. "Tarley can be as dirty as any *Drakon* Ranker battle. You will, no doubt, be reminded of what you used to be. This will be your last chance, Rae. If you truly have what it takes to be a Guardian, then prove it there."

RAE WAS SURPRISED by how quickly things shifted between himself and Alvis. The accuracy of his transference improved once Alvis made a conscious effort to keep his emotions reigned in, and when Rae was honest about when he needed time to calm down.

Alvis was more patient now. Not always, but more aware of why he needed to be, like he had taken on Rae's fears and cries, memorizing each one to keep them close to himself. Unlike before, Alvis's unrestrained compassion was a distracting warmth. A flutter in Rae's stomach, reminding him to breathe without the word echoing in his mind. A force promising it was okay to share when he was struggling and wasn't sure how to steady himself.

Alvis was simple, straightforward—not stupid, despite Rae sometimes mumbling otherwise. He was able to reach out and bend for others without getting bent out of shape himself. His honest, transparent nature made Alvis the most uncomplicated person Rae had ever met.

Why then, Rae thought to himself, *was Alvis so confusing?* Why did he make Rae's head so frustratingly muddled?

"You're an idiot," Zaile stated, after Rae had shared a little of his confusion with her during their Guardian spar on a training field.

Rae crinkled his brow. "Excuse me?"

"You. Are. An. Idiot." Zaile reappeared, already throwing a punch. Rae blocked it like he had every time so far. "How are you overcomplicating *Alvis* of all people?" she said, once she'd teleported a few feet away again. "I always assumed *you* were the smart one!"

"I'm *not* overcomplicating him," Rae replied, trying to gauge where Zaile may appear next. In a blink, she teleported above him—her heel slashed down, but Rae rolled away before she could hit his shoulder.

"Alvis told you exactly what he wants from you," Zaile said. She took a second to catch her breath. Hands on her hips, she looked at Rae like she truly did think he was hopeless. "Why can't you just believe him?"

Rae brushed his sweaty bangs out of his eyes, taking in her words. He *was* doing his best to believe Alvis and rely on him—as much as his own self-doubts allowed him to, at least. "I'm not talking about opening up to him," Rae clarified. How could he clearly explain how he felt when he could barely put it into words? "Alvis is working on keeping his emotions under control, so they don't affect me. But containing them doesn't mean he isn't still feeling them. I know he's struggling with what happened in Bellow—with what happened to his father. Since he offered to help me, I feel it's only fair, as his Guardian, to help him, as well. I'm just . . . uncertain of what I can do for him."

Realization dawned on Zaile, russet eyes lighting up. "Oh—so you want to know how he's *doing*! Well, that's easy," she said, and shrugged a shoulder. "Just ask him."

" . . . Ask him?"

There was a beat of silence.

"Oh my *god*, Rae!" Zaile cackled, half in disbelief, half in genuine amusement. "Come here, right now! I'm going to smack you over the head, and you aren't allowed to use your shield to block it!"

"I would prefer not to . . ." Rae mumbled, still unsure of why what he said was so hilarious to her.

"Repeat after me," Zaile said, once she had calmed down. " 'Hi, Alvis. How are you doing?' "

Rae frowned. "I didn't ask to be mocked."

"I'm not mocking you! It really is that simple. Once you get past that, the conversation will be easy." Zaile giggled again, more endeared this time. "Good for you for seeking advice, by the way. Whatever happened the other night between you two must have been really im-*Pact*ful."

Rae didn't deign to acknowledge her pun—and he didn't need Zaile reminding him of what happened that night on the beach. Memories still flashed: Alvis above him, hair wet and moon shining behind him. Alvis in front of him, pushing away Rae's doubts with a single press of their foreheads. Alvis's pulse beating wild under his touch.

Wind brushed against Rae's nose as Zaile appeared

in front of him. She poked at his heated cheeks with her pointer fingers. "Well, aren't you the cutest little tomato!"

Rae's next kick contained every ounce of his magic he could use without the hardened skin dragging his leg down. But it was still too slow, as Zaile teleported away, cackling.

"THE HELL ARE you doing?"

With one foot in their room and one outside, holding the wooden door open, Rae swayed awkwardly between his two choices: talk to Alvis or run away. "Nothing," he replied, trying to sound casual. This vacillating was getting ridiculous. How hard was it to just choose one action?

"Are you a vampire?" Alvis asked, the bright, red paint on his fingers too fitting for the conversation. He stood next to the open, balcony door and the afternoon light was dancing around his outline. "Are you waiting for me to invite you in or something? This is our room."

Rae forced his other foot into their room. The door closed heavy behind him, knocking him forward another inch when it hit his back. Not one of his best entrances. He straightened. "Are you sure it's 'our' room?" Rae gestured towards the canvases and portraits everywhere—including Rae's *bed*—and crinkled his nose at the cloying scent of house paint. Alvis must have painted *even more* today. "And isn't it bad to be smelling paint all day?"

"Yeah, yeah, stop fussing." Alvis leveled him with a look. "Where have *you* been?"

"Training. With Zaile."

The swipe of red Alvis was throwing against the canvas landed where Alvis didn't want it to. He cursed around a groan, then raised his eyebrows at Rae. "You were with Zaile?" he asked. "And she didn't teleport you into the ocean?"

"I guess she likes me enough now to not do that." Rae toed out of his shoes, continuing to focus on charging forward instead of running away. His heart was pounding far too hard. "I wanted Zaile to teach me how to be a better Guardian, but all she did was call me an idiot."

Alvis burst into a laugh. "Sounds like she was messing with you, dude."

"I know that."

Rae sighed, subtly rubbing his sweating palms against his pants. For the past few days, Alvis had done nothing but talk, promise, and ease Rae's worries. Rae was hard-pressed to remember if Alvis talked about his feelings at all since that night on the beach.

I can do this, Rae thought. *The hardest part is starting.* "I want to know how you're doing," Rae said, a little more loudly than he intended.

Alvis's head spun to him. "You . . . *what?*"

Managing to keep his face neutral, Rae tried again. "I—I want to know how you're . . . doing?"

Mouth falling open and closing repeatedly, Alvis searched for words. His expression would have been funny if Rae didn't feel like he'd just jumped over a cliff and was hurtling towards the ground.

Finally, Alvis said, "That would probably be more convincing if you didn't have that scrunched up, constipated look on your face."

Rae's stoicism slipped. "I'm serious."

Alvis watched him silently, then held up his hand. "C'mere."

"Why?"

Alvis sat down on the floor, then pointed to the empty space next to him. "Because if you wanna know my feelings, then come paint with me."

It was an invitation Rae had received many times. But it still ignited weird flutters in his stomach and sent his flight instinct running wild.

Alvis was patient, though. His hand was steady like he knew Rae would take it if he did nothing to startle him. Like he knew Rae would give in if he bent enough to accommodate him.

The distance between them was easy to close, once Rae remembered he didn't want to be the only one accommodated to anymore. A small warmth of appreciation bloomed in Rae's chest when Alvis reached for Rae's right arm, but at the last second grabbed his left instead—the one without his scar. Alvis was gentle when he tugged, until Rae sat down next to him. He kept a mindful but intimate distance between them.

"You can practice transference if you want," Alvis said, flippant, like Rae using it on him while he painted wouldn't bother him. Alvis softly turned Rae's left arm, examining its surface. "Do you care what I paint on you?"

Rae wasn't sure he wanted Alvis to paint *anything* on him. He shook his head and did his best to ignore the way his stomach danced when Alvis grinned.

As the touch of Alvis's fingers on the canvas in front of them turned into a slow line of dark blue, Rae took in the large paintings around them. There wasn't much of a difference between throwing paint and throwing punches. Rae had seen Alvis throw his arm with the same conviction, sending greens and yellows across the canvas, his lips pursed, and eyes wide like a child told to go wild. Alvis looked the same painting as he did when fighting.

However, here in their room, surrounded by beautiful paintings, it wasn't blood that dusted Alvis's face. It was a smear of yellow across his cheek and a smudge of black on the tip of his nose, like he had scratched it and the paint was such an extension of himself that he didn't notice.

Rae knew Alvis had a scar above his lip, but he'd never noticed the other ones; there was one above his left eyebrow, and a thin one beneath his strong jaw, leading partway down his neck. Rae's eyes continued to follow the lines that made up Alvis. He wasn't broad or a heavy weight, but was well-defined, from his jaw, to his arms, to his long legs, and the hard muscles of his stomach. Even his boyish charm and smile was defining, wide and bright like a beacon calling weary sailors home.

As though he could feel Rae's stare, Alvis raised his eyes. The green sparkled in the late afternoon sun, slipping in through the windows. Rae had always thought he noticed specks of gold in them, and when they were this clear and open and *close*, he could make the flecks out clearly. Something about them made Rae's heart pound too hard.

Rae slammed his skin-hardening attribute heavily onto Alvis's shoulder, making the taller boy jump. "Woah— hey! Give me a warning if you're going to do that!"

Without an apology, Rae released his attribute, then put it in the same spot, more gently than before. They went on like that for a while, both working silently. Each time Rae grew too conscious of Alvis's touch, he focused his magic onto a different part of Alvis's body. He was growing more accurate, and Alvis was accepting each piece of Rae's magic like he had always been familiar with it.

"When did you start painting?" Rae finally asked, managing to keep his voice steady.

"When I was seven," Alvis replied. "I always wanted to be a mechanic like Dad, but I couldn't once I got my powers. One day I came home, and Dad had a large, white tarp hanging across the entire wall of the workshop. He'd spent a month's wages on it, then he shoved a paint can at me and said, 'Now you won't have to use a brush!' "

The deeper tone Alvis took on in his impression was the same Rae remembered Michael having. It drew a small smile out of Rae.

"I tried to paint a starry sky, but I didn't realize yellow, blue, and red made brown, so it looked like shit." Alvis's eyes lit up when Rae's smile turned into a short chuckle beneath his breath. "It was nice, though. Like I was finally free from my powers for the first time since I got them."

Rae furrowed his brow. "I thought you liked having your magic?"

"Now I do," said Alvis. "But a Wielder's powers only appear when the previous Wielder dies." Sudden anguish sent a scream through Rae's entire body. Alvis tried to push the pain away but wasn't able to hide his growing tears.

Your pain is my pain.

"You can keep talking—or not," Rae said in a rush.

Alvis waited another moment, ensuring Rae was okay. Rae glared back—this was supposed to be about Rae assessing Alvis's feelings.

"I was sparring with a neighbor kid when my attribute appeared," Alvis continued. "I grabbed his leg and snapped it. I had no idea what was going on. Or that Mom was dead until I got home. She'd been sick for a long time. I mean, I was a kid, so I didn't understand how sick—but suddenly losing her made accepting my powers hard. I *hated* them. They were why Mom died. They were why I couldn't become a mechanic like Dad. Other kids didn't want to play with me anymore. It sucked."

Rae's gaze drifted down to Alvis's locket, hanging free from his shirt for once. "What changed?" asked Rae.

"I don't know," Alvis said, wiping at stray tears with the back of his hand and smudging some more paint on his face. "Dad helped a lot, even if he thought the best thing was to hide my powers. Maybe I liked them more after I saved someone for the first time? Maybe I was just growing up." He smiled, sad and soft. "Somewhere, along the way, they became a reminder Mom was still here with me. There's no way I can hate them now."

Zaile had said there was no way to overcomplicate Alvis, yet Rae was back against that wall again. How could Alvis be so optimistic after everything he went through? When Mr. Bremmet had promised him that Hanah would be kept safe as long as he'd won, won, *won*, Rae had hinged every hope on it. He had believed it would eventually stop Hanah from looking at him like she despised him more with each victory. Now she was gone. His old life was gone. But the pain of it still burned like a fresh wound. How did someone face this pain each day with a smile?

Rae fought the urge to jump when Alvis blew on his wrist, drying the paint faster so he could add whatever the next part of his vision was. He sighed. "Man, talking about my powers makes me really wish I could use them during our matches. I know we'll still win, but I feel like it would just help more."

We. Rae still wasn't sure how to believe in that word.

Alvis's tears were dry, but his lips had turned down in a pout. Rae was used to rolling his eyes when Alvis pulled a face like that. This time, Rae sucked in a harsh, startled breath. A realization hit him: Alvis was restricted from using his magic. He had it, and unlike Rae, he didn't depend on anyone to use it. But instead of learning to grow his attribute, Alvis was forced to push it down and hide his magic away. Even now, as he ran a pinky along the crease of Rae's elbow, tickling, Alvis's brow was furrowed in concentration. If he didn't focus that hard, would he hurt Rae with his powerful strength without meaning to?

Alvis raised a brow when Rae's attribute appeared on Rae's skin under his touch. It followed the same path of Alvis's finger, syncing like they were one and the same. An invitation for Alvis to stop holding back while touching Rae.

"If the chance comes, I'll do what I can to let you use your magic." Rae focused on where their skin touched instead of Alvis's eyes. "I think it's a good thing you like your powers now, since your magic is why you were able to save me."

Alvis took a sudden breath, then immediately released it like he had been punched in the stomach. Rae's gaze fluttered up—Alvis's face was closer than it was a minute before and Rae was paralyzed, his heart the only part of him sprinting away.

The tip of Alvis's nose brushed Rae's, but he didn't move closer. A single breath lay between them. A patient breath. A breath asking permission. A breath Rae leaned into with shaky lips.

The kiss was gentle and quick. An innocent press of lips before they both pulled back, slow and reluctant.

A blush dusted Alvis's cheeks red. Or maybe it was the sunset making them look that way. Rae didn't spend energy trying to figure it out—Alvis was moving towards him again, and Rae met him before he could make it half-way. The smell of paint was intense, but so was the grip Alvis used to press their lips harder together. His hand slid into Rae's hair, paint smearing across Rae's skin and streaking the white strands blue. Rae didn't mind.

He was absorbed in this chance to finally learn how to

kiss, to follow Alvis's lead and tilt his face just so—

Alvis hit his knee against a metal can, and it tumbled over, spilling yellow paint across their white tile floors. "*Shit*," he said, yanking away to try and control the mess with a towel.

The curse hit Rae like a splash of cold water. The clatter of the can had broken whatever spell was cast over him anytime Alvis was close. A spell that told him kissing Alvis would be a good idea, when Rae still didn't understand what being a Guardian meant.

"I have to go." Rae stood up too quickly. He nearly slipped in the paint as he shuffled around Alvis, towards the door and away from talking about what they just did. About how many kisses? About what they meant. What they could lead to. What they could end.

The bedroom door slammed heavy behind him and he fell against it, desperate to catch his breath. When he ran his hand over his face, it burned like fire beneath his palm. The color on his arm moved into focus and Rae's heart took off running once again.

Alvis had painted his Pact tattoo onto Rae's arm. When did Alvis find the time to create something so intricate so quickly? Or had Rae been that distracted by Alvis's green eyes, speckled with gold? By Alvis talking about his childhood, unbothered by Rae's lack of replies. By Alvis's touch, sparking Rae's attribute here and there, but never for long, because it was *Alvis*.

The plummeting of his stomach was back, and Rae realized it was a mixture of excitement and reticence. The latter was more familiar; it was safer, a grounding reminder that one misstep could make everything worthless. The two of them were finally moving forward together—adding another layer to their relationship was going to do nothing more than complicate it.

Rae looked at his arm once more, memorizing the painting, then hating himself for doing it. He rubbed it away on his white shirt, smearing it into lines of black.

CHAPTER 33

CIAN

CIAN HAD ENTERED THE FOYER on the second floor of Mr. Bremmet's mansion. He had been freshly showered after his match—which had been a resounding victory, of course. He'd followed the sounds of a soft piano playing a familiar tune. Rae had once told him it was the song he and Hanah had sung for fun when they were children. These days, Rae had played it for an entirely different reason.

Cian had tied his hair into a perfect braid, and it had swayed in time with his strides as he sauntered across the room. When he'd reached the piano, he had perched his elbow on the top of the polished, black wood. Even hunched like this, Cian's most recent growth spurt had made him tower over Rae. The younger Bremmet hadn't glanced up at him, but the barest hint of a smile had appeared on his lips.

"You missed a note," Cian had sung, teasingly.

Rae had pursed his lips like he did whenever he received criticism.

"What are you doing here, all alone, when you won your Ranker match earlier?" Cian had rubbed a finger on the piano's polish, smudging it. "Hanah won't see you again?"

Rae's fingers had continued to play the notes smoothly. "Commander Volos was there. I'm planning to go back after dinner."

"Did Hanah tell you to visit later or are you deciding on your own again?"

Rae had pushed the next keys harder but said nothing.

Cian had hummed along to Rae's playing, then helpfully pointed out, "I believe you missed another note."

Frustrated, Rae had yanked his hands from the keys and dropped them into his lap. "Why are you here, Cian?"

"To tell you the wonderful news, of course!" Cian had leaned down to whisper in Rae's ear like he was about to share a grand secret. "I won today."

Rae had rolled his eyes. It was a habit that years of being a Bremmet still hadn't broken him of. "I don't see anything special about you winning," Rae had said as he'd turned back to the keys. "You win all the time."

Cian had smirked. "My win today secures my place in the finals tomorrow. Against *you*. I hope you know how satisfying it will be to defeat you."

"You shouldn't be so excited until you manage to do it."

Rae had suddenly let out a small yelp, pulling his

312

fingertips away as the ivory keys turned to ice.

"Don't be so arrogant, Rae," Cian had chided, frowning.

"I'm not being arrogant," Rae had replied, rubbing his fingertips. "I'm being honest."

Rae's pout hadn't work on Cian as well anymore, but to his displeasure it had still been effective, occasionally.

Cian had flicked Rae in the forehead. "When you say it so seriously, it comes across as arrogant."

"It does not," Rae had rebuked, rubbing his forehead, even though his attribute had stopped Cian from hurting him. Then, violet eyes shining bright, Rae had smiled. One of the genuine ones he reserved for those closest to him. "Congrats on your victory, Cian."

The genuine warmth of the sentiment had been jarring compared to the stoic persona Rae had been cultivating as a Ranker champion. It had still taken Cian by surprise, even though he'd seen these rare glimpses more often than most. "There we go, little champion!" Cian had recovered and returned Rae's grin. "Finally, you're learning to respect your elders."

"Thank you for your endless wisdom, Oh Wise One," Rae had said, returning to his normal monotone. "Can you unfreeze the keys now?"

"You little bastard." Smacking his hand onto Rae's head, Cian had roughly ruffled the pale locks. Rae had laughed, trying to push Cian's cold fingers away.

A soft knock on the doorway had interrupted their laughter.

"I pardon the interruption," a servant had said, bowing. "Cian, Sir Bremmet would like to speak with you."

A shiver had run down Cian's spine. He'd wracked his brain, searching for what he could have done to warrant a call into Mr. Bremmet's office so suddenly. "Did Mr. Bremmet say why?" Cian had asked, forcing his voice to be steady.

The servant had shaken her head. "No, he didn't. He did say it was urgent, and you are to report immediately."

Rae had begun watching him, brow pinched in apprehension. He understood the yawning fear that came with a trip to their owner's office.

"Don't look at me like that, Rae," Cian had said, trying to sound collected. "Practice playing instead of pointlessly worrying about me."

"I'm not worried," Rae had replied, but didn't turn away. "Besides, the keys are still frozen."

Cian had known Rae for four years now. Why he'd underestimated Cian's ability to read him like an open book, Cian would never know.

"RAE WILL SOON BE KNOWN *as one of the greatest Rankers in our history,*" Mr. Bremmet had said. "*I need you to stay in second place and help defend against any other Rankers threatening his spot.*"

Mr. Bremmet's smile had been warm but his hands on Cian's shoulders had been freezing. "*Tomorrow, you will give an entertaining fight but in the end you will forfeit. I need you to become my number two, Cian."*

The conversation from the day before had replayed in Cian's mind as he dragged his feet towards his owner's office again, sweat dripping from his brow. Every small shift of his right arm—hanging broken at his side—had sent a new wave of nausea throughout his body. He could still remember the neon lights flashing Rae's victory across the Calamity Stadium's screens.

Cian had done what Mr. Bremmet had ordered. He had forfeited the match.

But, in an unusual, childish fit of rage, Cian had forfeited with *shame*. He had waited for the match bell to sound. No sooner than it did, Cian had transformed back into his human form. Surrounded by the crowd's confused murmurings, Cian had looked into Rae's confused, violet eyes. Then he'd casually pulled his own shoulder free of its socket.

Now Cian's forfeit had left his name on people's lips, but for all the wrong reasons. He'd undermined Rae's victory in the finals, disappointed top spenders who'd been looking forward to the two top *Drakon* Rankers fighting each other and brought embarrassment to the Bremmet family for such a brazen display of disobedience.

Number two? Mr. Bremmet had wanted Cian to become *number two*? Hadn't he once told Cian he may become the greatest Ranker he'd ever seen? And now he wanted Cian to be number *fucking* two. To become nothing more than a stepping stone for Rae's rise to greatness.

All for Rae. *Always* for *Rae*.

Rae and his still warm violet eyes, always making Cian forget he was supposed to be coldhearted. *Rae* and his heroic drive to protect a sister who despised him more each day. *Rae* and his impenetrable shield that now blocked Cian from achieving what he was destined to do.

By the time Cian had opened the door to Mr. Bremmet's office, he had become lightheaded from the pain in his arm and the effort of biting back tears. He had taken a step forward into the lavish room, but then cried out as a burning pain stabbed his chest, like his heart being ripped from him. Cian's knees had buckled, and he collapsed to the floor, cradling his broken arm.

Without a word, Mr. Bremmet had moved his finger away from Cian's stone on his *Drakon* bracelet. He had casually knelt in front of Cian and dug his hand into Cian's sweaty, blonde hair. His owner had yanked Cian's head towards him, forcing Cian to hold his gaze. "After you apologize for the embarrassment you caused Rae, you should thank him. If not for him pleading your case, you would already be a *Kon*," Mr. Bremmet had hissed. "Don't interfere again with Rae's path. I will not hesitate ripping that gemstone from your chest and sending you to the slums of Bellow."

Mr. Bremmet had released Cian's hair, his touch careful despite his harsh words. Like his owner had recognized Cian was still a valuable product and wanted Cian to know he remained important to him.

Mr. Bremmet had stood, straightening his coat, and then tapped the same spot on his bracelet. The pain in Cian's chest had receded immediately. Mr. Bremmet had then readjusted the cuff of his suit back over the bracelet, and leisurely walked to his desk, settling into his expensive, leather chair. He had lifted a document from his desk and glanced at it, ignoring the crumpled ice-*Drakon* on his plush rug. "Go to the infirmary and tend to your arm. Tell the doctor you aren't allowed painkillers until after the Closing Ceremony Ball tomorrow night."

CIAN HAD BEEN UNSURPRISED to find Rae leaning against the hallway wall outside Mr. Bremmet's office. Once the door had closed, the younger boy had rushed to his side immediately.

"Cian!" Rae had said, frantic. He'd reached for Cian's injured arm but stopped himself from touching it. "Are you okay?"

Cian had swallowed a growl. The audacity Rae had to look at Cian with teary eyes. So ignorant. So unaware of how he had limited Cian's future to nothing but second best.

A realization had hit Cian like a lightning bolt: Rae's tears were why *Drakon* were taught to ignore compassion. The concern Rae had held for Cian, instead of pride at winning their match, reminded Cian why feelings of love and comradery were such a hindrance. Rae's innocence and admiration of his mentor had stupidly made Cian feel safe; enough to forget all his training and fight with his emotions instead.

You will do whatever it takes to succeed, or risk sacrificing what you fight for. Cian's own words to Rae had echoed back to him.

Cian had lifted his hand and laid it carefully on Rae's shoulder. He'd given it a reassuring squeeze. The muscles beneath his palm had remained pliant, Rae's attribute sensing no threat or need to protect him. "I'm sorry I tainted our last match so horribly," Cian had said, pushing the words out. "I'll be supporting you from the shadows from now on, understand?"

Cian had dropped his hand and forced a smiled. Rae had returned it with a frown, recognizing something was off in the twist of Cian's lips. "Shadows? Last match?" Rae's voice had been barely more than a whisper, his violet eyes darkening in confusion. "What are you talking abo—wait! Cian? Where are you going—Cian!"

Cian had brushed past Rae and walked down the hall, desperately putting distance between them. Rae had called his name again, but Cian had refused to look back.

CHAPTER 34

"ARE YOU GOING TO THE FESTIVAL?" ALVIS ASKED, as he pulled on a pair of black, lace-up shoes. "Do you want to go together?"

Ever since Princess Meera had mentioned the festival earlier that day at the Linless meeting, Rae knew the question was coming, but he still flinched. He glanced over, only briefly meeting Alvis's questioning gaze before turning back to the notes he was copying from a textbook about the Ten Talismans and their Wielders. "No, thank you," he replied, and tried to convince himself Alvis looked painfully boring in his white, fitted shirt.

The patient yet, impatient look Alvis gave him had been constant since their . . . *moment* three days ago. Alvis shrugged, tossing a wave over his shoulder as he headed out the door. The tension in Rae's entire body left with him and he heaved a heavy sigh.

The kiss replayed in his mind, *again*. Rae scribbled faster to push away what the touch of Alvis's lips felt like on his. He had assumed replaying the moment would make the memory mundane and fade, but it only made it linger more.

"Damn, what did that paper ever do to you?"

Alvis was back in the doorway. He raised an eyebrow at the piece of paper in Rae's hands, crumpled from his frustrations. Rae had no idea when he'd stopped writing. He flattened the paper back onto the desk. "Nothing," he said, trying to adopt a cool tone. "I thought you had left."

Alvis said nothing as he made his way made to his own desk. It was far messier than Rae's. How he could find anything was beyond Rae's comprehension. "I forgot my Palace identification card."

"Why are you so forgetful?"

Alvis raised an eyebrow and Rae's defenses flared. "You really wanna do questions right now?"

Instead of walking back towards the door, Alvis closed the short distance between them. He leaned his hip against the desk, enjoying Rae's blatant annoyance at it. "Okay, then. Don't you think we should talk about it?"

" 'It'?" said Rae, playing dumb.

"The kissing thing we did?"

Absolutely not, Rae thought. "No," he said.

The playfulness in Alvis's eyes turned to hurt, like a puppy dog who had been scolded. "C'mon, dude."

"No."

Alvis began to lean closer. Rae's glare held him in place, but it wasn't enough to stop him from talking—it never was. Then realization dawned on Alvis's face. "Wait, wait. Was that your first—"

Rae's glare turned into a glower. Watching Alvis fumble with words was nearly worth his own embarrassment.

"Shit, I'm sorry. I should've asked first."

"It's fine," said Rae, harsh without meaning to be, because even though it *was* weirdly fine, how was he supposed to say something so embarrassing out loud? The legs of his chair screeched as he pushed it back to put more space between them. "If you want to make it up to me, then stop talking about it."

Alvis's lips pressed into a thin line. "If that's what you want," he said, standing and walking towards the door, feet dragging a bit and shoulders slouching.

Guilt stabbed at Rae as he watched Alvis walk away. Behind Rae's embarrassment was the truth: Rae was the one who closed the distance and made the first move. Alvis looked ashamed when he didn't deserve to be.

"W-Wait." Rae cringed at the stutter. He cleared his throat and wiped his sweaty palms on his pant legs. "I'll . . . I'll join you at the festival tonight."

Alvis's back froze. When he turned around, his eyes were as wide as they could go, his jaw slack. But he was quick as always to find his bearings. "You really suck at being honest, you know," he teased, then flashed a beaming smile.

Rae bristled, stuffing down the fluttering in his stomach. "Fine. Forget I said anything."

"Nope," Alvis said, popping the 'p' and steering Rae out the door. "No take-backs."

RAE HAD BEEN to plenty of festivals. Nerwen City was plentiful with them. There was always someone or something to celebrate: The King's birthday, the country of Zen's great achievements throughout history. And perhaps, most importantly, the Festival of Victory. It was the event following the Opening Ceremony for the biggest, most important Ranker tournament in the world.

For seven years, Rae's attendance had been mandatory. He was expected to be by Mr. Bremmet's side with the family's other Rankers, prepared to impress, to put on display why he was known as the Bloodied Champion. He wore countless suits, never the same one twice. Dances were held in the Palace of Nerwen City, so he had perfected every kind of waltz and ballroom dance there was.

But Torne's festival was nothing like Nerwen City's.

The city square smelled of cooked fish: smoked, spiced, lemony, and mouthwatering. The aroma weaved itself through the countless other delicious smells, like fried cakes and folded dumplings filled with vegetables and meats. One entire alley was blocked off for some sort of group dance that was mostly coordinated, but it didn't seem to matter if someone spun the wrong way or broke off to do a different dance entirely.

Rae and Alvis listened to the music in the square. When Alvis said he was completely tone-deaf, Rae mentioned he knew how to play the piano. And he should have known Alvis would then demand Rae play for him sometime.

Alvis decided to pick out food for Rae, and Rae did the same for him. But Alvis immediately regretted it when Rae found Papa Bob and his "spiciest filet of salmon in Torne."

"You stand out," Alvis observed after chugging down a cup of ice cream to ease the sting.

Slowly, Rae pulled his spoon out of his mouth, missing Alvis's eyes following the movement. "How so?"

"Your clothes."

"This is what most people in the Palace wear."

"And your face."

"What's wrong with my—"

"And the air around you. Something like that." He nodded his head towards a group of people a stall down. "They're all staring at you like you're elite. Though you kinda are, I guess."

The group of people turned away when Rae glanced over, giggling like they didn't mind being caught. "I highly doubt that's how they see me. I think you're who they're looking at." It sounded too soft, too revealing of something Rae hadn't thought through, so he quickly added, "Probably not used to seeing giants."

Alvis snorted. "If only they knew what a little shit you are. I'm only a giant next to you—oh, hey! There're the others!"

The others being who Rae would expect: Tal and Aella, Zaile and Lamont, and—

And Tahtsu.

Since their first real encounter in the warehouse, Rae had seen Tahtsu around, but his glare always told Rae to stay away. Now, though, Tahtsu's scowl was meaningless. The others all announced in unison the need to find more food and drinks, leaving Tahtsu and Rae alone.

Annoyingly obvious, Rae thought. Tahtsu's eyeroll ensured he was thinking the same thing. Tahtsu made no move to speak first, but when Rae turned away to watch the dancers, Tahtsu sighed, long and dramatic. "Listen, I still don't like you," he began, his tone far from delicate. "But everyone I *do* tolerate says you're turning out to be not a bad person and I should give you a chance. So, I want you to know it's not because of you *personally* that I don't like you."

Rae frowned. "I'm not sure the appropriate response to that."

"When I think about you, I remember my grandmother's death," Tahtsu ran his hand down his left arm. "I remember what it was like to watch her mark disappear. So, I know it's unfair to blame you, but it's kind of where I'm still at right now. Sorry about that whole thing at the lab, though. Grandmother Ellian probably would've kicked my ass for treating you like I did."

"It's alright," Rae replied, his eyes traveling to his left own arm where Alvis had painted his Pact tattoo design. "I understand. For what it's worth, I am sorry your grandmother lost her life. I'm . . . doing my best to make sure that never happens again."

Tahtsu observed Rae silently, searching for any cracks or lies in Rae's expression, but he apparently found none. He nodded and then they fell into silence, not comfortable, but far from the awkwardness it was originally.

Thankfully, it was only a few minutes later when Alvis reappeared, laughing, with a bowl of fruit in his hand and Rival next to him. When Rival saw Tahtsu, his expression changed lightning quick.

"Oh, hello," Rival said, an attractive drawl around the words.

Tahtsu raised a finely trimmed eyebrow at him but didn't seem put off. Far from it, if his slow glance up and down Rival's entire body was anything to go by. "Who the hell are you?" He reached out and grabbed one of the drinks from Rival's hands without waiting for a reply. The drink didn't seem like it was intended for Tahtsu, but Rival responded with a low whistle, intrigued.

A piece of pineapple between his teeth, Alvis handed Rae the bowl, then began to usher him away. "We should leave them before it goes where I know it's about to go," Alvis whispered.

Rae blushed and stabbed Alvis in the ribs with his elbow.

The rest of the evening carried on simple and easy. Tal's large, blue eyes lit up every time Rae offered something about himself, taking each piece like it was a special treasure. Zaile pulled Rae's arms and forced him to dance. Alvis laughed with no intention of stopping and Rae wanted to make sure Alvis would never need to.

"You okay?" Alvis asked after midnight, as they sat on a random doorstep and watched the festivities still going strong.

"Yes," Rae replied, smiling and not minding the soft brush of Alvis's shoulder against his. "I really think I am."

CHAPTER 35

CIAN

THE WEEK BEFORE CIAN had been set to become Commander Volos's newest captain, he'd had a single request for Mr. Bremmet: "Please let me challenge Rae one last time."

The Calamity Arena had sold out within minutes. The headlines had been extravagant: *The Final Matchup of the Bremmet Two! Cian vs Rae! The Ranker Match of the Decade!* Video from their previous matches had been edited together like movie trailers and splashed across every billboard and screen in Nerwen City.

And now the match was over.

Cian had won.

In the contestants' locker room, Cian had leaned back heavily against a row of lockers. Screams of terror and confusion had sounded from outside. The walls had shaken as *Drakon* took their dragon form to chase Rae down. Rae—who now had Mr. Bremmet's blood smeared across his claws after he'd discovered the truth about Hanah. The truth Cian had exposed and gleefully watched as it had broken through Rae's remaining slivers of control.

Cian had laughed. Soft and disbelieving at first, with his filthy hands covering his eyes. Then his laugh had begun to boil out of him, louder and louder, until he had doubled over, gasping between peals, the echo of it ricocheting off the tiled walls and turning back on him. Tears had slid from his eyes, between his hands, and down his cheeks, mixing with the blood on his lips.

For years Cian had fought as second best. Now, he was again number one.

So why did it feel like he had lost everything?

THE WHISKEY BURNED as it slid down Cian's throat. He wasn't used to any kind of heat, but this fire was pleasant. With a loud clink, he harshly placed the short, chipped glass back onto the grimy bar, then signaled the bartender for another.

Around Cian was boisterous chatter; roars of laughter between friends and threats made between the people gambling in the corner.

How long had Cian been in this disgusting, rundown town, where it was near impossible to tell Guardians from humans? Two weeks? Three? Ever since Commander Volos had ripped away his *Drakon* gemstone in punishment for killing Michael Witt, the days had bled together. The pain from the wound on his chest was finally beginning to dull. But no matter what he touched, nothing turned into ice anymore. His sword was now useless at his side. His ice magic was gone. Cian Bremmet, *Drakon* Captain, former reigning Ranker champion, was Fallen. A *Kon. Disgraced.* He gritted his teeth.

"You plannin' on payin' tonight, for once?" the barkeep asked. She poured another finger of cheap whiskey into a glass and slid it to him. "Or you just here to whine 'bout your lost magic again?"

Cian threw back the drink, not dignifying her with a reply. A pathetic Guardian like her, who had never accessed her attribute, who had never ascended to the power and prestige of a *Drakon*, could *never* possibly understand the endless agony of losing it all. Couldn't possibly understand how great of a failure Cian's life had become.

He paused, fingers flexing on the glass but still unable to send frost creeping over it.

A failure?

Bullshit.

How could he have possibly known Michael Witt was such an important person to Commander Volos and the Royal Family of Zen? If Cian had known about Michael, he never would have killed him. He would have found another way to capture Rae and Alvis.

Alvis and Rae. Cian's other screw up, but that one would be more easily reconciled. He knew Linless's plans to give Rae a Charge and create the "greatest Pact in the world." Jazz had spilled all sorts of Linless secrets before Cian had slit his throat.

Linless was impressively thorough in their secrecy and gathering information on them often amounted to nothing. But Alvis and Rae were somewhere out there, and Cian would find them. They were the key to his redemption. He would drag them back to Zen, screaming if he had to, and Commander Volos would be so impressed that his gemstone and rank would be restored.

Cian ran a hand through his greasy, blonde hair, tugging at his scalp. Then he pressed the palm of his hand into his eyepatch. He could still feel the power in the hand that had taken his eye away. He couldn't wait to return the favor tenfold.

Laughter burst from him like water from a broken dam. The bartender stepped away, startled. The noise around them quieted, and all the other eyes in the pub were suddenly focused warily on him. More laughter shook his shoulders, and he welcomed the stares—he had always enjoyed undivided attention. Through his frenzied giggles, Cian said, "Dear barkeep, do tell me."

The barkeep eyed him cautiously. "Tell ya what?"

"Where I can find one of these precious Charges you filthy Guardians all love so much?"

CHAPTER 36

THE OLDEST CITY-STATE ON THE CONTINENT, Tarley was home to the foul and forgotten.

Pirates, prostitutes, the greedy and most desolate the world had to offer—they all made their home there. And Tarley welcomed them with open arms, a safe harbor for all those searching for their place and finding it amongst the lost. The rules other countries used to maintain power didn't exist there. No police force to decide who was bad and who was lawful. No difference between a Pact and a Guardian with a gemstone.

When the sport of Rankers was created, it didn't take long for it to make its way to a crooked place like Tarley, but there was one key difference in its Ranker tournament: free will. Unlike Zen, Guardians in Tarley were not forced into battles, but did so of their own volition. Tarley became a refuge for many Guardians who had been exiled from their own countries and Charges searching for someone to win gold with.

Other nations had long since accepted it as fact and left Tarley alone, their previous attempts at changing the country's ways all spectacular failures, thanks to the strength of the citizens and their lack of propriety when it came to fighting. It had become an unspoken rule that if Tarley kept to itself, the rest of the world would leave them to do as they pleased.

The most southeastern territory in the land, Tarley rested between the borders of Coral and Drev. Cradled into a fjord, it was carved into the cliffs and open to the sea where the air wasn't as brisk. Fog settled heavy for most of the day and the waterfall to the north was relaxing background noise to the madness of the city life.

Next to the waterfall was the June Stadium, the city-state's most prized possession. It was clean and a gleaming gray, currently filled to the brim with fans watching two Pacts compete. The cacophony of the crowd cheering nearly rumbled the cliffs itself.

Beyond the arena, there wasn't anything outright breathtaking about Tarley. It was dull gray and brown. It was probably the ugliest city in the world, but Alvis's attention still skipped from one detail to the next. He absorbed everything from the foggy sky when they flew towards the landing station, then as they walked through the streets towards their inn.

To people who grew up somewhere like Torne or Nerwen, Tarley might have been off-putting and foreign, but for Alvis, it reminded him so much of Bellow he couldn't help the pricks of longing for his old home. Buildings crowded together with twisting alleyways in an endless weave of hidden shops and houses. Cracked, wooden signs hung from storefronts. Lampposts with burnt out bulbs lined the streets. The cobblestone sidewalk that lined the path was cracked throughout. It made it diffi-cult to tell if they were walking through the 'good' part of town or not. But Alvis was starting to think there wasn't a clearly drawn line for that here. No towering wall to separate the radiant from the shadows like back in Ner-wen City and Bellow. The stench of dead fish coated the air, mixing in with other food and item vendors. Thick clouds casted a gray hue over the afternoon, threatening to rain.

Despite all that, Tarley was alive. At the center square was a stage, musicians were playing handmade instru-ments, the crowd laughed and clapped along with each out-of-tune note. Boisterous chatter filled the air. Some folks shared laughs and bottles despite the relatively early time of day, while others exchanged fists as their comrades whooped and hollered around them. Couples openly touched, pressed against each other, their clothes ripped, skin streaked with dirt, and who knows what else. If this was how the Tarlies acted during the afternoon, who knew how they were when the sun set.

"Are you looking for someone?" asked Tal when he caught Alvis searching the crowd.

"Rival said he was going to be here for the tourna-ment," Alvis said. "But this place is insane."

Tal smiled. "Tournaments are always like this! I don't

think I've ever been to one that doesn't make the town a spectacle. Tarley's is one of my favorites."

"Why's that?" Alvis asked.

"The food is surprisingly good, and the tournament is so fun! This is where we recruited Tahtsu and Ellian a few years back." Tal looked at Aella, blue eyes sparkling. "And, they never expect us to win a fight."

THE INN THEY WERE STAYING AT wasn't fancy, but it was near the center of town and decently sized.

On the bottom floor was a small restaurant, communal bathing rooms, and a lounge. The shorter ceilings of the stairs forced Alvis to duck or risk scrapping the door-frame with his head. The wood creaked beneath Alvis and Rae's feet as they climbed the three flights to their room, leaving Lamont, Zaile and the rest to their own rooms. Before he turned away, Lamont told them to take a few minutes to settle in before they set headed to the arena to watch Aella and Tal compete.

Alvis and Rae's tiny room was barely big enough to share, but Alvis registered the bed in the center before he noticed the size of the room itself.

Bed. Singular. One.

Already sensing Rae's frantic internal crisis, Alvis grabbed one of the pillows and tossed it into an empty space below the window. "I'll go ask the front desk if they have any extra blankets," he said, then hurried out the door before Rae could reply.

Once he was down the hall, Alvis leaned against the wall and sighed.

A week ago, sleeping in the same bed with Rae wouldn't have mattered. Alvis never had trouble sharing beds. Rae was far worse with lack of personal space, but Alvis didn't doubt he would've handled it fine.

Now sleeping in the same bed meant being too close. Closeness meant remembering what kissing Rae was like, and Alvis already spent too much time thinking about it. About how much he liked Rae moving in first on the second kiss, and that it was *Rae* who gasped and held tight to Alvis's shirt.

And it didn't help Alvis how close him and Rae had had to be in the days leading up to Tarley. It had been all *touching*. Alvis touching Rae's forehead. Rae's attribute on Alvis's neck leaving a lingering tickle behind when it withdrew. And there was all the non-touching, too. Like *not* pushing Rae's hair behind his ear and *not* kissing Rae again.

But Rae had started asking Alvis how he was, and his transference grew more precise by the day, and Alvis had seen him smile three more times now.

And, honestly, that more than made up for the no touching.

CHAPTER 37

WEEKS HAD PASSED since Rae had been in a stadium, but it felt like eons. Had it really only been weeks since he fought in one or sat in the stands. He'd logged hundreds of matches, hundreds of victories . . . but the crowd's cheers here in Tarley's June Stadium were some of the loudest he'd ever heard.

Every breath Rae took was calculated to keep himself still. He counted down the seconds until Tal and Aella's match started, the ball of nerves in his stomach continually tightening.

Rae had never fought in June Stadium, but the tournaments weren't much different than what Rae was used to; the master of ceremonies introduced the participants, the barrier to protect the crowd had risen, and a gong had sounded. And killing your opponent was still the best route to victory.

The oval arena wasn't as massive as Nerwen City's but still tall enough for a Guardian to stand on their dragon form's hind legs with space to comfortably spread their wings and fly. The field below was made of dirt, already distressed from the previous battles that had taken place that morning. Two decently sized stages made of stone sat on opposite sides of the field from one another, one for each of the dueling Pacts. Referees waited on the sidelines, preparing to use their attributes when someone overstepped the rules. Surrounding the entire battleground was a clear wall, invisible if not for the sun catching it. It protected the crowd from stray attributes or limp bodies.

Next to Rae, Alvis was grinning. Rae couldn't blame him—tournaments were exhilarating the first time you saw one.

But the first time you killed in one . . .

The crowd screamed with the end of the current match. Too loud, too close. A wave of nausea washed over Rae again. He tried to fight it, crossing his arms tightly across his chest. He focused on breathing, knowing the sweat on his temple would give him away, but he felt helpless to stop his nerves breaking free. Crossing his arms made it easier to scratch at his scar—

There was a gentle nudge against Rae's shoulder. Rae jerked away, but Alvis wasn't perturbed. "Are you okay?" he asked, bending close to Rae's ear to be heard.

"I'm fine," replied Rae, not bothering to care if Alvis heard him or not.

Alvis's eyes fluttered across Rae's face, then down to the red scratches Rae's nails were leaving behind on his right forearm. "Rae, what do you need?"

And don't lie. Alvis said through their Pact link.

I don't know.

Do you need to leave?

Rae shook his head. It was the truth. Rae already felt less light-headed focusing on Alvis instead of the crowd. Slowly, he dragged his fingers away from his arm, but the evidence of his anxiety remained.

Switch seats with me, said Alvis.

Rae crinkled his eyebrows. *Why?*

Alvis was already standing. *Don't make me pick you up and move you.*

Rae stood quickly and squeezed himself into the narrow space between Alvis and the seat. As soon as they were sitting again, Alvis held up the hand closest to Rae, offering it. *Hand,* he said, motioning at Rae.

What?

Give me your hand. You can squeeze as hard as you need to.

Rae's mouth dropped open, then closed, then dropped again, no words coming out. Next to him, Zaile nudged him with her elbow, letting out an innocent, low whistle when Rae barely stopped himself from reciprocating.

"I . . . I . . ." Rae wasn't sure how he wanted to finish the sentence. *I don't see how that'll help*, he wanted to say. Except he knew he couldn't scratch at his scar if his hand was preoccupied. He wanted to protest, *I don't hold hands.* Which was true, but for some reason, if it was Alvis's, holding hands didn't seem particularly odd. They *had* already kissed—

Rae slammed his palm into Alvis's hand so hard it

hurt, but the sting was a perfect distraction from the ending of his previous thought. He refused to look at Alvis or Zaile's grin, so he made a point of staring straight ahead and pretending his ears weren't burning.

Alvis didn't intertwine their fingers; he merely clasped their hands together with his usual confidence. When he ran his calloused thumb over Rae's, the awkwardness gradually faded. And when the crowd's roar swelled to a fever pitch again, Alvis tightened his hold, keeping Rae grounded.

"TO MY LEFT, WE HAVE our three-time champions: Picket and Feray!" the master of ceremonies shouted into his microphone. The crowd was already cheering their names.

The two men were of equal, towering height. Muscles so excessively large they could break someone's neck without trying. From their seats, it was impossible to tell which man was the Guardian and the Charge: they both wore long sleeves and twin snarls—intimidating and obnoxious—the kind Rae thought Alvis probably hated and didn't feel guilty about punching.

"And their opponents: Aella and her Charge, Tal!"

The shouts around them started again, and they were far less welcoming.

On the opposite side of the field, standing on their own stage, were Aella and Tal. Tal's smile was timid as he waved at the unimpressed crowd. Aella stood behind him, holding onto the handles of his wheelchair, golden eyes unimpressed. She walked him forward until it was dangerously close to the stage's edge. She slipped Tal's bow and arrow from her back and handed them to him, smiling softly when he beamed up at her.

In terms of obvious strength and star power, Aella and Tal were at a disadvantage, and their opponents knew it. The men both let out boisterous laughs, as mocking as someone could possibly be. It got the crowd going again. People started laughing along with them. They shouted insults at Aella and Tal, telling them to give up already, mocking Tal's wheelchair, and yelling less than favorable things about Aella.

Soon the screams turned into demands. Chants of "Transform!" echoed throughout the stadium. Happy to oblige, Picket raised his arm with a theatrical flair. Feray roared and called for the crowd to get louder. Then, Picket put his left hand to Feray's head, and there was a burst of maroon light. Feray's dark, red limbs stretched and pulled, until he was roaring again, balls of flames shooting into the sky, strong even against the rain starting to drizzle down.

Tal clapped along with everyone else, smiling ecstatically at the successful Release. The complete picture of childish joy, he didn't look like he belonged fighting against monsters three times his size. Aella knelt beside him, almost in a bow, her hair tucked behind her ears. Tal's smile somehow brightened even further. He leaned forward until their foreheads touched. Their eyes closed for the briefest of moments. It was intimate; out of place among the impending fight and calls for blood. Tal spoke to her, a single word. A quick parting of his lips, then they backed away from each other. Tal's tattooed, left hand was slow and gentle as he set it against her forehead.

Light filled the stadium once more. It faded, and Aella rose, her movements meticulous and cautious as she straightened her long, slender neck. She was so at ease in her sparkling, purple dragon form. When the weak sunlight hit her scales, they captivatingly sparked like the facets of an amethyst. She looked like a grand jewel perched in the dirt of the arena.

The crowd was silent. The distant call of seagulls was the only noise piercing the stunned quiet.

Aella had *no wings*.

After they collected themselves, Picket and Feray roared with laughter. It was enough to break the rest of the crowd out of its stupor. Everyone started shouting again, the taunts becoming personal in their wrath.

"What the hell is this!"

"Get that wingless trash out of here!"

There was so much being shouted now, Tal and Aella couldn't possibly hear or make it all out. They both remained calm, Tal still smiling despite the onslaught. Aella's tail slithered around Tal's wheelchair, protective.

The gong sounded.

There was a loud clash of claws lashing against each other. Aella and Feray were in the center, dust swirling around them as they stood on their hind legs and claws pressed against one another, each doing their best to push the other back. Feray was considerably taller, and he tilted his head down to snarl into Aella's face. Aella was unaffected by the display—she'd clearly seen it plenty of times before.

It was a breathtaking image: a rich red Guardian with outstretched wings, and a brilliant purple one without, straining against each other on equal ground.

The broad claws of Feray's foot curled and dug into the dirt when Aella gained a brief upper hand. Feray stretched his wings out farther and flapped them, a burst of air pulling up at the same time his feet slammed into her stomach. Aella tumbled onto her back, stopping short of the stage Tal remained on, and when she straightened, it was to see a cyclone of fire rushing towards her.

She raised her hand—a sharp, swirling air burst forth from between her claws, meeting the flames head-on. They sliced through the fire, disbursing and extinguishing it.

Feray's eyes widened, caught off guard by the sudden nullification of his magic. Then he chuckled, entertained. "A wind attribute, I see. Isn't that some delicious irony—" His words halted in a startled gasp.

Aella's feet had begun to float above the ground.

Feray tried to cover his shock with a patronizing sneer. "A measly attribute can't compete against true wings, sweetheart."

Aella's feet lifted higher and higher, until she was the one staring down her nose. "Should we find out?"

Then, Aella was off, a burst of rainwater in her wake.

Feray was after her in an instant. His wings slashed through the air, harmonizing with his laughter and arrogant taunts as he chased her. Feray threw fireballs Aella's way, but intentionally, none of them came close to meeting their target, and instead smashed into the barrier. Screams and cheers roared, the crowd clearly enjoying the spectacle of the wingless Guardian running away from the already decided victor.

Feray was right, Rae hated to admit, having wings was glaringly different from using an attribute to fly. Aella's movements were choppy—she couldn't move consistently in a single line or curve when she needed to change direction like a Guardian with wings could. Instead, Aella jumped from one circle of air to the next, creating surfaces for herself to settle on. When she needed to fight against Feray's flame, she dropped heavy and fast to the ground with no way to ease her fall. It left her vulnerable, and the more agitated Feray got at Aella's clever escapes, the more accurate his flames became. If Aella made the slightest miscalculation, she would be burned.

Tal was an ignored shadow, lost in the brilliance of the Guardians' aerial fight. His chair was still perched at the edge of the stage, his bow and arrows sat neatly in his lap. He watched Aella and Feray with sparkling, blue eyes and an enchanted smile.

Picket didn't seem to mind Tal's lack of concern. He stretched his large arms above his head and cracked his neck. With a drawn-out sigh, he hopped off the other stage at the far end of the stadium and reached for the belt around his waist. Metal flashed in the sunlight. With an intentionally sluggish movement, he withdrew one of his knives and tossed it up. He caught the handle with his palm before doing it again. "I almost feel bad fighting against you, kid," he shouted, as he made his way across the field towards the other stage. He added more flair to the next toss when Tal dropped his attention to him. When the handle landed in his palm again, Picket motioned to Tal's legs with the blade. "It's not too fulfillin' breaking something that's already broken."

"They're not broken," Tal told him. He lifted one leg to prove his point, wiggling it a little, then flinched. His leg dropped back down heavily against the footrest. Still, he smiled. "They just don't work as well as they used to."

Picket didn't look impressed and continued to smirk. He pointed a finger up to the clashing Guardians in the sky. "I wasn't only talkin' about you." Picket tossed the knife again, talented enough to do it absentmindedly, as he craned his head back. "Your Guardian should stay in her human form. Much more attractive that way."

The clinking of metal-on-metal ringed through the stands above the stadium noise. When Picket grabbed for his falling knife, his fingers wrapped around nothing. Startled, he snapped his attention behind him—the blade lay covered in dirt. Innocently resting next to it was an arrow, its point buried into the ground.

When Picket turned back around, anger already started to cover his surprise and pull his lips into a sneer.

Tal's smile was gone. A terrifying calm was now in its place, and an irate flush was dusting his pale, long face pink. "I'd appreciate it if you didn't talk about her like that." Tal's bow was back in his lap, but his posture was far less inviting. "It's harder to avoid arteries when I'm angry."

A snarl rumbled deep in Picket's throat. He was tall enough that leaping at the stage was an easy feat—with a simple running lunge he was in the air, a fresh knife raised and aimed for Tal's throat. He growled as he swung it down—only for it to meet a solid force of air as Aella activated her transference. The blade bounced off, and Picket was pushed backwards, breath rushing out of him.

Above them, Aella roared and returned to the ground—Feray had scorched her soft underbelly with a line of fire, so hot the smell of her burning flesh filled the stands. It was the same move Aella had easily combated before. Tal's face visibly strained against the phantom pain of the burn radiating through his own body, but he remained composed.

For a brief moment, Picket locked gazes with Tal's owlishly wide eyes, expecting to see amusement for Picket falling into his and Aella's transference trap, or maybe excitement at having the upper hand. Picket didn't expect Tal's face to be grimacing with pity.

"How—" Picket started, but a gasp tore itself out of him as he was hurled backwards into the dirt, rolling, until he dragged himself to a stop.

Aella lifted off the ground again, higher than she did before. Feray chased after her, using his impressive, sharp wings to maneuver above her with a smug scoff—it broke off when Aella began to drop again, her eyes never leaving Feray's.

On the ground, there was no finesse in Picket's onslaught of thrown daggers aimed at Tal. His rage only increased as the blades met Aella's attribute and she simply dropped them back to the ground.

Tal sent a volley of well-aimed arrows, each catching

the tiniest bit of Picket's skin, even as the larger man dashed and dodged across the arena. The cuts were barely knicks, but enough to annoy him and Feray, if the frustrated looks Picket kept throwing into the sky at his Guardian were anything to go off of.

All the while, Tal remained unperturbed—each arrow he released hit its mark; whether as a tease or a warning. His motions were poised and fluid, despite the threat continually closing in on him. Aella's attribute protected or aided, changing the speed of the arrows when Tal needed her to.

Aella and Tal's teamwork was a flawless execution of what it meant to be a Pact.

Rae's hand flexed in Alvis's, then tightened, harder this time. "Is it really possible to trust someone that much?" Rae murmured, breathless. *Do I deserve to be trusted that much?* He hadn't realized he'd said that through their Pact link until Alvis replied, *Yeah.*

Aella hissed as Feray's flame licked her shoulder this time, sliding beneath her scales and burning her sensitive skin.

Zaile leaned to Rae. "It *is* possible to have that level of trust in a Pact. Because Tal believes in Aella—"

A knife halted in the wind a breath before Tal's face. He didn't flinch, and the sharp blade flew backwards in the same path it had come.

"—and Aella believes in Tal."

Tal released an arrow, it flew like a beast closing in on its prey, chasing after the returning knife. When Picket held his hand out, prepared to snatch his weapon back, he didn't realize it wasn't the handle of his knife fitting into his palm until pain wrenched a scream from his throat.

With all of Picket's bragging about his knife skills, one would think he'd never been injured by something sharp. The point of the arrow had sliced neatly into his palm, the shaft sticking out from the other side. When Picket glanced at it, he paled, then bit his lip against another howl of pain. His Guardian in the sky could only be feeling just as much agony through their Pact connection.

Another arrow pierced Picket's thigh, cutting into the muscle and nerves. He stumbled forward, staring at his leg in disbelief. His teeth ground together as he twisted his head around, breathing heavily. He took an aggressive step towards Tal. "I'm going to *kill* you."

Tal already had another arrow notched. But it wasn't aimed at Picket—it was pointed steadily into the sky. "I'm sorry, sir, but if you're going to blame someone, then you should blame your Guardian."

The stadium seemed to hold its breath—all noise suddenly gone. The only sound was the bow string snapping and the arrow cutting through the air—it picked up speed as a strong burst of magic-fueled air pushed it faster and faster. Picket screamed at Feray, and the dragon opened his jaws to unleashed another torrent of flames, but it wasn't fast enough, and the arrow buried itself into the soft skin of Feray's neck. He roared a shrill scream that shook the walls, the barrier, and rattled Rae's teeth.

Tal lowered his bow, the pity returning to pinch his brow. "Concede, please."

Picket dropped to a knee, gripping the phantom pain

in his neck and spat, "We refuse to lose to a pathetic Pact like you—"

Feray slammed into the ground behind him. Aella landed softly onto his back, the graceful motion at odds with the violent grip she held Feray's red wings. Feray growled, heat building beneath Aella's hand—she flinched but tightened her hold. Her lip turned up in a snarl and she closed her eyes, concentrating, and then the heat was put out, smoke slipping between her fingers into the sky. Feray tried again, breath growing heavier with each failure. Then he and Picket gasped together when another arrow sliced into the black, swirling flames of their Pact tattoo on Picket's arm.

"Concede," Tal repeated firmly.

When Picket said nothing, Aella raised her head and zoned in on him, eyes boring into his. Her grip on Feray's wing tightened, and she pulled.

A nauseating crack filled the air—an agonizing, screeching roar followed. Then there was a flash of maroon light, and the winner of the match was declared.

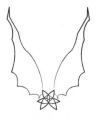

CHAPTER 38

"HOLY SHIT, YOU GUYS, you were *amazing!*" Alvis gushed to Aella and Tal, as they settled into the booth across from them at a nearby bar.

Alvis hadn't had a chance to find them immediately after their amazing match to drop every compliment possible on them. Lamont had ordered Alvis and Rae to go practice before the next match had started. Alvis had tried to push back, reminding Lamont that the training fields would be packed. But it completely backfired when Lamont responded, "Then go practice in your room." It was an effective suggestion, so Alvis and Rae had headed to the shoreline to practice, and now they smelled heavily of fish and salt.

Tal smiled at Alvis, pride dusting his pale face red. "Thank you! Wasn't Aella so cool? I bet you've never seen someone fly without wings! So cool, right? Right?"

"That's enough," Aella said, monotone, but her own beige face was lit up in a blush she didn't try to hide.

Tal seemed ready to tease her more, but he settled on another grin before diving into a conversation with Lamont about any potential Pacts from the tournament that they could recruit for Linless.

Watching how Aella and Tal interacted, Alvis understood why their match was the one Lamont wanted Rae and him to see. They leaned in together, arms unconsciously brushing against the other's. Being near Tal made Aella more open and less guarded. She was a textbook example of a Guardian: protecting Tal at the expense of her own safety, while still balancing her fight against Feray. And Tal carried his own weight, facing his opponent with confidence in both himself and Aella.

Alvis glanced Rae's way and wasn't surprised to see Rae was watching Aella and Tal, too. And Alvis knew Rae was thinking something self-deprecating like, "I can never be a Guardian like that." Or maybe it was, "Alvis is too hotheaded—I wish I had a Charge like Tal."

"Stop worrying," Alvis told him.

"I'm not worrying. I'm thinking," Rae replied. Then quickly added, "Which are *not* the same."

Except, as Alvis had told him at least fifty times already, they weren't *not* the same thing. But before he had a chance to repeat the same argument, Tal asked them, "Do you guys know when your match will be?"

"Not yet," Alvis said. He turned to Lamont. "Do *you* know when our match is?"

"Tomorrow," replied Lamont. "We're currently working

out the details with the tournament organizers."

Alvis grinned, suddenly giddy. He had never experienced crowds of people screaming and cheering or booing, their entire attention focused on a fight he was in. And tomorrow—*tomorrow*—he would be down on that field himself. Energy thrummed through his veins and his legs bounced, craving to be down on that field *yesterday*.

Next to him, Rae was quiet again, unengaged from the conversation, but looking towards whoever was talking. He didn't look out of place next to Lamont or Zaile whose clothes were just as clean and high-end. But that thing was happening again where people stared at Rae simply because of how unapproachable he seemed and what that meant he may be hiding. Some of them dropped their eyes when they caught Alvis glaring from over Rae's head. Others raised an eyebrow in challenge.

Rae wasn't a baby—anyone who tried to mess with him would find themselves slammed face-first into a wall. But Alvis still grabbed the sleeve of Rae's striped sweater. "Let's go get drinks from the bar!"

Relief made Rae's eyes soften and he nodded. He even let Alvis take him by the hand and pull him away from the table.

The tavern they were in was loud and crowded, bodies pushed against each other, so Alvis didn't bother dropping Rae's hand. It was nice being tall sometimes because people made space for *him*, which made it easier to tug Rae along behind him, ignoring each of Rae's annoyed grunts.

They were half-way to the bar when, above the din of the crowd, a familiar voice yelled, "Alvy!"

Alvis immediately recognized the large arms wrapping themselves around his shoulders and yanking him into a hug.

"Rival!" Alvis laughed into Rival's neck. He patted Rival's back as he stepped away. "I can't believe you found me!"

"Same here. Have you had your match yet?"

"We have one tomorrow," said Alvis, nodding towards Rae with his head. "Don't know against who, but we're ready."

Rival's gaze dropped down to Alvis and Rae's locked hands. "You two seem to be doing better since the last time we talked." He raised an eyebrow, amused, when both Alvis and Rae blushed a hot red. "Oh, *so much* better."

Rae yanked his hand free of Alvis's like it burned.

With a harsh elbow into Rival's ribs, Alvis finally got Rival to bite off his next laugh, gasping. Then Rival's arm caught Alvis's eye.

"Wait, did you find a Guardian?" Alvis grabbed Rival's arm, twisting it, and taking in the tattoo's harsh lines. It reminded Alvis of sharp, icy diamonds.

Not minding Alvis's manhandling, Rival grinned. "I told you, Tarley's got one of the biggest payouts outside of Zen, so plenty of powerful Guardians hang out here looking for Charges. My new one's pretty strong. Kind of a dick but that's not surprising. I'll introduce you, but I'm empty here," Rival said, raising his cup. "So, I'll find you again."

"Do you like that nickname?" asked Rae when Rival was out of earshot.

" 'Alvy'?"

"A lot of people call me that." Alvis grinned. "You can call me it, too, if you wanna."

Rae tried to keep his face placid. "I don't participate in nicknames—" He froze.

In an instant, Rae's face turned whiter than normal, replaced with the paleness only panic brings. His mouth dropped open as he stared, transfixed, at something over Alvis's shoulder. Alvis followed Rae's gaze—what the hell could make him look like *that*—

A yelp startled from him when Rae grabbed onto his shirt and started pulling him back through the crowd with a series of hard yanks. Alvis's stomach leapt—Rae was frantic with fear.

"Rae?" Alvis tried to gently loosen the death grip Rae had on him. "Hey, what's wrong—"

"Well, well, well," said a chilling, familiar voice behind them. "Isn't this a wonderful surprise?"

The laughs of drunken men and women faded as the world focused on that smooth, playful voice. Alvis couldn't tell if the pressure on his chest was from Rae tugging on his shirt, or his heart slamming against his ribs, trying to break free.

Alvis slowly turned. Cian's sharp grin was the same as the one branded into his memories. Suddenly, he was back on his street in Bellow. His dad was smiling at him through the blood streaming past his lips. Cian's sword was sinking into his dad's chest while Cian smiled.

And now that ice demon from his nightmares was standing only six feet away in front of him.

"Alvis—" Rae choked off with a groan, the pain of Alvis's memories and hate coursing through him. Alvis felt a distant pang of regret, and that small rational voice in the back of his head was trying desperately to tell him something, but his fury was too consuming.

Rae released Alvis's shirt to grab at his own hair. "Let's go. Please, Alvis, we need to go."

No, they didn't.

Cian's shirt was unbuttoned enough to reveal his dirt smeared, white chest. Enough to see what was there. And what wasn't.

Rae was now in front of Alvis, blocking his path, though Alvis hadn't moved yet. *"Think,"* Rae said desperately. A thin line of sweat was forming on his forehead. "He may not have his gemstone anymore, but he could still be in a Pact—"

"There you guys are!" Rival appeared from the line of people to throw an arm over Alvis's shoulders.

Cian's laughter was piercing. It burst from him with force, cutting through the racket of the bar. The musicians' hands faltered, their instruments screeching to a halt. People turned; annoyance written on some faces, confusion on others, but excitement on most when they saw the standoff taking form in front of them.

"What an unexpectedly wonderful night!" Cian crooned, hand slapping his knee in pure delight. He slowly straightened, like a cobra sizing up its prey. "I didn't realize my *precious* Charge had made such special friends!"

Rival pulled a face, something between confusion and disdain. "The hell you are calling me 'precious' for?"

With a shuttering breath, Alvis trailed his eyes over the Pact tattoo on Rival's arm that had reminded him of icy diamonds. His stomach dropped, and dread gripped him, mixing forcefully with his anger. He faltered a half step back from Rival's touch.

"Alvy?" Rival's smile turned into a questioning frown.

Cian cackled again.

In a blink, Cian's collar was gripped in Alvis's hand. Strength quickly building to uncontrolled, he yanked hard enough for the fabric to rip, and then he spun. Cian gasped as Alvis slammed him down onto the ground, the wood beneath splintering and cracking. Dust kicked up around them, it stung in Alvis's eyes and tears began to slide from their corners, but all he could smell was the metallic of Cian's blood when his fist connected with the hidden eye. Cian grinned up at him, so Alvis punched that, too.

Cian's grip on his forearm burned—ice was burrowing in, slicing the skin with a surgeon's precision. Alvis felt the ice sear around the fibers of his muscles and veins, chilling his blood and numbing his arm.

Lamont pushed through the crowd. "Zaile!"

Alvis's next punch met the floor, the sting of splinters breaking the skin of his knuckles feather light. He twisted his head around and searched for Cian with a madman's frenzy.

Cian suddenly reappeared near Rival in a swirl of wind, bloody and blinking. Thrown off by Zaile's teleportation, he stumbled into his Charge, who barely managed to steady him. Cian brushed him off, jerking his elbow from Rival's hold and snarled at Alvis. Blood slid from under his eyepatch and nose, and when he spit at Alvis's feet, it was more red than clear. He raised his hand, frost starting to form on it, but Rival grabbed his arm and forced it down. He was unfazed when Cian turned his snarl on him, barely flinching at the flash of frost slicing into his fingertips, like he had experienced the pain before.

The barkeep stepped up, clapping his hands in a harsh, jarring slap. "Break it up!" he shouted. The old man huffed and pointed from Alvis to Cian. "Ya know the rules—if you want to fight each other, you do it on the battlefield. Not in my bar."

At the mention of the tournament, their audience became boisterous, whooping and hollering.

Alvis raised his head. When their smirks met, Cian's was a satisfying red. "Tomorrow, I'm gonna beat your ass into the ground, *Captain* Cian."

CHAPTER 39

"YOU FOOL. YOU ABSOLUTE *FOOL*."

In the alleyway five blocks over from the bar, Lamont slammed Alvis up against the wall. His head smacked against it. It would probably hurt tomorrow, but right then every part of him was too numb with bitter fury to register it.

On the ground across from him, Rae sat huddled in a ball, face buried in his knees and hands covering his ears.

"We came here to compete, right?" Alvis snapped at Lamont. The wound Cian seared into Alvis's arm still stung. "All I did was get us a match."

Zaile's jaw worked, like she didn't want to be short with Alvis but could only think of how *stupid* he was being. "Against an exiled *Drakon*." She gestured from Alvis to Rae. "One with a big fucking grudge against *both* of you."

"It's not just any *Drakon*," Alvis said darkly, catching Zaile's eyes over Lamont's shoulder. "It's Cian, the bastard who *killed* my dad."

"And what about Rival?" Zaile snapped.

For the first time, Alvis faltered because Zaile was right. Goddammit, *Rival*. Of all the Guardians he could've pick in this fighting town, he landed on fucking *Cian*.

As Alvis struggled for a response, Lamont released him with a harsh shove. "We're withdrawing you from the tournament," he growled. "And you will return to Torne tonight."

"No, I'm not," Alvis bit out through grinding teeth. "I'm fighting Cian tomorrow whether you want me to or not."

Lamont shook his head, frustration peaking. "Tarley was intended to be a test, not a way to call Zen's attention to Rae—or worse—get the two of you killed. Linless has plans for the two of you. What we stand to lose is far greater than a selfish desire for revenge. You can mourn the loss of your father for the rest of your life, but you don't have a right to ruin plans you have agreed to fulfill."

"Then I quit—"

"That is not your decision to make," Aella interrupted. The burning tone of her voice struck Alvis to his core—this was the first time her anger had been directed at him. It wasn't an open anger like Lamont's or Zaile's. There was something much more intimidating in the shine of her hooded, golden eyes. Alvis finally felt himself sobering to the situation—the cold, damp air nipping his nose and ears, the trash-strewn alleyway, and stress emanating from the friends around him.

Goosebumps from the chilly night decorated Aella's skin. She turned her intimidating gaze from Alvis to Rae. She crouched and draped her jacket over Rae's hunched shoulders but refrained from touching him otherwise. Her gold eyes returned to Alvis and the message was clear—she would stand between him and Rae, if it came to that. "After everything Rae has done to get here, you do not get the option of throwing it all away without his consent," Aella said, the biting cold in her voice matching the chill in the air. "If you feel no guilt over the torment you cause your Guardian, then how are you any different from the evil in the world you have chosen to fight against?"

Guilt made the back of Alvis's neck burn. "Th-that's not what this is about! I'm not—"

"I want to fight." Rae still had his head down; the posture was a stark contrast to the conviction in his words. Slowly, he pushed himself to his feet. He raised his head, and in the night shadows of the alleyway, the violet of his eyes glowed, a steeled determination shining through.

"I want to fight tomorrow," Rae repeated. "If quitting Linless is the only way, then so be it."

"Rae—" Zaile and Aella both started to say, but Lamont held up his hand to stop them. "I will contact Princess Meera," he said, sounding displeased but resigned. "If she decides to allow it, I will ensure your match occurs tomorrow."

WHEN LAMONT, ZAILE, AND AELLA LEFT them for the inn and were out of sight, Rae slid back down the alley wall, landing on the moldy concrete with hardly a sound. The trembling in his shoulders eased, but he didn't lift his head when Alvis knelt in front of him.

"Are you able to walk?" Alvis asked quietly.

"My legs aren't injured."

"Not what I asked." Alvis sighed, then turned away, back towards Rae. "C'mon."

There was a brief pause where Alvis knew Rae was scrutinizing every inch of his back. Then Rae's arms wound around Alvis's neck, the weight of him slightly jarring. But it only took a breath for Alvis to dip into his power, holding onto Rae's thighs and easily hiking him up onto his back as he stood. Rae made a small high-pitched noise, surprised, not used to being shuffled around so easily.

Halfway to their inn, Alvis said, "If you don't want to fight tomorrow, you don't need to. It's wouldn't be fair to drag you into something I know will be triggering for you."

Even with Aella's jacket, Rae was shivering. Alvis felt each one against his back, along with the beating of Rae's heart. The tips of Rae's fingers slid beneath the collar of Alvis's shirt and tapped a steady beat against the metal chain, finding comfort in it the same way Alvis did.

"You aren't dragging me into anything," Rae whispered. "I already said I'm doing the match because I want to."

The rest of the walk back to the inn was quiet. When they reached their room, Alvis set Rae down gently before tossing off his shoes. By the time Alvis was changed into sleeping clothes, Rae still hadn't moved or spoken, lost somewhere in his head, and purposefully keeping Alvis out. Alvis was fine letting Rae come to an answer himself. But he also knew how close Rae was to tumbling into an anxious spiral as he hyper-focused on every self-doubt, instead of what they could do if they worked together.

Finally, Alvis grabbed Rae's hand and gently tugged him forward. "Would you be okay if I slept in the bed with you?" he asked, softly, reassuring he would respect Rae's wishes either way.

Rae jerked at Alvis's voice and touch, coming back to the present. His doe-eyes looked at the empty mattress, then the make-shift bed Alvis had made after they reached the inn. The limited light did little to hide the flush on Rae's cheeks. It was plenty obvious what he was thinking of and it made Alvis blush, too.

"Sleeping only," Alvis said quickly. But then he quirked an eyebrow at Rae, challenging. "Unless you'd rather do something else."

Rae took the bait easily, embarrassment easing at the tease. "I'm not thinking anything like that," he clarified. "Sleep where you want."

Alvis laughed. He flopped gracelessly onto one side of the bed, turning his head away to give Rae privacy.

Rae quickly changed out of his clothes and into his night things, then slid under the sheets, making a point to linger as close to the edge of his side of the bed as possible.

The silence was tense. Their private, silent thoughts weighed heavily around them.

Alvis's revenge on Cian wasn't playing out how he thought it would. He wasn't supposed to run into Cian in some random bar. His friend, Rival, wasn't supposed to be Cian's *Charge*—Cian wasn't even supposed to be *in* a Pact. And just as frustrating, Alvis couldn't use his magic tomorrow, when using his strength to overpower and break Cian had been what he'd wanted since his father's death. And now he was leaving the ultimate decision to take on Cian, his moral enemy, in someone else's hands.

"You're anxious about tomorrow."

Crinkling his eyebrow, Alvis turned his head. Rae was an arm's length away, on his back and staring at the same spot on the ceiling Alvis had been. The strain on Alvis's face evened out when he focused on who was in front of him instead of what was coming for them tomorrow. "Yeah, I'm worried."

Rae still stared at the ceiling. "I don't think I've seen you nervous before."

Alvis couldn't remember the last time he was foot-shaking, restless finger-tapping anxious, either. "What about you?"

"Yes," said Rae without hesitation. "Being this nervous is a bizarre feeling. I've always been calm before a match, but this is so . . . different. I don't know what the outcome of this fight may be."

Gnawing on his bottom lip, Rae lifted his left arm and tapped his fingers against the scar above his right wrist. "Tomorrow, I'm scared I'll screw up. That I won't be able to protect—" *you*. Alvis watched Rae swallow. "To protect someone again. I'm still not able to use transference when we spar against other people. Something in me gets frightened and I'm suddenly back to relying on what I know."

Alvis's fingers drifted across the mattress. They tapped against Rae's arm, then reached out and wiggled beneath Rae's palm. Alvis carefully took Rae's hand in his, and Rae let him. "My locket hasn't calmed down since we saw Cian," Alvis said. "All this power is flowing through me and I know I won't be able to use it tomorrow. Not to mention, out of millions of Charges, Cian ends up with Rival. *Rival*. And I have to fight like that doesn't matter, that I won't hurt my friend when I beat the crap out of Cian. I've never fought against someone I care about like this. I want to make this as easy as possible for you, but, *shit*, I don't know how to handle these feelings."

Alvis's voice must have shaken more than he thought it did, because Rae reached out and slid his hand through Alvis's already messy black hair. Alvis stiffened, but when Rae started to pull back, he said, "You don't need to stop."

"You did it to me when you were drunk," Rae quickly explained, the hand less confident, but continuing. From Alvis's bangs around the side and to the back, until the tips slid out from between his fingers. "Even though you were mad at me, you said you were comforting me."

Alvis would be lying if he said he remembered every-thing from that night, but he smiled and nuzzled his head into Rae's touch. "It's what my dad used to do."

Rae was always quick to avert his gaze when he was uncomfortable, so when he met Alvis's eyes, Alvis knew right away where Rae's mind was at.

Maybe they should have talked about strategy. And figured out how exactly Alvis would take on Rival and how Rae would handle Cian. But it was the night before the biggest fight of their lives, and they were both tilting and spinning, while Rae's mantra of breathing pulsed between them. They ached for an anchor in the chaos and uncertainty, and they found it in each other.

Rae's lips pressed against Alvis's first, hesitant and chaste. Alvis responded eagerly, and Rae seemed to lose any reservations holding him back. Hand still buried in Alvis's hair, Rae used his hold to deepen the kiss and turn it into two, then three, then more. His soft gasp as Alvis slid his hands down his back was addicting, so Alvis let his hands roam more. First over Rae's shirt, then under. He stroked his fingertips over Rae's abs and thundering heartbeat but avoided his gemstone scar.

Rae's gasped again when Alvis kissed his neck, nib-bling at the sensitive spot beneath his jaw until Alvis felt the full-body shiver rake through him. Electricity shot down Alvis's own spine; Rae's hands slid from his hair to grip at his biceps and explore his arms, and Alvis was reminded again of how smooth Rae's palms were. Like Alvis was being caressed by hot silk, leaving trails of fire across his skin.

Time slipped away with every breath Rae stole from Alvis's lips. How long had they been kissing now? Was it for minutes or hours? The intensity was beginning to shift, a question mark building between them, until Rae signaled he wasn't ready for more, and Alvis rolled away.

Rae's cheeks were painted red, visible even in the dim light of their room. His lips were swollen, and his breathing was hard like Alvis's. Neither of them had space to think about anything but how the other's touch had felt.

After a moment, Rae inched closer to Alvis again, then inched away, face torn. After the third attempt, Alvis huffed a laugh. Rae glared, then Alvis wrapped his arms around Rae's waist and shuffled forward, burying his face into Rae's chest. He smirked at Rae's confused sputter and at one of his arms sticking straight up in the air like a startled cat's tail.

"Wh-What are you doing?" Rae managed to ask. Any heat in his words was lost when he made no actual move to shake off Alvis. Slowly, Rae lowered his arm, draping it over Alvis's shoulder. Not hugging back, just resting.

"I like that I can touch you without hurting you," Alvis said. He couldn't see Rae's skin turn red again, but he felt the heat of it against his nose.

"Stop saying things like that."

"How about 'I believe in you, Rae'?"

Rae's chuckle was a quick, exasperated exhale through his nose, but Alvis knew his lips were quirking upwards. "No. That's still embarrassing."

" 'Tomorrow, we'll win together'?"

"That's acceptable, I suppose."

"Tomorrow, we'll win together."

"Together . . . as Pact . . . Partners," Rae agreed.

Alvis laughed into Rae's chest, into his pounding heartbeat, and held on tighter. "Yeah, as Pact Partners."

CHAPTER 40

THE FOLLOWING DAY CAME TOO QUICKLY.

The fog was heavy in the morning and lingered through the day. Mist slowly dampened clothes, and the sky was dark and threating rain.

Rae hoped the inclement weather would deter a crowd, and he and Alvis were a last-minute exhibition match before the semi-finals—no doubt secretly bribed into existence by Linless. June stadium was at full capacity—word had apparently still gotten out that two Pacts fighting today had a personal grudge. Combined with the semi matches, no one in Tarley would dare miss an event like this. Rae looked out at the sea of faces above them. Old panoramas of past tournament crowds tried to superimpose over his vision. Tarley had no bright screens with closeups of Rae's face or his name being cheered even before he was victorious. Rae had hoped it would loosen the gross twist of nerves in the pit of his stomach, but the knot was still wound tight.

There was a reassuring squeeze on Rae's shoulder. "Don't focus on them," said Alvis, breath warm against his ear. He nodded across the field. "Focus on *him*."

On the opposite stone stage stood Cian and Rival. Cian looked maniacally giddy, so unable to control his excitement that his breaths were icing the air. Next to him, Rival seemed far less amused. Arms crossed, he stared at his feet, twin knives still sheathed.

"I've never gone into a fight with Cian where I wasn't sure I could win," Rae said. He looked from Rival to Alvis. "Are you going to be okay against him?"

Alvis hesitated, then shrugged, not forcing a smile. "I'll need to be. At least I've sparred against him before, so I'll know how he moves."

The gong sounded. And the crowd roared. Ready or not, it was time to prove the last month had been worth it.

Cian hadn't transformed yet, despite the cheers demanding it. He made his way across the field to greet Alvis and Rae in the middle, Rival trailing behind him at a much slower pace. Cian never dropped his gaze, watching Alvis with an eerie intensity.

"This makes me quite happy," Cian purred, as they all congregated at the center of the arena. "I didn't believe I would have the opportunity to repay you so soon."

Alvis's jaw worked; fists already prepared to unleash revenge. "You killed my dad, *Cian*," he growled.

"And you cost *me* everything, *Alvis Witt*." Cian tapped the black patch stretched across his face. "An eye for an eye.

Commander Volos will be pleased when I return with your—"

"You are speaking to my Charge, Cian," Rae stated, the words like unrelenting venom. "I suggest biting your tongue."

Something like heartbreak passed through Cian's expression, but he sneered before Rae could hope against hope that Cian still cared about him. That this brokenness between them could be fixed. "You have become a disgrace, Rae," Cian spat bitterly. "Our family name was wasted on you."

The audience's howls were growing impatient.

Alvis and Rae each took one last, long breath. When Alvis placed his left palm on Rae's forehead, Rae allowed himself to lean into it.

"Hey," said Alvis.

Rae raised his eyes. Violet met green, determination offering comfort.

"We've got this."

All Rae could do was nod.

"*Release.*" The crowd roared as brilliant purple light filled the arena.

Rae landed next to Alvis with hardly a sound. Without hesitation, Alvis lifted a hand, resting it on Rae's long, pale neck just below his soft, purple mane. The warmth of his scales was a calming pressure against his thundering heart.

A radiant blue light flashed, and Cian roared and flared his cobalt blue dragon wings. One of his sapphire eyes was gone, a scar across the lid. The light barely had time to clear before his sword, made of sharpened ice, cut through the mist, destination evident. But Rae was there before it could land on Alvis, easily stopping it with his claw. He spread his purple wings and propelled himself forward. Cian didn't fight back as Rae pushed them to the other side of the field, then slammed him up against the invisible stadium wall, cheers erupting.

"Very good!" Cian sang, pure mockery. His wings were splayed out around him; they blocked enough of the cheering audience for Rae's focus to remain on his thrilled expression. "Welcome back, Bloodied Champion!"

ALVIS SAW RAE SLAM CIAN up against the wall, and he probably should have been focused on it to make sure Rae was okay, but he couldn't turn away from the outline becoming clearer with each spiral of settling dust.

Rival was staring at him, too. Neither of them moved.

Alvis was used to standoffs and waiting to see who would throw the first punch. He gladly took those on. But this was different. Words needed to happen, but he had no idea who was supposed to begin, or what the first ones should be.

Finally, Alvis groaned. "Why are you in a Pact with someone like *him*?"

Rival shrugged before Alvis finished. "You don't come across many former *Drakon* in these parts. A strong Guardian means easier wins, which means more money."

He tilted his head back towards a shrill, excited roar. Cian and Rae were above them now, exchanging even blows mid-air, neither gaining an inch. "Didn't realize you knew each other, or that Rae used to be a Ranker. But there are a lot of things you left out. Right, *Chosen One*?"

Alvis flinched. He hadn't thought about Cian dropping Alvis's secret to Rival after last night, but he couldn't say he was surprised. Of course, Cian would rile Rival up and drive a wedge between his and Alvis's friendship. Make him angry to ensure he didn't hold himself back when he and Alvis fought against each other.

"C'mon, Rival," said Alvis, trying to quell the fire rising in Rival's eyes. "It's not like I wanted you to find out from that bastard, but you know why I couldn't tell you. You know how I feel about you. Just because I'm a Chosen One doesn't change that I'm your friend."

There was still anger simmering in Rival's eyes, but Alvis knew which kind of anger it was.

"Have you been holding back against me this entire time?" asked Rival.

"No," replied Alvis. He wasn't lying; there had been more than once where Alvis had used his magic to break out of Rival's hold. And when Rival won, it hadn't been because Alvis was letting him do it. "If someone sucks at fighting, they'd lose a lot quicker than you ever did."

Rival softened, relieved. Then, he closed the distance between them in a few short steps. He wrapped his arms around Alvis's shoulder and pulled him forward into a hug, and Alvis leaned into it easily. "Man, I really don't want to fight you," Alvis mumbled into Rival's shoulder.

Rival exhaled a gentle laugh. It took Alvis back to that first night in the bar, when Rival decided Alvis was an okay person to sit with, and their laughter led to sparring in the parks or Rival's backyard, and Rival giving Alvis unhelpful advice every time he complained about Rae-this and Rae-that.

Now, they stood on opposite sides, fighting for an audience that would settle for nothing less than full out attacks and blood.

But Rival would never be Cian's Charge—to Alvis, Rival would only be Rival.

Arms wrapped around Rival like he was a lifeline, Alvis said, "Thanks for being my friend."

There was a gentle pat against Alvis's shoulder, an unspoken agreement. Then a knee drove up into his stomach.

"Dude!" Alvis choked out, hunched over and coughing. "Cheap shot!"

Rival grinned, shrugging. "You shouldn't let your guard down so eas—"

The words cut off into a wheeze as Alvis's foot collided with his unguarded ribs. Rival groaned, grabbing at his now aching side while Alvis quickly put distance between them, fists raised and ready. "Shouldn't let your guard down so easily," Alvis sang, enjoying the way Rival's eyes lit up through his pain at the challenge. He tightened his stance and mirrored Rival's smile from before.

"Cheeky lil' shit." Rival straightened, pushing away the hit with a stretch. He grasped the handles of his knives, slid them free, and swung them forward in one fluid motion. "Let's see you try."

CHAPTER 41

"A PACT WORKS WELL FOR YOU," CIAN SAID. "Unsurprising, given how far you've fallen."

Rae fluttered his wings, unaffected. "Perhaps that's why you've taken to it so well yourself."

Cian growled and adjusted his grip on the hilt of his sword, swinging it into Rae's side hard enough to send him flying despite not penetrating. "Once I bring you and Alvis back to Zen, Commander Volos will cheer my name." Cian grinned, breath shaking with glee. "She will return my gemstone, and I will kill Rival like I never dirtied my hands with such filth."

A sudden surge of anger at Cian's threat made Rae rush forward. He slammed the palm of his left dragon hand into Cian's hollowed eye socket and snarled, "I will *never* let you kill a Charge."

The stadium shook as Cian crashed into the ground,

the crowd cheering. Rae ignored them, but then a stinging pang startled him from diving in and landing another
blow. Rae grabbed at his side, initially wondering if Cian
had pierced him with an icicle, but there was no wound.

ALVIS HATED KNIVES. He really freakin' *hated* knives.

Rival stared down at one of his own curved blades.
Blood dripped from the very edge. He whistled, impressed. "Nice dodge."

It didn't *feel* like a nice dodge. With a huff, Alvis put
more pressure onto the fresh gash above his hip. His hand
came away red, but it could have come away redder, so
hopefully it wasn't as bad as it felt.

Alvis shook it off and lunged. He sidestepped Rival's
next slice, then spun to grab Rival's open arm. He dug his
elbow into the tender spot behind his collarbone before
he twisted the arm behind his back. Alvis curled his foot
around Rival's opposite ankle and jerked, sending them
tumbling to the ground, knee pressed into Rival's lower
back. Rival groaned when his arm was tugged further
back until the socket threatened to pop.

"Damn," Rival breathed into the dirt when Alvis
pushed his face into it, equal parts winded from the fight
and impressed. Alvis relented enough for him to turn his
face to the side and smirk up at him.

Opposite sides or not, Alvis couldn't repress his beaming grin under the compliment. Then reality settled on

him again when Rival tried to pull himself free of Alvis's hold.

Alvis caught a peek of Rae from the corner of his eye. Alvis needed to break Rival's arm, incapacitate him enough to where it either forced Cian out of his Guardian form or gave Rae an easier time against him. It was an easy thing to do. He knew how to do it by heart. But, still, he hesitated. Rival's pulse was racing against his fingertips. Alvis liked Rival's voice—he didn't want to hear what it sounded like when he screamed in pain.

Rival's wrist was suddenly stinging cold beneath his palm. Alvis yelped and yanked his hand back, flinching as he stumbled away. When he looked at his hand, his eyes widened at the freezing blisters forming along his palm.

Cian cackled from across the field. He lounged casually in the crater he'd made from Rae's attack. One of his long claws was raised and pointed in their direction.

How? asked Rae through their Pact link.

Ignore it, Rae, Alvis said back, keeping his voice steady where Rae's shook.

But how?

Alvis's jaw worked and he swung towards Rae. But Rae was too focused on Cian's pointing claw, eyes unseeing to anything beyond it.

Rae, ignore *it. So, Cian can use transference. Just keep doing what you're already doing. Rae!*

"Y'know," said Rival. "I think I figured out why you're staying with Rae." Rival stood, rolling the strain out of his arm, and glanced over his shoulder to where Rae was crouched, wings drawn back against his shoulders. "You've been confusing me this whole time, since you could have picked any Guardian who actually gave a shit about protecting you."

"I don't *need* him to protect me." Alvis shook out his hand, but all it did was make the blisters sting more. "You have no idea what Rae is dealing with."

"And that's the reason you're with him. He's broken and you think you can fix him."

Alvis's stomach did a weird plummeting thing he couldn't explain. Rival had hit a nail on the head, but Alvis didn't know what to make of it, or why it made him feel so *guilty*. "Rae isn't broken," he responded through grinding teeth.

It was true—Rae was closed off. He was also passive aggressive. And he wore anxiety on his shoulders like a cloak. Rae was many difficult things, but Alvis had never once thought of him as broken.

Alvis lunged—this was a fight. Alvis wasn't interested in talking about this nonsense when he knew this battle couldn't drag on. The crowd turned Rae into a ticking time bomb. If they didn't finish quickly, the more opportunity Cian had to push Rae over the edge.

Rival was prepared for Alvis's charge. He sprinted forward—blades raised. Alvis twisted backwards as the right one cut into the air where he'd previously stood.

"I've told you before, you can learn a lot from switching Guardians," Rival said. "Like how you need at least a *bit* of mutual trust."

The next fist aimed for Rival's face was well-timed,

but Alvis's stance was sloppy thanks to his injury. Rival ducked and kicked Alvis's feet out from under him, sending him to the ground with an aggravated grunt.

"Here you are, believing in him, trying for him—" Rival dug his heel into the wound at Alvis's side. Alvis covered his pain with a growl. Rival nudged the underside of Alvis's chin with the tip of his left blade, forcing him to look Rival in the eyes. "And how's he trying to support you?"

CHAPTER 42

RAE WAS LOSING.

Alvis was getting hurt—Rae wasn't protecting him.

Logic told him Alvis was trying to pull him back from the looming edge of his sanity. But logic was losing its hold as every thought began and ended with a pounding between his ears, punctuated by screams.

He couldn't stop himself from circling back—*how* was Cian able to use transference so successfully?

Cian, who planned to kill his Charge, who had only been in a Pact for days. How was he able to do what Rae had so desperately been trying to do for weeks? Cian had easily used transference in the middle of his fight with Rae—he'd been paying attention to his Charge, despite the battle and the fact he was planning to later kill Rival.

Rae was scared of looking at Alvis. Of breaking his concentration on Cian, because if he did, the crowd might permeate the white noise he was forcing to keep them out.

Claws suddenly wrapped around his throat.

"Distracted in a fight?" sneered Cian, squeezing tighter. "How unlike you, Bloodied Champion."

Rae fought against the lurch in his stomach at the name.

There was a wild giddiness in Cian's eyes. "Does it still bother you to hear your true name? Or perhaps you need to hear it more?"

Rae gritted his sharp teeth, refusing to answer as he slammed a claw harder than steel into Cian's face. It was a punch fueled by desperation. Cian's hold faltered and he put distance between them again, but the joy in his eyes didn't lessen. "Ladies and gentlemen!" Cian spun to address the crowd in a projecting voice, his blue scales catching the weak light. All eyes were suddenly on him. "Are you aware what *special* guest you have the honor to see tonight?"

Rae's eyes widened. "Stop it."

"I present to you . . ."

Rae grabbed at Cian's throat with a snarl, ready to clench his fingers until his trachea shattered and he gagged his final breath. But he was too slow.

"The *Bloodied Champion*, himself! Zen's greatest Ranker in history!"

Rae froze—so fast his wings stopped working and he dropped to the ground, landing harshly on all fours. His long neck was tense, pulled tight and straight as he stared at the ground before him. There was a deafening silence throughout the entire stadium. Then mumblings started, building quickly, as realization began to dawn on spectator after spectator.

" 'Bloodied Champion?' Isn't that—"

No—this wasn't happening.

"Zen's strongest Ranker?"

Please stop. Please don't ruin this—

"The actual Bloodied Champion!"

I'm a Guardian, I'm not the—

"What was it they used to cheer for you?" asked Cian, his words too loud, too innocent. He landed softly in front of Rae. Cian lowered his head and pushed his face into Rae's, their snouts nearly pressing against each other. "Champion." The breath of it danced across Rae's face. "Champion. Champion! Champion!"

"Champion!" The crowd picked up the chant. "Champion! *Champion!*"

At first, Rae's head was utterly quiet. Maybe it would be different this time, he thought. Maybe everything he had been working on since being in the Pact would change things. But the hope was shorter than a panted breath. He should have known better. The screaming voice in his head was growing again, mixing with the chants of the bloodthirsty crowd. That bottomless black pit was opening up inside him, sucking him in. He was spiraling towards it and his defenses were crumbling.

"CHAMPION! CHAMPION! CHAMPION!"

Rae shook himself, hard enough that his head slammed against the clear barrier around the stadium. It felt like nothing, and maybe it would shake the screams from his head, so he did it again, then again. But from behind the barrier, *that* name was so loud, too loud—or was that the screaming?

It was *himself* screaming.

He lashed out with his claw, slamming it into the transparent wall. He scratched as hard as he could, because if he could destroy something, then maybe he wouldn't be the one to break. But the wall didn't give.

With a terrified cry, he rushed backwards and away, claws catching in the ground and making him flail.

"CHAMPION! CHAMPION! CHAMPION!"

The chants didn't stop—why didn't they stop? Didn't everyone know how *scary* that name was? They should be too scared to say it.

Rae's breaths were coming out wild and frantic. He wrapped his wings around himself—they were his last, pathetic defense. How else was he going to protect himself . . .

Breathe, breathe, breathe, breathe . . .

CHAMPION! CHAMPION! CHAMPION!

Rae roared.

THE CHANTS WERE DEAFENING.

Alvis screamed Rae's name as he lay pinned in the dirt. A screech answered him back, so loud in his head he flinched and covered his ears. It faded but didn't disappear, lingering at the back of his head, growing louder, then retreating again in a continuous wave.

" 'Bloodied Champion'?" murmured Rival. Awe fell over his rugged face as his brown eyes snapped back down to Alvis under his boot. Apparently, Cian had kept at least one secret about him and Rae. "Wait—*Rae* is Zen's Bloodied Champion?"

There was another biting screech in Alvis's head. He pounded his temple with the heel of his hand, fending it off. "*Don't* call him that," Alvis hissed through gritted teeth.

Rae was backed up to the stadium wall, side flattened against it. His wings curled around his back like a comforting blanket as he trembled. His white lips were pulled as far back as possible, threatening fangs bared, and breaths so heavy, dust swirled around him every time he exhaled.

The crowd chanted louder than before. Rae roared again, the painful plea of a desperate animal. He crouched on all fours and scratched at the ground with his hind legs. Roaring again, he slammed his head into the ground. Again, and again. Alvis felt the ache of it beneath the front of his skull.

Alvis needed to get to Rae. Now. He grabbed at the duller edge of Rival's knife, prepared to shatter it if Rival didn't drop it away. "Let me go, Rival. I don't want to hurt you."

The words weren't intended as a challenge, but Alvis should have known Rival would take them that way. Alvis would have, too, if he had just found out his opponent— his *friend*—was a Chosen One. And his friend's Charge was the frickin' Bloodied Champion of Zen. "*Rival*—"

"If I let you up so easily, it will be the same as me throwing the match," said Rival. His left blade pressed even further into Alvis's neck, leaving the sliver of a cut. "I can't do that. Even for you."

Rae's claws ran across his own snout, over and over. Never deep enough to bleed, but hard enough that he and Alvis felt the scratches left behind. It was like Rae was stopping himself from doing something far more terrifying with them.

Alvis pulled his knees to his chest and kicked, both feet nailing Rival perfectly in the stomach with more force than necessary. The sudden intensity of it caught Rival off guard, he stumbled backwards without raising his blade far enough away—it sliced through Alvis's shirt and split his skin in a long cut from his collarbone to the top of his ribcage. Perfectly through the Pact tattoo on his chest shaped liked a metal flower.

A howl tore from Rae.

Alvis stumbled into a sprint—and slid to a stop, wounds screaming at the lurch.

Taller than most Guardians, Cian walked in his dragon form the same way he did as a human; a sluggish stalk with long, sliding steps, like he knew the prey was already his. "Your father's sacrifice is quite pitiful now; dying to help you escape, and here you are, mine for the taking." Cian's sword dragged in the dirt, leaving ice in its wake. "What was it you said? You would 'beat me into the ground?' What empty words."

The hairs on the back of Alvis's neck stood up. Cian's towering dragon form stepped between him and Rae. Alvis's mind raced, searching through every previous fight, every other training session—*everything*—trying desperately to figure out what would help him win here.

A tortured cry resounded in his mind. Alvis blinked against the tears blurring his vision. Another cry reached his ears. He followed the sound—Rae was still writhing and hissing on the ground. His violet eyes were dangerous, frantic. They craved blood. They cried for help.

The words were slow to gather themselves, but when they did, Alvis felt a frightening calm settle over him. "I'm not fighting alone," he whispered.

Rae screeched again.

Alvis dug his heels into the ground.

"Alvis, run away!" Rival called from somewhere behind him, smart enough to stand far away from Cian. "You can't fight against a Guardian in their dragon form by yourself!"

"I'm not fighting alone." Alvis repeated louder.

Rae's next scream fell into a desperate wail.

Cian cackled—it was the obnoxious one he did when he knew things were going his way and it was hilarious to see Alvis think otherwise. It bounced and echoed off the stadium walls, making it seem endless. "You believe *he* can help you? Rae is nothing but a broken excuse of a Guardian. He's a *Kon*—a Fallen *Drakon*, and he can never amount to anything more!"

"I'm *not* fighting *alone!*" It echoed against the chants tearing Rae apart.

Cian growled. "Stop *saying* that."

Alvis grabbed at his own chest, sliced and bleeding. He balled his fist and pounded it against his racing heart. Against his Talisman, burning hot and glowing gold.

383

Against the Pact tattoo of swirling metal that connected him to something more. He raised his head, craned his neck back as far as it would go, and pushed back against Cian's frightening glare with one of his own.

Hey, Rae, Alvis said through their link.

"Come at me with whatever you want, you ugly lizard." Alvis relaxed his fist and splayed his fingers over his and Rae's Pact tattoo. He dug his nails into the already broken skin until it bled even more.

I'm about to do something really *stupid, Rae.*

"Because I'm going to catch that stupid sword—"

I'm trusting you to help me out, okay?

"—and then punch your fuckin' face in."

It was with a madman's fury that Cian howled and slashed his sword down at him, all reason gone and every piece of strength he possessed going into the swing of it.

Alvis raised his hands.

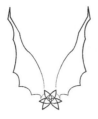

CHAPTER 43

IT WAS FINALLY QUIET.

The screaming and chants had finally been swallowed by the gloom embracing him. The relief of it rocked through him. Rae wished he could stay here forever. No more pain. No more screaming. No more fighting. Just quiet and solitude.

He stood there for a moment, still afraid to open his eyes and unclench his hands from his ears, in case it was all a cruel lie.

Fingers slid through Rae's own. Interlocking, they gently tugged them off Rae's ears, pried them loose from his hair. It took all of Rae's effort to unclench his eyelids and open his eyes, blinking hard against the sudden brightness around him.

In front of him was a figure he didn't know. But this person had been in Rae's dreams lately, ever since Alvis and Rae had grown closer.

The figure never said anything in those dreams. But if they did, Rae somehow knew he would recognize their voice in an instant. Around their neck was the outline of a necklace, a blinding light holding back the darkness around them.

Unlike all the other dreams, the fuzzy gray surrounding the figure was fading. The face beneath was finally revealed.

It was one Rae knew too well.

"Hello, Rae."

Rae's eyes widened. "You're . . ." He had been wrong—he barely recognized the voice even though it was his own. This other Rae's sounded so much lighter; so . . . *at ease.* And that smile—how many times had Rae seen his smile in the mirror? When was the last time he allowed himself to see its rarity again?

"I'm you," the Other Rae confirmed, using a sarcasm Rae usually reserved for the stupidest of responses. The Other Rae smiled again. "And I'm here to bring you back."

"I can't go back," Rae said, quivering. "It's shameful. How can I—everyone has seen it. See me *fail.*"

Linless. Cian. The crowd. They had all bared witness to his weakness and shame, unwillingly thrown on display.

Alvis.

Alvis had promised to help Rae stop tumbling, but this wasn't a simple burden. His was a monster finally released. "*Alvis* has seen me fail." That admission hurt worse than the others combined.

"Alvis is helping you because you let him see you."

"I'm *broken.*"

"You aren't broken, Rae."

Cold hands tightened around his own. They turned Rae's arm over and swiped a hand over his scar. Not to make it disappear, but to piece it back together, make it something new. "You're breaking down—there's a difference."

"You sound like Alvis," Rae said.

"He's influencing us, I suppose," replied the Other Rae, offering a small smile. He reached under the collar of his shirt and pulled a chain over his neck, then cradled it in his open palm. Rae leaned forward for a glance—it was a small piece of metal. Black with a tint of red, it was an impossible design of countless chains linked together. From the center grew flaring petals, sharp edged like a blade, then a stem of two lines of metal forming into a delicate hook.

Rae knew what it was. He had seen the mark on Alvis's chest. It had long been seared into his mind as the piece of himself he had given away.

The Other Rae smiled again, peaceful, calm, and relieved. "Breaking down isn't the end, Rae. You're *rebuilding*."

Suddenly, the small flower began to unfold, like dominos falling into place, pulling itself into a fully bloomed flower, floating above the Other Rae's palm. It was shining silver, flawless, and beautiful.

"Now, prove it," said the Other Rae. "Show them you belong to no one, Rae. Reclaim yourself—" The rose settled into Rae's waiting hand and it was like finding his wings for the first time. "—and *breathe*."

CIAN'S SWORD CUT THROUGH THE AIR on its downward slash.

Alvis never expected he would be *this* calm as he watched death fall towards him.

Then there was pressure. Something strong slammed into him, forcing itself against his open palms. Beneath the skin of his hands, something heavy and deep pulsed—a protective callus he had felt only a handful of times before and could never forget. The pressure was both cold and warm. It thrilled him and wrapped him in comfort. The force folded around his bones, branding them, until they were surly glowing. The design of his Pact tattoo lit up, shining violet through his shirt and down his left arm.

The ground cracked under Alvis's feet as he bent his knees. The cut on his chest burned as he reached up, but he screamed against it. He screamed so loud his throat ached. Screamed louder than Cian laughed. Screamed louder than the screech that had tormented Rae's mind.

From the corner of his eye, Alvis saw him: Saw Rae, panting like he was coming up for air, hand raised and steady with three claws curled.

Alvis's hands connected with the icy blade of Cian's giant sword.

It stopped dead.

Dust plumed as the earth shook around him with the reverberation of the blow, casting chunks of mud aside.

This was crazy, Alvis thought. But it felt so natural, like he should've always been stopping giant ice swords with his bare hands.

Alvis twisted, and with a shout, threw the ice sword with enough strength for Cian to tumble along with it. He and the blade flew. The sword scratched against the ground, throwing dirt and ice into the air as Cian attempted to use it to pull himself to a stop.

Alvis raced to Rae's side. He gently cupped Rae's snout in his hands and helped him raise his elegant head.

Violet met green.

"You did it," Alvis said, breathless. "Rae, you fuckin' *did it*. You used transference! Your attribute saved me— saved *us*."

Beneath his hands, Rae's scales grew warm like gratitude, comfort, and relief all rolled into one. Slowly Rae bent his head— an offering for Alvis to climb.

Heart beating like mad, and excitement making him feel invincible, Alvis stepped forward without hesitation. Steadily gripping the white horns adorning Rae's head, Alvis pulled himself up behind his ears, ahead of the spikes running down Rae's spine. Rae's purple wings spread and flapped, calm and controlled, so unlike how he was minutes before.

Across the field, Cian pulled himself up onto all fours, snarling. His white-hot rage grew when he caught Alvis grinning down at him. Spears of ice as long as Cian formed in the air, one after another, in a semi-circle around him. But before Cian could shoot them off, Alvis slid off Rae into his outstretched and waiting claw.

"This is the best you can come up with, Bloodied Champion? The human boy?" Cian jeered, but there was a new edge to his smile, one Alvis recognized as disguising doubt.

Cian adjusted his clawed hand—his icicles ready to meet Rae and Alvis's attack head-on. "A mere human can't fight against a Guardian alone!"

Rae's wings stretched, threatening, as the scaled arm holding Alvis gradually raised him past Rae's ear and behind his head, then higher still, until Rae's arm was wound up as far as it could.

Out of the corner of his eye, Alvis saw Rae grin. A coy pull of the lips and flash of dragon teeth that was so different from his human smile but just as captivating.

This, Alvis thought. *This is my Guardian.*

Rae gently tightened his claws around Alvis. "My Charge is not fighting alone."

Alvis felt Rae's arm move forward with all his strength. His grip loosened until Alvis was hurtling headfirst, cutting through the air towards Cian.

The warm-cold brand around Alvis's bones surged to life again, setting his Pact tattoo ablaze, flaring like he was a star streaking across the night sky.

With an animalistic growl, Cian released his icicle spears at Alvis. They cut through the air—and shattered uselessly against Alvis's arms, torso, and legs.

Alvis's momentum was buffeted by the blow, and Rae's skin-hardening attribute had increased his weight, but Rae's throw was strong and perfectly aimed.

Alvis curled his fingers into a fist. Rae's attribute

coiled around Alvis's knuckles and hugged his wrist. It whispered a promise to Alvis to put his all into this next move.

For once in his life, Alvis didn't need to hold back.

He didn't have to concern himself with hitting too hard. He could pour every ounce of his attribute into this single punch. A punch for his dad's death, a punch for Rae's pain, and a punch for all those who had fallen to Cian.

The grotesque crack of Cian's blue jaw beneath his fist was euphoric. The way his lengthy, scaled neck twisted from the force was the most satisfying thing Alvis had ever experienced.

Cian's towering dragon body twirled and slammed into the ground, so hard the stands shook. He lay still. Then a flash a blue light returned him to his crumpled, human form.

The crowd sat stunned. Then, in a burst, cheers erupted, boisterous and unrestrained, rattling the arena and Alvis's ears.

He lifted his gaze from the crowd to the sky. He smiled up at Rae.

They had won.

CHAPTER 44

THEY HAD WON.

They had *won!*

Rae flew over and came to a rest beside Alvis. After barely a single beat of silence, Alvis jumped and wrapped his arms around his scaled neck, burying his face into it as he laughed.

Rae's white scales burned in a red flush. He contracted his limbs, and in a flash of purple light he was suddenly back in his human form. Rae quickly stepped to the side, letting Alvis stumble face first to the ground from the sudden change.

Rival snorted, catching Rae's attention. Rival quirked an eyebrow. "Only a Charge, huh?"

With ears burning red, Rae said, "I don't know what you're saying."

Suddenly, the cacophony in the stadium dropped into confused murmurings.

Into the overhead speakers, the master of ceremony's voice said, "Excuse me! The field is for participants and referees only. Please exit the arena, now!"

In what had been an empty center field seconds ago, now stood three cloaked figures. Heat suddenly drained from Rae's body.

One of the referees stepped forward and held up his hand, attribute prepared. "Remove yourselves!"

"Destre," said the shortest of the three people. Her voice was oddly light and familiar—it sent a sudden shiver down Rae's spine. Behind her, the one called Destre reached out their hand and placed it on the speaker's shoulder.

Suddenly, the shortest figure was gone.

A teleportation technique—almost identical to Zaile's. Rae would have easily mistaken the two if he hadn't fought against Zaile countless times. Where she used air to pull people to where she wanted them, this was a water-based attribute. It called water molecules into the ground, then slid them and the object being transported in a blink. A temperamental attribute that thrived on moisture and was a risk to use when there was none.

Here in the mist, it was dangerously accurate.

The referee opened his mouth to shout again, but the short figure appeared in front of him. She tapped his knuckles playfully before stepping back. The referee made a motion to call his magic, but his water attribute barely formed on his fingertips before it vanished. Confused, he tried again, twisting his fingers and straining, his arms shaking with the attempt. He tried again, and again, sweat growing on his brow and expression bending into fear.

The figure turned to rejoin their companions, tossing back the hood of the coal-black cloak. "No need to worry," she said brightly. "Your attribute will return shortly."

Rae's stomach dropped.

There was only one Guardian—one *Drakon*—who could take powers away as easily as she could make them stronger. The King's right-hand since the age of fifteen. The *Drakon* every other *Drakon* was smart enough to fear.

"Rae?" asked Alvis, when Rae grabbed his arm and tugged him behind himself, attribute briefly attaching itself to Alvis's entire skin on instinct.

"It's Commander Volos," Rae hissed back. The spike of fear Rae felt from Alvis rivaled his own.

"What? How the hell would she know we're here?"

Volos looked exactly how Rae remembered her: Bright, blue hair fluorescent against her white skin. Eyes a combination of honey gold and neon pink. Lips painted silver to match her nails. The giddy, genuine smile on her face as a she skipped over to where Cian lay splayed on the ground, crouching next to him.

"C-Commander," Cian wheezed, the words pushing past the swelling on his face. "I—"

Volos pressed her finger into Cian's fractured jaw, forcing him to gag. "Cian, Cian," she chided, still smiling. "What have you done?"

"I saw Rae . . . I wanted to bring him back . . . ! Like you and the King wanted!"

Volos's gaze moved to Rae, to Alvis, then back to Cian. A perfectly filed nail dragged down Cian's broken cheek. She tilted his chin back, her gold and pink eyes softening as they met the hope in his blue ones. "Your ambition is admirable as always, Cian." Then Volos grabbed Cian's chin and pulled, popping his tender jaw out of place. Tears streaked down Cian's cheeks. "However, an ambitious traitor is still a traitor. Flaunting a Pact so publicly?" Volos clicked her tongue. "Now, now, Cian! You should know better."

Volos released him—Cian's entire jaw hung loose, tongue trying to form words but only managing slurred syllables. Without a pause, Volos dug her hand into Cian's blonde hair and yanked, craning his neck back, the twist of it almost unnatural. She held him steady, forcing his gaze to Alvis, Rae, and Rival. She leaned into Cian's ear. "Allow me to remind you how fragile a Pact truly is."

Destre—the water-*Drakon*—touched the shoulder of Volos's unnamed companion and they vanished. When they reappeared, their hand was pressed against Rival's chest before he could so much as blink, or Cian could do more than choke out a desperate plea. Blood burst from between Rival's shoulder blades and out his back in a grotesque spray, stunning the stadium into silence.

The blade made of hardened scales slid itself free. Rival stumbled backwards and Alvis reached his arms out, catching him. Red stained and foamed from Rival's lips when he coughed.

The hood of Rival's murderer fell away, and Rae's world tilted.

The young woman's eyes were the same dark purple he remembered. Her white hair was now a copper black, but Rae still knew her face as well as he knew his own.

Like dust blowing away in the breeze, the Pact tattoo on Rival's arm disappeared, and the life faded from Cian's eyes.

Bright blood dripping from her pale fingertips, Hanah turned to Rae and smiled. "Hello, Rae."

CHAPTER 45

THE BLOOD RUNNING FROM RIVAL'S CHEST WAS warm—too warm for a heart to be so still beneath Alvis's palm.

"Hey," said Alvis, gently shaking his friend. "Rival, get up. C'mon, dude, *get up*." But Rival's eyes remained open and staring, glossed over. And his lips were parted, instead of smirking.

Strand by strand, Volos released Cian's hair, until his head fell limp into the dirt. She clapped her hands together, cleaning them of stains and the grime of someone else's life.

Fingers shaking, Alvis closed Rival's eyes, the picture of their emptiness seared into his own. He knew Rae could feel it—the white, hot rage pulsing throughout his body. The heat from his locket as he tried to maintain control over it.

The girl with ebony hair that had stolen Rival's life must have sensed something, too, because Alvis had barely stood before she lunged at him. Rae jumped between them, throwing up his arm, hardened skin shining. A screeching whistle pierced the air as metal met metal, the force of it pushing Rae into Alvis's chest, both of their heels digging into the ground to stop them from falling.

Rival's blood dripped from the girl's blade made of scales and onto Rae's arm, turning the reflective skin red. She pressed harder—it was easy to see now that her weapon was a part of her; skin that flowed seamlessly into scales that hardened into a blade. Magic that was the perfect offensive twin to Rae's defensive attribute.

It clicked in Alvis's mind. The same attribute; the same violet eyes and face . . .

"Why, Hanah?" whispered Rae. "Why do you have an attribute? Why are you *alive*?"

Hanah stared at him over their straining arms, violet clashing with violet. "Do not speak to me as though we are equals, *brother*. Not when you gave up *everything* I helped you create. Not when you gave up on *me* and fell so low you created a Pact."

A sob tore itself from Rae's throat and he faltered. Alvis could feel Rae's heart breaking and his shoulders shaking against him, the sweat and misting rain clinging their shirts together.

How dare she.

Alvis's rage was beginning to boil to the surface, spurred by the heat of his Talisman.

How dare Rae's sister appear from the dead. How dare

she stab at Rae with tormenting words the same ways she stabbed Rival through the heart.

Alvis took hold of Rae's shoulder—ignoring his surprised gasp—and pushed him out of the way. Hanah stumbled forward with a jerk, and before she could regain her balance, Alvis grabbed the sensitive part of her arm where skin turned to scales. He felt a sick satisfaction watching Hanah's eyes widen with fear—she wasn't prepared for the emerald fire of his gaze searing into her wide, purple eyes. "If you think Pacts are so worthless," he growled. "Then we'll show you just how *worthless* we can be."

Beneath his grip, the top of Hanah's blade cracked. She screamed and Alvis let her pull her arm away. His leg connected with her side, and she barely bit back another scream at the nauseating crack. She sailed through the air then crashed into the ground, rolling back towards Volos like she was nothing more than a ragdoll. Alvis lunged after her—he was running on animal instinct now; his fury focused and strength unrestrained.

He would kill them. All of them. Pull them apart until they were as still as Rival—

Stop! Please!

Rae slammed himself against Alvis's stomach and dug his heels into the ground, pushing them to a stop. His nails were digging into the open wound on Alvis's chest, but neither of them could feel the pain. Anger still pulsed through Alvis's limbs and made his teeth clench around growls and heavy exhales. But the fog in Alvis's mind cleared enough for him to hear the screeching static in Rae's head.

"Alvis Witt," said Volos over the commotion. She moved around Hanah struggling up from the dirt and towards them, strides quick and short, and her words a happy chirp. "Who knew a Chosen One had been living so close to Nerwen City for so long? I do think it's time for you to come home, Alvis—"

Metal cut through the air and impaled itself into the ground at Volos's foot just short of her next step. With a slow drag of her eyes, Volos followed the trail of the arrow.

From the lower stands, bicep flexed and tattoo proudly on display, Tal stood. His gaze was unyielding as he held Volos's eyes.

Volos's expression darkened. She began to snarl, teeth barred—and then she giggled and turned away from Tal. "Well, well," she sang, tossing her arms up in a theatrical shrug. "Looks like Zen isn't the only one interested in *using* you, Chosen One."

"Commander, we must leave before the mist disperses," Destre said in a deep voice. He gathered Cian's limp body like he was picking up discarded paper. Then his large, hooded form began to glow yellow, his black skin turning to marigold scales.

Wings pushed themselves from Volos's back, a dark light surrounding her. Her limbs stretched and grew. Her black scales swallowed the light, but the white gemstone on her chest glistened. Next to her, Hanah stood straighter, injured arm cradled tight against her side. The purple glow wrapping around her was too familiar, and Alvis frowned because it wasn't right to see it on someone else.

Volos's finely trimmed claws pulled off the ground. "Do well to remember this, people of Tarley. People of *Linless*," she called into the stands, forcing everyone to hear her words. "Zen will not stop until every dragon is free from the grips of humans. *Peera Drakon Ah*."

Reptilian, violet eyes locked with her brother's, Hanah repeated, "*Peera Drakon Ah*."

In a burst of wind and rain, they vanished into the mist.

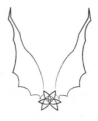

CHAPTER 46

THE CHAIR RAE SAT IN WAS BIG ENOUGH for him to pull his knees to his chest and curl further into himself.

On the bed in front of him, Alvis slept soundly, eyebrows pinching together every so often before the lines smoothed out. He was shirtless, healing injuries covered in bandages. The Talisman was still around Alvis's neck—it had burned Dr. Sienya when she had tried to take it off.

The locket rested perfectly on top of Alvis's Pact tattoo. Rae didn't know how many times in the last few hours his eyes had traced over the tattoo's design; the way the locket blended into the visible, red-tinted black lines curling down Alvis's arm. The locket and tattoo were the only comforts Rae could find in the mess of his thoughts.

Hanah was still alive.

She had an attribute. And hatred of Pacts was so ingrained she had no hesitation taking a Charge's life.

But she was *alive*. Misguided as he once was, but alive. The whirlwind relief of that truth was nauseating. Rae lifted his arm and rested the scar against his forehead—it was suddenly easier to breathe now than it had been since Hanah's apparent death.

"You could've slept in the bed, dumbass."

Alvis's voice was still sluggish with sleep. Rae unwound himself like he had been caught doing something wrong. He straightened his shoulders and folded his hands in his lap. The tile was cold beneath his bare feet. "I wasn't sleeping. If I had been, I would have missed Princess Meera stopping by earlier." Even though Meera's visit had filled Rae with endless relief, it was still a struggle to smile. "She said to tell you, 'Welcome to Linless.' "

Happiness surged through their bond and it turned Rae's smile from forced to real, Alvis's joy allowing Rae to feel safe with his own.

"I told you, you did it!" Alvis said, grinning.

"*We* did it." Rae's correction was mumbled but Alvis beamed. The excitement faded, though, as he dragged his gaze across the multiple shallow scratches on Rae's face left behind by Cian's ice spears and Rae's own claws.

"Are you doing okay?" Alvis tapped his own temple when Rae crinkled his brow. "Here, I mean."

Fear clenched the air in Rae's chest, then eased its way out when he remembered he had space to breathe here. His perfect posture fell away, shoulders curling in on themselves again. "I don't know," Rae admitted. "I don't feel out of control, but it doesn't feel right either."

Rae didn't realize he was only a step away from breaking

into a sob until a single tear fell onto his hand.

There was the gentle sound of shuffling, then Alvis said, "Come here." Careful of his injuries, Alvis had moved himself to the other side of the bed. Back pressed against the railing, the empty space he left open wasn't much, but Rae still found himself fitting into it. Their knees pressed together, but Alvis didn't reach to pull Rae closer against him.

"What are you thinking about?" asked Alvis, when the silence stretched between them.

The words were slow to come out. Thinking them was enough for them to get lodged in Rae's throat. "Now that Cian is dead, you have no reason to stay in a Pact with me. However, Hanah is alive. I couldn't save her before. I don't know if I should try to save her again now, but I need the chance to figure it out. I understand how horrible it is to ask this of you after what Hanah did to Rival, but please, let me keep fighting alongside you."

There wasn't a single beat of silence between Rae's words and Alvis harshly ruffling Rae's hair. "Dumbass," Alvis sang, until every silver lock was mused.

A smile bloomed on Rae's lips. If he were being honest with himself, he expected this would be Alvis's response.

"Don't smile when you're being dramatic," Alvis said. He softly traced his thumb over one of the cuts on Rae's cheek. "Obviously, we're keeping this Pact. You think I'm happy with how this whole thing played out? First my dad, and now Rival? Cian may be dead, but there's plenty of Zen that can't be left alone. The world depends on Linless. It depends on *us*."

Such heroic words. Cheesy and overused, but this was Alvis, always straightforward. When he said words like those, Rae found himself believing each one.

Their hands were still resting between them on the sheets—Rae slid his fingers into Alvis's. Alvis squeezed back, strong and reassuring. And as Rae drifted off to sleep, the only mantra he could hear was the softness of their breaths, together, rising and falling.

ACKNOWLEDGEMENTS

Thank you to my husband and forever teammate, David. Sorry for spoiling things, but I appreciate your ears and every time you cackled because you thought an idea was badass. And thank you for the endless cold brew supply and supporting me on this journey.

Hey, Kaylee and Elliot, my little Captains: Mommy loves you. Thank you for being cuddly, hilarious, intelligent, and weird. And thank you for loving me, too.

Endless thank you to my first editor, Rebecca Faith Heyman, for tackling my novice writer ego and encouraging me to grow past my first draft. Thank you for your advice and honesty, *especially* on that second draft where I for some reason thought eating raw bread dough was a good idea??? And thank you to my second editor, Allison Davis Salcido, for pushing me to put as much effort into describing buildings as I do smooches. Your proofreading and notes helped finalize this novel and make me confident it's completely done!

To my amazing sensitivity reader, Oderas, thank you for your wonderful and helpful feedback!

To my mama Karenita for chasing around the kiddos while shooing me away to my office so I could get some hundred words in. You've read every version of this book and still call Alvis "Avis" and I hope that never changes.

To my besties, Allison and Brooke, thank you for reading all the drafts from when it was word-mush to full sentences.

To my Gamestation writer's group: Geoff, Will, and Phil. Without you and your years of encouragement, this book would be nothing more than another discarded NaNoWriMo draft. Thank you for your infinite input and laughter. Phil, I'm glad your video is no longer the X-split logo.

BETA BAES. Thank you for your eyes and comments! Especially for the push to include a Cian chapter, which I think was a wonderful idea I loved writing!

Toni Infante! I know every interaction of our is basically me being, "I LOVE YOUR ART NEVER STOP CREATING IT" but.... that's cause it's true. Thank you for creating the breathtaking book cover and art print! And thank you to my aunt, Deb Lee, for the logo design!!

While my HappiLeeErin anituber days have kind of come to a bittersweet end, I will never forget all the support I've had from all my viewers over the years. Not only on my book, but on all the silly videos I made with all the dumb faces and noises. Thank you for not judging me on my Angel Beats review where I bawled like a baby (understandably, but still). And same for my twitter and Instagram followers! I love your messages and will always talk Kuroko no Basuke and Hisoka booty with you. THAT WILL NEVER CHANGE. And of course, thank you to all the anituber friends I've met and my Mangapod crew, Dodger, Lou, and Moeka!

When I decided to crowdfund The Guardian, I *never* thought I would gain as much support as I did. Thank you to every single one of you who put faith into my book baby and me. AND FOR YOUR PATIENCE!!!

To the Last Dragons and Dragon Queens: Ben Sutherland, arimaythea, Arnar Bjornsson, Dylan Thomas-Bouchier, Christina Benesh, Phillip Lockhart, Marc Herrmann, Sophie Jennings, Jens Banning, Mikael Karlsen, Leon Pennington, Caroline Leah, Jeffrey Baltazar, Simon C., and Ethan Fickle.

And, finally, to those who need someone to believe in them, I hope this story tells you I do. You've got this <3

Lightning Source UK Ltd.
Milton Keynes UK
UKHW041906161122
412313UK00005B/345